ARROWHEAD | BOOK TWO

THE ARROWHEAD PROTOCOL

BRET HURST

Black Rose Writing | Texas

ISBN: 978-1-68513-544-7
PUBLISHED BY BLACK ROSE WRITING
www.blackrosewriting.com

Printed in the United States of America
Suggested Retail Price (SRP) $27.95

The Arrowhead Protocol is printed in Garamond Premier Pro

*As a planet-friendly publisher, Black Rose Writing does its best to eliminate unnecessary waste to reduce paper usage and energy costs, while never compromising the reading experience. As a result, the final word count vs. page count may not meet common expectations.

For my wife, Terri
My children, Josh, Jessica, and Jacob
My parents, Steve, and Ethel.
And to Jay Black.
I couldn't have done this without the help all of you gave me.
I thank God for each of you and this book.

THE
ARROWHEAD
PROTOCOL

Prologue

Nothing in life is quite like a missing person. We bury our dead, rehab our injuries, and cover our scars as best we can, but there is no closure for the missing. It puts life in a kind of holding pattern. Things are no longer the same, but the new state of being remains undefined. A wife has not yet become a widow, and a child is somewhere between daughter and orphan.

At least that's how Susan Leonette saw things. Actually, it was worse than that for her. Everyone believed her father was dead—not missing. They assumed her new status was determined, but she knew in her heart he was still alive. She could feel it in her bones. Her life simply paused five years ago, and since then she had burned through her money, dreams, and hope—and she was close to the end of all three.

Resting her forehead on the steering wheel of her beat-up old Civic, she tried to calm her thoughts and dredge up some enthusiasm. She'd invested so much financially, emotionally, and even spiritually in this search. How much longer could it go on? He'd been missing for five years—five Christmases, birthdays, and July Fourths.

Susan raked her fingers through short, light brown hair and sighed. This would be her last try. This strange meeting would be her last attempt for now, and then she would turn back and focus on her *own* life before *it* was over—maybe even go on a date.

She stepped out of the car and straightened her back, steadying herself for what was to come. She was short, but curvaceous and muscular. Exercise had been the only therapy she'd allowed herself during this time, and as a result, her fitness was one of the few bright spots in an otherwise overcast life.

Walking across the parking lot, she shoved her hands deep in the pockets of her hoodie. Fall was fading into winter and the wind here outside Charlotte was chilly as it whipped around the buildings.

With the money she'd scraped together by waitressing, she'd worked her way through private eyes. The latest was a man named Dickson from Baltimore, another one who was supposed to be a missing person specialist.

Susan hadn't liked his vibe, but she was running out of options, and he seemed to believe her story. So, she'd given him a retainer a little over a month ago and since then, he'd emailed the same generic "no progress" report every week.

As a result, it surprised her when this other P.I., Frank Carson, had reached out. At first, Susan assumed he was looking for more money. He'd been firm, however, that Dickson's fee covered his work, so she agreed to meet him. She really didn't have a reason not to.

Approaching the restaurant, she picked Frank out immediately. He sat at a round, metal table outside the sandwich shop. Over the past half-decade, she'd become something of an expert on private eyes. This man didn't fit the mold at all. He looked much more like a soldier than an investigator. He was big and muscular, with leathery skin and a salt and pepper flat-top haircut.

What was most disconcerting was that he was watching her from the second she turned the corner, like he'd known she was coming at that precise moment. A small shiver ran through her. This was a dangerous man with merciless, cold, calculating eyes.

He stood as she neared. "Miss Leonette?"

She nodded and shook his hand. "Call me Susan."

"My name's Frank Carson." He looked over his shoulder. "Would you prefer to go inside?"

Susan shook her head. "Where's Dickson?"

He turned back, his dark eyes steady on hers. "He's not coming. Our investigations overlapped, and I said I would pass this information onto you." Frank sat back down and gestured for her to follow suit.

She remained standing. "What's in it for you?" she snapped, no longer having the patience for pleasantries with these men.

He frowned and scratched a puckered white scar on the side of his neck. "I'm doing a separate investigation for a different client." He paused, studying her. "It's possible that your answers might assist us in our investigation."

She narrowed her eyes. "What client and what investigation?"

Frank shrugged one massive shoulder. "I'm not at liberty to reveal that information."

Susan crossed her arms over her chest. In her experience, if something sounded too good to be true, it usually was.

Frank held up his hands in a placating gesture. "Just have a seat. I don't want anything from you, Miss Leonette."

She reluctantly sat. "It's Susan."

Again, Frank held her gaze with steady, dark eyes.

She resisted the urge to squirm and look away. She'd been at this too long to let this man intimidate her and she was out of money, anyway.

Frank let out a slow breath through his nose. "I think we may be looking at different sides of the same mystery. What helps you might help us. You have nothing to lose and maybe, just maybe, this will lead to the break you've been looking for."

Susan refused to hope. She'd had a hundred conversations that *could* lead somewhere over the years. She would not allow herself to believe that this would be any different. "If you don't need anything from me, then why are you here?"

Unexpectedly, Frank smiled. "You are direct, Susan. I like that." He pursed his lips. "I do need something from you. It's just not money. There's a, uh, I guess you'd call them a group of private investigators in Miami that are very good at this kind of thing." Susan opened her mouth, but he forestalled her with a hand. "These guys are very selective about who they represent, but all their work is pro bono. If they take your case, it's free."

Susan leaned back, crossing her arms again. "So, why don't you hire them?"

Frank frowned. "Because they won't work with me. We've had a few disagreements in the past, but they don't know you. You can probably convince them to help you. All I ask is that you share whatever you discover. Maybe we can all win in this situation."

Susan had been down this road too many times before. Her heart had become calloused now and was not so easily snared. "I've hired everyone who's anyone in the missing person's racket. Why would these guys be any different?"

A slight smile touched the corner of Frank's lips.

She got the vague impression that he liked her, and Susan wasn't sure that was a good thing.

Frank said, "They aren't washed-out ex-cops. They were with the Agency, probably other departments you've never heard of. They're a different breed."

This got Susan's attention. Her father had been working for the government in some capacity when he disappeared. She understood Frank wanted to use her as a pawn in whatever game he was playing with these men, but this did sound different. If it helped her find her father, she had to try. Just one more time. "Who are they, and how do I get in touch with them?"

Frank slid a card across the table. "They take clients through their front man, a guy named Jeff Lansing. This is the number of a friend of his named Brenda Taylor. This group helped her out with a situation. Tell her you heard she knew some people who could do the impossible. Be vague and don't tell them about me. She'll get you in touch with Jeff, and then you'll be good to go."

Susan ran a finger over her chin and sighed. "Where are they?"

Frank grinned. "They work out of Miami. Think of it as a vacation."

Susan's forehead creased. "I can't afford—"

He held up his hand again. "I know." He pushed a second piece of paper across the table. "I paid for a two-week reservation at a hotel in Miami. It's not much to look at, but it's the least I can do for your help."

She looked hard at Frank's lined face. "No bullshit, Frank. Are these guys really that good?"

His smile faded, and he nodded. "I give my word, Susan. They're the best I've ever seen."

Part 1

Chapter 1

Eddie Mason was working the opposite of a missing person's case. He had the person, but no idea where he came from, and he wasn't making any progress. He'd started thinking of this mystery as a long stretch of untouched beach. Just an endless collection of white sand, every grain exactly the same, no pattern emerging. Hell, he wasn't even leaving any footprints of note.

It still mystified him how he had landed in this position, saddled with this puzzle. His life had followed a long and twisting path that somehow ended with him leading a rag-tag group here in Miami. They took on little missions using their skills, experience, and contacts to help people in special circumstances. Definitely not a nine-to-five job, and he didn't think it counted as a small business, either, because they never collected a fee. Eddie's Agency mission had left him with a nice little nest egg and a house free and clear. As a result, he felt it was his duty to live off this money while helping others.

This *team* included himself, another ex-CIA agent, an ex-special forces soldier, a limey hacker, and a quirky civilian who knew everyone. He really needed to give this group some sort of name, because when you described it like that, it sounded like a bad cartoon.

A year ago, while doing a protection detail for a U.S. senator on a mysterious trip, Eddie discovered a strange man living in a cave on an island in the Caribbean. This Caveman, as he started calling him, didn't know who he was or how he'd gotten there, but he saved Eddie's life. He promised to put his team and their considerable talents to work discovering Caveman's story. Since that time, they had made no progress at all, and he was getting discouraged.

He drove today's nondescript, light blue sedan into what his team referred to as the Langer building and passed under the heavy garage door and into one of the concrete slips. As he stepped out, he could still feel the Miami sun beating down on the roof, and it fueled his sour mood. It was November, for God's sake; it was supposed to be fall. He clicked a button on his fob and the garage door descended. His dark, light-weight jacket and light shirt were good for changing his look and profile in a second, but they were a bitch in this heat.

Eddie walked up the steps and punched a code into the keypad next to a steel door with a small bullet proof window at eye level. With a click, it popped open, Eddie stepped inside, closed it behind him, and sent the "all clear" text.

He pulled off the jacket as he walked down a short hallway into what had been a break room when this building was some sort of factory. As he took a bottled water from the fridge, he heard the rumble as one of the garage doors opened again. He rubbed his palm on his jeans and loosened the Sig pistol in his holster.

It was his team's standard practice that each member was inside before the next arrived, making it impossible to catch all of them in the confined space and vulnerable. Eddie walked back to the door and pushed the red mushroom button on the wall, deactivating the small door's keypad. He bent down and looked through the glass.

An old, rusty pickup truck pulled in next to the sedan. Luis stepped out and surveyed the area. The garage door closed again. He was slightly shorter than Eddie, in loose pants and a light-colored jacket. His dark hair was pulled back into a short ponytail and the bastard didn't look to be at all affected by the heat.

Luis jogged gracefully up the stairs and gave him a thumbs up.

Eddie popped the mushroom button up, opened the door, ushered his friend inside, and closed it behind him.

Luis asked, "Any trouble?"

Eddie shook his head. "Not yet, and I'm trying to keep it that way."

He raised his eyebrows as he sent his "all-clear" text. "So, what, now we don't take on any new cases?"

Eddie shrugged and opened the bottled water. "I wouldn't. Not until we get Caveman sorted out."

Luis grabbed the index finger of one hand and popped a knuckle. "And what if that never happens?"

"We haven't been at this long enough to say that yet."

The garage door rumbled again, and Luis hit the disconnect button with the side of his fist. "Eddie, we've got no leads. We're dead in the water. If we can help someone in the meantime, we should. If nothing else, to let our minds work on something else for a while. We can come back to Caveman with a fresh perspective."

A faded red minivan pulled into the garage and then the heavy metal door rattled closed behind it. Loren stepped out, and Luis let her in through the door.

She was tall with shoulder-length blonde hair and honey colored skin. As soon as she was inside, she searched Eddie's face with concerned green eyes.

Every time he saw her, she affected him, which made him nervous and also fueled his foul mood, and he frowned.

Loren turned to Luis, "Is he still being stubborn?"

He didn't look up from texting the next "all clear" as he nodded and imitated Eddie, "We need to stay focused on Cavemen for now."

Eddie looked down his nose at the two of them. "We know nothing about this girl."

Loren grinned and turned to Luis, "You owe me five bucks."

He scowled, hit the red button door again, and turned to Eddie. "Come on, man. 'We don't know them' is always at least your third excuse why we shouldn't help someone."

Eddie looked from one to the other. "Bite me. You all remember a little while ago when we almost died in the middle of the ocean."

Loren shook her head. "We've done two missions since then, no issues."

Eddie sighed, his brow furrowing, and looked at Loren. "We've made no progress. Nothing."

Her expression softened. "I know."

The garage door rose again.

Luis walked down the hall to the kitchen and said over his shoulder, "We can do this one quick thing and then get back to the business at hand."

Eddie leaned down and looked through the window. "One quick thing—famous last words."

Another unremarkable sedan pulled in and parked. Jeff, a short, redheaded man in a black Chicago Bulls jacket, emerged and tried two or three times before getting his fob to close the garage door behind him. He walked up the stairs and Eddie let him in.

Jeff looked past him to Loren and Luis. "So, are we doing this or what?"

Luis shook his head. "No, we're still in the Eddie worrying phase. We're at least a half hour away from agreeing to do this."

Jeff assumed a serious expression and looked over at Eddie. "Can't we rush the process along a little?"

He looked at each of them. "You can all kiss my ass." He pushed past their grinning faces and started down the hall, but stopped and turned back. "All joking aside. This time, it's not even someone Jeff knows. It's someone who just met someone Jeff knows."

The three of them stopped and their smiles faded a bit.

Eddie continued walking. "All I'm saying is that we should be careful."

The team had purchased this long dormant factory in west Miami because of its unusual design. Four medium-sized buildings situated across public streets from one another, connected by underground. Because of this design, if anyone followed a member of the team here, it would be very difficult to anticipate where they would depart the complex.

There were two small locker rooms down the hallway, and they had gotten into the habit of changing all their clothes, just in case someone had slipped a tracking device onto any of them.

They'd made little progress finding out who Caveman was, where he came from, or who put him on the island, but that didn't mean that they'd made no progress. Unfortunately, everything that they'd learned made the situation even more treacherous.

Though Caveman couldn't remember anything about himself, he seemed to know a lot of CIA secrets that he shouldn't know. Making matters worse, they were pretty sure Caveman was a product of a mothballed Agency program. And worse still, Treleous, a well-funded, organized, and ruthless secret organization, was after that information.

Now his team was trying to learn anything they could about Caveman, while keeping Treleous from discovering his existence–and keeping him out of their hands.

He guessed they also had a side mission to oppose Treleous in all of its pursuits, but they hadn't advanced any on that front either. To that end, they always met here at the Langer building in one set of cars, changed, and left in different vehicles. They were acutely aware that Caveman's life was in danger, not to mention the absolute necessity to keep the secrets in his head out of enemy hands.

They stood in the hallway, looking at him expectantly.

Eddie opened his mouth to respond, when Jeff said, "I've got another reason we should take the case."

All eyes turned to him in surprise.

"This girl, that reached out to us for help. I checked. Her father is number sixteen on the green list, and Susan herself is number seventeen."

Among the top-secret information some unknown person had put in Caveman's head was a chart of good guys, the "green list," and bad guys, the "red list."

A moment stretched between them, the only sound a drip echoing somewhere down the passageway.

Luis chuckled. "How do you know that?"

Jeff shrugged. "I've been getting Caveman to write things down. To see if it helped him remember. Anyway, I've started checking those lists."

Eddie blew out a breath. "That's not necessarily a good thing. Don't you all find it convenient that someone on a list in Caveman's head shows up and just happens to ask us for help?"

Loren's attention stayed on Jeff. "Yes, but it's also the only lead we've had." She looked over at Eddie and shrugged. "And she is on the green list."

He rolled his eyes. "So what? I'm on the red list!"

Luis cocked his head to one side. "Yeah, but that was legit."

Eddie shot him a look.

Luis grinned. "I'm just saying. We've got to at least hear what this girl has to say."

Eddie rubbed his face and turned to start back down the hallway, calling back over his shoulder. "I still don't like it."

They split up. Jeff and Loren headed toward the northeast building as decoys, while Eddie and Luis continued in the opposite direction.

Eddie pulled out his cell phone and dialed Piper, the team's hacker and computer expert in London.

He answered with a deep yawn. "You all getting ready to go?"

Eddie said, "Any minute now. Are we clear?"

Piper smacked his lips. "I've checked all the camera feeds for the last twenty-four hours and ran an algorithm on all the footage. No one is watching the Langer building that I can see."

"Great, thanks." Eddie hung up.

Luis drove them out of the southeast corner building in a mid-eighties Camaro and turned south.

Both men carefully watched their surroundings as they took a roundabout route to the interstate before continuing toward their ultimate destination.

They rode along in silence before Eddie shook his head and asked, "All right, what's this girl's story?"

Luis's eyes never left the road, but he grinned. "Her name is Susan Leonette. She's from Charlotte, and her father disappeared a few years ago."

Eddie frowned. "Why's he on the green list? What did he do?"

Luis shrugged. "Worked for the government in some capacity, I'm not sure. She's convinced it has something to do with his disappearance, though."

Against his better judgment, Eddie had to admit that piqued his curiosity. "I don't think we should tell Caveman this girl's name yet. I don't want to get him all excited. Let's ease him into this, okay?"

Chapter 2

Frank stood in the fishing boat's bow as it motored out of Miami harbor toward a massive yacht anchored offshore. After his last adventure on the high seas, he'd taken a personal oath never to go back out on the water for the rest of his life. He sighed. Like a thousand other promises made in the heat of battle, this one didn't appear to be sticking, either.

He studied the craft and thought about the organization that employed him. Frank wasn't really a zealot, a patriot, or any other believer. From long years of combat, black ops, and a host of illegal activities, he thought of the world in two groups: the controllers and the controlled. He saw very little gray in this distinction. Working with this organization attracted him because he saw them as firmly in the first category. It also didn't hurt that they paid well.

The organization itself had a belief system, though—a goal, and an endgame. Born out of the Cold War, which was such a strange conflict. Not really a war, but a prolonged standoff, each side looking to tip the scales of power in their direction. All the while making sure the other wasn't doing the same.

If the USSR had ten nuclear bombs, then America needed at least eleven. If America had a presence in Latin America, then the Soviets needed two. This fierce competition didn't stop there, however. Technology was also a weapon that each side refused to cede to the other. They pushed for faster planes, quieter submarines, and even the macabre and crazy. This led to projects like MKULTRA and others.

This race continued on even after the Cold War. Once the machine was moving, it didn't just stop. It continued on for decades, and in some ways pushed the envelope further in all directions.

A scientist named Parker Mendelson worked on a group of these science fiction type projects long after the fall of the Soviet Union. Someone in power discovered the details of his work and decided they were over the line and pulled the plug.

Frank turned and spat into the passing ocean. The people who started this organization that employed him thought these projects were too important to mothball. That they had to stop the Russians and all other interests working against America—at all costs. So, they organized to keep that work going in secret.

The fishing boat's driver motored in a wide circle around the yacht until someone onboard waved a green flag. Only then did he approach.

Supposedly, there was a secret cache with all the details of Mendelson's work hidden somewhere in the world. This organization wanted it, and it was Frank's mission to find it. They were close last year. His team had followed a foolish senator who led them right to the location. An island in the middle of the damned Caribbean. It was supposed to be the easiest job in the world. Kill the senator and take what was there.

That's when everything went to hell, and Frank learned other forces were involved. Forces that wanted to stop his employers. A small group, that he was convinced was based here in Miami, got the jump on them. They stole whatever was there and saved the senator.

A muscle bulged in Frank's cheek. He didn't lose very often, and the thought still pissed him off. However, he kept his cool. Over the past year, he had tracked them to a mysterious group of do-gooders here in Miami. He was going to get them, steal back whatever they took, and kill them all. Even the score, so to speak.

The fishing boat pulled alongside the larger vessel, and Frank leaped over and climbed the stairs. He reached under his denim jacket and grazed his fingertips over the Glock in his holster. It was a subconscious act as he stepped onto unfamiliar ground.

Armed men with submachine guns stood fore and aft, and a third on the roof stared down at him through dark glasses. They no longer asked Frank for his gun whenever he visited Gemini, but he was still a visitor. He didn't know these men and was acutely aware of his vulnerability out here in the ocean. Another sign that he was part of the organization, but not in upper management. Not some foot soldier, but not one of the top floor types, either.

Gemini sat behind a large desk in the main stateroom and looked up as he entered. "Is everything ready?"

Frank shrugged as he took a seat opposite him. "We've dropped the bait in the water. Let's see if they take a bite."

Gemini frowned and steepled long, slender fingers. He sat ramrod straight in a khaki hunting jacket with a leather shoulder patch, his silver hair slicked down and parted to one side. "I'm still not sure I understand why all this is necessary."

Frank had expected the question, though it still irritated him. "Since determining who caused us so much trouble, we've tried several ways to get to them without success. They're smart, careful, and this is their home turf. They got the drop on us last time because they aren't amateurs."

Gemini nodded slowly. "And this woman, Susan Leonette, you think she can draw them out?"

Frank shrugged again. "If our information is correct, this is exactly the situation they go for. A woman in distress, against a powerful foe. I got her name from you, because she's loosely connected to what we've been working toward. It seems like that would interest them."

Gemini sighed. "We thought she might have had some kind of correlation, but it turned out to be a dead end."

"We know that, but maybe they don't. All we need them to do is take a nibble."

"And if they do, how are you going to take them down?"

Frank said, "I have a full team here in Miami, ready to go. We've bugged her hotel room and her phone, put a tracker on her car, and I have Mack carefully trailing her. If our quarry moves, we'll be ready."

Gemini narrowed steel-gray eyes. "Good. This has taken too long, and I want to get back to business."

Frank nodded. "If they meet her, we'll spring the trap and solve this problem once and for all."

Chapter 3

As Luis and Eddie headed southwest of Miami, the buildings gave way to neighborhoods, then to farms and groves. When they were certain no one had followed them, they focused their route and finally arrived at a stone wall nestled among dense foliage. Using a code, they opened the steel gates and drove down the main road, past rows and rows of avocado trees, to a house near the center. Several windows were missing, stacks of lumber lay on the ground, and a shop full of power tools stood next to the main building.

They'd stashed Caveman in this safe-house, while they tried to figure out where he came from, and almost immediately the strange man started remodeling the place. Eddie's team supported this because it gave him something to do while hidden away here.

Caveman appeared in the doorway, a screw gun in one hand, as four German shepherds rushed past him and greeted Eddie and Luis with wagging tails and whines.

Luis lifted a small sack off the front seat and held it up. "I have Cuban sandwiches from Mamacita's."

Cavemen smiled. "Well, bring them in. I'm starved." Inside, he placed a piece of plywood across two sawhorses as Eddie and Luis pulled up chairs and distributed the food.

The three men ate in silence for a moment and then Eddie said, glancing around the half-finished kitchen. "It's coming along nicely."

Caveman shrugged. "It's getting there." He continued to study them, eyes narrowed, before asking, "What's up?"

Eddie wiped his mouth and shrugged.

Luis said, "We have another potential job, but Mr. Hesitant here is worried about taking it."

Caveman asked, "Why?"

Eddie gave Luis an exasperated look before turning back to Caveman. "I'm trying to stay focused on helping you."

He snorted. "We seem to be at a dead end, Eddie. Whoever did whatever they did to me was very connected and thorough. We shouldn't have expected anything different." He picked up his sandwich. "Look, I haven't lost faith. I believe we'll figure this out, I really do, but it's going to take some kind of break. It'll come, but we can't make it happen any faster. You might as well help people if you can in the meantime."

Eddie leaned back in his chair and sighed. Amazing how much more comfortable and assertive Caveman had become. Gone was the hesitant man he'd found on the island.

The troublesome part was that this girl might actually be the clue they'd been waiting for. But, without letting Caveman know too much, Eddie felt obligated to reiterate the risks. "I get what you're saying, and I appreciate it Caveman, I really do. But every time we do a job, the chances of us getting discovered gets greater."

Caveman nodded. "I understand."

He continued, "If we get compromised, that puts *you* in danger. We're keeping you safe with secrecy more than any other protection."

Caveman took a bite and chewed thoughtfully. "I can't imagine what could happen that would lead back to me. If we can connect this mystery to me and the men who want what's in my head, then maybe, but that doesn't seem likely. Who else would care about me?"

Eddie and Luis exchanged a quick glance.

Caveman shrugged. "Even if the worst happens, that this is somehow connected to me, that could be the break we need. Maybe that's what it will take to make some progress. None of us thought that pursuing this was going to be without some risk. I'm comfortable with that. What I'm not comfortable with is you all not helping people that need you because of me."

He held Eddie's gaze. "I can't live with that, Eddie. Do what you do. Something will help with my mystery when it's time. I can feel it."

Eddie sighed. He didn't like this. His gut told him something was wrong with this situation. He'd ignored that instinct before, and it almost cost them everything. Of course, it also led them to Caveman, the mission he believed he was meant to work on. Maybe he shouldn't heed this inner voice by avoiding the situation, but approach it with extreme caution. "Are you sure?"

Caveman nodded. "I am. I'm serious. Do what you do."

Eddie sighed and turned to Luis, "Call Jeff and tell him to set up a meeting."

Chapter 4

Frank looked up from his newspaper.

One of his men, listening through a pair of headphones, suddenly held up a finger. "It's Jeff calling her back."

He swung his legs off the bed, his heart rate quickening. Was this it? Had his trap really worked? He rubbed his thick-fingered hands together.

His man grinned. "We're a go. They want to meet in thirty minutes. They'll call her with a location."

Frank frowned. He guessed it was too much to hope that this adversary would give the location up front—they were too sharp for that kind of mistake. That's why they needed a trap like this. He stood and leaned through the open door into the adjacent room. "We're on, let's get ready."

He had five teams of two, ready to follow Susan wherever she went. The pairs were all well-trained, and he had chosen their vehicles to blend in. He figured five was enough to help conceal the tail, especially if they worked together. He and Mack would hold back in a sixth car, ready to jump in wherever the action was. "Remember, I need someone alive." He turned and looked Mack directly in the eyes. "Alive." To the other men, he said, "I don't care about anything else, but I need at least one of these people she's meeting."

He desperately hoped they wouldn't send a cutout. Some middleman who couldn't be traced back. That would put a kink in his plan. No, they were too small and tight-knit. He didn't see them using any kind of outsider. This was the play.

He was nervous as he watched his team walk out to their cars, which was unusual for him. Sometimes he became keyed up before a fight, but rarely anxious. It was these bastards he was trying to catch. They always seem to get the jump on him. "Check your radios and weapons. We only have one shot at these people." He knew he didn't need to tell the men that, but he just couldn't help himself.

He slid into the passenger's seat of the beat-up old Ford Explorer.

Mack patted his short blond mohawk and grinned at Frank as he took the wheel. "Don't worry. We've got these guys. They took the bait."

Frank scratched at a white puckered scar on his neck. "Don't get ahead of yourself. The fish isn't in the boat yet."

The team's rag-tag collection of vehicles pulled out and again he mulled over their number. It was a delicate thing, a rotating tail team. Too many cars or too few looked unnatural and would stick out to a professional. It had to be the right amount, so that occasionally each driver could pass the person they were tailing as if it didn't matter. He assumed that the people he was trying to snare would follow Susan to the rendezvous point and then watch for anything out of the ordinary.

Frank lifted his radio and said, "Remember. They'll probably make the target move to several stops before they make contact. Be patient and smart." He set the radio back in his lap.

Mack looked over. "Relax, we're ready."

Chapter 5

Eddie stared out the kitchen window, his mind working over the details as he sipped his coffee. His team was based here in Coral Gables in a house the CIA "had given" him as a sort of settlement after the scandal and false accusations. Two separate stucco structures and a four-car garage surrounded a circular, brick parking area. The mustard walls and barrel-tile roofs were common here in Miami. Having grown up in West Texas, he was still amazed by the fruit trees that dotted the five-acre compound. A beautiful place, but it still didn't feel like home, which added to his unease. The damn place was too large and ostentatious for a simple country boy.

Luis and Jeff lived in two of the four suites in the second building, and he and Loren had sort of fallen into living with each other here in the main house. After their little adventure in the ocean, where they discovered Caveman, Treleous learned her identity. As a result, she couldn't return home, but their relationship, if you could even call it that then, was brand new.

Hell, they'd never really even dated. So, she moved into the second building, and they started "going out." It went well and over the next four months, she went back to her room less and less until she rarely returned there at all.

They'd never really discussed her moving in. It just sort of happened, and neither brought it up. Was that the sign of a healthy, mature relationship, or the opposite? Eddie wasn't sure.

He liked things settled. He wasn't sure he really understood that about himself for most of his life, but he did now. Maybe it took the CIA ripping all his life's structure away for him to realize that he missed it. For him to recognize he needed a task he believed in, work that mattered to him, and a woman who brought out the best in him.

They had a mission now, and Eddie believed in it, but their lack of progress bothered him. The same thing was true of his relationship with Loren. She was the one. He knew that, so shouldn't their relationship also be making some sort of progress? Shouldn't it be going somewhere? Eddie was also at his core a religious person, and this caused their current status to weigh on his mind as well. He wanted to marry her, but they'd never discussed it. Would she want that, too? He thought so, but she was cagey about anything on the topic. So, until they talked about it...

Luis, Loren, and Jeff entered the kitchen. Each poured a cup of coffee, then sat around the table.

Eddie joined them, pushing these thoughts to the back of his mind. Their standard operational procedure for this type of job was for Jeff to meet potential clients first, while the team watched from a distance. It allowed them to better cover the area and reduced the chances of walking into a trap.

Usually, however, Jeff knew the person they were meeting. This was the first time that an unknown person had reached out to someone he knew for help. These meetings always made Eddie nervous, but this additional separation really bothered him. It didn't help that she was on a list in Caveman's head. "I think we should change it up a little."

All eyes swiveled to him, eyebrows raised.

Loren asked, "Change what?"

Jeff was the only member of the team with no official training, and he seemed exposed to Eddie. He shrugged. "I'm not sure why, but something's nagging at me about this. I think we should put Luis in the car with Jeff."

Luis said, "Okay, but if there's any kind of trouble, it only leaves the two of you to watch our backs. That's not very good coverage. Harder to see a trap before it's sprung."

Eddie nodded and sighed. "I know. I just have a feeling."

Luis studied him, his dark brown eyes steady and unblinking. "Then that's what we'll do. Your gut's served us well in the past."

Jeff and Loren nodded.

"All right. We do checkout plan 3, the one that ends at Naranja Lakes Park. That's a nice open place. I'll take the south side, and Loren, you take the north. Keep your guns ready."

Everyone nodded.

Luis said, "Okay, let's do this."

Chapter 6

Luis slid into the passenger's seat next to Jeff. The team used a collection of cheap nondescript cars for losing tails. For meetings like this, however, they kept the "Mules" in the garage at the house. Three souped-up BMW M3 sedans with bulletproof glass and steel plates in the doors.

Jeff started the car and grinned at the rumble that filled the interior. "You ready?"

Luis unconsciously laid a hand on the Sig in his holster and nodded. "Let's roll."

As they drove out the front gates and toward the first stop, Luis stared out the window. It was always like this before a mission. A tightening across his ribs. Not really a nervousness, but more of a gathering before the jump. He'd learned a long time ago in the Gulf to avoid expelling energy too early. He let a long slow breath and focused on his fingertips and the balls of his feet, relaxing each muscle.

Luis wasn't really into this Tai Chi crap. He was a good Cuban Catholic after all, and if he told his mother about any eastern religion stuff, she would immediately cross herself and start lamenting in Spanish. But at Fort Bragg, they introduced him to a lot of alternative thinking and some of it actually worked. He relaxed and focused on the task at hand. He'd spent years on missions all over the world, so the waiting process was nothing new to him.

They parked down the street from the first meeting place. Soon Susan arrived in her small gray Civic. She stepped out, shading her eyes from the sun as she scanned the area.

Luis studied her through a pair of binoculars, then lifted his radio. "How are we looking?"

Loren answered first. "Looks clear on my side."

Eddie's response followed. "Me, too."

Luis liked the look of her. She had an earnest and honest appearance. Also, some other quality that differed from the women Luis grew up with, that he couldn't quite put his finger on. These subtle cultural differences fascinated him. She was pretty, too. He turned to Jeff. "Okay, let's move her on to stop two."

Jeff nodded and dialed a number.

Through the binoculars, Luis saw Susan answer, look around frowning, and then slip back into her car.

Loren's voice came over the radio. "I'm going to zip over to the second stop."

"10-4," Eddie responded.

Jeff waited a beat before pulling into traffic a suitable distance behind Susan.

Luis studied the road and cars around them. It was an eleven-mile trip to the second stop, all of it on side streets. Knowing the final destination allowed them to hang back and observe the route. He noticed several cars that he recognized, but none behaved like a tail. So far, so good.

Loren's voice came over the radio again. "I'm in place at stop two. All appears clear."

Luis mentally catalogued the cars. He saw a small red sedan, a gray pickup, and a green Mercedes. The second stop was a Home Depot, where they directed Susan to park at the very edge of the lot.

Once again, she stepped out of the car and looked around expectantly.

Luis lifted the binoculars and surveyed the area. "She's short."

The radio crackled and Eddie said, "All looks clear to me, but it feels off. Stay frosty. I'm moving to the next stop."

Loren responded. "10-4."

Luis studied the woman again. He sensed nothing off yet, but he trusted Eddie's instincts. He lifted the radio. "Okay, we're sending her on the last leg."

Jeff called her again.

This time Susan looked impatient and irritated as she climbed back into her car.

He set down the binoculars. "Let's roll."

Jeff pulled out into traffic. "You think Eddie is just being paranoid?"

Luis shrugged. "We're about to find out."

Chapter 7

Frank held his radio close to his ear, engrossed in the chatter between his teams, a muscle pulsating in his jaw. This was the moment he'd worked toward for over a year. They'd taken something from that damned island that was important to his organization. Frank cared about that too, but not nearly as much as getting his hands on these people. These bastards had gotten the best of him for the last time.

Mack followed the chase. Hanging back, close enough to stay engaged, but far enough to stay free from the automotive ballet the team was performing. Usually chatty, today he was quiet and focused.

Frank was sure the entire team could feel his intensity. That was fine. He wanted every one of them to feel the urgency. To be at the top of their game.

Mack slowed and stopped on the side of the road as Susan pulled into some park. He turned to Frank. "Stop one. How many do you think they'll run her through?"

Frank scratched the puckered white scar on his neck. "At least two more." He lifted the mic. "This is Actual. Stay alert out there. These stops are to catch you all. Over."

A few moments later, one of his men called in across the radio. "This is Two. She's on the move, heading east. Over."

Mack put the car in gear and pulled into traffic.

Frank ground his teeth through the next stop at Home Depot. He was so full of the adrenaline that he could feel each heartbeat. He knew he needed to relax, but he'd never wanted to get his hands on an adversary this badly. These sons-a-bitches had embarrassed him.

Once again, his team called in to say that they were on the move, and Mack kept pace.

Frank stared out the window. This mission had put him here in Miami for too long, and he was sick of the place. It was just too damned hot and not enough people spoke English. Frank spoke a little Spanish, but he couldn't communicate clearly in a crisis, and that was a problem. He didn't like problems, especially if they could affect a mission.

The girl stopped at a parking lot for a moment before continuing on.

The radio crackled. "This is Three. Tango has turned east onto Hibiscus Way, over."

Frank sat forward in his seat. This was it.

"This is Five. She's slowing down. Tango has turned into Naranja Lakes Park. Continuing past target, over."

"This is Two. I got her. I'm parked across the street, over."

"This is Four. I also have eyes on the prize. Tango is looking around the park, over."

Frank studied the radio, waiting as the minutes passed.

"This is Two. This is longer than the first two stops. This could be the one, over."

"Three to Actual, over."

Frank lifted the Radio. "This is Actual, go ahead."

"Three understands mission is to grab anyone meeting Tango. Repeat R.E. for the tango, over."

Frank scowled. "All units, this is Actual. Mission is to grab anyone meeting the tango. Anything you have to do to achieve that aim is cleared. I don't care about the tango. I just want anyone meeting her alive. Understood? Over."

"This is Three, solid copy, over."

Chapter 8

Luis focused the binoculars on Susan as she stepped out of the little car and waited. She seemed irritated and unsure. Once again, she shaded her eyes from the sun and looked around the park. A group of young boys played basketball on the court just beyond her. Nothing seemed out of order. He lifted his radio. "How does it look?"

Loren answered first. "All looks clear to me."

Eddie's voice followed. "Same here. Be careful."

Luis said, "10-4", and dropped the radio into his lap. He pulled his Sig from its holster and nodded to Jeff. "Let's go."

They eased forward and into the parking lot. Luis felt a vibration is his fingertips. Something was wrong. He glanced over his shoulder and then turned his attention back to the girl.

As they rolled toward her, she turned in their direction, tilting her hand to keep her eyes shaded. Luis noticed Susan's eyes narrow and then focus behind them. Something about it bothered him and the vibration increased. "Speed up a little."

Jeff glanced over but eased down the accelerator.

Luis looked over his shoulder again and noticed a red car. He'd seen one similar earlier. Had he seen it more than once, or was it just a coincidence?

He turned back to the girl. Her eyes were wide at their increased speed. She'd hunkered down and lifted her arms in a defensive posture. Her eyes didn't move back to the red car. If this was a trap, then Luis decided Susan wasn't in on it.

Jeff slammed on the brakes and slid to a stop in front of her.

Luis stepped out of his side before the car was even at rest. He lifted his pistol and turned to look back toward the red car. He asked, "Are you alone?"

She looked wildly around. "What? Yes, why?"

The red car was still moving in their direction and Luis tracked it until a pickup truck slightly to this left caught his attention. Pivoting, he saw the passenger lift a pistol. Luis fired one shot into the windshield.

Susan shrieked and then moved toward her car.

Luis leaned into the BMW and yelled at Jeff. "Go!" He slammed the door, then said, "Get in the passenger's side and watch my back."

The BMW's tires squealed, spewing a cloud of blue gray smoke. It slid a few inches before the rubber caught and the car lurched forward.

The truck skidded to a stop and then raced back.

Children on the basketball court scattered.

Luis rotated and squeezed off a round at the red sedan as it raced down the road toward them. The front right tire exploded, and it ground to a halt.

The door swung open, and the driver fired a quick shot at Luis, who hustled around behind Susan's sedan for cover.

She followed him and then yelled, "Behind you!"

Luis spun, conscious that he was putting his back on the driver of the red car, but not having a choice.

A white car turned off the road and streaked across the grass towards them. It fishtailed as it left the road and the engine roared as the driver accelerated and corrected back toward them. Luis leveled the Sig and fired.

Two more shots rang out and Luis whirled to see the driver of the red car slump to the ground. Eddie or Loren covering him.

He turned again and noticed that the white car was slowing and fading off the left. His bullet must have found flesh. He yelled at Susan, "Get in the car!"

A large truck turned off the main road and rumbled in their direction. Luis jumped into the driver's side of the compact sedan and yelled, "Keys!"

Susan fumbled for a second before handing them over.

Luis started the car just as the truck struck the back-quarter panel.

The little Civic spun with the impact. Luis was thrown into the steering wheel, knocking the gun from his hand.

Someone in the truck started shooting down into the car. Luis instinctively ducked away and felt a line of fire along his right thigh. Susan stared up at him wide-eyed, blood trickling down from a cut on her forehead.

Luis said, "Put your seatbelt on and find my gun!" He jammed the accelerator down and was relieved when the car immediately moved.

Susan threw herself back into the seat and, with a couple of yanks, got the strap around her and clicked into place. Feeling around with her feet, she discovered the gun and leaned down to retrieve it.

Luis raced out the entrance, the little car straining forward with only a slight vibration in the steering wheel. He pulled on his own belt and then accepted the gun from her.

At the entrance, a large black SUV slid around the corner into their path.

Chapter 9

Frank gritted his teeth as Mack pulled the SUV into the path of the escaping silver Civic. He lifted his Glock to shoot, but before he could pull the trigger, their truck rocked with impact. Another vehicle had rammed them from behind.

Mack pulled his pistol and squeezed off two rounds wildly through the back window.

The ramming car was already pulling back, and Frank glimpsed the driver's blond hair beneath a ball cap. It was her. It had to be that damned Loren Malen who'd escaped from Gemini.

The Civic angled across the grass away from them. The driver leaned down and fired.

Frank threw himself back against the seat just as a perfectly round hole appeared in the middle of the window. That was a hell of a shot. If Frank hadn't moved, that bastard would've hit him.

The Civic bumped over the curb and entered the road. The blue BMW that had rear-ended them pulled in behind it.

Mack jammed down on the gas, the SUV skidded around, and shot off in pursuit.

A burst of static came from Frank's radio. "This is Three. I have them in sight. I'm coming around the southeast corner in pursuit. Over."

Frank lifted the Mic. "This is Actual. Who else is engaged? Over."

"This is Two. I'm hit, repeat, I'm hit. Stay in pursuit. I'm stable but cannot drive. Four is done. Over and out."

Frank slammed the side of his fist into the dashboard, creating a spiderweb of cracks in the plastic.

"This is Five. I'm in pursuit, but my vehicle is damaged."

The Civic and the blue BMW turned right out of their sight.

Frank said into the radio, "This is Actual. The tango and the second car helping them have turned north. Over." In the rear-view mirror, he could see the truck driven by Five pull in behind them. Ahead, he saw a beige SUV driven by Six join them and screech around the corner, chasing the target.

Frank hit the dashboard again.

"Actual, this is Six. The two vehicles are separating. Do I stay with the tango?"

That was a good question. He was pretty sure that woman in the car was Loren. Regardless, this whole charade was to get at least one of the people they were after. The girl meant nothing, but she was now with one of them in a car. Frank ground his teeth, causing a muscle to bulge in his jaw. "Affirmative. Stay with her. Go for the easier car to catch. Over"

"10-4. BMW has turned east. Over."

Mack pulled around the corner and shot up the road.

"This is Six. Tango has turned west on Margaret Street. I'm gaining on him."

Frank grabbed the handle above the door as Mack turned to follow them. Six's SUV was right on the Civic's tail.

Mack said, "I think we got him."

A green BMW burst out of the side street between Frank's SUV and Six.

"Crap!" Frank exclaimed as he pulled his pistol and leaned out the window.

The BMW swerved and pulled alongside the beige SUV.

Frank leveled his Glock, but before he could fire, the driver of the BMW shot out Six's front tire. Immediately, the SUV lost momentum. Mack slammed on the brakes, and they slid forward, crashing into the slowing vehicle.

The BMW veered back onto the road behind the Civic.

Two passed them in his truck, but Frank could see steam boiling out from under the hood.

Mack reversed and the two cars resisted pulling apart before finally popping free.

Ahead, Frank saw the blue car driven by Loren appear from a side street behind Two. Now they had his last remaining car boxed in.

Mack swore, and Frank looked over. As the truck accelerated, it began to shake.

Frank leaned out and tried to look beyond all the vehicles. Her Civic was long gone. Catching Loren or the son-of-a-bitch in the green BMW was their only hope now.

"This is Two. I'm overheating. I'll be out in minutes. Can anyone help? Over."

Suddenly, the two BMWs swerved onto side streets in opposite directions. Two's truck came to a stop in the middle of the road, unmoving.

Mack fought the shaking steering wheel and asked through gritted teeth, "Which one?"

"The blue one with the girl."

Mack wrestled the truck around the corner, and the street was empty.

Frank pounded the dashboard with his fist until the plastic fell to the floorboards in splinters.

Chapter 10

Luis made another sharp turn, his eyes darting to the rear-view mirror, pretty sure he'd lost all of his tails. He glanced over at Susan, who held onto her shoulder strap with both hands, her knuckles white, but her eyes were clear and alert. Her breathing was rapid, but not panicked.

He asked, "Are you okay?"

She shook her head. "No! What the hell just happened? There's been some kind of mistake. You need to let me out."

Luis placed a hand gently on her forearm. "Your safe now, and when I'm sure we aren't being followed, I'll let you go, if that's what you want."

Susan looked at his hand and then back up, her thin eyebrows drawn together.

He squeezed once and then returned his hand to the wheel. "What mistake? Are you not looking for your father?"

She took a deep breath and let it out slowly. "I am, but," her voice rose an octave, "but that was a shootout. My father is just missing, it's not, it's..." She faltered and let go of the strap, then folded her hands in her lap. She studied her thumb, scratching at the nail. One tear rolled down her cheek. "He's just missing. No one is trying to hurt me or anything. Until now."

Luis sighed. "Did you know those men were going to be there?"

She looked over sharply, a crease forming in her forehead. "No. I don't know who those men were." She hesitated. "Except one."

Luis looked sidelong at her. "Which one?"

"The big man in the passenger's seat of the SUV that tried to cut us off. He's, well, I'm pretty sure he's the one who told me to go to you." She looked over, a painful cast in her hazel eyes. "He's how I found out about you."

Not good. At least it was a decent sign that she was forthcoming with that information, though. She didn't seem complicit in this attack.

Susan asked, "Who are you?"

"My name's Luis. You're Susan, yes?"

She nodded and shuddered. "I think you might have saved me."

Luis nodded. "That's a good bet."

"Thank you." She looked down again, hunched her shoulders, and absentmindedly rubbed her forehead. She noticed a small smear of blood on her fingers, pulled down the visor, and studied her injury.

"You okay?"

Susan nodded and glanced over at Luis, giving him a once-over before noticing his leg. "You're bleeding!"

He shrugged. "It's okay, it just grazed me."

Her eyes flew open wide. "A bullet?"

"I'm fine. This guy in the SUV, he told you about us?"

Susan's attention darted between his face and his injured thigh. "Yes. I'm sorry. That man, Frank, he said his name was, told me y'all didn't like each other. I didn't mean to lead him to you."

Interesting. He definitely needed to find out more about that later. "It's okay. I appreciate your honesty."

They rode along in silence for a moment.

Luis glanced in the rear-view mirror. "Is there anything in this car you're attached to?"

Susan frowned. "What? Why?"

Luis shrugged. "You can't keep it anymore. We're going to have to dump it. Is there anything in here you want?"

"Dump it! Why?"

Luis responded without looking at her. "Because those people want us, and if they can use you to get to us, they obviously will. You've gotten yourself mixed up with some evil men, Susan. It's almost certain that they're tracking this car in some form or fashion. So, I'm sorry, but is there anything in this car you want?"

Her eyes widened. "What would I do for a car, then?" she asked, her voice rising again.

Luis responded in a soothing tone. "One problem at a time. We'll help with that, but for now, we need to get away from this car. Is there anything in it you need?"

Sus shook her head. "No. My luggage is in my hotel room." She reached down and pulled her phone charge cable free. "That's it."

Luis grinned, and Susan returned a weak smile. He handed her his cell phone. "Now please turn your phone and mine off for now. They can be tracked as well."

She accepted his phone and considered his words before complying.

They continued into an industrial section, where soon all the signs were only in Spanish. He pulled up to a flat gray roll-up door in a tan building and beeped the horn twice.

A short Hispanic man in a denim, button-up shirt peered around the corner.

Luis nodded at him.

The man disappeared, and a moment later, the door rolled up.

Luis pulled inside. It was a large area with several cars in various stages of disassembly.

Susan leaned over, her eyes wide, and said under her breath, "This is a chop shop."

Luis grinned. "It sure is. There's no faster place on earth to make a car disappear than a chop shop in Miami." He stepped out as a stocky man with dark glasses and a bandana tied around his forehead walked over.

He grasped Luis's hand and gave him a half chest bump, half hug. The man frowned at the circle of blood on Luis' pants. "You okay?"

Luis nodded. "Fine. Listen, this little pony needs to disappear. My guess is it has a Lo-jack or some kind of tracker on it."

The man with the glasses frowned. "No problem. Antonio, silence this one for me."

A young man jogged over and crawled under the Civic.

Luis grasped the man's shoulder. "I appreciate it. Got some wheels I can borrow for a few days?"

He nodded and led them through the workshop to a board on the far wall. He pulled down a pair of keys and handed them to Luis. "It's for the mostly blue pickup out back."

Luis accepted them. "Gracias. I owe you one."

Outside, Luis and Susan climbed into a light blue mid 1970s Ford pickup, its hood and front right fender painted a matte primer gray.

Luis began to put the car in drive, but Susan stopped him. "Wait. So, what, I just lose my car now?"

Luis shrugged. "It was pretty beat up."

She threw up her hands. "That may be, but it's mine."

Luis nodded. "It was. Now you're going to have to say someone stole it from the hotel parking lot. It's Miami. No one will even blink an eye."

Her brow furrowed. "And what did you mean it's being tracked?"

Luis shrugged. "If those men used you to trap us, it's a pretty good bet they put a tracker in your car. I would have."

Susan gaped at him.

He reached over and gently closed her mouth with a bent knuckle. "Look, I know this is all crazy."

She sat back and crossed her arms. "Crazy? This is beyond crazy."

Luis' smile faded, and he bore into her with cold, dark eyes. "Listen to me. I know you don't want to be in the middle of this, but you are. Nothing in the world will change that. Some bad guys used you to get to us, and now you're stuck. I promise I will get you out of all of this as soon as I can. But for now, you need to just accept it and help me keep you safe. Understand?"

She looked over and stuck out her jaw, but resisted arguing with him. "Who's us? And why do those men want to find you?"

Luis put the car in drive and pulled out. "I'm not sure we're ready for you to know any of that yet."

Chapter 11

Eddie pulled into the Langer building and closed the garage door behind him.

As he stepped out of the car, Jeff's head appeared in the door window, a crease visible on his forehead.

Eddie knew how he felt. He stepped inside and took in Jeff and Loren standing behind him. As he gave each of them a quick hug, he asked, "Nothing from Luis yet?"

Loren shook her head.

Eddie rubbed his forehead with his fingertips. "I knew something seemed wrong about this."

Jeff asked, "Who do you think it is?"

Eddie sighed. "Did you see the big man in the black SUV that tried to cut Luis off? He looked an awful lot like the man who tried to kill Sam and me on the island."

Loren covered her mouth with long, slender fingers. "So, they've found us?"

Eddied shrugged. "Well, not yet, but they're getting awful close."

Jeff asked, "What do you think we should do now?"

Eddie paced back and forth. "Well, first is this about Caveman? Loren, you and Jeff get back to the house in the Mules and be ready to help Luis when he calls. I'm going to go to the safe-house. I think someone needs to be with Caveman, in case this was just something to draw us away from him."

Jeff's eyes widened. "Like a diversion?"

Loren asked. "Did you call him?"

Eddie nodded. "No answer. But you know how he is when he gets working." He shrugged again. "I'm going to go down there just in case. I'll leave from the northeast corner."

Loren kissed him. "Be careful."

• • •

It was nearly an hour before Eddie made it to the safe-house, as he'd taken an overly cautious route, doubling back again and again.

The people from the island had finally found them. Or gotten close enough that they knew the work they did and how to draw them out. Exactly what he'd been dreading had happened. He didn't believe that they'd discovered Caveman's whereabouts. They'd been too careful about that, but he would feel better when he saw his friend with his own eyes. He punched in the code and drove down the long driveway.

Caveman was in the shop cutting boards on a power saw.

Eddie let out a slow breath and stepped out of the car.

Caveman turned, and then his smile faded. "What's wrong?"

"It was a trap."

Caveman's eyes widened. "Is everyone okay?"

Eddie lifted one shoulder. "I'm not sure. Luis jumped in the car with the girl we were meeting and took off. We ran interference for them and I'm almost positive they got away, but haven't heard from him since."

Caveman studied the ground between them. "Was the girl part of the trap?"

Eddie frowned. "I'm not sure. Luis didn't seem to think so. For whatever reason, he told Jeff to get out of there and he stayed with her."

Caveman scowled. "He must've had a reason, a hunch that she was a victim, too."

Eddie nodded. "I hope he's right."

The two men walked into the house.

Eddie asked, "Everything been quiet here?"

Caveman nodded and picked up his phone from the counter. "Oh crap. I didn't hear that you called—I was out cutting the inserts. I'm so sorry."

Eddie put a hand on his shoulder. "It's okay. I'm just glad you're safe. You better text Loren and Jeff that you're good."

Caveman nodded, began to text, and then glanced up. "The girl has to be okay. Why else would Luis put himself in jeopardy for her?"

Eddie cocked his head to one side. "Sometimes Luis does impulsive things. I'm pretty sure the big man who tried to kill us on your island was there."

Caveman sank down into a kitchen chair and looked through Eddie. "So, they finally found us?"

Eddie shrugged. "They're close, at least."

Caveman sent the text, then set the phone down and frowned. "I wonder where they found this girl. What did she want us to do for her again?"

"Find her missing father."

Caveman's brow furrowed. "Why did she come to us for that?"

Eddie shrugged. "Her father did something with the government."

This caused Caveman's eyebrows to shoot up. "Well, maybe there's something in my head that could help. What was her father's name?"

Eddie narrowed his eyes, trying to remember. "Benjamin. Um, Leonette, that's it. Benjamin Leonette."

Caveman's eyes rolled up into his head. His limbs snapped into a rigid state for a few seconds and then he sagged, falling out of the chair.

Eddie rushed forward, grabbed him around the torso, and eased him to the ground. "Caveman! Caveman!"

He lay peacefully on the floor, breathing steadily, but not responding at all.

Chapter 12

Frank burst into the hotel room in a rage and hurled a chair into the television. He hated these people. They'd gotten away once again and left him with one dead and two injured. His men gave him a wide berth as they tentatively entered in his wake. He turned on them and roared, "Clean the room of everything, including prints, and we're out of here in five minutes!"

They nodded and scrambled to each of their rooms.

Frank grabbed his suitcase and walked back outside. Was the dead man traceable back to him or these hotel rooms? He didn't think so. Now the question was, did they have to move hotels or leave Miami all together? Throwing the suitcase into the back of the SUV, he climbed into the passenger's seat and willed the storm of anger in his mind to cool. He needed to go see Gemini and face the music. Once again, this quarry had gotten the best of him. Worse than that, they now knew Frank was close, making it even harder to try again.

He balled a massive fist and squeezed his eyes shut. What was his next move? He sensed someone near him and opened his eyes to find Mack waiting. "Did the tracker lead us anywhere?":

The younger man shook his head. "We found it in a dumpster in Overtown."

Frank sighed. He figured this group would check for trackers or bugs.

"What are your orders, boss?"

He let out a long breath. "Tell the men to head south and find another hotel to set up in. But first, take me to the marina. I need to go tell Gemini."

Mack studied him with cold, blue eyes. "You need some back-up?"

Frank considered the question and then shook his head. "Thanks, but I don't think we're there yet."

Mack drove him to the coast and once again Frank took the launch out to the yacht and Gemini's judgment. He analyzed the morning's activities. As usual, the problem was how prepared and professional these adversaries were.

The two cars waiting in the wings were a good play. By staying on the sidelines until Frank's men acted, they put them in a vise. Then their hit-and-run tactics spoke of training and experience.

Frank shook his head. It was very hard to get your hands on a small, well trained, and disciplined team. He wasn't afraid of telling Gemini he'd lost them. He was worried about telling him he had no Plan B.

· · ·

Back on the ship, the gunmen were in the same place, but their posture remained unchanged. He didn't appear to be in real trouble yet.

Gemini stood in his standard khaki shirt and jacket in the center of the room, staring out at the sea. "They gave us the slip?" he asked without turning.

"I'm afraid so, sir."

Gemini didn't turn. "Tell me what happened."

Frank relayed the events of the morning.

Gemini frowned and remained silent for several minutes, his eyes looking inward, his expression pensive. Finally, he focused on Frank. "So, they took the girl and got rid of the tracker. I find that interesting."

Frank considered that. "Why? As opposed to what?"

"Well, think about it. Once they knew it was a trap, the reasonable thing to do was run. But they put themselves in harm's way to take the girl. Why? They don't know her. As far as they were concerned, she could've been working with us. But they took her. And then they didn't just dump her. They took the time to make sure we couldn't follow. Very interesting."

Frank nodded slowly. "Okay, but how do we use that?"

Gemini paced back and forth. "You know when we followed the senator to that island to find Mendelson's repository?"

"I remember."

"Susan's father was a scientist who worked for Mandelson. He disappeared right about the time the government shut everything down. Poof, he just vanished."

Frank narrowed his eyes. That was interesting. "From where?"

"Washington D.C. He lived in Georgetown. I have the entire FBI file on the missing person." He walked over to his desk. "If they took the girl, my guess is they intend to help her. Or at least use her. They must not have gotten everything they needed from the island. Not if they want to find Benjamin Leonette." He handed Frank the folder.

It was heavy. "So, if they look for Benjamin, we might know where they'll do that."

Gemini nodded. "That will also take them away from their home turf, where it appears we will never get to them."

Frank scratched his scar and held up the file. "I'll look through this and get some men to D.C. today."

Gemini nodded. "All is not lost, my friend. We'll get them."

Chapter 13

Luis drove the old pickup truck into the parking lot of a shopping center and backed up against the building's side. Close enough to be a public place, somewhere she would feel safe, but far enough back that he could monitor his surroundings. He turned off the engine.

Susan sat slightly hunched forward, taut as a bowstring. Her eyes narrowed, and she set her jaw.

He said, "You have a decision to make, Susan."

She turned to him, the question shaking her from her thoughts. "What decision is that?"

Luis gestured toward the stores across the way with his chin. "You can just walk away. Go over there and call an Uber back to your hotel. Report your car stolen and go home."

Susan scowled and sat back. "What do you mean?"

"I mean, you aren't a prisoner. You're free to do whatever you want. I have some suggestions, but I don't want you to think that you're being held captive or anything like that."

"Suggestions? Are you saying you can't help me?"

Luis shook his head. "I don't know. But stuff got pretty crazy back there and I understand if this is getting to be more than you bargained for."

Susan studied him for a long moment. "What suggestions?"

Luis sighed. "You seem to have gotten yourself caught up with some bad guys. People very interested in getting to us. My guess is that if you go back to your hotel, they'll be waiting."

Susan closed her eyes and shook her head. "So, you're telling me I'm screwed."

A smile touched Luis' lips. "Not necessarily. You can come with us. We can help you find your dad, and you can help us find out who these guys are."

"You don't know who they are?"

Luis shrugged again. "I have a guess."

"Why do they want to get to you?"

Luis scratched his chin. "I don't think we know each other well enough for that yet. What did they say to you about us?"

Susan took a deep breath. "I don't know. He said—"

Luis interjected, "Who's he?"

"Uh, Frank something."

"The man you maybe saw this morning at the park?"

Susan looked past him, remembering. "I think so. The one in the SUV that tried to cut us off. The dark-haired one."

Luis nodded. "Go on."

"Frank came to see me in Charlotte. He said that he was looking for information that might involve my father. That if it helped me, it might help them. He said that y'all had a falling out so you wouldn't help him, but you might help me."

Luis considered this. He didn't think she was lying. He wondered if she was just bait or if the disappearance of her father really was connected to Treleous or Caveman. "That's it. That's the last time you saw him before today?"

She nodded, her eyes widening. "Yes. I didn't even know he was in Florida. You have to believe me."

Luis considered her. "I think I do. So, what do you want to do?"

Susan let out a long breath through her nose. She looked sidelong at Luis before asking, "Do you still think you can help me find my father?"

"Possibly."

She turned to him, her eyes pleading. "Will you?"

Luis liked her, and he wanted to help, but Eddie was going to be beside himself. "My boss isn't going to be happy about this morning. Let's call him and check in."

Chapter 14

Eddie sat back on his haunches and frowned at Caveman. He'd tried everything to revive his friend. He'd coaxed him, shook him, splashed him with ice water, and even slapped him, but Caveman hadn't reacted at all.

His gut told him this wasn't medical. That it was part of Caveman's programming. Some sort of failsafe to put him into a kind of catatonic state if someone tried to access certain information. Eddie prayed it wasn't permanent.

He glanced at his watch. Adding to his worry, he still hadn't heard from Luis. He shook his head. How was it they were in the middle of a storm again? Eddie flinched in anger. He knew they shouldn't have taken this case.

Then a thought struck. How is it that this woman had reached out to them with a name that would trigger Caveman? Was that somehow the intention? Was this all just to sabotage him? Did that mean that Luis was in trouble?

One thing at a time. He couldn't stay here, and Caveman required help. What if he remained like this for days? Eddie squeezed his eyes shut. He couldn't leave him here, so he'd have to risk moving him somewhere else.

Collecting some scrap wood, he made a makeshift stretcher, hauled Caveman onto it, and strapped him down. He grabbed one end, dragged his motionless friend out to the SUV, and loaded him into the back. Struggling with the dead weight, he finally closed the rear door and leaned against the vehicle, panting. Taking Caveman from here was a risk. Especially since Treleous was so close, but what choice did he have?

He put out some food for the dogs, then after checking on Caveman one more time, he climbed in and drove out the front gate.

Once again, Eddie took a roundabout path back north. Should he take Caveman to the house or the Langer building? If he needed to bring outsiders in, which would be the least exposure? He decided the Langer building would be the harder resource to replace, so he headed toward the house.

His attention darted all over the traffic, looking for a tail. Alone, it was much harder to detect one, and the three of them hadn't noticed the surveillance this morning. Just how compromised were they?

He pulled out his pistol and placed it in his lap for easy access. Tilting down the rear-view mirror, he studied Caveman. Still breathing, thank God.

Eddie wanted to call Loren and Jeff, but resisted the distraction. He had to ensure no one was following him. He noticed a black minivan behind him for a while, and monitoring it, abruptly turned at the next light and doubled back. The van didn't follow. Was he being too paranoid?

Eddie repeated this same process for the next hour as he migrated in the house's direction. The muscles in his back were tense, and the stress was draining him. But he stayed vigilant and focused until he finally pulled down their driveway.

Jeff and Loren stepped outside to meet him.

Seeing Eddie's face, she asked, "What's wrong?"

"It's Caveman. He's catatonic and unresponsive. Jeff, help me get him inside."

Loren's eyes widened.

Eddie opened the rear and slid Caveman back some.

Loren leaned down and checked his pulse. "He's breathing." She lifted an eyelid. His eyes were white, with his pupils completely rolled back. She felt his forehead. "How long has he been this way?"

Eddie looked at his watch. "About an hour. Maybe a little more. I was discussing this morning's events with him. He asked who the girl was searching for. I said the name Benjamin Leonette, and he turned off like that." He snapped his fingers.

Jeff covered his mouth with one hand. "Do we move him to a bed?"

Eddie nodded. "I think so. At least we can make him comfortable."

Loren asked, "Have you heard from Luis?"

Eddie shook his head. "Not yet. I take it you haven't, either. We know he got away, though, so until we hear something…"

Jeff and Eddie lifted the makeshift stretcher and carried Caveman inside the house. They walked him down the hallway to a guest room and laid him on the bed.

Caveman looked peaceful, breathing in and out in a steady rhythm, but didn't move or fidget at all.

After a moment, Eddie led them from the room and back down the hall to the kitchen table, where he slumped down in a chair. "What are we going to do now? It's very worrisome that this woman, what's her name, Susan, came to us asking about a person who just happened to shut Caveman down."

Jeff cocked an eyebrow. "So, you think this is all about him?"

Loren stood and pulled a glass from the cabinet. "Well, it's too coincidental that she would know something that would trigger Caveman like that. At the very least, it's someone gunning for us, and it's connected to him."

Eddie rubbed his forehead. "Agreed. I'm pretty sure the passenger in the black SUV was the man who tried to kill Sam and me on that island."

"You said that earlier. Then, at least we know it's Treleous. Whether they know about Caveman is another question."

Jeff shook his head. "I don't see how they could."

Loren sighed. "They certainly haven't acted like they knew about him so far. How could they have discovered him? And if they knew about him or where he was, then they would have attacked him there."

Jeff said, "Then it might not be all bad. Obviously, this was a trap, but the name she used affected Caveman. Assuming he snaps out of it, this might be our first break in the case."

Loren looked over at Eddie. "That's a good point."

"It's a possibility." What should they do now? Who was Benjamin Leonette? "Maybe this is one of those times we should involve the Agency, or at least Craig. Ask him what he knows about this."

Loren poured herself a glass of water and returned to the table. "Maybe you're right. Maybe something he can give us will trigger him to wake up."

Eddie sighed. "All right. If he's not up by tomorrow, then we call Craig. Agreed?"

Loren nodded.

The group of them walked back down the hall to check on Caveman. They were staring down at his still unmoving form when Luis called.

Eddie answered on speaker. "Are you okay?"

Luis replied, "We're good."

Jeff sagged in relief and sat on the bed.

Loren put a hand on his shoulder and squeezed.

We're good? Already speaking like he and the girl were on the same team. Interesting. "Why did you leave and go with her when everything went down?"

Luis said, "I saw her face. She didn't know. My instinct told me if I left her, she was dead."

Eddie sighed. "Where are you?"

"Out and about. I'm going to find someplace I trust and wait for the heat to die down. Maybe until the morning."

"Makes sense. We have another problem. I was telling our guest about this morning's events, and when I said her father's name, he slipped into some sort of coma. Like I turned him off or something."

Luis asked, "Is he okay?"

"I don't know. He's breathing, but unresponsive." Eddie scratched his scalp. "I brought him to the house."

"What do you want me to do?"

"Stay put for now. Is Susan freaking out?"

Eddie could hear the smile in Luis's voice. "Kind of. I convinced her she had to stay with us for now. We're going to help her, right?"

Eddie shrugged. "Jeff says it's the first clue we have about Caveman so far. So, I suppose we'll do something. Hold tight and turn your phone on at the top of every hour."

"Roger," said Luis before hanging up.

Jeff stood. "So, he's convinced she was an innocent this morning?"

Eddie nodded. "Yeah. And he's committed us now, so I guess we'll have to at least hear her story."

Loren brushed Caveman's hair back from his forehead. "They know we have her now. So, whatever information we can get, it's a good bet Treleous will have access to it as well. Meaning, even if she's on the level, if we look into this, we'll probably be walking into another trap."

Eddie let out a long breath through his nose. "That's true. The question is, do they know what we look like now? I mean, they've seen you, Loren, and I guess now they've seen Luis. Are Jeff and I still a mystery to them?"

Jeff shrugged. "I was in the car, so they at least have a sense of what I look like with my red hair and all." He motioned with his chin at Eddie. "You're the one who's least likely to be recognized."

Eddie frowned. "Possibly. Before we do anything else, I want to talk to this girl. Look her in the face."

Chapter 15

Luis put the truck in gear and pulled out of the parking lot. Still unsure if he could entirely trust this woman, he had to stash her somewhere not connected to the team. Maybe until tomorrow. He couldn't risk taking her to a hotel, either. "You hungry?"

Susan had been staring straight ahead, deep in thought. She turned and nodded. "Actually, I'm starved."

Luis turned onto the main road. "You like Cuban food?"

She shrugged. "Never had it."

Luis scowled. "That sounds like the first problem we have to solve." He continued into an industrial section and then to a small two-story cinderblock building with most of its pink paint peeled away.

Susan raised her eyebrows.

Luis grinned. "Best food in the city outside my mama's house." Inside, he led her to a table in the rear. "You like pork?"

Susan looked down her nose at him. "I'm from North Carolina. Yes, I like pork."

Luis grinned and ordered for both of them in Spanish. He liked this girl. So different from the women he'd grown up with. He leaned back and surveyed the mostly empty restaurant. "How long have you been looking for your father?"

"A long time."

Luis wanted to hug her, but knew he often had trouble understanding the right way to comfort white people sometimes.

Susan asked, "What now?"

"You mean how do we help you? Well, for starters, we don't like how the meeting went this morning. So, my boss is checking through some stuff, and you and I are going to lie low until he thinks things are clear. Maybe until tomorrow morning."

She raised her eyebrows. "Where are we going to do that?"

Luis shrugged. "I'm working on it."

The waiter brought the food and Luis leaned in and asked him in Spanish, "Does your brother still have that little warehouse he's selling?"

He nodded.

"Ask him if I can rent it for one night. Tell him I'll make it worth his while."

The waiter nodded and shuffled off.

Susan took a forkful of black beans and rice. Her eyes widened. "This is really good."

"Told you."

Susan's gaze traveled over Luis's face. "Who's your boss and how did y'all get into this kind of work?"

Luis grinned. "Eddie runs our team, and we just sort of fell into it, I guess you'd say."

She leaned back. "That's all I'm going to get, huh?"

Luis shrugged. "Until we get a little more comfortable."

Afterward, Luis took them to a Walmart where he purchased sleeping bags, pillows, a camp stove, and a coffee pot.

Susan surveyed the cart. "Are we going camping?"

He shook his head. "No, but we are staying in a little warehouse. There's nothing but a bathroom and a bare floor. You want to get a toothbrush? Stuff like that?"

She ran her fingers through short, light brown hair. "Please."

Luis collected a pair of shorts and some first aid supplies, then checked out and headed south. They fell into a companionable silence as they drove. This was also new and strange to Luis. He'd never ridden this long with any woman without talking before.

He pulled into a small street with a long rectangular building, orange garage doors running its entire length. Luis pulled up to the fourth one, which had a 'For Sale by Owner' sign taped to the front. Luis opened the combination lock, lifted the door, and turned on the switch. The unit was empty, with only a bare concrete floor and a bathroom in the rear.

Susan hesitated at the entrance and looked around tentatively.

Luis said, "Don't worry, you're safe."

She crossed her arms over her chest. "Smart girls don't go into empty warehouses with men they just met."

Luis shrugged one shoulder. "True. So, what do you want to do?"

She paced back and forth just outside the door. "I'm not sure. What choice do I have?"

Luis dropped his chin to his chest and considered the problem. "Do you know how to shoot?"

Susan turned to him. "Shoot what?"

Luis pulled his Sig from his waistband. "A pistol."

Once again, she looked down her nose at him. "I'm from North Carolina. Yes, I know how to shoot a pistol."

Luis turned the weapon and held it out, handle first. "Would you feel more comfortable if you were the one with the gun?"

Susan arched an eyebrow. "Yeah, that would make me feel a bit better." She leaned forward and took the pistol. Keeping an eye on Luis, she popped the clip and checked it before sliding it back into place.

Luis grinned. He really did like this girl. They set up the camp stove and placed a sleeping bag on each side. Luis put a teapot in the flame. He raised his eyebrows. "Tea? I have Chamomile."

Susan snorted.

Luis stopped and looked up. "What?"

"You're not what I expected."

Luis pulled out two mugs and put a tea bag in each one. "How so?"

Susan lifted her hand, made a gesture, and then dropped it. "I don't know, you aren't like any of the other P.I.'s I've used over the years."

Luis shrugged. "That's because we're not private eyes."

Susan crossed her legs and laid the pistol in her lap. "Then what are you?"

Luis centered the teapot over the flame and let a slow breath. "I don't know. Capable people for hire."

Susan looked down her nose at him again. "Capable people who charge nothing?"

Luis scowled. "Well, it's complicated."

Susan studied him, appearing to wait for him to continue.

Luis stood and carried the pair of shorts to the bathroom, leaving the door cracked, just to make sure Susan didn't run, before pulling off his boots and then trying to pull his jeans off. The dried blood on his thigh stuck to the pants and he ground his teeth as it pulled part of the scab. Finally getting them off, he pulled on the shorts; he sat on the toilet, examining the channel along his right thigh that was now bleeding again. He pulled some gauze from the bag and then looked up.

Susan stood in the doorway, scowling at his wound. "Are you all right?"

"I've had worse."

Susan raised her eyebrows. "Been shot a lot, have you?"

He shrugged. "A few times."

She snorted. "I was kidding." She knelt down and took the bandage from him. "Let me."

Luis flinched. "You know a lot about first aid?"

"I didn't really have a mother, and I had an accident-prone father. You learn fast." She cleaned the wound, then taped the bandage in place. Shen sat back on her haunches, inspecting her work.

"Looks good. Thanks."

They walked back to the camp stove, and he poured the now boiling water over the tea bags.

She accepted a mug. "How can you help my father? What can you do that all the other investigators couldn't?"

"Do you know what your father did for the government? I mean, exactly what he did?"

Susan shook her head. "Not really. He was a professor in materials engineering, but he was always vague on what his job really was."

Luis said, "And none of these investigators found out, either?"

"Nope."

"Well, that's where we'll probably start. We know people, high up people in the government. We can find out what he was working on. Who he was working with. If the normal ways of finding someone haven't worked, we can start with a different angle."

Susan raised her eyebrows. "And you can find out that kind of information?"

Luis smiled. "We can."

She took a sip of tea and stared at the floor.

Luis could see the day's adrenaline spike fade, leaving the inevitable fall. It was what had surprised him at first about combat. Your body had trouble handling a sustained period of adrenaline rushes and then falls. In his experience, until you got used to it, it inevitably led to a kind of low-level depression and a lingering sense of doubt.

She looked up at him. "What am I doing?"

"Trying to find your dad."

She sighed. "But this is crazy. People are shooting at me. My car is gone. I'm hiding out in a warehouse. This is really crazy."

Luis nodded. "True. But maybe it will take a little crazy to find him." He shrugged. "How much progress has the sane approach produced?"

She fought back a smile. "That's your answer? Maybe crazy will get us some progress?"

"You never know. Besides, what's it going to hurt you? Pursue this for a few days. Do you have something to get back to?"

She dropped her eyes. "No." She looked back up and shook her head. "I've got nothing to get back to. I've put my whole life on hold to find him."

He didn't mean to make her feel bad. "Then a couple more days seems like a small price to pay."

She gave him that look that woman give men when they've said the wrong thing, but then she nodded. "I guess you're right. It would all be worth it if I could just find him."

Chapter 16

A little after midnight, Eddie padded down the hallway to the guest room, wearing shorts and a tee shirt. He examined Caveman, who lay on his back, breathing steadily. His friend didn't fidget or move to get more comfortable. He simply slept on, motionless. It was freaking Eddie out a little. How long should he wait before he took Caveman to get help?

If he decided to take him to a doctor, the question was, which one? He couldn't just take him to the hospital. Hell, he didn't even have any kind of identification.

Eddie remembered that Senator Hawthorne had access to some sort of concierge doctor. Maybe he could get him to help. But that would mean letting the Senator in further than they had so far. All those plans and protections would be for nothing, however, if Caveman died.

He returned to his room, these questions and concerns swirling around in his head until he finally faded off into a shallow sleep.

Later, a clank punctured his slumber and Eddie snapped awake and half stood, grabbing the pistol from the nightstand. He stood motionless. The sound came from the kitchen.

Loren was awake now too, and Eddie held a finger up to his lips.

She collected her pistol, and the two of them moved quietly down the hallway.

The sun was just a brushing on the horizon and Caveman stood at the coffee maker yawning and scratching his hip. "That was really weird. How'd I get here?"

Loren lowered her pistol, walked over and hugged Caveman, then stepped back and brushed his light hair from his forehead. "How are you feeling?"

He half shrugged and looked from her to Eddie. "Strange. Hungry."

The side door opened, and Jeff walked into the kitchen. "I saw the light. I couldn't sleep–" he noticed Caveman and his face split into a grin. "Good to have you back, buddy."

Caveman frowned. "From where? What happened?"

Eddie gestured everyone to the table. "I was talking to you about our case, and I mentioned a name and it made you pass out like a switch was turned off inside you."

Caveman's eyes went out of focus for a second, and he nodded. "Oh, right. Benjamin Leonette, right?"

Eddie nodded, thankful that the name didn't knock Caveman out again. "Right."

Caveman looked at Eddie. "You remember on the island, you'd ask me a question, and I didn't know I knew the answer until after you asked it?"

Eddie nodded.

Caveman shrugged. "Well, that's kind of what happened when you said that name, except this time, it, well, it opened up a lot of information. Overloaded my mind until I couldn't assimilate it all."

Jeff grinned. "Your hard drive ran out of resources."

Caveman chuckled. "Sort of."

Eddie said, "So, is this guy legit? This Benjamin Leonette?"

Caveman nodded. "Yes. He's on the green list. His daughter too."

Jeff said, "I told them."

Caveman raised his eyebrows at Jeff, nodded, and turned back to Eddie. "Do you have a picture of his daughter?"

"I do." Jeff grabbed his camera and brought her image up on the screen.

Caveman frowned at the picture. "That's her. She's really his daughter." He looked up at Eddie. "Bring her here. I want to talk to her."

Eddie frowned. "Are you sure?"

"Yes." Caveman's gaze lingered on the photo. "I'm going to take a shower and try to sort through all the new stuff in my head. Get her here and we'll take the next step." He handed the camera back to Jeff and poured himself a cup of coffee.

Loren reached out and touched his arm. "Did it dislodge any memories of who you are or where you came from?"

Caveman studied the floor. "I don't think so. It unlocked a bunch of stuff that's weird." He looked up into her concerned green eyes. "I just need to sort through all of it. Try to figure it out." He took a sip of the coffee and his eyes crinkled at the corners. "And I really think this is going to take caffeine and a shower."

She squeezed his forearm and let him go.

Eddie watched Caveman disappear into the bathroom, and then turned back to Loren and Jeff. "He seem okay?"

Loren shrugged. "As okay as he ever was."

Jeff frowned. "Whatever they pushed into his head the first time, it pushed out his real name and where he came from. It makes me nervous that if we keep opening stuff inside him, what else is going to get pushed out? I mean, maybe he forgets who we are after one of these episodes."

Eddie looked back toward the bathroom. "That's a real positive thought. Thanks, Jeff."

He shrugged. "I'm just saying."

Eddie said, "Actually, I think the opposite might be happening. Doesn't he seem a lot more assertive than before? More human, I mean."

Loren pulled a coffee mug from the cabinet. "True, he wasn't his normal, docile self, was he?"

Eddie smiled. "Nope. Maybe some of his original personality is shining through." His smile faded. "He wants us to bring that girl here. I don't like it. I'm going to have Luis blindfold her."

Loren arched an eyebrow. "I'm not sure how long we can control the situation like that, but I get it."

Eddie nodded. "Even if Caveman is right, and she's on the level. The bad guys know who she is, and if they get her later, she can lead them here. We have to at least avoid that as long as possible."

Loren sighed and poured herself a cup of coffee. "You're right. What are you going to tell her about Caveman?"

Eddie picked up the phone. "I don't know. Why do we have to tell her anything? He's just part of the team."

Loren shrugged. "It seems like he's going to know things about her dad. How do we explain that?"

Eddie tapped the phone against his chin. "We'll just say he's our research guy, and he's looked into her dad."

Loren frowned. "I suppose that's as good a lie as any."

Eddie said, "Let's hope so."

Chapter 17

Luis was sitting beside the camp stove with Susan, drinking their morning coffee, when the call from Eddie came in, and he noted how closely she watched the conversation. Surprisingly, his boss suddenly wanted him to bring her to the house. He'd always been super protective of Caveman, and Luis wondered what had changed.

Susan asked, "What's wrong?"

Luis shrugged. "Nothing's wrong. My boss just asked me to bring you someplace that I didn't expect."

"Where's that?"

Luis stood. "One of our safe-houses."

They'd engaged in small talk late into the evening and he didn't think she'd slept a wink, but he couldn't really blame her. She was in the middle of nowhere with a strange man. He watched her stretch, his Sig 9 mm still clutched in one hand.

Luis said, "He's also bringing our, uh, research man, who may have some information about your dad."

Her hazel eyes widened in surprise, and then the look faded as quickly as it had appeared. Susan crossed her arms. "What information?"

She must have had a lot of disappointments over the years. Luis shrugged. "I don't know yet. Let's go find out."

They climbed into the truck, and Luis pulled away from the warehouse. Now that they were once again around other people, Susan offered his pistol back to him.

Luis shook his head. "You hold on to it."

Susan looked mildly surprised but kept it. "How could your people already have information on my father?

Luis looked sidelong at her. "I told you, we have access to different resources than the people you've hired in the past. Besides, you don't think we did some digging before we agreed to meet you?"

Susan cocked her head to one side. "How? Who are you guys, or who did you used to be?"

Luis shrugged one shoulder. "Eddie will decide what to tell you. For now, you're just going to have to trust me."

Susan sighed and sat back.

Luis reached into his pocket and pulled out a bandana. "And I'm sorry, but I'm going to have to blindfold you."

She looked over, eyebrows raised.

Luis continued. "Those guys have already used you once. We can't take any chances of them finding us. We can't let those men who've already used you once to find us get any more information."

Susan nodded. "I suppose I did lead them to you before. I'm sorry about that." She took the cloth and tied it around her eyes. "How long until we get there?"

Luis looked back at the road. "Not long."

She sighed. "My first time in Miami, and I'm not getting to see very much."

"This is your first time here?"

She shrugged one shoulder. "My first time anywhere, really."

Chapter 18

Frank pushed away from the computer and arched his back. He'd stayed here on the yacht, going through the files on Benjamin Leonette.

Gemini entered the room fully dressed and bent to look out the window at the rising sun. "Have you been at this all night?"

Frank stood. "I have."

Gemini nodded. "Then you're going to need some coffee." He pulled out the pot and smelled the aroma. "Find anything interesting?"

Frank walked over. "Not much. This guy just vanished one day, and no one's seen him since. The FBI had only one lead. In the last few days leading up to his disappearance, Leonette made several phone calls to the Paleo Pipe Shop in Georgetown." Frank lifted a piece of paper and read. "Let me see—yes, to an Amsu Dakarai."

Gemini poured the coffee. "I remember reading that."

Frank shrugged. "Amsu reported that Leonette was just interested in a certain type of pipe tobacco." He glanced down at the paper again and read, "Lanceolate. Amsu said that he tried to find it for him but couldn't. Apparently, that was the end of that story."

Gemini took a sip and frowned. "Is that it?"

Frank shook his head. "I noticed a few other things that I found interesting." Frank picked up another piece of paper. "The top one is, three months before he disappeared, he made a cell phone call to his daughter. This call hit tower eNB 10406, which is in Wheatland County, Montana. There's no record of him going there. No plane ticket, nothing. The day before and the day after, he made calls that hit a tower in Georgetown. So, how'd he get to Montana and back so fast, and why?"

Gemini frowned. "Could it be a mistake?"

Frank picked up his mug of coffee. "I don't think so. I'm not so concerned with how he got there, but I wonder what a scientist like Dr. Leonette was doing in the middle of Montana. This place is northeast of Yellowstone. It's in the middle of nowhere."

Gemini asked, "Why didn't the FBI find this?"

Frank took a sip. "I'm sure they did, but since it's a single data point months before his disappearance, there was no reason to pursue it."

Gemini said, "But you think there is?"

Frank shrugged. "If I understand your notes, we don't think the professor was grabbed. We think he disappeared. Well, men like Leonette don't do anything without a plan—without some kind of preparation. If you could get there without being detected, central Montana might as well be on the moon. No one in the world would ever find him there."

"So, you want to send someone to this Wheatland, Montana?"

Frank nodded. "I think we should cover all our bases. If we assume that these guys now with Susan are going to start this investigation over again, then we should have at least a sense of where they're going. I would send one team to D.C. to cover the shop and I'll take a team to Montana."

Gemini arched a silver eyebrow. "You want to be the one out there?"

"I do. I have a hunch that this means something. And every time we've dealt with these people, they do something unexpected. Act on information we don't have. Going there is just the kind of thing they'd do."

Gemini frowned.

Frank continued. "Besides, let's not lose track of what our goal is. It's not just getting these people that gave us the slip yesterday. It's getting Mendelson's work. Maybe we don't catch Susan's friends, but maybe we're able to get a line on Leonette. Wouldn't that be more valuable?"

Gemini's gray eyes narrowed. "Yes, I think it would."

"Then, getting Leonette might be as important as whatever these bastards found on that island, right?"

Gemini sighed and nodded. "Okay. I'm convinced. Send Mack to D.C. and you go prowl around Montana. Let's see if we get lucky."

Frank nodded. "We're due a little luck." He gave Gemini a half salute and ambled out to the launch. He knew Gemini cared about getting the information above all else. That meant that Leonette was more important than the people on the island to Gemini.

Not for Frank, though. He just told Gemini what he wanted to hear. Frank wanted the people who got the best of him, and he wanted to kill them. His gut told him they would be in Montana. It was time to get back in the game and catch these bastards.

Chapter 19

Eddie sat with Loren, Jeff, and Caveman at the kitchen table, eating breakfast. He smiled to himself. Actually, they were mostly watching Caveman shovel in food like he'd just returned from a week lost in the woods.

Loren asked, suppressing a smile, "Are we not feeding you enough at the house?"

Caveman looked up. "Whatever made me pass out, I don't know. It kind of depleted me. I'm starving." He took another large bite of eggs.

Eddie asked, "Are you sure you *need* to meet this girl, Susan, in person? Can't we just talk to her and tell you what we learn?"

Caveman shook his head. "I don't exactly know why, but I need to talk to her face to face."

Eddie pursed his lips. "I don't like it."

Caveman let out a long, slow breath and looked down. "We *need* to help her. It's, It's…"

Eddie studied him, his concern rising again. "It's what?"

Caveman looked back up. "Connected to me. Somehow connected to me."

Eddie rubbed his forehead. "That doesn't make me feel any better, Caveman. If she really is related to you, the bad guys just used her to ambush us."

Caveman nodded. "I know. But she's not bad. I'm sure of it."

Eddie sighed. "How?"

Caveman shrugged. "I just am."

"Even if that's true, if she finds out about you, then someday we're going to have to let her leave and she'll know. She'll be out in the world with knowledge about you."

Caveman squeezed his eyes shut. "I get it." His face cleared, and he smiled. "We'll just have to keep me a mystery. Convince her I'm just another member of the team. That there's nothing special about me."

Loren arched an eyebrow. "It's going to be hard to do that with a name like Caveman."

He stopped chewing and frowned. "That's true. I'll need some kind of normal name. What should we call me then?"

Eddie sipped his coffee. "It has to be something that you'll remember. Something you'll answer to."

They silently contemplated the problem for a moment, and then Jeff grinned. "Why don't we say his name is Cayman? Like the islands. It's a little hippy but believable, and it would be an easy cover up if we slip."

Loren said, "That's a great idea."

Eddie chuckled. "We're going to make a spy out of you yet."

Jeff puffed up and leaned back in his chair.

Eddie said, "Cayman it is. Now, how are we going to explain the things you know? What kind of questions do you want to ask her?"

Caveman set down his fork and hunched over. He looked a little sick.

Loren leaned forward. "You okay, sweetie?"

Worry spread up over Eddie's chest and shoulders.

Caveman sighed. "I'm okay, but I think maybe I was wrong about why I passed out yesterday. I don't think it was because I was processing so much information anymore." He looked over at Eddie. "I'm starting to think it was more of an intentional block. Thinking about this is getting harder. It's like the programming in my head is fighting me." He looked down at the floor. "Like before."

Eddie furrowed his brow. "Can we help?"

Caveman shook his head. "I just have to push through it, I think. Also, I don't understand a lot of what's in my brain now. And, when I try to make sense of it, something tries to stop me. It almost hurts, but I'm pushing past it. The problem is what I'm going to want to ask her is going to sound weird."

Loren said, "We were thinking we can say you are some kind of researcher. That you've read files related to her father, but not specifically about him." She shrugged. "Something like that."

Caveman nodded.

Eddie shrugged. "I guess that's as good an idea as any right now. We just need to make it seem like most of the questions are coming from us, and Caveman, you just sort of feed us lines of inquiry. Agreed?"

They all nodded.

• • •

It was a weird moment when Luis and Susan made it to the house and hustled inside. She was shorter than Eddie had expected and when they removed her blindfold, her eyes darted nervously around the room.

Eddie believed the fear and trepidation he saw on her face was genuine. Relaxing a fraction, he held out his hand. "I'm Eddie, and this is Loren, Jeff, and Cayman. Like the islands."

Luis looked over Susan's head at Eddie with raised eyebrows. Eddie suppressed a smile and gave a small shrug.

She returned a firm shake. "Susan." She glanced furtively at the others. "I'm really sorry for the trouble I caused y'all yesterday."

Eddie shrugged. "Luis seems to think that it surprised you as much as us, so that's good enough for me—for now." He ushered everyone into the living room.

The team settled onto the two couches while Susan sat across from them next to a small table topped with several figurines. She stayed perched on the edge, as if ready to bolt at any moment.

Jeff said to her, "Can we get you a drink or something?"

She shook her head. "No. Thanks, I'm fine."

Caveman moved to get comfortable, and Eddie's heart rate kicked up a notch. They'd never let anyone *know* about Caveman before, much less let someone *see* him. He pushed down his anxiety and turned his attention back to Susan. "Why don't you tell us your story?"

She folded her arms over her chest. "What story? You mean about my father's disappearance?"

Eddie nodded.

Susan took a deep breath and then hesitated. "You know, it's weird. I've told this a million times, but this time I don't know where to begin."

Jeff cocked his head to one side. "Do we make you uncomfortable?"

Susan shook her head. "No, nothing like that. It's just, I don't know, this seems different." She picked up a crystal panther from a side table and toyed with it. The figurine had come with the house, and Eddie wasn't sure he'd ever really noticed it before.

Susan set it back in place. "My mom died when I was really young. My dad was a professor at Duke, so from since before I could remember, until I was maybe fifteen or so, it was just me and him in a tiny house off campus." She sighed. "Then he got this job offer from the government." She smiled weakly. "He was so excited, but he knew it was a big change. I was still in high school, and we'd have to move to D.C. He left it up to me, but I could tell he really wanted to go." She shrugged, "So we took it."

Loren studied her. "That's a big change from Durham."

She chuckled. "It was. But it was fine. I made it through high school all right. When it was time to go to college, though, I just wanted to go back south, you know?"

Loren nodded.

"So, I went to Duke." Her eyes misted a bit. "Everything seemed fine. We texted all the time, and we had a long talk every Sunday night. May of my junior year, he didn't answer the phone one Sunday. It was weird. We'd texted the day before. He didn't answer the next morning, either. So, I called his work number, and it was disconnected." A tear rolled down her cheek and Luis jumped up and grabbed a napkin from the kitchen.

Eddie repressed a smile. This was unusually sensitive for Luis. This girl really seemed to have affected him.

Susan thanked him and wiped her eyes. "I took a flight to D.C. that afternoon. His place in Georgetown was trashed, and he was nowhere to be found." She shrugged again. "So, I called the police."

Eddie believed her. The story seemed genuine to him. "And no one ever found anything?"

She shook her head. "No. Even the FBI got involved. Nothing." She hunched over and picked up the leopard again. "I withdrew from school and stayed there for months." Realizing she was still holding the crystal figurine, she smiled sheepishly and put it back. When she looked up, her eyes were red and sunken. "Finally, there was nothing left to do. So I went home. Then I got the last kick in the gut. When I got back to my apartment in Durham, I discovered I'd been robbed." She smiled weakly. "It's been steadily downhill from there."

A crease formed at the top of Loren's nose. "What do you mean, robbed?"

Susan shrugged. "My place was trashed, too."

Eddie asked, "Was anything missing?"

Susan hesitated. "A few things. I had an envelope in my bottom drawer with some cash, my passport, stuff like that. I was supposed to go to Spain that summer for a study abroad program."

Luis asked, "Nothing else? No jewelry."

Susan shook her head. "I don't really wear jewelry. The only other thing of value I owned was my laptop, and I had it with me."

Eddie frowned. It was too coincidental that someone ransacked both her and her father's apartments. "Did your dad ever give you anything to hold for him?"

She shook her head again. "The cops asked me the same question. Nothing."

Eddie considered that. "And your father was Benjamin? Benjamin Leonette?"

Caveman flinched slightly.

Eddie glanced over, but Caveman's eyes never left the girl. He exchanged a look with Loren, turned back to Susan, and opened his mouth to ask her another question when Caveman broke in. "Benjamin Leonette, PhD in materials engineering, Duke University, 1983?"

Susan's eyes widened. "Yes, how did you—"

Caveman continued, "And he worked for Major Kinston. Mark Kinston?"

Susan's brow furrowed, and she shrugged one shoulder. "I heard him mention that name, but I don't know who he worked for. He could never tell me anything about his work."

Caveman abruptly stood and paced the room.

Susan looked over at Eddie, eyebrows raised.

Eddie held up a hand to her and slowly stood. "You okay, Cayman?"

Caveman nodded, flinched again, and then said to Eddie, "Can we have a moment?"

Eddie nodded, held up a finger to Susan and gave her a reassured smile, before following Caveman down the hall.

They went inside the room where he'd spent the previous night and closed the door.

Eddie asked, "Are you alright?"

Caveman rubbed one hand over his mouth and nodded, but his eyes remained focused on something far away. After a moment, he turned back to Eddie. "It's definitely some kind of security protocol in my head. I don't want to remember this stuff. I don't want to go there, but I can't help it now. It's like it's too late. I already jumped off the cliff. I'm already falling."

Pinpricks of worry raced down Eddie's arms. "Do you want to sit down on the bed?"

Caveman waved that away impatiently. "No. No, it's not like that." A pleading, desperate look came into his eyes. "I *know* about this girl. I *know* about her father."

He paced a few times, his eyes darting back and forth. "I want to protect them. I need to help her. But the things I know don't make any sense. They're like nonsense or some sort of code." He stopped and turned back to Eddie again. "She's good. I know we can trust her, but I'm going to have to ask her some questions that I can't explain. Questions that are going to make me look strange."

Eddie suppressed a smile.

Caveman grinned. "It's one thing for you all to think I'm strange. You *know* I'm strange. *She* doesn't know that."

Eddie nodded, and his smile faded. "It's a risk. Maybe I can ask the questions you're talking about."

Cavemen shook his head. "It's not like that. I have to ask them. We'll just have to play this as best as we can."

Not a good plan. He was about to make another argument when Caveman abruptly opened the door and started back down the hallway, Eddie rushing after him.

The awkward small talk in the living room ended abruptly when they returned.

Loren asked Caveman, "You okay, sweetie?"

He nodded but spoke to Susan. "Yes. I'm sorry. I have a lot of things I'm trying to keep straight in my mind. I did some research into your situation and I'm just trying to keep it all straight." He hesitated. "It's how I do research. I beg your patience with how my mind works."

A smile quirked at the corner of Susan's mouth. "My father's a professor. I'm used to academic types and their idiosyncrasies. Don't worry about it."

This seemed to break some of the tension in the room. Eddie remained standing, but Caveman sank back down onto the couch and frowned. "I read, uh, several files about your dad and some of his work. So, do you mind if I ask you about some things and see if they ring a bell with you?"

Susan shrugged. "Sure, okay."

Caveman scratched at this cheek. "How about Arrowhead? Or Arrowhead ranch? Or Arrowhead train station? Do any of those mean anything to you?"

Susan looked at him blankly and shook her head.

Caveman sighed. "How about Paleo—"

Susan shot to her feet. "How do you know about that?"

Eddie stepped forward, looking from Caveman to Susan. "Know about what?"

Susan's brow remained furrowed, and it was a second before she moved her attention from Caveman to Eddie and held up one small finger. "The

FBI had only one lead that they followed. The week before my father disappeared, he made several calls to the Paleo Pipe Shop in Georgetown."

Caveman nodded, as if finally understanding something. "Yes. A pipe shop. Run by a..." He snapped his fingers a few times, "Amsu Dakarai."

Susan turned back to him. "Yes. How do you know that?"

Caveman raised his eyebrows. "I read the file."

Susan looked around the room and then back at Caveman. "What file? What did you learn about my father's work?"

Caveman shrugged and adjusted himself on the chair. "I read some files on it, a—uh, a while back."

Susan bit her lip. "Do you a have a photographic or eidetic memory?"

Caveman titled his head to one side. "Yes. Kind of. Something like that."

Loren looked over at Eddie, eyebrows raised.

He gave a small shrug in return.

Susan nodded and turned back to Caveman, her tone calm and coaxing. "My father used to work with people like that. I understand. So, you read a file about him and his work?"

Caveman said, "Kind of. It was about some way to contact or follow your father. Like instructions about a train, or highway called Lingtrack from the Paleo Pipe Shop to Arrowhead in Montana. But it's like the message was from Lingtrack, not necessarily about Lingtrack. It was confusing."

Susan's eyes widened. "Montana? Are you sure? I don't think my father's ever been to Montana." She looked over at Eddie. "What does that mean?"

Eddie's attention darted from Susan to Caveman and back. "I'm not sure. That's what we're going to try to figure out."

Chapter 20

Eddie ushered everyone into the kitchen where Jeff pulled out his laptop and asked Susan, "Why did the man at the pipe shop say your father called again?"

She shrugged. "He said that he wanted to know if they had a specific brand of pipe tobacco, Lanceolate. The shop owner told my dad he'd see if he could special order it." She frowned and shook her head. "But evidently there's no such brand. What's even weirder is, my dad doesn't smoke a pipe. It was all very strange."

Jeff did a quick search and looked up. "Google agrees, there's no such brand."

Susan said, "I even went to the shop myself. The owner was a nice, old Indian man. But he knew nothing about my dad. He seemed genuinely bewildered by the whole affair."

Luis leaned back against the counter. "And you've never heard of Arrowhead? Ranch or whatever?"

Susan shook her head. "No, and I've never heard of him going to Montana. Not in my lifetime, anyway."

Jeff continued typing. "There is also no train, or anything called Lingtrack. There is an Arrowhead Ranch outside the town of Beaver Ruin, right around the middle of the state." He read a few more lines. "It's just a cattle ranch. Nothing about it seems odd or special."

Eddie turned to Caveman. "And you think these things are connected?"

Caveman nodded. "It's like a type of train or transportation, a track between the shop and the ranch."

Loren frowned. "Maybe it's a communication path?"

Caveman narrowed his eyes. "Maybe. That could be it."

Eddie sighed. "It seems as good a place as any to start."

Susan looked up sharply, her eyes wide. "So, you'll help me?"

Eddie made a quick circuit of the team and all nodded. He turned back to Susan. "I make no promises, but we'll check these leads and then see where we go from there."

Susan abruptly jumped up and hugged Eddie. "Thank you so much. I can never thank you enough."

Eddie hugged her back and then held her at arm's length. "After yesterday, you can see why we are very careful with our security. You'll have to follow our lead."

Susan nodded. "I understand."

Eddie let go of her, walked into the kitchen, and paced. "The ranch is easy. The shop is the one that concerns me. The people who tried to use Susan as bait know about her and her father. How else could they have found her? And if they know about them, then we have to assume that they know about the whole situation. Including the original investigation. So now that we have her, it appears likely that they'll be waiting there for us."

Loren nodded. "It seems like the answers are more likely to be in Montana, though. Right? The FBI didn't find anything at the pipe shop, but didn't even know about the ranch."

Caveman frowned. "Something about that doesn't seem quite right. I'm not sure why, but I think we need to check out both."

Eddie said to Luis, "They got a look at you yesterday, so they might recognize you now. So, if Loren's right, maybe you should go check out the ranch."

Luis shrugged. "Sounds good to me."

Eddie stopped and leaned on the counter. "I'm the least likely to be known, so I'll go to the pipe shop."

Susan said, "I want to go. I have to help."

Eddie shook his head. "Those men from yesterday know you, Susan."

She crossed her arms. "Then I'm going with Luis. I can help."

Eddie shook his head. "I don't—"

Susan continued, "Look, I'm his daughter. If people know my dad there, then they're more likely to help me," she pointed at Luis, "than him." She grimaced before adding, "No offense."

Luis grinned. "None taken. I don't mind. She could be a help."

Eddie kept his attention on Luis for a second. Something was definitely going on with him. "Okay."

Loren said to Eddie, "And I'm going with you."

He scowled. "They know you, Loren, you can't."

She waved this away. "I know. I'll stay out of sight, but there's no way I'm letting you go alone. With no one watching your back."

Eddie started to argue, took in her expression, and thought better of it.

Caveman said, "What about me and Jeff?"

This was as far as Eddie was willing to go. "You two are staying here in reserve. Ready if one of us needs you."

They looked unhappy, but remained silent.

Eddie said, "The question is, how do we get there, and then where do we stay once we get there? We have to assume they'll be watching airports and hotels."

Loren asked, "You think it's time to get Sam's help?"

Eddie stood and started pacing again. "Maybe. Jeff, why don't we start with you tapping into your network? See if you can get us someplace to stay? Near the pipe shop, no one will be watching. And find someone to lend us some wheels in Montana."

"I'm on it."

Chapter 21

Frank stepped off the launch and walked down the pier to where Mack waited in a red pickup truck he'd never seen before. That was good. They were already cleaning things up after the fiasco yesterday. He slid into the passenger's seat. "What's the situation?"

Mack pulled away from the curb. "We sanitized and cleared out of the hotels and relocated. We used our contacts to put out an APB on Susan's Civic. Nothing. It disappeared. She hasn't returned to her hotel, but her stuff's still there and I have Clyde watching it."

Frank nodded. "Good. I find it interesting that they took Susan. When we pounced, the logical thing to do was bolt. But the dark, talented guy took her with him. Why?"

Mack shrugged. "Maybe because they're Boy Scouts? Do-gooders?"

Frank frowned. "Maybe, but why keep her, then? We used her as bait because her father was part of the work Gemini cares about."

Mack glanced over. "You mean the same work that led us to that damned island?"

"The same."

Mack scowled. "Why didn't we just keep her, then?"

Frank sighed. "Because when her dad disappeared, we determined it was a dead end. Our employers closed the file, so to speak. But if it really was a dead end, then why did they keep her?"

Mack turned onto the highway. "You think we missed something?"

He shrugged. "Maybe. Or could be, they don't know it's a dead end and now they'll go through the same investigation we already did."

Mack grinned. "So, we might know where they're going?"

"That's the hope. We have two places I want to watch. A little town in Montana, called Beaver Ruin. And a store in Georgetown."

"That's a strange pairing."

Frank nodded. "Susan's dad made a call from that town once and called that store a few times before he disappeared."

Mack nodded. "So, you want me to go to Montana?"

Frank shook his head. "No, I'm going to go there. I want to you to go to D.C. and watch the shop."

Mack looked over, eyebrows raised.

Frank continued. "I have a gut feeling."

Mack shrugged. "Okay."

"I want us to have eyes on the hotels and airport. And the shop itself. But don't be seen. We don't want to spook them away. We know what Loren looks like and the dark, talented guy. We really need a nickname for him. Other than that, just track everyone coming and going and let me know if anything seems off or interesting."

"I'm on it. One of these times, we're going to catch a break with these bastards."

Chapter 22

Eddie frowned as Caveman shuffled back to his room for a nap. The whole discussion seemed to wipe him out, like trying to figure this out was exhausting work.

Luis looked Susan up and down. "I assume your clothes are back at the hotel."

Her eyes widened. "They are."

"She can't go to the mountains in shorts."

Jeff grinned. "No, she can't." He asked Susan, "What are your sizes?"

Eddie led Loren away from this discussion and down the hall to the master bedroom.

Loren grinned. "Luis seems very taken by Susan."

Eddie furrowed his brow. "I know. I'm surprised."

Loren shrugged. "He's done it before."

"True. Especially with a woman in distress. What do you think of Susan?"

"I believe her. I think we can help her, and I think it may even help Caveman."

Eddie sighed. "I agree. I also think you're right. We need Sam's help. The question is, how much do we tell him?"

She sat on the bed and frowned. "We have to at least give him the basics for now. Probably more when we see him."

Eddie dialed him and put it on speaker. "Good morning, Sam. I have Loren here as well."

Sam's voice was serious. "What's up?"

Eddie answered, "We have a lead we're chasing down."

Sam sounded excited. "About Caveman? How did you find it?"

Eddie sighed. "Actually, it sort of found us. In your investigations into Mendelson's work, did you ever come across the name Benjamin Leonette?"

Sam let out a slow breath. "Yes, he was a scientist working on the projects. I believe he disappeared, right?"

Eddie said, "Right. His daughter contacted us. She wants us to help her find him."

Sam hesitated. "I'm stunned. How did she find you?"

Eddie said, "We'll fill you in on all of that later. We've looked into this a bit, with Caveman's help, and we think there's two things we need to check out. So, here's where we need your help. We have to get Loren and me to D.C. and Luis to Montana without anyone noticing. Can you help?"

Sam said, "Certainly. Can we use my jet for either?"

Eddie nodded. "For Loren and me, I think so. It's going right back to D.C. So that will just look like you're traveling. Can we get a plane not connected to you for Luis?"

"Of course. How soon do you need them?"

Eddie said, "Sometime today, if possible, would be great."

Sam said, "Done. You want to fill me in?"

Eddie raised his eyebrows at Loren.

She shook her head. "When we get up there."

Sam said, "Okay. Do you want to stay with me?"

Loren frowned. "No, Jeff's going to find us some place no one knows about. I'll explain later."

After they hung up, Eddie called Piper, their hacker, in London. "Good evening, I mean, morning for you guys. What's up?"

Eddie said, "There's a shop in Georgetown we're interested in. The Paleo Pipe Shop. We want to know anything that seems odd or interesting. We're probably going to be in the air, so can you send whatever you initially find over to Sam?"

"On it."

Eddie hung up and held Loren's gaze for a moment. "I agree we have to pursue this, and I'm all for following Caveman's leads." He sighed. "It just worries me that this is a lot of exposure, for what may be a long shot or nothing."

She nodded. "Agreed, but again, this is the only lead we have."

Eddie frowned and looked away. "I know."

They walked back down the hallway and Loren took Susan across to her apartment so she could shower and clean up. Luis appeared like he wanted to follow and paced nervously as the two women left.

Eddie chuckled. "What's with you?"

Luis looked over, eyebrows raised, and then shrugged with a grin. "I don't know. I feel protective of her."

Eddie frowned sarcastically. "So that's what you kids call it nowadays."

Luis shook his head. "No, I just want to keep her safe." He grinned. "She's awful cute, though, isn't she?"

"Don't lose your head, Luis."

The smile vanished. "Never."

Edie rolled his eyes. He knew he didn't have to worry about Luis taking the job seriously. "I take it her car is no longer a problem?"

Luis held out both hands, palms up. "I don't know what happened. It just disappeared."

Eddie shook his head. "Funny how that happens in Miami."

Luis grinned. "Isn't it."

Part 2

Chapter 23

As Loren walked Susan across to her apartment, the young woman was suddenly silent, and her eyes brimmed with unshed tears.

Loren put her arm around her. "You okay?"

Susan nodded. "Yeah, it's just that—well, all of this has happened so fast, and it's been a weird couple of days." She threw up her hands. "I mean, I just wrote down all my sizes for a complete stranger."

Loren grinned. "That is pretty weird. Jeff will take good care of you, though. Don't worry about it." She opened the door and led Susan up the stairs.

"You all already seem to know more than anyone else has ever come up with. I just don't want to get my hopes up again."

Loren nodded. "I don't know what we'll find, but I promise you, we're not like anyone you've ever used before." She let her into her apartment.

Susan studied the place. "It's nice. You and Eddie aren't..."

Loren shrugged. "We are, but it started out kind of weird. So, this is—or maybe used to be—my place."

Susan considered that. "How did you get in with this crew, anyway?"

Loren sat on the desk chair. "I used to work for the CIA. I met them through my work there."

Susan's eyes widened. "Is it hard being the only woman?"

"It's a lot of testosterone, that's for sure, but they're really good guys."

"Yeah, Luis knew I was nervous spending the night last night with a man I didn't know, so he gave me the pistol. It was very chivalrous."

Loren snorted.

Susan raised her eyebrows. "What?"

"That was nice of him, and you never have to worry about Luis, but that was a symbolic gesture."

Susan furrowed her brow. "What do you mean?"

"Luis is about as dangerous a man as I ever met. If you had that gun, two pit bulls and a hand grenade, it wouldn't have stopped Luis if he really wanted to hurt you."

Susan's eyes widened. "I saw some of that yesterday. I'm pretty sure he saved my life."

Loren nodded. "Probably. He's a good man to have around. Go take a shower and relax. You've been through a lot."

Susan stood and wiped her eyes. "I can't thank you all enough." She walked into the bathroom and closed the door.

Loren heard the shower start and considered Susan. She was young, maybe twenty-five, and clearly running on fumes. What an ordeal this must have been for her.

She smiled. Susan has certainly gotten Luis's attention. She'd rarely seen a woman affect him like this. She considered Susan's question about being the only girl in the group. Loren had never really had any girlfriends. Not out of choice, but more out of circumstance. She spent most of her early life on the road with her father.

The closest she'd ever had to girlfriends were the other women involved in her CIA mission. Clay Pigeon was a high-risk, high-reward project that placed five female agents into the lives of key members of the Saud family. The goal was to determine who in that group was working with the U.S. and who was working against us.

Each woman trained for five years in a secret location, Loren being the first, with the others straggled in over the years. But for two special years, all five overlapped. Loren remembered that time fondly, but none of them really ended up close. They were all different from her, and Loren became more like an older sister than a friend to them.

That one operation had changed her life, though. Really, it had changed Eddie, Luis, and Jeff's life as well. Loren hugged her knees. Eddie's job for the CIA was to protect and bring in agents on the run in Europe. Four of the five Clay Pigeons came to him on the run. She sighed. That one operation really blew up Eddie's life. She smiled. But it brought them together. And the fourth Clay Pigeon, Ellen, introduced the team to Luis.

She paused, her thoughts returning to the lack of girlfriends in her life. Loren had recently discovered that over the years she had just learned to push on through any circumstance she was in. Never really allowing herself self-examination. This discovery surprised her. She didn't really have any close female friends and she never would have thought about it until Susan asked the question. Now she couldn't unsee it. Why didn't she? She stood and smiled. It wasn't that she didn't like the guys. They were great, but they were—well, men.

The water stopped, and Loren turned her thoughts back to Susan. She really hoped they could help her. Which really meant that she hoped Caveman was right, and he hadn't finally gone over the edge. Of course, none of that mattered if Susan's dad wasn't alive anymore.

Chapter 24

Eddie watched Loren and Susan walk across to the courtyard to the apartments in the other building, before sitting beside Luis at the table.

Jeff collected his laptop, fist bumped each of them, and headed toward the door. "I've got a lot of calls to make. I'll catch up with you in a bit."

Luis asked, "You think the stuff in Caveman's head is legit?"

Eddie shrugged. "I don't know. He hasn't been wrong about anything yet." He sighed. "It makes me nervous as hell, though, that a woman on a list in his head just happened to show up at our door."

Luis frowned. "That's not true. They used someone on a list in his head as bait against us. That's not the same thing."

Eddie nodded. "Fair enough. This remind you of the time we met?"

"Yep." Luis stood and grabbed Eddie's shoulder as he headed for the door. "And we had to help her, too. I'm going to go pack."

Eddie drummed his finger on the table. It was uncanny how much that situation and the one now with Susan were alike. He shook his head. His job for the CIA had been to protect and bring in agents in danger or on the run, and it seemed like during his time on the job he had to save every damned one of the Clay Pigeons—Loren's stupid, dangerous project.

Eddie sighed. That wasn't fair. It was an important mission that uncovered a cancer within the CIA itself. It was the Project that both gave and took away.

Loren was the first Clay Pigeon he saved. That's how he met her. She brought something back from her mission, something that scared some pretty powerful people. Scared them so much that they set out to secure a mole inside the Agency itself, and they succeeded.

The second Clay Pigeon Eddie saved—or tried to save—was Nikki. He shook his head at the memory. He'd set up the hand-off with the agency like always, but the mole was in place this time. So, it was a trap. He ground his teeth. They killed Nikki, but Eddie escaped. Got away with that stupid beaded clutch she had been so obsessed with.

At least she didn't die for nothing. In that clutch was an encrypted thumb drive. The third clay pigeon, Amy, brought back the key to break the encryption. It contained all the answers, gave his life back to him, and exposed the bad guys, whoever they were. No one ever told Eddie the details.

He adjusted his coffee cup on the table, surprised by how angry it still made him. But Clay Pigeon still changed his life one more time. Literally the day he saved Amy, the third, the fourth reached out to him. Changing the course of his life again, this time leading him to meet Luis. Clay Pigeon gave and took away. His mind wandered back to that hotel room that day in France.

He could still remember the ugly blue and yellow carpet as he made his way down the hallway. Eddie hated hotels. Each floor a canyon, leaving him vulnerable to attack from either end.

He knocked softly on the door, and Loren ushered him inside before returning to Amy, who lay sobbing on the bed. She brushed her hair back and spoke soothingly to the crying girl.

Worry about her spread out across Eddie's chest. "Was what she brought back valuable?"

Loren nodded. "From what I hear, very. Valuable enough to prove that they set you up." She pointed to the dresser. "Your official 'no longer on the most wanted list' paper is on the dresser. Signed by the deputy directors of both the CIA and the FBI."

Eddie picked it up and studied the page. It seemed legitimate. Something like this had to come with strings, though, didn't it? Eddie looked down at his shoes. "So it was worth it?"

Loren sighed. "That's the question, isn't it? It gave your life back to you, so that's something." She shrugged. "The way the Bureau and Agency people were acting, I say yes. She brought back something that was definitely worth it." She studied Eddie's face. "You don't believe the document?"

He sighed. "I don't know. I don't trust any of them."

She nodded. "I know some powerful people, Eddie. I sent a copy to a friend of mine. You're not alone anymore."

His brow furrowed as he looked into her eyes. "Thank you, but I can't stay here."

Loren looked back at Amy. "I understand, but I can't leave her, Eddie. She has no one else. I can't let them debrief her without someone to stand by her. Someone to advocate for her."

The thought of parting from Loren again tightened around his heart like a fist. He understood, though. It was tough coming in from the cold, and this young woman, who had cleared his name, was all alone.

Eddie had to go, however. He had to get some space from the men downstairs. To test their word. He wrapped his arms around Loren. He couldn't remain, and she couldn't go. It was always the story of their relationship. He kissed the top of her head. "Afterward, get word to me."

She looked up into his eyes. "I will. I promise."

He left the hotel by the rear entrance and jogged across the parking lot, stopping at the far edge under a group of trees. Still early, the evening traffic and pedestrians moved back and forth—but no one seemed interested in him.

Was he really free? Was no one going to tail him away from here? A hotel where the FBI, the CIA, Interpol—and probably most of the European intelligence agencies—were currently in conference.

He simply could not believe that none of them were going to follow. He crossed Erignac Square and stopped in a doorframe. Still, nothing caught his eye or tugged at his instinct. He moved down a few more blocks before doubling back and changing direction. Still clear. Maybe everyone still thought he was in the hotel room with Loren and Amy. He pulled out his burner cell phone and called Jeff. "Where are you?"

"I'm parked in front of the Ferris wheel in Honfleur."

"Okay, come across the A29 bridge. I'm near the Le Havre city hall. There's a Burger King across from it. I'll meet you there."

"10-4," Jeff replied and hung up.

Eddie did another quick sweep of the area when his burner phone rang. He stiffened. Only three people had this number. "Hello."

"It's Piper. Got a second?"

"What's up?" Why was his British hacker buddy calling him now?

After a hesitation, Piper said, "Your old, retired communication channel has become a grand central station."

Eddie guffawed. "You've got to be kidding me."

"Nope. She says her name's Ellen, she knows Loren, and that she's in trouble."

He rubbed his forehead. He and Loren had literally just saved Amy, the third Clay Pigeon, earlier that day. Was it possible that suspicion was falling on all American women—and that the remaining Pigeons were caught up in the wash? If so, then it would make sense that Ellen was suddenly in trouble.

Could it be a trap? Maybe, but who had set it? They'd already turned Amy over to the Agency, so what value could Eddie have for anyone now? Whatever she'd brought back had been delivered. "Okay, thanks. Give me the number." He hung up and checked his surroundings one more time before calling Loren.

•   •   •

Loren put a hand on his arm, snapping him back to the kitchen and reality. She looked at him, brow furrowed. "You okay?"

Behind her, Susan looked clean, refreshed, and a little less stressed.

Eddie nodded. "I'm okay. I was just thinking about Ellen."

Loren tousled his hair. "Me too. You hungry?"

Eddie nodded.

During lunch, a delivery van arrived. Jeff ran outside and returned with several bags and packages for Susan.

She stared at the pile wide-eyed. Lifting a hiking boot, she said, "I can't accept all of this."

Jeff waved it away. "Of course you can. A professional shopper friend of mine did this. You should have everything you need."

Eddie shook his head. "Never underestimate Jeff's friend network."

"Seriously. It's too generous."

Loren said, "Don't worry about it. This is stuff you needed and we're happy to help."

Jeff set his laptop on the table and checked his email. "The rest of my job is coming together." He turned to Luis. "I assume you all have to fly into Bozeman. It's a couple of hours from Beaver Ruin, so a four-wheel-drive pickup will be waiting for you there." He moved his attention to Eddie and Loren. "I have a place for you to stay just a block or so down from the pipe shop. It's with a dear friend of mine named Emily."

Eddie snorted. "You've been a busy boy."

Jeff shrugged. "It's what I do."

Eddied frowned. "But I'm not sure we want to stay with someone, Jeff—"

"No, don't worry, it will be perfect. She has a garage at the back side of her place, away from the street. Trust me, it'll be a perfect setup."

Eddie opened his mouth, but Loren put her hand on his arm. "That's great, Jeff. Thanks."

Caveman entered, yawning, and filled his plate. "I'm starving."

Once again, the amount of food Caveman consumed stunned Eddie. Like a marathon runner, the day after a race. What was going on inside him?

Chapter 25

That afternoon at the Miami Opa Locka airport, Luis pulled four duffle bags from the trunk and led Susan to one plane, waving to Eddie and Loren as they headed to another.

Susan looked them over. "How long are we going for?"

"The advantage of private air service is no bag limit." He pointed to each as he rattled off their contents. "I have cold weather gear, camping gear, guns, equipment, ammo, food, and water."

Her eyes widened. "You think we'll need all that?"

"No idea. But I learned a long time ago, better to have equipment and not need it, than the other way around."

They boarded a blue and white G3 owned by an oil baron friend of the senator. Susan was wide-eyed as she climbed aboard and took a plush leather seat. "Are y'all really rich?"

Luis shook his head. "No. Eddie and Jeff have money, but mostly we have rich friends who have other rich friends."

She shrugged one shoulder. "That must be nice."

Luis took a seat across from her. "It can be."

She glanced nervously up to the cockpit. "I've only flown like three times ever."

Luis raised his eyebrows and frowned. "I've flown on just about everything that makes it into the air."

She turned her large blue eyes back to him. "In the Army?"

He nodded.

She hesitated. "In the war? In the Gulf?"

He nodded again. "And some other places."

"What did you do?"

He shrugged. "Fought, mostly."

She looked away. "I'm sorry if that was a personal question. I'm just curious. I've lived a sheltered life, I guess. I never really thought about it before, but I've never gone anywhere, or done anything."

The jet taxied out onto the runway.

Susan grabbed each armrest, her knuckles white.

Luis suppressed a smile. "What were you studying?"

She reluctantly pulled her attention from the side window back to him. "Chemistry."

"Wow. Impressive. I wasn't very good at school. Never liked being cooped up in a classroom."

She examined one of her new boots and said partially to herself. "It was my favorite place in the world. I loved being in class and in the lab, but I didn't realize how little life I had outside it."

Luis frowned. "You were a kid, doing what you were good at. Just because something came and turned your life upside down doesn't mean it was wrong before."

Susan looked up, searching his face. "You say that like you are speaking from experience."

He really hadn't meant to walk into that cobweb. He was just trying to distract her, but she was perceptive, and looked so earnest and sympathetic. "I was on a mission that went bad." He shrugged again. "Real bad."

She leaned forward and for a second, Luis thought she was going to take his hand, but she remained on the edge of her seat. "I'm sorry, Luis. I didn't mean to pry."

He smiled weakly. "It's okay. I was injured. My team was killed. I suddenly had my whole life turned upside down, just like you did. So, at least on some level, I can understand."

"I'm so sorry."

He waved this away. "It was a long time ago. But I can relate. I had to rebuild my life. It was hard, but I did it. You will, too."

The jet leveled out and some of the tension eased out of her posture.

He smiled. It was strange to go back to that memory now. There'd been a girl then too, who in some ways reminded him of Susan. Sometimes change is like a lightning bolt and sometimes it's like waves from a storm coming ashore. Waves that keep knocking you off your feet, and an undertow trying to drag you under.

Susan looked back at the window, and Luis' mind returned unbidden to his storm. Right after the ambush, they airlifted him from Iraq to Ramstein Air Base in Germany. At the Landstuhl Medical Center, he underwent three surgeries, and he lived. Which was better than the rest of his team.

He understood that people in those situations often suffered from survivors' guilt. His Catholic upbringing mostly insulated him from that. Things were what they were, according to a larger plan, beyond his comprehension. If he didn't die that day, it was for a reason. He had other things he needed to accomplish.

What haunted him was, what would he do next? He couldn't face starting over with another unit, being the new guy on an established team. But he also couldn't imagine what he would do outside the Army. He didn't realize it then, but the ambush was just the first wave. The second came three months later.

The military bureaucracy somehow lost him, and he was stuck in Germany doing rehab and waiting. For once, their incompetence was really a kind of blessing. Luis wasn't sure what he was going to do, and the limbo gave him time to contemplate his choices.

A man could only think so much, however, and soon he developed cabin fever. It wasn't in his nature to sit inside, in little rooms, under florescent lighting. So, between rehab sessions, he started taking the shuttle into the nearby town of Kaiserslautern to limp around and get some fresh air. To try to keep this funk from sliding into depression. That was what he was doing the day the second wave hit him.

It was a gray overcast day as he stepped off the bus in town. Luis' unit was often deployed behind enemy lines or in disputed territory, and this kind of work quickly taught you to watch the civilians for signs of danger. A mother hustling her children off the street. An old man darting his eyes toward one specific alley. People just appearing anxious, coiled, and ready to run. It was this last type that caught his attention as he searched for a place to eat and read the paper.

A young woman stood at the corner of a building, near the edge of the outdoor seating. Her posture was tense, and her wide eyes darted back and forth. Eaten up with fear. She didn't appear to be looking for a haven to run to. She was looking for the monster to run from.

Without even really thinking about it, Luis altered course and headed casually in her direction. He still had a slight limp and was acutely aware that he had no weapon. Pulling off his sunglasses, he held them up to the sun, and cleaned them on his shirt, covertly scouting the area. Aside from the young woman, no one appeared to be searching or watching. If there was a threat here on the street, Luis didn't recognize it.

He casually turned his attention back to her. She was average height and build, but striking, with straight glossy black hair under a gray beret. She was very attractive, in a sweater and blue jeans that looked new and expensive. Like a model on a photo shoot. What could make such a person this scared? His fingertips tingled.

She looked over in his direction, so Luis casually took a seat at a small, round metal table and opened his paper. Out of the corner of his eye, he saw her turn away and suddenly snap her head back in his direction.

Luis didn't think he'd done anything to attract her attention, so he scanned the crowd again, and that's when he saw him. He was dark, in hair and complexion, and moved with a grace and posture that spoke of capability and training. The bulge of a pistol was visible in his jacket.

As the man moved in the woman's direction, his path took him right by Luis. Training was not the same as experience, and he revealed himself as a rookie when he latched onto the girl and never looked away. Like a quarterback staring down his receiver from the snap.

In his mind, Luis tagged him with the nickname Semipro and glanced back at the girl. Who was the bad guy here? Before he inserted himself into a situation, he needed to make sure he wasn't missing something. That he wasn't entering the fray on the wrong side. In the end, the fact that the man wasn't identifying himself, as well as the woman's palpable fear, pushed Luis to her side.

Semipro reached into his jacket for the gun just as he passed by Luis. His expression was that of anger and the desire to commit violence.

In one fluid motion, Luis stood, seized the man's wrist, and spun him to the concrete. Semipro's head cracked against the ground as he went down. Luis gave him a sharp punch to the jaw and pulled the gun free. His eyes fluttered, and he shook his head, trying to clear it.

Luis stood, holding the pistol at his side, and hurried to the girl.

Bystanders began to notice the man on the ground, but everything had occurred so quickly, the crowd was unclear what had happened. Some moved forward to help, and a few looked after Luis, unsure of what to do.

The woman's eyes darted back and forth between him and the man on the ground a few times in shock. Then she collected herself to run.

"Wait," Luis said. "I'm trying to help you. Are you in some kind of trouble?"

She hesitated.

He kept the pistol down by his side and held up his other hand, palm out. "It's okay. Was that man trying to hurt you?" he asked as he closed the distance between them.

Her attention moved over his right shoulder, eyes widening. "They are."

Luis shot a quick glance back and noted two other men swiftly making their way through the crowd. He gently grabbed her elbow. "My name's Luis. I'm not going to let anyone hurt you."

She looked between him and the men pursuing her, as Luis eased her behind the building.

"What's your name?"

She swallowed. "Ellen. You don't understand, those are very dangerous men."

Luis kept an eye behind them as he steered her between two trash dumpsters. He smiled faintly. "I'm pretty capable myself."

She studied him, her dark blue eyes holding his. "Are you a soldier? An American soldier?"

He nodded and pushed Ellen through a line of bushes into a parking lot, and then behind a panel van. He checked the pistol, a Sig Sauer P229 9mm. An excellent weapon—easily concealed. He peeked around the edge of the van and saw the two men enter the area and then fan out. One was skinny and the other's enormous stomach spilled over his belt. As was his habit, Luis tagged them Laurel and Hardy in his mind.

He pulled back and turned to Ellen. "Can we go to the police?"

Her eyes widened. "No. I'm fine. I appreciate the help, but I can take it from here."

Luis made another quick check on the men. "I don't think so. Not yet. I'll just help you get out of here. Why no police? You in trouble?"

She shook her head. "No. I just can't trust them."

Luis pulled her down low, and they moved down a few more rows behind another truck.

"These guys chasing you. They're not the police?"

She shook her head. Her breathing hadn't slowed, and though she was keeping her wits about her, the fear was genuine. No, it was more than fear. She was terrified.

Luis darted a quick glance again, and this time Hardy saw him and squeezed off a round. Surprising that they were shooting already. Taking a blind shot at someone in a public place completely changed the situation. This was more serious than he'd thought.

He and Ellen continued down and over a few rows. "Okay, I'll help you get out of here, but what the hell is going on?"

"I can't tell you. I'm sorry and I appreciate the help. Just help me get away, please."

At that moment, Laurel burst around the corner and aimed at Ellen. Without even thinking, Luis spun and put a round right through the skinny man's chest.

Chapter 26

Frank savored the smell as he poured coffee from a metal thermos into the lid. From up on this rise, he could see the whole town of Beaver Ruin. It was smaller than he expected. Just five or six buildings clustered together at the intersection of two roads.

The sun was setting, and the temperature had already dropped significantly. He rubbed his hands together. It was cold in the cab of the beat-up old pickup he'd acquired. Quite a shock to the system going from Miami to the beginning of real winter.

What was some nerdy scientist doing here? A man like that would stick out like a sore thumb in a place like this. He was sure if Leonette had been here for any time at all, folks would remember him. But Frank knew from experience that you had to be careful in a place like this. People here would be suspicious of outsiders, and once you made the wrong impression, it would be nearly impossible to recover.

He laid one thick hand atop a paper on the seat next to him. It was a fake work order to do maintenance on the cell tower behind him, giving him a reason to be here. The four men he'd brought were probably overkill, but that was his way. He wasn't sure what he was walking into here. He left two at the airport. It was not a big place, but too much for just one person. The other two he brought here with him, stationed down each of the roads, telling them to be careful. To be as inconspicuous as possible. He watched an old Ford pickup pull up to the feed store, and a large man in overalls walk inside. Everything about this looked like a wild goose chase, but Frank's gut told him this was the place to be.

His phone rang. "This is Frank," he answered in a clipped voice.

Mack's voice came over the phone. "We're set up here in Georgetown, but this is a lot of ground to cover."

Frank scratched a puckered scar on his neck. "What's the layout?"

"It's too hard to watch the pipe shop itself without giving ourselves away, so we have three well hidden cameras on the front and back. I've got guys at all the airports watching everything coming in from Miami and Ft. Lauderdale, and the rest I have making their way through every hotel in the damned city, paying off bellmen to call us if they see anyone we have a picture of. Which is only the girl."

Frank nodded to himself. "Good work. Stay alert."

Mack hesitated. "How likely you think it is that's someone is actually going to come here?"

Frank sat up. "Very likely. Listen, Mack, this isn't busy work. Stay sharp. You know how slippery these bastards are."

Mack's voice turned placating. "I'm on it. I was just curious. Don't worry. I've also set the cameras to record everyone who comes in and out of the store. We can rewind and examine each person while they're still inside and I got tails ready for anyone that feels off. I'm not loafing. I was just asking, relax."

Frank sighed. "I'm not relaxing until I have my hands wrapped around the neck of someone from that island."

He could hear the smile in Mack's voice. "You and me both."

"Keep me in the loop." He hung up and lifted a pair of binoculars from the seat, focusing on the Mired Mule Bar and Grill in the center of town. If he'd come here looking for someone, that's where he'd start. Three men in jeans and cowboy hats approached and opened the door. He studied each of their faces and then placed the binoculars back down on the seat.

Pulling out a cigar, he stuck it unlit into his mouth. He hoped one of these traps worked better than the last time, because he was done losing to these bastards.

Chapter 27

Luis glanced over at Susan, who sat staring out the jet's window. He leaned back, crossing his legs at the ankles.

In the years that followed, Luis often wondered what would have happened if he and Ellen had made it out of that parking lot in Germany unscathed. If they'd escaped without him having killed anyone. Would he have let her go? He would never know, but the minute he shot that man, it committed him. There was no turning back after that.

Susan brought him back to the present. "What are you thinking about?"

He gave a sheepish smile. "Just the time I was telling you about when my life changed as well."

Her brow furrowed. "I'm sorry to dredge up unpleasant memories."

Luis shrugged. "It's not necessarily a bad memory. It was hard at the time, but it led to better things. Eventually, this will work out for you as well."

Susan held his eyes for a long time before answering, "I hope so. I'd hate to think that all I've accomplished was bringing my troubles to y'all."

• • •

It was dark by the time they landed at the Bozeman Yellowstone International Airport. As their plane taxied over to a private hangar, Susan unzipped her bag and pulled out a powder blue jacket and shrugged it on.

Luis shook his head at the color as he pulled on his own dark brown coat.

Susan noticed his expression and looked down at herself. "What's wrong with it?"

Luis fought back a smile. "Nothing, it's just awful bright is all."

"Well, I think it's nice." Then almost to herself. "Probably the nicest I've ever owned."

As they walked down the stairs, a big man in a denim jacket and cowboy hat approached. "You Luis?"

He nodded and shook his hand.

"Folks call me Buddy. Jeff said you all needed a good set of wheels." He held up a keyring and pointed at an orange hard topped Jeep Wrangler with oversized tires. "She should be able to get you anywhere you want to go around here."

Luis took them. "I really appreciate it."

"No problem, anything for Jeff."

"We're on our way to Beaver Ruin. How long of a drive is that?"

Buddy rubbed his chin. "Two, maybe two and half hours. Just down I-90 and then up 191. You all will want to get someplace to stay near here and then head up in the morning, though. Not much in Beaver Ruin."

Luis nodded. "Thanks, any suggestions?"

"Yeah, I'd stay at the Blue Moon Motel and get a steak at Charlie's."

Once again, Luis shook his hand. "I appreciate it."

"Anything for Jeff, I told you. Just leave the keys with Melinda at the desk in there when you're done with her." He turned and ambled off across the parking lot.

Luis turned to Susan. "Hungry?"

She nodded "Starved."

Luis led her over to the Jeep. Hopefully, tomorrow would lead to some answers.

Chapter 28

As the senator's plane leveled out, Eddie unbuckled and turned to Loren. "Who's this person Jeff set us up with? I don't like the idea of staying with someone. I thought he was going to get us a house or something."

Loren shrugged. "Some woman named Emily. We didn't give him much time. Besides, Jeff has a good nose for things like this. If he says it'll be okay, I trust him."

Eddie shrugged. "I suppose. Besides, it's done now, I guess. The question is, how much do we tell Sam and how much do we involve Craig?"

"I'm okay telling Sam everything. Craig, that's a tougher question."

Eddie frowned. The risks were piling up here, and he didn't like it.

Loren studied his face and took his hand. "One problem at a time."

The jet landed at the private section of Dulles airport, and they descended the stairs to find Senator Sam Hawthorne himself standing in front of a large black Mercedes.

Eddie leaned back and said out of the corner of his mouth, "Did you know he was picking us up himself?"

"No, but we should have guessed." She hugged the senator.

Eddie shook his hand before sliding into the back seat.

Loren got in next to Sam and asked, "No driver?"

Sam shook his head. "Not for this, and I had the car checked. It's not being bugged or tracked. Where are we headed?"

Eddie handed him a paper with Emily's address.

Sam took it and passed a thin folder to Loren as he drove out of the airport. "This is everything your friend Piper found on the pipe shop in

Georgetown. There's not much. No shell corporations or partners. The same guy has owned it for thirty years and he purchased it from a family that owned it for a long time before that."

Eddie glanced over his shoulder as they pulled onto the interstate. No one appeared to follow them.

Sam continued, "I looked into it a bit as well. I don't see how this is connected to Treleous or even the scientist's disappearance. It looks like a dead end."

Eddie shrugged. "It may be, but Caveman wants us to investigate it."

Sam glanced up at the rearview mirror. "Really?"

Eddie nodded. "It's the first clue we have, so even if it turns out to be nothing, we had to look at it. But we have a problem."

The Senator's light blue eyes shot up to the mirror again. "What's that?"

Eddie sighed. "Like we told you earlier, Treleous tried to use his daughter Susan as bait to get to us."

A muscle bulged in Sam's cheek. "I take it everyone escaped?"

Loren said, "We did, but now that we have her, we'll have to assume that they'll watch the shop and anywhere else obvious we go to find her father."

Sam nodded. "That's why you're not staying with me. Do you trust her?"

Eddie shrugged. "Caveman does. And he trusts her father. He really wants us to check out here and a ranch in Montana. Does the name Arrowhead mean anything to you?"

Sam shook his head. "Should it?"

Eddie shrugged. "Caveman thinks it's somehow connected to Leonette and the shop."

Sam frowned. "I found out something else out that's interesting. I'm pretty sure Craig was involved in the original investigation when her father disappeared."

Eddie raised his eyebrows. "Really? That is interesting."

Sam said, "Have you thought about getting his help on this?"

Loren nodded. "We have."

"But I take it you're leaning against it?"

Eddie pursed his lips. "I think we could use his help. I'm just not sure we can trust him. Sure that he's not with Treleous."

Sam looked up into the rear-view mirror again and sighed. "I don't see how, either. It's a shame, though."

·   ·   ·

The address Jeff gave them was for a three-story brick row house in Georgetown with two garages and a regular door facing an alley behind it.

Eddie pressed the intercom as Jeff's instructions directed. With a loud buzz, the door opened. He pushed cautiously into an open area with the elevator at the far side. No one was there. He looked back at Loren and Sam.

She shrugged.

A woman's voice came over the intercom. "You coming in or what?"

Eddie raised his eyebrows. "Are you Emily?"

"I am. Come in and ride the elevator to the second floor."

Sam suppressed a smile. "If this doesn't work out, call me and you can have a guest room. Please keep me in the loop and let me know if I can help in any way." He walked back to his car and drove away.

Chapter 29

Mack carried the box of donuts into the hotel room and glanced at the three monitors on the desk. Two showed the front of the Paleo Pipe Shop and one showed the rear.

Chip, his heavy-set surveillance guy, was leaning back in the chair, his eyes on the images. He looked up, grinned, and pulled one from the box. "You're a Godsend."

Mack asked. "Anything?"

Chip shook his head. "Nope. The old man closed up right at nine and walked home. We followed him." He reached over and unplugged his headphones, and the sounds of a TV and pots and pans clanking played from the speaker. "We have ears in his house. Nothing unusual." He turned in his chair and pulled a stack of papers off the printer. "This is everyone that went in and out of the shop today."

Mack flipped through the pages. "Any of them look suspicious?"

Chip shrugged. "Not to me. I've fed them into the computer to see if we get a hit from any database we have access to, but nothing popped."

Mack frowned at the picture of Loren taped to the wall. This wasn't going to work. These people they were after knew they could identify her. There was no way she was going to walk into that shop.

He sighed. They didn't know what anyone else looked like, except the Hispanic-looking guy who'd snatched Susan at the meet. That wasn't much of a description either. They couldn't tag everyone with dark hair and a tan.

Mack set the papers down and poured himself a tumbler of Scotch from a makeshift bar in the corner. He was convinced the guy who saved Susan was the same son of a bitch that blew up his boat back on that damned island—the guy they'd dubbed Mr. Talented. He wanted to get into a fight with that guy in the worst way. Taking a sip, he stewed on the memory. He didn't care about the organization or what they were interested in. His goal was to get paid and commit violence. He didn't mind work like this as long as it felt more like a hunt and less like a stakeout. This didn't feel like a hunt at all, and these bastards were going to slip through their fingers again.

He stood, picked up the police file from Benjamin Leonette's disappearance, and flipped to the page about the shop they were watching. The professor had asked for Lanceolate tobacco and the owner said he couldn't find the brand. He turned to Chip. "Google Lanceolate tobacco." He spelled the name.

Chip typed it into his computer and then turned with a shake of his head. "Nothing."

Mack scowled. This was the key. It had to be a code. "First thing in the morning, I want to hide a microphone inside the shop. Do we have that kind of equipment with us?"

Chip bobbed his head back and forth. "Yeah, we have something that will work. We'd have to distract the owner for a few minutes. Why?"

Mack scratched his chin. "Because I want to know anyone that asks for Lanceolate tobacco. That's how we'll catch them."

Chapter 30

Eddie and Loren carried their bags inside and closed the door. The small ante room had clean white walls free of any adornments or decorations. A camera watched them from above the elevator. He leaned into Loren as they crossed the area and said sotto voce, "What's Jeff gotten us into?"

Loren shrugged, pushed the button, and the elevator doors opened, exposing an interior of polished mahogany and brass.

Up one floor, they exited into a large butler's pantry with coat hooks and cubby holes containing rain boots and shopping bags.

A short, attractive woman who looked to be in her early sixties stood in the doorway, looking at them expectantly. She wore blue jeans and a red V-neck tee shirt, with her silver hair pulled back into two short ponytails.

He liked her immediately. "I'm Eddie and this is Loren. We really appreciate this."

She waved this away. "I'm Emily. Anything for Jeff."

Loren furrowed her brow. "How did you know it was us, and not some bad guys?"

She raised her eyebrows. "I took a chance that Senator Sam Hawthorne wasn't moonlighting as a getaway driver for a gang robbing houses by ringing the doorbell. Come on, I'll show you to your room."

Eddie suppressed a smile and exchanged a look with Loren as they followed. "Do you know Sam?"

Emily shook her head. "Only what he looks like." She led them out into a vast, open living room with several couches. Along one wall was a line of large, framed book cover posters.

Loren came to a stop in front of the first.

It was the silhouette of a palm tree against an orange sunset background with the title, *The Last Vacation*, and the author's name, *E. L. Bryant,* below it in black.

Eddie had heard the name but had read none of them.

Loren turned from the poster with wide eyes. "Are you E. L. Bryant?"

Emily gave a small nod. "I am."

Loren grinned. "I love these books. I've read all..." She faltered and her grin faded. "So you write Blake Stanton?"

Emily shook her head as if she'd heard the question a hundred times before. "I do. You find that surprising?"

Loren shrugged one shoulder. "Yeah, I just thought that he'd be..."

Emily rolled her eyes and continued on across the living room. "Written by a man?"

Loren said, "Well, kind of." She looked over at Eddie as they followed. "Have you ever read any of her work?"

Eddie fought back a smile. "Can't say that I've had the pleasure, but I'm intrigued."

Loren looked surprised. "They're great, and the TV show is excellent as well."

Emily led them down the hallway into a large room with a bath. "You all can stay in here. Drop off your stuff and come on."

She swept from the room, and Eddie and Loren had to rush to keep up.

Emily took them back to the elevator, asked over her shoulder, "Why did you think a man wrote it?"

Loren scowled. "Because Blake is such a misogynist."

Emily stopped and held up a finger. "He's not a misogynist. He does not hate women. He's a male chauvinist, there's a big difference."

Loren nodded noncommittally. "That's true. So why do you write him like that?"

Emily shrugged and continued on. "Why do you read him? Because he's interesting." She pushed the button to call the elevator and leaned into Loren with a conspiratorial glint in her eye. "Don't you love it when a smart woman proves Bryant wrong? And don't you just hate it when a dumb woman proves him right? It's delicious and interesting."

Loren grinned. "I do."

The doors opened, and they stepped inside. Emily chose the button for the roof. "People today are too easily offended. If you try to avoid all of that, you'd have very bland characters. I prefer to throw gasoline on the fire right from the start."

The doors opened onto a wide-open roof with a kitchen, fire pit with chairs surrounding it, several raised beds, and a glass hot house in one corner.

Emily continued across to the far side. A four-foot-high concrete wall encircled the edge of the roof, and she rested her arms on top of it. "At the end of the block there, if you turn left, your pipe shop is about three doors down. You won't be able to see who comes and goes, unfortunately. The only thing across from it is a gaudy fitness place."

Eddie cocked his head and looked at her. "How much has Jeff told you?"

Emily shrugged and led them back to the chairs around the fire pit. "That you all are some kind of private eyes searching for a missing person who may have some connection to that shop."

She sat and gestured for them to follow suit.

Eddie needed to have a talk with Jeff about confidentiality.

Emily read his expression. "Oh, don't worry about me. I can keep a secret, and even if I couldn't, I don't leave this place anymore."

Loren's eyebrows shot up. "Ever?"

Emily shook her head. "Not in three or four years. We live in a wonderful time. They bring groceries to me. I shop online. Even doctors and dentists will come right here."

Eddie sat forward. "Don't you miss it?"

Emily scowled. "The world? Not really." She gestured around her. "I can come up here. See the sky and do a little gardening. People visit me all the time. I always have guests. I have quiet to write. I'm happy here."

Loren shook her head. "And what about meeting someone?"

Emily's eyebrows shot up. "You mean men?" She smiled with a shrug. "I've had two wonderful love affairs in my life, and they were enough for me." She looked out into the night for a moment and then said, "So, I got a copy of the police report from the Leonette disappearance. The shop seemed like a dead end. What makes you think differently?"

Eddie's eyebrows shot up. What the hell?

Loren fought back another smile. "You got a copy of the file?"

Emily waved her hand. "I had myself set up as a consultant for the police years ago. This is a five-year-old cold case. The chief just gave it to me."

Chapter 31

Loren's mind was still reeling with the fact that she was having a conversation with E. L. Bryant.

The author stood, stretched, and walked over to a small refrigerator. Pulling out a bottle of wine, she raised her eyebrows. "Feel like a glass?"

Loren and Eddie nodded.

Emily dropped the bottle and a corkscrew into Eddie's lap and grinned. "I'll be right back." She scurried off to the elevator.

Eddie shook his head and chuckled. "She is something else."

Loren grinned. "I love her. She's fantastic."

"I don't know how I'm going to get back control of our investigation."

"Oh, you're not getting her out of this. You might as well just go with it."

Eddie's smile faded. "You know this is all supposed to be a secret, right?"

"All she knows is that we're looking for a missing person. Who knows, she might be a help."

Emily returned with a folder under one arm and handed each a glass. "This is the police report. So, why do you think this shop down the street isn't a dead end?"

Eddie rolled his eyes and peeled the foil off the bottle.

Loren shrugged. "We have some separate information that leads us to the belief that there might be more to it."

Emily frowned. "Credible information, I assume."

Eddie pulled the cork from the bottle and filled each glass. "We think so."

Emily asked, "So what's the plan, then? How are you going to get something that the police couldn't?"

Loren exchanged a look with Eddie.

Eddie shrugged. "I don't know." He took a sip of wine. "It doesn't seem that the owner is the connection. Maybe there's a message in the shop itself."

Emily frowned and opened the folder. "What about this tobacco he asked for?" She skimmed the folder. "Lanceolate?"

Loren answered, "There doesn't seem to be such a brand."

Emily cocked her head to one side. "Well, it's a type of leaf, and probably some tobacco plants have it."

Loren sat forward. This was a different way of thinking about this. "Is there anything special about that type of leaf?"

Emily shrugged. "Not really. It's long and pointed, kind of shaped like an arrowhead."

Holy crap. And just like that, the two items Caveman focused on suddenly had a connection. She looked over at Eddie, whose eyes were wide.

Emily stopped. "What? What just happened?"

Loren exchanged another look with Eddie and then replied, "One of the other pieces of information we received was the name Arrowhead."

Emily slapped her thigh. "Excellent! You've made your first clue connection."

Loren said, "Maybe we should look for something in the shop that looks like an arrowhead."

Eddie said, "I could tell the owner I want to buy a gift for someone, ask if he minds me taking pictures? Then we can look at them, see if something reminds us of an arrowhead."

Emily nodded. "So, you two are planning on visiting the shop tomorrow?"

Loren hesitated. "Eddie's going."

Emily looked at Eddie and then turned to Loren. "Can he be a little like Blake?"

Loren laughed. "No. No, it's just, well, someone might recognize me."

Emily's eyebrows rose. "Ah. The plot thickens. This is fantastic."

Eddie exchanged another look with Loren.

Chapter 32

After dinner, Luis checked them into a large rustic room at the Blue Moon Hotel.

Susan entered, took in the two beds, and crossed her arms over her chest.

Even though they'd spent the night in the little warehouse, somehow the presence of actual beds made it more awkward. There was no way he could let her have her own room, however. Again, Luis was unsure how to handle this unusual woman. "I think it's safer this way."

Susan nodded. "I know. I know it is." She hesitated. "Loren said that your giving me the gun last night was like, uh, a symbolic gesture." She met Luis' eyes. "That if you wanted to hurt me, it wouldn't have made any difference."

Luis frowned. Why would Loren have told her such a thing? He wasn't sure how to respond to that. That seemed like a good thing, since she had made it to the next morning undamaged and unmolested.

Susan sensed his confusion and smiled. "It's okay. I trust you. It's just, well, weird. I've never spent a night in a hotel with a guy I knew—"

"Much less a stranger."

She nodded. "Yes. I mean, you're not really a stranger. But I don't know you that well, either."

Luis stood in the doorway, unsure of what to say or do. He walked over to a side wall and dropped two duffle bags there. "Freshen up. I'll go get the other bags."

A smile flickered in Susan's eyes, and she nodded.

Luis walked outside. Women, especially white women, were always a mystery to him. How had she gone from scared to amused so quickly, and why? Was that a good thing? Did that mean that she'd accepted the situation, or did he still need to make her feel at ease? He carried the remaining bags and two backpacks into the room and locked the door.

Susan came out of the bathroom and, once again, there was an awkward silence.

This made Luis uncomfortable, so he knelt and unzipped the two packs just to keep busy.

"Why do we need a backpack, anyway?"

Luis shrugged. "We're out in the country trying to get to a ranch. I don't know how far it is. And you never know when you have to make a run for it. I also have a tent, overnight supplies, tools, and guns." He grinned. "Lots of guns."

She studied him with steady blue eyes. "Y'all are the strangest group of people I've ever encountered.

Luis looked up and shrugged. He couldn't really argue with that.

•   •   •

The day was clear and cold when Luis stepped out of the hotel room the following morning. He took in the mountains and rubbed his hands together. It felt like the preparation before a battle. He hoped that wasn't a harbinger of things to come.

They loaded their luggage into the Jeep and ate breakfast at a diner in town. Afterwards, Luis unzipped a duffle bag and pulled out two pistols.

Susan raised her eyebrows as she watched him check the weapons.

Luis shrugged. "I don't know anything about this place, and I never go someplace I don't know without some firepower."

She frowned. "Should I have one?"

Luis shrugged and handed her a Sig 9 mm.

She accepted the pistol, racked the slide, checked it, and put it in her purse.

He liked this girl.

The scenery was spectacular as they headed east, then north toward Beaver Ruin.

Susan looked over with a big grin. "I've never seen the mountains before. Not real ones like this."

They were beautiful, but Luis discovered that when he caught sight of them out of the corner of his eye, they reminded him of the Hindu Kush. His reaction to this surprised him. It wasn't adverse or like something as simple as PTSD. It was more like an echo of a long dormant mindset.

There was nothing out here. Just ranches and open land as far as the eye could see. He glanced over at Susan. It didn't seem like a place some professor type would go. He wondered if this was just some wild goose chase. Hell, Caveman wasn't even sure what any of this meant.

When they finally arrived at Beaver Ruin, the town was even smaller than Luis had expected. He cruised through the little collection of buildings before pulling a U-turn and heading back. Glancing at his watch, he realized it was not quite lunchtime, so he pulled into the gas station and filled up the Jeep. "I think the best place to start would be at the bar and grill. What do you think?"

She shrugged and smiled. "Agreed. Besides, how could we go wrong with a name like the Mired Mule?"

Luis chuckled, then his face grew more serious. "Does this look like a place your father would go?"

Susan sighed. "Not really. He wasn't very outdoorsy. I learned about camping and guns from other people in my life, not Dad. He's a stereotypical academic. You think it's a mistake?"

"I don't know. But it'll be simple enough to find out."

They parked outside the restaurant and waited, watching the few locals go about their business. Nothing seemed out of the ordinary. At eleven on the dot, the door opened and a tall, thin man with a long straggly beard flipped the sign to open.

Luis checked the pistol one last time and looked over at Susan. "Ready?"

A crease formed in her forehead, and she nodded.

The interior was dim and rustic. The man was now behind a long bar, stacking glasses. Spaced along its length were clusters of napkin holders and ketchup and mustard bottles.

In the far corner, a waitress poured salt from a cardboard container into shakers. An overweight man in a chef's apron sat across from her, smoking a cigarette.

Everyone looked up when they entered, but no one greeted them. It was Luis's experience that people in small towns were usually friendly, especially to strangers. This reaction seemed wrong. He glanced over at Susan.

She raised her eyebrows and shrugged at him.

After a beat, the waitress and the cook went back to their conversation.

Luis walked up to the bar and smiled. "How's it going? I was wondering if you could help us."

The bartender shrugged. "If I can."

Luis nodded in Susan's direction. "We're looking for a place called Arrowhead Ranch. Have you heard of it?"

The room went silent again.

The man behind the bar's face darkened. "Now, why would you want to know about that place?"

Luis hadn't expected the response or the question and hesitated, fumbling for an answer. Should he bring up Susan's father?

A chair scrapped on the floor behind him, and the bartender's attention darted under the bar for a second. Right where you'd keep a shotgun.

Luis turned so he could also see the chef, now standing, eyes riveted on them. He held up a hand in an attempt to calm everyone down. Suddenly, the bartender lunged under the counter.

In a flash, Luis grabbed a metal napkin holder and threw it at him.

Chapter 33

Eddie stared down at the case of disguises and frowned. What was the best approach?

Loren picked up a slim package. "I say we gray your hair a bit and add a salt and pepper beard. Then put on the big coat we brought and have you move like you're older. What do you think?"

Eddie shrugged. "I don't have a better idea."

He sat and Loren began to work on his hair.

It wasn't common for them to use disguises in their work. Even rarer for Eddie to be the one wearing it. He wasn't usually the man out front, and he wasn't comfortable with this role, but it was the only option.

When finished, she helped him into the oversized tweed coat, and Eddie shuffled into the living room.

Emily's eyebrows shot up as she exclaimed, "Holy shit!" She put a hand to her chest. "Pardon my French, but that transformation is amazing. Where did you..." She held up a hand. "Forgive me, I shouldn't ask that, I know."

Loren handed Eddie an earpiece and tested it with the handset radio she held.

He gave her a thumbs up.

•   •   •

It was cold outside, and the wind cut through the coat and gave Eddie a shiver as he walked out the rear and down a block.

At a little after ten, the street was mostly clear from rush hour traffic, and only a few pedestrians walked the sidewalk.

Eddie eased into his role. Careful not to be too obvious as he checked his surroundings. Resisting his training as he shambled along. No one stood out to him. Not loitering nearby, or sitting idly at an outside table, or in a parked car near the store.

Did that mean they weren't here? No, he was sure someone was watching. Probably electronically. He came to a stop at an intersection and glanced up at the traffic light. He could see two cameras mounted beside it. Another stood halfway down the block on a pole.

They could be hijacked or even be unofficial surveillance hiding in plain sight.

He covertly studied each street, alley, and doorway. The light turned red, and as he crossed the intersection, he visualized escape routes and options. If he had to run, he didn't want to lead the enemy back to Loren. Just before the shop was a narrow alley leading behind this line of stores. Eddie's instinct was to wander down it and get the lay of the land in the rear, but he resisted the impulse. He had to avoid doing anything to attract the attention of whoever might be watching.

A sharply dressed woman in a cashmere overcoat entered the shop just before he reached it, which was a relief. Better if he wasn't the only person in the place.

A small brass bell clanged as he opened the door and a skinny, Indian man with white hair and beard looked up from the woman and gave him a nod.

The shop was smaller than he expected, maybe fifteen by twenty. Round metal tins with colorful labels stood in rows on shelf after shelf to the left. To his right stood a counter holding large glass jars filled with tobacco with a scoop and bags. Ahead was the counter and cash register—ornately carved wooden pipes displayed beneath the glass countertop.

Nothing struck Eddie as odd or unusual. The number of brands and types surprised him, however. It was overwhelming. He didn't know that there'd be so many choices, and he chastised himself for not doing more research. They'd been too cavalier about this, and now he wasn't sure what to do. Nothing replaced preparation. Not training, talent, or skill. Now it would be odd to leave and return to the shop later, and he thought the original plan of taking pictures wouldn't be practical.

The woman completed her purchase, and with a nod to Eddie, left the store.

The owner turned to him with eyebrows raised. "May I help you?"

Eddie rubbed his chin. "You'll have to forgive me. I'm here to buy a gift for my friend, and," he shrugged, "I don't really smoke a pipe, so I'm at a bit of a loss."

The owner smiled. "Not to worry. Do you know what type they like? Aromatic or non-aromatic? Maybe English?"

Crap. He was hoping to play this off, but how? He grimaced. "Uh, I'm sorry. I didn't realize there were so many options."

The man smiled indulgently. "Quite a few. Pipe smoking is a very personal undertaking."

In all of his years of training, one thing the Agency had drilled into him was controlling your mental impulses. When lying off the cuff, there was always the urge to skip ahead in the deception, to rush right to the information you were after.

They drilled on it so much because it was so hard to resist. Even pros, long experienced in the field, had to rehearse resisting this all the time. For it actually denied your brain's focus, which was to complete the task at hand. It went against your natural programming.

Eddie was out of practice at this, and it was never really his original mission or training. His lack of preparation and planning was putting him in a bind, and almost before he realized what he was doing it, he asked, "Have you ever heard of the brand Lanceolate?"

The minute the words left his mouth, he knew he'd made a mistake.

Chapter 34

Frank sat forward so quickly he spilled hot coffee onto his lap. Mr. Talented and Susan just walked in the front door of the stupid bar and grill! They were here!

He grabbed the radio. "This is Frank. I've got eyes on them! The girl and the son of a bitch that saved her. They're walking into the bar. Tom, watch the back. Marco, converge on the front with me. Move! Over."

He sprayed gravel as he jammed down the accelerator and raced down the dirt road. The bar was a great place for a trap. The front and back doors were the only two exits. Both opened into open space, offering little coverage, and no easy escape routes.

He pulled the Glock from his holster and steered around a turn with one hand. If this turned into a gunfight, the nearest police station of any kind was in Harlowton, about twenty minutes away at best.

In a town like this, however, everyone had a damned gun. The goal was to snatch the talented guy, who was a fighter, and Frank assumed it would require injuring him. Incapacitate the target, get him out of here as clean as possible, and then keep him alive. They had a jet ready at Bozeman, and he'd brought two men with experience in combat field triage and treatment. He turned again, now on flat ground, the town just ahead.

Marco slid around the corner at the other end of town in a beat-up, old Dodge pickup and raced in from the opposite direction.

A burst of static came over the radio. "This is Tom. I'm on site entering from the rear. Over."

Frank reached the Mired Mule first and skidded to a stop. He leapt from the truck and leveled his pistol just as the front door burst open.

Mr. Talented and Susan raced out, hunched over, and scrambled for the Jeep.

Frank gritted his teeth and aimed low, but a tall, gangly man with a pump shotgun charged out, hot on their heels.

Shotgun snapped his attention from Mr. Talented to Frank and his pistol. He threw himself backward, swinging the weapon around, and squeezed off a round.

Frank ducked down and heard the pellets rip into his truck's far fender. "What the hell! How did these guys already have back up? Again?"

He heard two more shots and peered up just enough to see Mr. Talented jump into the Jeep, before turning back to the door.

Shotgun was now aiming at the Jeep? What the hell was going on? Those two weren't in the bar for more than a minute. That wasn't much time to piss the bartender off this much.

Mr. Talented lurched the vehicle backward and leaned out, squeezing off two rounds, driving Shotgun back inside. Then, in a spray of sand, the orange vehicle flew away down the road.

Frank jumped in the cab, threw it into reverse, and jammed his boot down on the accelerator. He grabbed the radio and said through gritted teeth, "This is Frank. Get that bastard in the orange jeep! Over and out."

He didn't need to give that order. His men were good at what they did and were already moving. In his rearview mirror, he saw Marco, and then Tom, on the road behind him. He was just pissed that these bastards had slipped through his hands again.

Chapter 35

Some instinct told Eddie to run. He snapped his head around and saw through the front window two men racing toward the shop. The one in the lead wore camo pants and a military style jacket, a pistol held down at his side, and had a short, blond Mohawk.

The shop owner stood rigid, staring at him wide-eyed.

Eddie pushed the man down as he passed and leaped over the counter. He pulled his pistol free, cut between stacks of boxes in the back room, and kicked the rear door open.

He hesitated at the opening, darting his head in and out, pistol ready as he checked in both directions. It was clear, so he took off to his right, down the alley, away from Emily's house.

Loren's voice came into his earpiece. "What's going on?"

Eddie replied through heavy breathing. "Running from two armed pursuers. Heading west behind the shop." He ducked around a corner to his left and slid to a stop. Two more men were rushing toward him, guns drawn. These were different, however. They wore suits and looked like cops or feds. Eddie dove behind a dumpster, rolled, and came up running. He heard the men call out behind him, but couldn't discern what they said.

A bullet ripped a hole in the wooden side of a building just above his left shoulder. He glanced back and saw Mohawk, his pistol leveled, and then the two suited men collided with him.

Eddie turned down an alley to his right and came face to face with Mohawk's partner. He was big, but flabbier than his buddy. Eddie ducked under the man's swing and hit him in the face with the fist that held the pistol.

The flabby man grunted and fell.

Eddie hurdled him and continued down the passage which deposited him back onto the main road that fronted the pipe shop. It was still too hot to head back to Emily's, but if he continued down the main street, it would be easier for Loren to find him and hopefully Mohawk and his friend wouldn't be so aggressive in such a public space.

Hurrying down the sidewalk, he forced himself not to run and to appear as casual as possible. His ankle hurt, and his heart pounded in his ears. He slid the pistol back into the holster under his coat and glanced over his shoulder. But the sidewalk was mostly empty, and no one appeared to be chasing him.

Eddie estimated it was maybe twenty yards to the next intersection. An elderly couple stood at the light, waiting to cross. He studied them. Nothing out of Eddie's line of sight attracted their attention. Hopefully, that meant no one waited around the next corner. He flexed his ankle, trying to keep it loose and ready to run.

A door to his left banged opened, and he whirled, his hand going for his pistol, but it was just a delivery man.

He kept his eyes on the startled man as he passed, and then looked back to the intersection. Left or right? He scrolled through a mental map. Where was the best place to disappear and wait for Loren? As he continued toward the intersection, he considered and discarded several options before deciding to go right.

He looked at the couple again. They still looked calm, but hell, they could be deaf for all he knew. Slowing as he came to the corner, he scanned the opening area to his right, and slid his hand closer to his holstered pistol as he swiveled to peek around the blind corner to the left.

Two black Suburbans screeched to a halt at the intersection and suited men leaped out, guns drawn and pointed at Eddie.

The one closest to him held up a badge. "FBI!"

Chapter 36

Luis raced down the road at a breakneck speed. The oversized tires and four-wheel-drive strained to speed down the asphalt. This was really not this thing's natural habitat. He turned to Susan. "Watch behind us and tell me what's going on!" He brought up a mental picture of the surrounding area. Foothills and mountains of the national forest to the northwest. If he remembered correctly, they were about five miles away.

Susan said, "We've got three pickups behind us, closing fast."

He reduced his speed a hair, to keep the shimmy from ripping the steering wheel from his hands. He had to get off-road where he would have the advantage.

Susan darted a quick glance at him. "That didn't go very well."

"They certainly didn't like us asking about Arrowhead."

She shook her head. "And that big guy waiting for us outside was definitely Frank. The one who tried to use me as bait to trap y'all."

Luis blew out a long breath. "Well, we thought that might happen. What's weird is that the people from the bar didn't seem to be on the same side as Frank, did they?"

Susan furrowed her brow. "No, they didn't. It was odd, like everyone was shooting at each other." She looked back again, and her eyes widened. "Oh shit, there are two more black trucks coming after us, way back. That makes five."

Luis gritted his teeth. That was a lot of pursuit. And awfully quick. What had they walked into? "We can't outrun them on blacktop. We need to get off-road."

Susan nodded. "I agree. Let's do it."

The road curved around to the left, leading them away from the mountains. Luis pointed toward them in the distance. "I think they give us the best advantage." He suddenly swerved onto a smaller paved road heading that way.

Susan braced herself.

Luis said without looking over, "Sorry about that. You think you could lean out and squeeze off a few rounds behind us if need be?"

She looked over wide eyed. "Those are *people* back there."

"You're right, I'm sorry."

The Jeep rose and fell over a bump in the road.

Sometimes he forgot how far from normal his life had become. If he ever was that normal to begin with.

She shook her head. "No, I'm sorry. I know we're in danger, and if our lives are at risk, I'll—"

He put a hand on her arm. "I know. I was wrong to ask it. Are they still back there?"

She leaned out and looked back. "I see two of the pickups. Just two. The other one and the black ones aren't there anymore." She stretched up higher. "Yeah, I only see two. I don't think the others made the turn. But the first two are gaining on us."

Luis glanced at the side mirror. "Hold on." He turned onto a dirt road.

He heard the first truck slide on the gravel as it turned to follow.

The road swayed one way and then the other across the flat, grassy plain at the foot of the mountains looming up above them.

A crack sounded, and a bullet whistled overhead.

Susan scrunched down in her seat.

Luis slid around a sharper turn and gritted his teeth as the top-heavy Jeep strained to stay upright. Trees and shrubs grew along the road on both sides, making a low wall. Did they grow out of a ditch or were they just at the edge of the road?

A second shot rang out, and a ping sounded at the rear of the Jeep. Aiming for the tires, that's what he'd do in their position.

A gap opened in the roadside foliage off to his right, and Luis spun the wheel and crashed through it. He entered what looked like a wide, flat green plain. The grass was waist high, but the ground was rough and uneven, however, and he fought to keep the vehicle under control.

Susan sat up and looked back. "They're trying to follow."

Luis scanned the terrain ahead for a gap, a way through, or any kind of opening. Anything.

Susan said. "They're falling back, but they're still coming."

The Jeep rose and fell with the land, and Luis wrestled with the wheel. They raced toward a dense forest, and he noticed a gap to his right and headed toward it.

The grass suddenly ended, and they sailed over a ledge, the ground ten feet below them.

Chapter 37

Eddie lifted both hands quickly and said in a calm, clear voice, "I'm armed, and I have a permit for the weapon."

The Bureau men tensed.

A tall, thin man in the front said, "Thank you for telling me that. I'm Agent Barker. Where is this gun?"

"Holster on my left hip."

Barker kept his pistol aimed at Eddie's chest. "Nice and slow. Why don't you show me?"

Eddie opened the overcoat.

"Okay. Now slowly, pull it out and place it on the ground."

Eddie started to move.

The agent continued, "Real slow now."

Eddie nodded and pulled the Sig out, holding it between his thumb and forefinger.

Barker said, "Now place it on the ground in front of you, take a few steps back, lie on your stomach, and place your hands behind your head. All nice and slow."

They still thought Eddie was an old man, so he made a noise and appeared to be stiff, going to the ground, stopping on one knee. He used the ruse to scratch his ear and pull the earpiece out, with no one noticing. Then, trying to move to a lying position, he appeared to stumble and, with the motion, tossed the earpiece into a pile of trash at the edge of the sidewalk.

As soon as he was on his stomach, two agents moved forward and cuffed him.

Agent Barker picked up the gun. "You say this is registered. Do you have that registration on you?"

Eddie nodded. "In my rear pocket."

The agent that cuffed him helped Eddie to his feet. "Sir, do you have any other weapons, or needles, or anything else that could harm me as I search you?"

"No, sir."

The agent pulled the wallet out, handed it to Barker, and continued to search him.

Eddie said, "It's underneath the side with the credit cards. There is one for Florida and one for D.C."

Agent Barker opened the wallet. "So, tell me, Mr. Mason. How did you get approved for a permit here when, according to your driver's license, it's not your permanent residence? That's very unusual."

Eddie replied, "I'm a consultant."

Barker said, "What kind—"

The man searching Eddie said, "Sir, I, I think this man is in disguise."

Barker raised his eyebrows and pulled out the Florida driver's license. He looked from the picture to Eddie and raised his eyebrows. "Are you in disguise, Mr. Mason?"

There was no point denying it now, but how was he going to explain that? "I am."

Barker glanced at the permit again. "Just what kind of consultant are you?"

Eddie held his gaze for a moment. "Security."

Barker pursed his lips. "Why did you go into that store today?"

Eddie furrowed his brow. "To shop."

Barker tilted his head to one side. "In disguise?"

Eddie nodded.

"I see. And why did you run out the back door?"

That question was simple. "Because a man in a blond mohawk was chasing me. I believe your men saw him."

Barker rubbed his face. "Do you know who this man with the mohawk was?"

Eddie shook his head. "Never seen him before."

"Why do you think he was chasing you?"

Eddie shrugged. "No idea."

Barker snorted. "Mr. Mason. Put yourself in my shoes. I have an armed man, in disguise, a long way from home, walking into a place of interest—"

Eddie's eyebrows shot up. "Why's it a place of interest?"

Barker sighed. "I'm asking the questions, Mr. Mason. If you were me, wouldn't you think this looked a little like a problem?"

"I can certainly see your point of view."

"Anything else you want to tell me that would clear this up some?"

Eddie shook his head. "I was in there to shop, and," he shrugged, "My girlfriend likes me to dress up sometimes, so I thought I'd surprise her."

"I see. And where is this girlfriend?"

"On her way up from Florida. She's supposed to call me when she gets here."

Barker frowned. "Well, you can see how that doesn't help me very much, either, can't you?"

"I do," replied Eddie. "I wish I could be more help."

Barker sighed. "So do I. Okay, Mr. Mason, we're going to take you into custody for some questioning."

Eddie raised his eyebrows. "Am I being charged with something?"

"Not yet, Mr. Mason. But we're going to need to get more answers than we're obviously going to get standing here in the street."

Chapter 38

As the land fell away from the Jeep, Luis' stomach rose into his throat, and he braced for impact. It crashed into the ground, immediately bounced back up, and fell again. All the while racing toward the river ahead. He held the wheel in an iron grip, jammed down on the brakes, and hoped the water wasn't too deep.

They surged into the creek, throwing up a wave of water and slamming them against their seat belts. They kept going, though—thank God—and came up onto the opposite bank. It was a gentle rise that ended in a dense forest, but Luis resisted turning. He continued straight, trying to stay as small a target as possible.

A shot sounded out, and then two more.

Luis felt a bullet hit the Jeep just before they reached the tree line. He had to slow down to navigate through the trunks, but at least they had some cover now. After about twenty yards, he stopped and looked over as Susan hauled herself back up into her seat. She held onto her seatbelt in both fists, her hair mostly out of her ponytail and blowing around her face.

Luis asked, "You okay?"

She nodded. "My sternum isn't happy, but," she swallowed, "we're alive."

He smiled. "Stay here. I'll be right back." He stepped out, staying low and moving from cover to cover he made his way back to the edge, and peered around a bush.

The first pickup that had been pursuing them sat halfway down the drop off, its nose smashed into the ground and rear wheels near the top. Trying to stop had not been a great choice.

The big man Susan had called Frank was climbing back up the slope, and a second man stood at the top, pistol drawn, covering his boss.

Luis debated trying a shot, but it was a long way for a pistol, and it would reveal his location.

Frank made it to the lip and the two men shaded their eyes against the sun and looked back toward Luis, studying the forest.

Luis held his breath. After a few minutes, the two men climbed into the second truck and drove away, leaving their damaged pickup behind.

He walked back.

Susan paced around, hands on hips, stretching her back.

Luis asked, "You okay?"

Susan nodded. "Yeah, it just feels like I was inside a pinball machine." She twisted one way and then the other. "I take it we lost them?"

He nodded. "For now. And they're down a vehicle."

She gathered her hair in one hand and fixed her short ponytail. "What's going on?"

"That's a good question. I don't think the men in the bar were working for Treleous—"

"Treleous?" Susan asked with a furrowed brow.

Luis sighed. "That man, Frank, who used you to get to us. We think he works for an organization called Treleous."

"What kind of organization?"

Luis rubbed his face. "A bad one."

She raised her eyebrows. "That's all I'm going to get?"

"For now."

Susan said, "What does that have to do with my father?"

Luis sucked on his teeth. "I suspect they wanted your father to do bad things for them."

She studied the ground. "So, maybe that's why he disappeared?"

He shrugged. "Could be. Anyway, I don't think the people at the bar were *with* Frank."

She nodded. "Agreed."

"But they didn't like anyone asking about Arrowhead. Maybe because they were worried someone like Frank would come asking. Not someone like us."

She walked around in a small circle. "So maybe, if they knew we weren't with them, we might get a different reception?"

"Maybe."

He glanced back the way they'd come. Was Treleous regrouping to pursue? Where were they? He took a few steps back the way they'd come and cocked his head to listen.

Susan watched him, her expression curious but biting her tongue.

A smart girl.

There was no sound but the wind rustling overhead. Why had they stopped pursuit? How many people did they have on site? Luis frowned. Why were they here in the first place? The only answer he could come up with was to catch one of his team. So why stop pursuit now?

He turned to Susan. "Where are they? It doesn't make sense that they would come all the way here to catch us, and then give up so easy."

Susan shrugged. "They didn't really have a suitable vehicle for following us. Besides, the people at the bar seemed to be shooting at them as much as they were at us. Maybe they have more to deal with now. Or this was more than they bargained for."

Luis turned back and frowned. "Maybe."

After a moment of awkward silence, Susan asked, "What do you think we should do next?"

Luis shrugged and led her back to the Jeep. He rummaged around in his duffle bag, pulled out a map, and spread it out on the hood.

Susan studied it.

Luis pointed. "This is Beaver Ruin, and this red 'X' is Arrowhead Ranch." He moved his finger to the left. "We're here in Lewis and Clark National Forest. I think we could make our way down the base of the mountain here to the ranch. Stay out of sight until we're close and check it out. Maybe have time to tell someone who we are before they shoot us. What do you think?"

She shrugged. "It makes sense. I'm not sure what else we can do. That guy Frank is back the way we came."

Luis looked back over his shoulder. Where were they? Maybe they were lying in wait to trap them when they emerged from the woods or showed back up in town or at the airport. What were they doing?

Luis dragged his thoughts back to the problem at hand and frowned at the map. "The only thing is, we won't make it there before dark, so we'll have to sleep in the Jeep. You okay with camping?"

Susan looked down her nose at him. "I'm from North Carolina."

He snorted. "Got it."

She shrugged and half smiled. "Besides, I still have a gun, so I should be okay."

Chapter 39

Eddie sat in the empty FBI interrogation room, his handcuffed wrists resting on the table in front of him. After taking him into custody, the agents transported him to the Hoover building and placed him here. He glanced at his watch. That had been over an hour ago. Probably trying to decide what to do with him.

He had broken no laws, but clearly the Agents thought he was guilty of something, and he couldn't really blame them. No one had said a word after putting him in the Suburban, however. They just gave him suspicious looks and rode in silence.

Eddie sighed. Also, by now they had to know he was ex-CIA, which he was sure made everyone even more suspicious. What a mess.

The door opened and a tall, square-headed agent in a suit entered and handed him a bottle of water. "Do you need to use the facilities?"

Eddie shook his head. "No, thank you. Why am I here? Are you charging me with something?"

The man frowned. "Not yet."

Eddie raised his eyebrows. "Then you can't hold me. Can I go?"

The man sighed and eased down into the chair opposite him. "We're not holding you, Mr. Mason. You're merely here for questioning."

Eddie chuckled. "Really? Looks a lot like holding to me, what with the lack of questions and all. Do I get my phone call?"

The man pursed his lips. "I'm Agent Harkins. I'm sorry for the inconvenience. We're just waiting for the agent in charge to come question you. Before he begins, you'll have an opportunity to make a phone call and get representation."

Interesting. "Agent in charge of what?

Harkin laced his fingers and set them on the table. "Why were you at the Paleo Pipe Shop?"

Eddie raised his eyebrows. "That seems like a question."

Harkin nodded. "You don't have to answer it. I did not intend it as an official question. I was just curious."

Eddie said, "Shopping."

Agent Harkin nodded. "In disguise?"

Eddie shrugged. "I like to cosplay."

Harkin smiled slightly. "So you said to Agent Barker. Who was the gentleman with the mohawk?"

"No idea. That's why I was running from him."

The two men stared at each other for a long moment, and then Agent Harkin nodded and stood. "I'm sorry for the inconvenience. This will all be over soon." At the door, he stopped and turned. "You know, of course, that according to Executive Order 12333, it's illegal for the CIA to run domestic operations against American citizens."

Eddie raised his eyebrows. They thought he was still working for the Agency? Maybe in some unofficial capacity? Did that improve his situation or make it worse? "I don't work for them anymore."

Agent Hawkins nodded again and left the room, closing the door behind him.

Eddie took a sip of the water. Clearly, the FBI still had surveillance on the pipe shop. If it really was a dead end, then why were they still monitoring it five years later? Not only watching it, but with a multi-man team. Ready to make an arrest. That was very interesting.

He was almost positive that the man with the white mohawk was the one they'd run into before, back on the island. How many guys could there be with hair like that?

So, as expected, Treleous was watching the place as well. Were they working with the FBI? He didn't think so. They didn't seem to be cooperating, and Agent Harkin's question appeared to confirm that.

Harkin's inquiry also indicated that they didn't catch Mohawk. A shame. Of course, he was pretty sure that guy wasn't the type to go quietly.

Eddie sat back. He wasn't really worried. They couldn't charge him with anything. He had broken no laws. It could put him back on an FBI watch list again, however, and that would be a problem. No sense worrying about that yet.

He looked at his watch again. They really couldn't keep him like this. How long should he wait before causing a stink? He didn't really want to make an enemy of the Bureau if he didn't have to.

The door opened and Craig Black, his old CIA boss, walked into the room.

Eddie sat back. Of course. Just when he thought it couldn't get any worse.

Craig frowned at Eddie, dropped a plastic bag containing Eddie's fake beard on the table, and took a seat.

Silence stretched between them.

Craig gestured at the item. "Do you want to explain this?"

Once again, Eddie faced the question of how much to tell Craig. His being here didn't remove him from suspicion. They could've called Craig because Eddie used to work for him. Or they could have called him because he was still interested in the Pipe Shop. Which could mean that he was with Treleous.

Eddie shrugged. "I'm working on a case."

Craig sighed and drummed his fingers on the tabletop. "That's all you're going to give me?"

Eddie picked up his water bottle. "Why do you care what I was doing? Why does the FBI care? Why am I even here?"

Craig frowned at him. Then he flinched and face reddened.

He was angry. Maybe as mad as Eddie had ever seen him. What had suddenly pissed him off so much?

Craig shook his head, and he drew his brows together, his look melting into an expression that struck Eddie as sad. Then Craig looked away, and said half to himself, "I can't believe you're part of Treleous."

Chapter 40

Frank stood at the top of the drop-off and studied the tree line. The Jeep was nowhere in sight. He rubbed the scar on his neck. Why had he tried to stop? He balled his fists and forced down his rage. Even if he'd jammed on the gas and made it down there in one piece, there was no way he could keep up with that damned Jeep in this terrain. Then how the hell would he have gotten back out?

The bastards had gotten away again, which pissed him off, but some instinct told him something else was in play. He felt vulnerable, and he never ignored an instinct.

He lifted the radio. "This is Frank to Tom. Come in, Tom. Over." Silence. He glanced over at Marco, and asked, "When's the last time you saw him?"

Marco shrugged. "Before we turned off the main road, he was right behind us."

Frank looked back the way they'd come and frowned. Why wasn't he answering? He lifted the radio again. "Tom, do you copy? Are you there, Tom? Over." He turned back to the tree line. One problem at a time. "Let's go check on him." He climbed into the driver's side of Marco's truck and drove the two of them back across the field.

Frank's phone rang, and he answered it.

Over the speaker came Mack's voice. "We got problems."

Frank gritted his teeth. Of course they did. "What's up?"

Mack sounded out of breath. "Well, someone showed up and asked for that stupid tobacco. Probably in disguise. He looked like an old man but didn't run like one. Anyway, we went to grab him, and the damned FBI swarmed the place and arrested him."

Interesting. "Any of our people get taken?"

"No, but it was close. I got away by the hairs on my chin."

Frank doubted that. "Did you have to shoot any agents?"

He could hear the smile in Mack's voice. "Negative. I know how you frown on that, so I restrained myself."

Frank sighed. Thank God Mack had listened this time. "Okay, clean up and get back to the plane, ready to move. I'll call you shortly." He hung up.

They turned onto the main road and headed back toward Beaver Ruin.

They rode along in silence until Marco pointed. "That looks like his truck."

Sure enough, ahead, the other pickup sat parked on the side of the road.

Both men pulled out their pistols and held them ready as they parked nose to nose with the other vehicle. Frank killed the engine. The road was empty, not a car in sight for miles in either direction. The truck appeared to have been abandoned.

He rubbed his face and turned to Marco. "Watch my back. I'm going to check it out."

Marco nodded and the two men stepped out of the cab.

Nothing but open grassland on either side, a piss poor place for an ambush. He eased around the front and looked into the open driver's side window. The cab was empty, but Tom's radio sat on the seat. Right in the middle. Like someone deliberately placed it there. Frank picked it up. It was on, so not out of battery.

Frank looked up and down the road again. Was this a message? He stepped back. The rear tire was flat. A bullet hole in the fender. He reached down and rubbed a finger across it.

Marco walked up and looked over his shoulder. "You think someone got Tom?"

There was no blood. No body. So *got* was probably the night word. Frank nodded.

Marco scowled. "Who?"

That was a good question. He thought back to the bar. The people inside had chased Susan and the talented guy out, then shot at Frank. Did they pursue? Catch up with Tom first, and then what—kidnap him? Again, it didn't look like they killed him, so they took him. Where? Why? And why not come after Frank and Marco next?

He walked back to his truck, Marco trailing behind him. What had they stumbled into? Was this why Leonette had come here? Is this where he'd escaped to? Or had these people grabbed him, too?

Frank called Mack.

He answered on the second ring.

Frank's mind raced. "Mack, get everyone and head here to Bozeman as fast as you can. It looks like someone nabbed Tom."

"What do you mean, nabbed?"

"I don't know. But someone thinks they can mess with us."

"So you want me there to kick a little ass?"

Frank looked over at Marco and nodded. "Yes, I do. I think it's time we show these people who they're messing with."

Chapter 41

Eddie was at a loss for words. He was completely unprepared for Craig to accuse him of being part of Treleous. Did that mean Craig wasn't connected to them?

Eddie spoke under his breath. "I'm not, but do you think we should discuss that here?"

Craig held his gaze, his dark eyes bloodshot and steady.

Trust Craig or not? The decision point was upon them, and Eddie had to make a choice. Right now. He looked into Craig's eyes and believed him. Believed the anger Craig showed when he thought Eddie was part of Treleous. "I'm not with them."

Craig pursed his lips and sighed. "Tell them you don't want a lawyer and let them question you. They can't keep you. Afterward we'll talk."

Eddie nodded. "Call Loren and tell her I'm okay, please."

Craig nodded once, stood, and spoke over his shoulder. "All right, that's enough."

The door opened, Craig stepped out, and once again, Eddie was alone.

A few minutes later, Agent Harkin re-entered the room. "You can make a phone call now. Do you want representation before we question you?"

Answering too soon seemed like the wrong choice, so Eddie took a breath and then, shaking his head, replied calmly, "I've got nothing to hide. You can ask your questions."

Harkin said, "All right. Let's start with, what you were doing at the Paleo Pipe Shop?"

Eddie raised his eyebrows. "Shopping. Why does the Bureau care?"

"You know I can't tell you that. Why were you in disguise?"

How to answer that? "It's not always safe for me to return to Washington, because of my previous role at the Agency."

Harkin sighed. "Why is that?"

Eddie smiled. "You know I can't tell you that?"

Harkin looked down his nose at him. "So you wear a disguise every time you come back?"

Eddie asked, "Is that against the law?"

"Is that why you were armed?"

Eddie nodded. "It's not always safe for me to return to Washington."

"So you keep saying." Harkin frowned. "Who's the mohawk guy?"

"I told you. I don't know, but he looked like he meant me harm, so I ran."

Harkin sighed. "Is this all I'm going to get?"

He shrugged. "That's all there is."

•   •   •

Eddie walked out the front door a few minutes later. Harkin wasn't happy, but all he had was a suspicion. Unfortunately, he was now back on the Bureau's radar. That was a problem for another day, however.

At the street, Craig pulled up to the curb in a nondescript gray sedan and Eddie got in.

As Craig maneuvered the car back into traffic, he asked without looking over, "What the hell is going on?"

Where to begin? "How do you know what Treleous is?"

Craig glanced over. "I run special operations for the Central Intelligence Agency. Of course, I would know about something as large as that. How do you know about them?"

Eddie blew out a large breath. "Sam Hawthorne has been secretly working against them for years."

Craig's eyebrows shot up. "What do you mean, working against?" He frowned. "That's what all that nonsense on his boat last year was?" He glanced over again. "That's when what he sucked you in?"

Eddie nodded.

Craig asked, "Why didn't you all just bring this to me?"

"Think about it. How could we know for sure you weren't with them?"

Craig bobbed his head from side to side. "Okay, what's up with the pipe shop?"

"We're trying to find Benjamin Leonette."

Craig frowned. "Why?"

Eddie shrugged. "Because his daughter asked us to."

Craig shook his head as they passed the Capitol building and turned right. "How did you find Susan?"

Eddie smiled. "She found us. Actually, Treleous used her as bait to try to get to us."

Craig growled. "Who's us? Your merry band of vigilantes down in Miami?"

Eddie nodded.

Craig turned again and headed into a seedier section of town, then into the garage of a small house. He closed the door, led Eddie inside, and marched across the cramped and dated living room to a bar on the far side. Opening a bottle of Scotch, he poured two glasses and handed one to Eddie.

Craig held his up in salute and then downed the contents in one gulp. "And why did your band of do-gooders decide to help Susan?" He held up his hand, forestalling Eddie's answer. "I withdraw the question. The answer is too obvious. How did you know about Paleo?"

Eddie shrugged. "We have some sources of our own."

Craig nodded and poured another glass. "And you all thought Treleous would be there? Hence the disguise." He took a sip. "Were they?"

Eddie nodded. "Crazy man with a blond mohawk chased me. Unfortunately, the Bureau boys didn't catch him. Why were they there, anyway?"

Craig shrugged. "My people heard some chatter that Treleous might be looking at that shop again. So I asked them to stake it out."

Eddie raised his eyebrows. "You heard chatter from who?"

Craig smiled. "I have sources too, you know. I thought they were doing something. I just didn't realize they were trying to catch you. What do they want with you all, anyway?"

Eddie sighed. "They think we have something they want."

"Do you?"

Eddie shook his head. "Not what they think."

Craig sucked his teeth. "What do they think you have?"

"Supposedly, there is a record of all of Mendelson's work hidden somewhere."

He raised his eyebrows. "Parker Mendelson? The scientist? I suspected they wanted to continue his work and that would help. But you don't have it?"

Eddie shook his head. "Sam was convinced it was on that little island. But it wasn't."

Craig toyed with his glass. "What was there?"

"Not that." Eddie took a drink. "You don't happen to know what really happened to Leonette, do you?"

Craig held Eddie's gaze a long time before shaking his head. "Nope. And he's not the only Mendelson scientist to disappear, either."

Chapter 42

As Frank drove back toward the airport, he called Gemini. "Something's not right here."

"What do you mean?"

"Mr. Talented showed up here with Susan, but before we could get to them, the town drove them out at the end of a shotgun."

Gemini sounded surprised. "What do you mean, the town did?"

Frank said, "They went inside a restaurant and about thirty seconds later, some guy chased them out of the place at gunpoint. Even fired at us. We chased Mr. Talented into the woods, but along the way, someone nabbed Tom. Left his truck and his radio, but took him."

Gemini's voice turned to ice. "Someone from the town?"

"It would appear. It gets weirder. Someone else showed up at the shop in Georgetown and asked for that damned tobacco. Mack thinks he was in disguise, but before he could nab him, the FBI showed up and arrested the guy. So I told Mack to come here and we're going to kick some ass."

Gemini said, "Interesting. Slow down, Frank. I will find out who the FBI arrested, so at least we'll have their identity. We'll get your man back, but this seems important. Connected to Mendelson, somehow. I want you to go shopping. Buy motorcycles, ATVs, whatever your men feel you need up there. Get the services of a chopper if you think that will help. How many men do you have?"

Frank said, "Without Tom, I've got four, counting me. Mack's on his way, and he's got eight, but one of them is Chip."

"How many more do you need to do some careful reconnaissance, maybe go after Mr. Talented? Find out where to strike?"

Frank pushed down his anger. He would not leave his man behind, nor was he going to ignore this kind of disrespect, but he understood Gemini's thinking. They could kill Mr. Talented and maybe solve this Mendelson mystery in one final blow. What was the best way to approach this? "Understood. I'll start with the ones I got, and I'll get Mack to bring us the drones. I don't know yet. Let me find out what we're really up against here, and I'll let you know."

"I'll be ready. Let me know. Patience, Frank, I know you want to make these people pay, and I promise you, they will."

Chapter 43

Eddie studied Craig. "What do you mean, Leonette's not the only Mendelson scientist missing?"

Craig eased down into one of the living room chairs. "I think we need to go back to the beginning and tell each other what we know."

Eddie sat opposite him and nodded. He would not tell Craig about Caveman, but he thought he could open the kimono, so to speak, on everything else. "Okay."

Craig held his gaze. "Notice my words, Eddie. I didn't say I'll tell you everything I *can*. I said I will tell you everything I *know*. I'm not playing some dammed game like I do sometimes."

Wow. This was a new approach from Craig. Was it real? Eddie had never known the man to tell him an outright lie. His approach was usually of the half-truth variety. He nodded and made a go-ahead gesture.

Craig sat back. "Okay, let's see. You know about Mendelson?"

Eddie nodded again. "Evil secret CIA research man."

Craig raised his eyebrows. "Blunt, but true, I guess. Before they shut him down, across his operations, he had twenty-nine scientists. I can currently only account for six of them."

Eddie frowned. "What do you mean account for?"

Craig shrugged. "Twenty-one of them. I can't tell you where they are right now. Six died and I've validated their death. Seen the body, so to speak." He counted them off on his fingers. "Matheson, Elliot, Gordon, Karlsson, Koji, and Stein."

"Heinrich Stein?"

Craig raised thick, dark eyebrows. "Yes. Do you know him?"

Eddie said, "He's the one who recruited Sam into this fight."

"Really?" Craig rubbed his chin. "Interesting. I didn't know that." He focused back on Eddie. "Two more, Calvin Arturo, and Chin Ling," he made air quotes, "died, but no one found a body."

Eddie sat up. "I know the name Calvin Arturo."

Craig drew his brows together. "From where?"

Eddie shrugged. "I don't know. But I've heard it somewhere. I'll try to remember. I take it you don't believe they died?"

Craig shook his head. "I don't. Both were very convenient. The kind of situation where there would be no body."

Eddie asked, "Were they before or after Leonette?"

"Before. One a month and one three months before. If my timeline is correct, those were the first two to," he made air quotes with his fingers, "die or whatever. Then everyone else dies or disappears in short order after that."

Eddie frowned. "What does that mean?"

Craig took another sip of his drink. "I've no idea."

Could it be they disappeared to join the bad guys? Did someone kill them? "How do you know about Treleous?"

Craig let out a deep breath out through his nose. "About six years ago, some CIA operation intercepted a communique that simply said, 'Mendelson's work must continue, Treleous agreement in place, funds available.' Since the message included a prominent and controversial D.O.D. scientist by name, they passed it over to one of my departments." He shrugged. "We started calling it the Treleous case."

"Have you ever heard of Arrowhead? Or Arrowhead ranch?"

Craig shook his head. "I don't think so. Should I have?"

Eddie shrugged. "From the same source, we got the information about the pipe shop. We also got a tip that this ranch in Montana might be connected to his disappearance."

"Interesting. Did you check it out?"

"Luis is there now."

"I don't suppose you're going to tell me who this source of yours is."

Eddie shook his head. "I can't. But it's trustworthy."

Craig sighed. "Where's Loren? With Luis?"

"No. She's here in D.C. In Georgetown. We're staying with Emily Bryant."

Craig's eyes widened. "The author?"

Chapter 44

Loren was sitting at the kitchen table with Emily eating lunch when Luis called, and she stepped away to take it. "How's it going?"

Luis said, "Not great. Where's Eddie? He didn't answer."

Loren sighed. "He got arrested by the FBI."

She could hear the smile in Luis's voice. "Really? Wow! Maybe he's doing worse than me. We got to the town. It's really small, I mean tiny. Anyway, we go into the bar and grill and ask about Arrowhead Ranch, and everyone starts shooting at us!"

Loren's eyes widened. "Are you serious?"

"As a heart attack. So we ran outside and Treleous was waiting for us. Luckily, the two groups started shooting at each other and we escaped in the chaos."

"Holy cow. You two, okay?"

"A little frazzled, but fine."

Loren glanced over her shoulder. Emily remained at the table, eating. "Where are you now?"

"In the woods."

Loren raised her eyebrows. "What's your plan now?"

"I'm going to sneak down to the ranch and see if we can get a different reception. Was Treleous at the pipe shop?"

"I think so, yes. Why?"

"What's bothering me is, how did they know we'd be here? I mean, I understand that the shop was in the police report. But how did they know about the ranch? No one should have known about that but Caveman."

He was right. That was not good. How could they know? "Could Susan be a leak?"

"I thought about that. Maybe. But it would've made more sense to ambush us at the hotel last night. We would've been sitting ducks. If she'd tipped them off, that would've been the play. Instead, they were waiting for us at Beaver Ruin. It took longer to get there than Bozeman."

"Makes sense, but careful, Luis. We don't know her."

He sighed. "I know. I will. Tell Caveman what happened and see what he says."

"Will do."

"I don't know how long I'll have cell service. Just know that I'm in the Lewis and Clark National Forest trying to sneak my way down to the ranch from the west."

"Got it. Stay safe."

After disconnecting, Loren looked at the street below. How had they known about Montana? Susan was the only unknown person who knew they were going there. She closed her eyes, said a prayer that Luis wasn't walking into a trap, and then called Caveman.

It was a long time before he answered. "What's up?"

She said, "Treleous was waiting in Montana. How could they know that? Was that information stored anywhere else? Anywhere they could have access to it?"

Caveman immediately replied, "It wasn't Susan. I'm telling you she's good."

"I know you think that. So, where else could they have gotten the information?"

Caveman clucked his tongue. "I don't know. It's not referenced in anything else in my head. I don't believe it's Susan, though."

"Then we need to figure out where else they're getting their information before we run into more trouble."

"I understand. Let me think about it."

Loren hung up and looked at her watch. It had been almost two hours since Craig called to tell her that Eddie was okay. That was strange and unexpected. The question was, did that make the situation better or worse? She didn't know.

Where was Eddie, and what was he doing?

Chapter 45

Luis hung up the phone and walked back to Susan. Once again, she was watching him. Actually, that wasn't the right word. She was studying him. Like she was trying to understand him. Or like maybe, if she watched him close enough, she'd be able to ferret out answers to all the questions he wasn't answering.

She was probably smart enough to do it, too, if he wasn't careful. This one would be trouble if he didn't watch himself. The question was, was she also a plant? Caveman had confirmed she was Benjamin Leonette's daughter, and that he was good. So how could she benefit from selling out the team? Was she the reason they weren't being chased right now?

Susan furrowed her brow.

Luis wasn't a political creature. He wasn't a schemer like Craig Black, or even a planner like Eddie. With him, what you see is what you get.

She asked softly, "What's wrong?"

Luis forced a smile. "Not only was Treleous waiting for Eddie and Loren, but so was the FBI. Eddie went and got himself arrested."

Susan raised her eyebrows. "You don't seem anxious about that."

Luis shrugged. "Eddie can handle the Bureau."

Susan nodded, but her brow furrowed again. "No, that's not it. What's wrong?"

Luis was smart enough in his own way, but he was straightforward, and at his core, he was a soldier. If the situation supported it, a direct assault was always the simplest. "I'm just wondering how Treleous knew we'd be here." He held her eyes and waited.

Susan looked through him for a beat, nodded and then focused back on his face. "You think it's me? That somehow, I told them?"

Luis said, "I'm not accusing you of anything—"

"Yes, you are." She shrugged one shoulder. "I mean, I get why, but you are." She raked her fingers through her hair, then abruptly unzipped her jacket, and pulled her shirt up to her chin. "I'm not wearing any kind of wire. You took my cell phone. How could I even contact anyone?"

Luis took a step forward to stop her and then froze. It wasn't overly sexual or revealing. It was a simple dark blue cotton bra, not any different from seeing her in a bathing suit. But something about it affected Luis. She had a tight, flat stomach with just a hint of muscle underneath. Paler than the women Luis had grown up with, and that somehow added to the effect.

He made a downward movement with his hands. "Put your shirt down, you're going to freeze."

She didn't move. "No. I need you to believe me." She shook her head. "My life probably depends on it."

He closed the distance between them and gently pushed her hand down. "Okay. I understand, and I don't know how you could have signaled anyone. But we need to find out how they knew, because that information might be necessary to keep both of us alive. Now zip your jacket back up." Why did this woman affect him like this?

Luis walked over to the Jeep. Distraction was a tool used in almost all types of training, from hand-to-hand combat to spy craft. Was that little display an honest attempt to show she was on the level or a carefully crafted distraction from his suspicion?

Again, he kept returning to the question, what would she gain if she was working with Treleous? His gut told him she was okay, and it was true that there was no way for her to signal anyone. Then how did they find this place? He folded up the map. "I don't know if we're actually in the national park, or if we're allowed to drive here. Either way, we'd best get moving."

She looked at him, her eyes pleading. "Do you trust me, Luis?"

He frowned. "I do."

They drove east through the trees. Most of his life, girls had paid attention to Luis. He was quiet, especially when he was younger, and that made him seem mysterious. As a result, he learned to be comfortable around woman at an early age. He knew what signs to watch for. When to make a move and subtle ways to discourage someone if he wasn't interested.

Susan, however, wasn't like anyone he'd ever met before, much less been interested in. She was a white college girl from the deep south. That type usually only wanted someone like Luis for a weekend adventure. She didn't act that way around him, though. Never spoke down to him or acted superior.

He rubbed his face. Why had she gotten under his skin? It made him feel vulnerable. It wasn't an instinct that something was wrong or anything like that. More a sense that he was unprotected around her. From her or the people after them, he wasn't sure.

Chapter 46

Eddie took a sip of Scotch as he and Craig mulled over the information they'd just exchanged.

His old boss broke the silence. "So, since you got involved with this on that trip with Sam, does that mean that Selik is part of Treleous?"

"Absolutely. Did you not know that?"

Craig shook his head. "We knew he was a person of interest. That he was into bad stuff. That's all."

"Our source says his real name is Anton Selik."

Craig scowled. "How long have you known that?"

Eddie shrugged. "A while."

"And you didn't think you should pass that along?"

Eddie narrowed his eyes. "You haven't exactly been on our Christmas card list, Craig."

He looked over. "Why? Because I kept you from your girlfriend?"

A surge of anger coursed through Eddie. He squeezed his eyes shut. "No, you lied to the woman I love, and as a result, almost sabotaged our relationship."

Craig rolled his eyes. "I think you're being dramatic."

Eddie half stood and quietly said, "No. I'm not."

Craig drew back. His eyes darted back and forth across Eddie's face. "I didn't know it was serious. And look, it all worked out in the end."

Once again, Eddie pushed down his anger and said through gritted teeth, "By accident, it worked out, and you cost us years we'll never get back."

Craig sighed. "I told you, I didn't know you all were serious."

"That wasn't up to you, Craig. Why did you lie to her?"

Craig took a big gulp of his drink. "Look, your relationship was based on extraordinary circumstances. I thought of it as a form of Florence Nightingale syndrome." He sighed. "I thought you all were looking to reconnect out of a sense of obligation rather than any genuine connection." He held Eddie's angry, unwavering gaze. "Hell, you didn't know it was real, either."

"It doesn't matter. None of that was up to you. And how could you know how real it was? Sometimes it just happens like that. Like a lightning bolt."

Craig looked at him for a long time. "Not for me."

"Not to me either, before. But we don't work for you. So if you want to work *with* us now, you can't treat us like we do anymore. You have to promise to respect that. Treat us as partners, not employees."

Craig dropped his chin to his chest. "I still think you're being a little dramatic."

Eddie shook his head. "Craig, I'm two minutes from punching you in the throat and walking out the front door."

Craig raised his eyebrows. "You're serious?"

"As a heart attack."

Craig stood. "You're really pissed."

Eddie lifted both hands in a gesture of disbelief. "We're both really pissed. You meddled in our lives. Have you not met either of us?"

"Okay. Okay. I'm sorry I didn't realize—"

"How could you not realize?"

Craig shrugged. "I don't think like that. I'm married to the job. Every relationship I've ever had was a fling." He frowned. "Except maybe one. I didn't realize. I'm sorry. I really am." He held out his tumbler.

After a long moment, Eddie clinked his glass against it. "You really are an ass."

Craig nodded. "I can be sometimes." He poured them each a refill.

They returned to their seats and Craig said, "I don't get all the effort to find Mendelson's repository."

Eddie frowned. "What do you mean?"

"Well, think about it. The scientists that worked on the projects could have recreated most of it by now. What, they were waiting to work on these projects for years, until they found the repository?" Craig shrugged. "They shouldn't need it anymore. So why spend this time baiting Sam, trying to trap you? For what?"

Eddie took another sip. It was a good question.

Craig continued speaking to himself as much as Eddie. "With any size organization, it eventually all comes down to the bureaucracy. They've applied a lot of time, money, resources, and risk to this. What's the benefit?"

Eddie considered that. Sometimes the best lie contains a grain of the truth. It gives it substance and some connection to reality. He said, "I don't think the repository can be a complete red herring. It's too specific. If it wasn't the goal, it would too easily lead the team astray."

Craig sat forward. "Makes sense. So what are they're really after is related to the repository?"

"Maybe the repository contains more than just data from the projects."

"Something else they need—"

Eddie said, "Or want to keep hidden."

Craig nodded slowly. "Right. Something dangerous to them."

Eddie continued, "If you were one of these scientists and you knew this information could hurt Treleous, then you might want to disappear, too."

"Or fake your death."

Eddie raised his eyebrows. "Or fake your death. What about the others that died? How many did you say, four? That seems like a lot. Could those be hits?"

Craig frowned. "Possible. Especially if Treleous has access to professionals."

"They do. I know firsthand."

He blew out his breath. "What would be so damaging that they would spend so much effort and money to get?"

Chapter 47

Luis continued east, following the creek along the edge of the forest. Maybe five miles from the ranch, it became clear that they wouldn't be able to drive the entire way. Navigating through the trees was already becoming cumbersome and time consuming.

He turned to Susan. "In my pack are some snacks."

She unzipped it and looked over, eyebrows raised. "Did you think we were going away for a few weeks?"

Luis grinned. "I take my eating seriously, and when you're on a mission, you never know. I'll take a couple of granola bars."

She handed them to him and returned to her seat with a bag of chips.

As he chewed, the situation again drew his mind back to his time on the run with Ellen all those years ago. She'd been like Susan, but higher maintenance. Used to being the center of attention.

She'd been stunned when Luis shot the man in that German parking lot. He could remember her training flash past her eyes as she tried to decide what to do.

Ellen looked from the dead man back up at Luis.

He grabbed her elbow again. The body lying on the pavement would leave a trail. It would ensnare the authorities, and now it involved Luis. The conflict of whether it was worse to keep Luis with her, or to get away from him, was written across her face.

Luis said, "Look, either this is legitimate, and we wait to tell the police that this was self-defense, or this is something else? I need to know which, right now."

A siren wailed in the distance, quickly getting closer.

Ellen looked up at the sound and then back at him, her dark blue eyes intense and uncertain.

"I'm a soldier. I understand duty, keeping my mouth shut, and how we fight on the battlefield and behind the scenes. Tell me, or we're staying here until they arrive."

She shook her head. "No. Just let me go. You don't understand, I can't—"

He tightened his grip.

She looked around, but the parking lot was empty.

Luis narrowed his eyes. "You can yell, say I'm kidnapping you all you want, and it won't matter. I just killed a man, I have to face the music, with you as my witness or I need a damn good reason to the leave the scene of the crime."

Her attention darted back to the siren.

"You have about twenty seconds, or this decision is going to be made for you."

"Okay, I'm a CIA agent on the run. I need to get to someone that can help me. Now let me go."

Luis studied Ellen's face. He believed her. He'd done several missions with Agency types. She felt legitimate. He led her out of the parking lot, pushing her along with her elbow. "No. Without you as a witness, this would be very difficult to explain. Besides, as a member of the military, I think it's my duty to help you escape. Do you have a car?"

She tried to pull away from him. "Look, I appreciate your help but—"

The heavy-set man Luis thought of as Hardy appeared at the end of one aisle and took a wild shot at them.

They ducked down and kept moving.

Luis asked, though clinched teeth, "Do you have a car?"

"Yes, over behind that red building."

Hardy shot again, shattering a windshield just beyond them.

Keeping low, they weaved between vehicles, moving in the direction she'd indicated. They came to a street with shops and more people.

Luis said, "Don't even think about it."

She looked over at him, sighed, and gave a resigned nod.

They hustled around the end of the red building, and Ellen pointed. "That blue Mercedes, that's mine."

Luis said, "Give me the keys."

She hesitated and then dug them out of her purse.

They jumped into the car and Luis drove them out of the parking lot. "Have you reached out?"

She looked over. "To whom? My escape contact? Yes. He's going to meet me in Verdun. West of here."

Luis looked over his shoulder. A black Mercedes lurched around the car behind them. "I think we have company."

Ellen turned. "That's them. We have to lose them."

Luis turned left smoothly. No point giving away the fact that he was aware of them just yet. "How do we get to Verdun? The A4?"

She nodded. "Yes."

Luis glanced at the rear-view mirror. The black car was still behind them, gradually closing the distance. The light ahead turned yellow, and Luis slowed.

Ellen looked over, wide-eyed.

Luis came to an almost complete stop. Just as the light turned red, he jammed on the accelerator and shot across the intersection.

Cars beeped and swerved to avoid him, but he navigated through the gap and left the black Mercedes stuck at the intersection.

Ellen's shoulders sagged. "Nice."

Luis shrugged. "I learned to drive in Miami."

She smiled weakly. "Why did you help me? This could be a lot of trouble for you."

He glanced over. "I don't know. It seemed like the right thing to do." He shrugged again. "And maybe my duty. I've never left a woman in distress alone." He smiled ruefully. "In my whole life." He pulled out his cell phone and dialed. "Janet. I've run into some friends in town, and we've decided to go away for a few days. I'm going stir crazy. Can you sign me out, please? Thanks, I owe you one." He hung up and turned his phone off.

Ellen said, "You were at the medical center?"

He nodded. "I was."

Ellen rubbed her face. "I escaped in Frankfort, and I had a friend there who I thought could help me." She sighed. "But I just learned that they'd transferred him home already. I'd just found that out when I ran into you. You saved my life."

Luis looked over and waved that away. "My pleasure."

Her brow furrowed. "I'm so sorry I got you into this. You shot that man— with no hesitation."

"That's what they trained me to do. It was obviously him or us." He noticed a sign for the A4 highway and changed lanes. "Why do these people want you?"

She sighed. "Pride mostly. They discovered I was an agent assigned to spy on them." She shrugged. "I didn't even learn anything." She looked over. "We were in Frankfort, and I realized something was wrong. I don't even know what tipped them off. But I could sense it. So I ran."

Luis reached over and patted her arm. "Well, you're safe now. I won't let anything happen to you."

Ellen pursed her lips. "I should tell you. That was when I reached out to tell my handlers that I was in trouble. Something was wrong with the channel. So I had to go to an old contact. One that wasn't supposed to be active any longer." She let out a slow breath. "But by the grace of God, he answered and agreed to help."

Luis looked sidelong at her. "You trust this guy?"

She nodded. "I do. He's saved several of my friends already."

Chapter 48

Eddie stood, set his drink down on the counter, and turned to Craig. "Well, I need to get going. Is the FBI going to be any trouble for…"? He faded off and his eyes widened.

Craig frowned. "What?"

"Sam thinks Treleous is everywhere. Plugged into every government agency. Do you believe that?"

Craig frowned and nodded noncommittally. "Probably in some form or fashion. Why?"

"Do you think they have contacts in the FBI?"

"Yes."

Eddie yanked out his phone. "Crap."

"What?"

"Then they know who I am. The FBI will tell them who I am. That means Jeff and," he hesitated, "and someone we're watching could be in danger."

Craig drew thick, black eyebrows together. "Someone? Meaning your source?"

Eddie nodded. "How long do you think it will take them to untangle my trail and get to the house in Coral Gables?"

Craig titled his head to one side. "A while. You're pretty good at this kind of thing."

"So are they. Can you take me to Loren? In Georgetown?" Eddie dialed the phone. As soon as Jeff answered, Eddie said, "I think Treleous might be able to figure out where the house is. Call Piper and see if anyone is watching. Get a gun, then take our friend through the tunnel to your room. I'll call you shortly."

"Got it." Jeff hung up.

Eddie turned back to Craig. "Other than that, is the Bureau going to be a problem for me?"

"No, it will be more trouble for me than you."

Eddie nodded. "Yeah, I got the impression they thought I was still working for the Agency."

Craig shrugged. "Can't really blame them. What else are they supposed to think?" He rinsed out the two glasses. "So, what were you hoping to find at the pipe shop?"

Eddie shrugged. "I'm not sure. Leonette called there for a reason. A reason that we're convinced is connected to this ranch in Montana."

"Because of your source. I take it you didn't notice anything before you ran out the back door like a little girl?"

Eddie shot him the bird. "Emily tells us the name of the tobacco he asked for means an arrowhead shaped leaf."

"Just how do you know Emily Bryant?" Craig held up a hand. "Let me guess. Jeff knows her?"

"I told you, Jeff knows everyone. There is no such tobacco, and when I went into the store, I was shocked at the number of choices."

Craig looked down his nose at him. "So, what's your plan now?"

Eddie shrugged. "I'm not sure."

Craig held out a card. "This is how you can get touch with me any time of day or night."

Eddie took it with raised eyebrows. "I never got this privilege when I worked for you."

Craig glanced over. "Well, as you keep telling me, now you are working *with* me, not *for* me. All joking aside, please keep me in the loop."

"I will. You do the same."

Craig frowned. "If you're really getting worried about Jeff's safety, I happen to know that Luis' brother, Hector, is in Miami for the next few days."

Eddie looked over sharply. Eddie had never even met Hector. "How do you know that?"

Craig shrugged. "I know a lot of things."

Eddie's forehead creased. "Now, you see, you're back to being your old self again. How in the hell do you know where Luis' brother is? Why do you know where he is?"

Craig sucked his teeth.

Eddie crossed his arms.

Craig threw up his hands. "Okay, when it was apparent you and Luis were going to stay together, I had his brother transferred to a section I run."

Eddie guffawed. "You are unbelievable. That's pretty damn Machiavellian."

Craig grinned without showing his teeth. "It's why I'm so good at what I do. But seriously, if you're worried about Jeff, I can send him to help."

Eddie's eyes narrowed. "Just how dumb do you think I am, Craig? I have someone I told you I want to keep a secret, but you want me to just give him to your man?"

Craig scowled. "Don't be like that, Eddie. He's not my man. He's Luis' brother."

"Oh, really. Then how do you know where he is right now?"

Craig sighed. "He works for someone who works for me. He's not going to be more loyal to me than he is to Luis. It was just a suggestion. I'm not trying to play you, Eddie. This is too important."

Eddie looked at him for a long time. "Thanks for the offer of help. I think we'll handle this for now. Can you give me a ride to Georgetown?"

Craig led him to the garage.

Chapter 49

By late afternoon, the forest had become too dense to continue, so Luis parked the jeep behind a screen of brush. He checked his cell phone. No service. He pulled a handheld GPS from his bag and spread the map out on the hood, checking their position. He looked back behind them and listened. No motor sound in the distance.

Susan looked over his shoulder. "Where are we?"

Luis pointed. "Around here." He looked at his screen. "I'm pretty sure we're still in the park, so we'd best not start a fire. I'm afraid it's a cold dinner tonight."

"I've had worse."

Luis turned to look at her.

Susan shrugged. "I've spent every penny I have looking for my dad. I've had a lot of cold dinners."

Should he hug her? Squeeze her arm? Even being born and raised in the U.S., Luis still felt culturally out of step with everyone he met outside of Miami. He was never sure how to interact with them, especially in situations like this.

She shaded her eyes against the sun. "We probably only have two more hours of light. We'd better find a good place to camp."

Luis pulled out all of his duffle bags and lined them up next to the Jeep.

Susan walked over, hands on her hips.

Luis narrated as he pulled out what he wanted. "Okay. One tent, two backpacks, two subzero sleeping bags, Two pistols for me, and one for you—"

"Why do I only get one?"

He glanced up. "Everything you take, you have to carry."

Her eyes widened slightly. "One is fine."

"That's what I thought. One rifle with two scopes for me. Compass, GPS, satellite phone, can opener, lighter, knife, hatchet, two canteens, medical kit, bolt cutters—"

Susan's eyebrows shot up. "Bolt cutters? You think the weight of bolt cutters is worth it?"

Luis looked up at her and nodded. "I never go anywhere without bolt cutters. Small tool pouch," he tilted his head, "let's say two days' food and water." He pulled out and held up a roll. "And toilet paper."

She shook her head. "I'm impressed."

Luis deftly filled each backpack, put Susan's on her back, then leaned around. "Too heavy?"

She shook her head. "No, it feels good."

He zipped up the bags and loaded them back into the Jeep.

They hiked deeper into the woods, moving east at a good clip. Luis was impressed by her endurance. She was something else.

Susan said, "It really is beautiful out here."

"It is. I was on a long mission in the mountains of Afghanistan. It reminds me of that."

They climbed down an embankment and across a small stream.

Susan asked. "Do you not like thinking about the war?"

"No, there's just no point, really. It was horrible, exhilarating, terrible, fulfilling, sad, and, unfortunately, necessary." He stopped and drank from a canteen before handing it to Susan. "It's like being in a bad car accident. You're glad you survived, but you don't talk about it."

Susan furrowed her brow. "I'm not sure that's how most people think."

Luis grinned. "Maybe so. It wouldn't be the first time I was different."

About an hour before sunset, they found a nice clearing at the top of a rise beneath the canopy of a stand of trees.

They set up the tent and, once again, he found himself surprised by her mechanical aptitude and capability. "Pick out something for us to eat. I'm going to look around." He moved in a steady circle around the clearing.

Checking escape routes and imagining how it would look in the dark. A massive ponderosa pine lay on its side about fifty yards away. Luis marked the location in his mind, visualizing falling back here from the campsite.

When he returned, Susan was sitting cross-legged, snacks arrayed out in front of her. "What's on the menu tonight?"

Susan grinned and made a Vanna White movement with her hand. "We have two types of beef jerky and six types of granola bars," She looked up at him. "You really like your granola bars."

Luis shrugged. "If you saw the stuff they gave us to eat in the Gulf, you'd learn to love them, too."

"Yikes. Okay. Lots of chips, popcorn, and canned chicken and tuna."

Luis stroked his chin. "I think I'll have tuna, with a side granola bar variety."

"Excellent choice, sir. I'll have some chicken and potato chips."

He sat down next to her, opened the cans, and handed over hers. They ate as the curtain of darkness stretched across the horizon.

This also reminded Luis of the Gulf. Few places in America had this little light pollution. The stars literally dusted the sky. After dinner, they lay on their backs shoulder to shoulder, losing themselves in the expanse.

He could feel her mood slide. This was her first moment of downtime in forty-eight hours, other than when she had passed out in the hotel last night. The first time for her to really reflect since she'd been yanked out of her life and dragged along this surreal adventure.

Now the mental exhaustion was catching up with her, and the days of adrenaline would lead to the inevitable fall, like she'd had earlier. It was about time for it to happen again. Luis has seen it many times before.

Susan let out a long breath. "I'm sorry for all this trouble."

Luis grabbed her hand, waiting to see her reaction. To his surprise, she entwined her fingers in his and squeezed. It wasn't really a flirty gesture, more like she was holding on to keep from drowning. On the other hand, he didn't think it was entirely platonic, either, and he had to admit that he liked it.

In his experience, distraction was usually the best tonic in this kind of situation. "Have you thought about what you'll do when this is all over?"

"I don't know. My dad's friends keep me enrolled at Duke, so I remain an active student who just doesn't sign up for any classes. I guess I could go back there." She sighed. "It just doesn't hold the same joy for me that it used to."

Luis squeezed her hand. "Well, think about it this way. You're getting to see the Rockies up close."

"That's true. It is beautiful." Silence stretched between them. She shook her head. "This is ridiculous. I don't know why I'm even here." Her eyes misted a bit, and her voice caught. "What are the chances my dad came here? I got caught up in the possibilities. Now I'm here in the middle of nowhere on a wild good chase. I mean, this has to be a red herring, right?"

Luis wiped his mouth. "Wild geese rarely start shooting at you as soon as you ask about them. Something is going on here. And we're going to find out what it is."

She squeezed his hand and shuddered a few times before settling back into regular breathing. "It just seems too crazy. So impossible. But I can't thank you enough for helping me."

Susan rolled her head over and rested it on his shoulder. Luis smiled in the darkness, surprised by how right it felt. Soon he could tell by her steady breathing that she had finally faded off into sleep.

Chapter 50

Eddie surveyed the area as Craig backed out of the garage. "Nice neighborhood."

Craig grunted. "It's a safe-house. You want it to be in a place where people stay inside, behind their curtains."

"Makes sense." Craig always had an answer for any question. One that always seemed logical and reasonable, though often crafted out of half-truths and incomplete information. Eddie glanced at his phone. Luis hadn't answered a single text this morning. It was a little concerning, but he could take care of himself. He just hoped he hadn't walked into some sort of trap.

This whole situation continued to remind Eddie of the time he met Luis. The night when he first talked to the fourth Clay Pigeon, Ellen. He didn't know what he was walking into then, either. His mind wandered back to that night in France right after Piper first called him.

Eddie left the shadows under the awning of the Le Havre city hall and crossed the street. He moved away from the Burger King where he was supposed to meet Jeff, who wouldn't be here for at least ten minutes. He glanced at his watch, checked his surroundings, and dialed Loren.

"Are you all right?" she answered breathlessly.

"I'm fine, but you won't believe it. Another Clay Pigeon called asking for help."

"Who?" asked Loren, the surprise clear in her voice.

"Ellen. Do you know her?"

"There is an Ellen. Why would she be calling you now?"

"Who knows? Maybe now that they know about Amy, they're suspicious of everyone. I'm going to give you her number. Can you see if she's on the level?"

Loren sighed. "Of course. If she is, we have to help her."

Damn it. Why couldn't he just break free of this? Leave this life behind? He squeezed his eyes shut. "If she's legit, then you and Craig call me back."

"I will. Thank you, Eddie. Be careful."

He stepped into another doorway and slowly surveyed the area. How had he found himself in this situation again? He was free of these people. This wasn't his job anymore, and he certainly didn't owe these bastards anything. Of course, the wild card was Loren. What did he owe her?

He crossed the city hall grounds, the Burger King visible ahead. Slowing his pace, he wandered over to a group of people to his left. As he passed, he came to a stop, giving off the impression he was with them, before moving on a few steps.

Jeff's red Porsche turned onto the road and Eddie broke into a jog, intercepting him at the agreed upon meeting place and sliding into the passenger's seat. "Thanks."

He smoothly shifted gears and kept going. "No problem. I take it everything turned out okay?"

Eddie shrugged. "Yes, and supposedly, I'm a free man again."

Jeff fist bumped him. "Excellent."

"Thanks, man. I may need another favor."

Jeff glanced over. "Anything. What's up?"

Eddie's phone rang. He held up a finger, and he answered it.

Craig's voice came over the line. "Eddie, this is legit. This is our Ellen, and she's in trouble."

"So go help her."

Craig hesitated. "There's a problem."

Of course. "What problem?"

"Amy, the woman you just saved. Well, the information she brought back, the information that exonerated you, well, it seems to show that we have several moles in the Agency. I don't know who I can trust yet, so I need you to go get her."

Eddie squeezed his eyes shut and banged the phone on his forehead. "I don't work for you. This is not my job."

"Please, Eddie, I'll make it worth your while. Here's Loren."

Eddie said to himself through gritted teeth. "Make it worth my while. What could he possibly give me?"

Loren came on the line. "Eddie, she's in trouble. I hate to ask you this, but can you please help her?"

Eddie shook his head. "Where is she?"

"Kaiserslautern. It's in Germany—"

"I know where it is. The U.S. military medical center is there. Can she move?"

"Yes, she has a car."

Eddie turned to Jeff. "What's halfway between here and Germany?"

Jeff shrugged. "Reims?"

Eddie shook his head. "Too big." He said back into the phone. "How about Verdun? We'll meet her in Verdun. Tell Craig to figure out a place, tell Ellen, and let me know in the morning."

•   •   •

Craig snapped his fingers, bringing Eddie back to the present. "Where did you wander off to?"

Eddie sighed. "I was thinking about Ellen."

Craig glanced over. "The Clay Pigeon?"

Eddie nodded. "That's how I met Luis." And he just remembered that's how he'd acquired the house in Coral Gables. That had been Craig's idea of payment for services rendered.

"That's right. You worried about him? I wouldn't worry about Luis. He's a damn hard man to kill."

Chapter 51

An Army field surgeon once told Luis that he could sometimes sense what was going to happen in the operating room before it did. That a second prior, he felt it and could prevent disaster. The doc said that he didn't really understand it, but that he'd saved lives that way.

Luis' mom would say that was the Holy Spirt whispering in the surgeon's ear. He wasn't sure what he thought about that, but something similar happened to him from time to time. It was like he had his finger on a fine wire, like a guitar string, pulled incredibly tight—almost to the point of breaking. Occasionally, Luis could feel a vibration in this string, like an echo of future events floating back to him.

He felt it in Iraq before the ambush that wiped out his team and put him in the hospital. Had it helped? He still pondered this question as he lay here at the edge of the mountains that reminded him of the Gulf. Memories that turned his thoughts back to that night in Iraq.

The head of his unit was a freckle faced captain named Teddy Patterson, who the unit always called Tap. He twirled his finger in the air, and Luis and the rest of the team followed him up a rise to the main road. Flashes lit up the night sky and sounds of the battle floated in from the town of Ramadi.

They assembled in front of the colonel, who held a red flashlight up to a map. His voice was gravelly and matter-of-fact. "We're never going to run these bastards out of the city unless we can get some armor and mechanized units across the river." He glanced up at Tap, who nodded.

The colonel continued. "We have some pontoon bridges in route from Karbala that should be here by morning. You men need to wade across and scout for locations to deploy those temporary bridges. It needs to be flat ground and someplace we can cover the engineers while they set it up." He folded up the map. *"I know the enemy holds the other side, but the darkness should let you get in and out with no trouble. Questions?"*

There were none. They had undertaken countless missions like this, in the Gulf, in Africa, and even in a few other secret places.

War and God are funny things, though. Luis had seen a bullet miss killing one person by an inch, and a ricochet kill another sitting in a room, not even in the fight. Once the man upstairs decided your time was up, there was no outrunning the Grim Reaper.

The unit climbed up on what remained of the Omar Bridge and stood at the jagged end. Just like all the other bridges here, it was beaten, broken, and useless.

Tap lifted a pair of night vision binoculars and surveyed the opposite bank of the Euphrates. The chatter of automatic gunfire and muffled explosions continued uninterrupted. He pointed off to the right. "I see a good spot, about half a click down to cross." He took in each of the men. "Ready?"

That's when Luis felt it. The faint vibration in his fingertips. As they climbed down, he fell into step beside his lieutenant. "I got a feeling."

The team was used to Luis's intuitions and never ignored them.

Tap glanced over. "Trouble?"

Luis shrugged. "Something's ahead."

Tap clapped him on the shoulder. "Listen up guys, Luis' Cuban voodoo is talking to him, so stay frosty."

Luis cringed. His mom would tear him up if she heard them associate voodoo with him.

Each member of the unit tapped him on the helmet, as was their ritual whenever Luis had a feeling. They moved along the edge of the river and then slipped into the water—cold and inky black. It was awkward swimming with a rifle and equipment head to toe. Luis crossed using a kind of side kick that he'd found worked best. They spread out as they reached the middle, and Luis took his normal position on the far right. The current was swift, and he worked to resist it and keep close to the unit.

Lights were visible up the bank, but the gloom of the shore itself revealed nothing. No detail at all. When they were about two-thirds across, Luis twisted and brought his rifle up in front of him, ready to come out fighting.

A tracer round raced down into the river and a man yelled. Then the shore was alight with muzzle flashes as automatic weapons sprayed the river.

Luis turned, bringing his legs out in front so he could return fire. That's when the first bullet hit him.

•   •   •

The memory of that pain jolted him back to the present. The vibration he felt that night was foretelling an ISIS team on its own mission. Trying to sneak across the river to wreak some havoc before melting back into the city. It was just bad luck that the two groups encountered each other right as Luis' unit came out of the river on the enemy side.

He shied away from the memories of what came after, realizing that the recollection had settled upon him because his fingers were vibrating again now. He gently woke Susan. "I got a feeling trouble's coming. Get your pack and come with me." He led her out of the camp and up to the fallen tree. "Let's leave our stuff under here, sleep in your boots, and if we have to bug out tonight, come here and bring your sleeping bag with you if at all possible."

She nodded.

Luis unzipped his pack and took the scope off his rifle and switched it out with another.

Susan watched with interest. "Night vision?"

Luis shook his head. "Thermal. Almost the same thing." He checked the pistol under his arm, shoved a second in his pants, and gestured back to the clearing. "Picture this path in your mind. If we run into trouble, we'll pull back here in the dark. It's not a good place to sleep, but it's pretty good cover." He glanced over at her. "Got it?"

She frowned and nodded. "You really think we're going to have trouble?"

"I do."

Chapter 52

Loren paced back and forth on Emily's roof. The author had suddenly barricaded herself in her office, declaring that she needed to write.

She flopped down in a chair, full of nervous energy, but with nothing to work on. Eddie was off somewhere with Craig, of all people. Luis was in the woods after walking into a trap. A trap set by who knew. Blowing out a breath, Loren stood and returned to pacing. She hated waiting and inaction, and the feeling of being stuck in a dead end. It had been a long time since she'd felt like this, so helpless. Like a spectator, who couldn't even see the action.

She shook her head and smiled grimly. The last time was when Luis and Eddie saved Ellen, the fourth Clay Pigeon. With nothing else to chew on, her mind wandered back to that damned hotel room in France.

She sat on the bed holding Amy while she cried and cried. Loren had been on the same mission as the girl, so she knew what that assignment could do to a person. Especially to a woman. Loren's past and personality allowed her to separate herself from unpleasant and haunting things.

Clearly, Amy was not built the same way. So Loren stayed with her and stroked her hair and let her get it out. There was nothing else to do, so her mind was stuck worrying about Eddie and Ellen.

After everything that Eddie had done for all the Clay Pigeons, now when he finally had his life back, she'd asked him to put himself in danger one more time and save yet another one of her friends. She squeezed her eyes shut and worked to quell the worry. Eddie was a very capable man, and Ellen had found someone else to help her as well. Someone she'd met near the hospital. Craig arranged a meeting for them in Verdun. She glanced at her watch. In just a few hours, Ellen would be safe and it would all be over.

Amy's body finally relaxed, and she let out a little snore.

Loren released the tension in her shoulders. Sleep was what the girl needed more than anything else.

A sharp rap sounded at the door.

Loren started, leaped up, and tiptoed across the room before the sound woke Amy. It was not a good knock. The fierce sound and rhythm spoke of danger and impending doom. She opened it.

Craig stood there, his eyes wide, and his jaw clenched. He looked past her at Amy's sleeping form and then yanked Loren into the hallway and closed the door behind her.

"What is it?"

He looked up one way and then the other before dragging her a few steps down to the end of the hall. He rubbed his chin, his eyes darting back and forth.

Loren rolled her eyes. "What is it?"

Craig said under his breath. "That thumb drive Nikki had in that stupid beaded purse, the one Eddie had all this time?"

Loren nodded.

"Well," He hesitated, seemingly unsure how to explain. "Look, Clay Pigeon was supposed to help us find out who was our ally and who was our enemy in the Saud family."

Loren felt her chest tighten and her fingertips ache. "I know. I was one of them."

"Well, it turns out that we were fishing for minnows, and we caught a shark."

She balled her hands into fists. "Get to the point, Craig."

He leaned in closer. "It turns out that the Saudis who hated America had an entire spy network. Moles in every government agency."

It was a big revelation. Beyond what Loren had imagined, but though startling, she couldn't see how it was bad. "Okay?"

Craig held her gaze. "Including the CIA."

That wasn't good. Not good at all. But something about Craig's posture told her she was missing something. "And?"

"One name on the list was the contact I just used to set up the meeting later this morning between Eddie and Ellen."

•   •   •

Even after all these years, the memory sent a jolt through her, bringing her mind back to the present. It wasn't just Eddie and Ellen who were heading into a trap back then. It was Luis as well.

He'd helped save Ellen back then, and she hoped he had some more magic in him, because in her bones she could feel he was walking into trouble again.

Chapter 53

Eddie watched Craig drive away before entering the house.

Loren was standing there, brow furrowed, when the elevator doors opened. "You okay?"

"I'm fine."

She hugged him. "Did you punch Craig?"

Eddie chuckled. "I thought about it. It was good. I think we came to an understanding."

Emily stood in the kitchen wearing an apron, a platter with three large steaks on the counter in front of her. "Every time a man stays with me, I make them grill." She looked at Eddie. "You can grill, can't you?"

He shrugged and nodded. "Yes, Ma'am."

"Excellent. Go ahead upstairs and get the grill going, and you two can talk in private. I'll be up directly."

On the roof, Eddie uncovered the kitchen area and got the fire going, as he filled Loren on the arrest with the FBI, Craig, as well as Susan's father and the other scientists.

Loren spread out a tablecloth and set the table. "Well, at least we know we can depend on Craig. That's a big advantage." She told him about Luis' reception in Beaver Ruin and their current situation.

Eddie looked up with a look of concern. "Is he in trouble? Should we go?"

Loren shook her head. "He says he's good, but I'm worried about him. And Caveman is still convinced we need to stay and find whatever's here first."

"Why would they get a reception like that?"

"I don't know. At least that shows us we can depend on the information in Caveman's brain. Something's there."

Emily appeared, pushing a wheeled cart full of food. "Is it okay for me to be here? Or do you all need more time?"

Eddie accepted the meat from her. "No, it's fine. We're at a bit of a stalemate, anyway." He asked everyone how they liked their steaks.

Emily poured each of them a glass of wine. "Is it okay if I ask if you had any trouble with the G men?"

Eddie took the cup from her. "No, Ma'am, it's fine. They really couldn't charge me with anything."

She pursed her lips. "And I've seen that you all have influential friends. Not much luck down the street, I take it?"

"No. In the short time I was in the place, it was overwhelming. There were hundreds of brands in little cans and jars. I don't know what the clue is, but it's going to be like finding a needle in a haystack. I'm not sure what to do next." He looked over his shoulder at them. "Any suggestions?"

Loren gave him a helpless gesture.

Emily frowned. "But you're sure it's relevant? Not just some coincidence?"

Loren said, "We saw a document that showed it was connected. A communication path of some type."

They finished preparing the meal, sat, and began to eat.

Emily's forehead creased, and she stared off into space, chewing. After a moment, she opened the police report and read it again. She looked up at them, her eyes wide. "I don't mean to be all James Bond, but I have a thought."

Eddie raised his eyebrows. "We could use any help we can get. Lay it on us."

She glanced back down at the report. "Well, it doesn't say that Leonette ever went into the shop. It says he called it three times." She angled it over for Eddie to see. "Maybe we're not supposed to go inside."

Loren set down her fork and exchanged a look with Eddie. "You think?"

Eddie sat back. "That's a very interesting thought, Ms. Bryant."

"Call me Emily. So how would that work, then?"

Eddie cocked his head at Loren. "Could you scrape a line for a keyword?"

"You can do *anything*. The two questions are, what are his friends capable of, and could they do this five years ago?"

He leaned back and took a swallow of wine. "Could it be that simple?" He glanced at his watch: seven thirty. He stood, leaned over, and kissed Emily on the top of her head. "You're a genius."

She blushed. "It's only a theory. We haven't proved anything yet."

Eddie walked over to the elevator and said over his shoulder. "Get the number. I'll go grab one of the burner phones." He returned a moment later and dialed from a piece of paper Loren gave him.

After several rings, the owner answered. "Paleo Pipe Shop."

"Yes, do you have Lanceolate tobacco?"

"Sweet baby Buddha, don't eat my head. Why would you ask me such a thing?"

"I just want to know if you had Lanceolate tobacco."

"Who are you? Why are you troubling me?"

"So you don't have Lanceolate?"

The line went dead.

Loren raised her eyebrows. "Don't eat my head?"

Eddie shrugged.

They left the phone in the middle of the table, the three of them staring at it.

Emily refilled her glass. "How long would this take?"

Loren leaned back in her chair. "I've no idea." She took a drink. "It might not work at all."

Eddie walked over and started cleaning the grill. "If it doesn't, I'm not sure what to do next."

Loren stood and stacked the plates. "I'm not sure either. I guess if we don't hear something soon, we'll go help Luis."

The phone rang.

The three of them exchanged a look.

It rang again.

Eddie walked over and answered it on speaker. "Hello."

Over the phone, a man responded in a gruff voice. "Who are you?"

Chapter 54

Loren looked from the phone to Eddie, eyes wide.

He lurched forward and said in a rush, "I am a friend of Susan Leonette's. I'm trying to get in touch with her father. I'm a friend."

Silence. "How did you know about this channel?"

Loren rubbed her face, looked over at Eddie, and shrugged.

Eddie answered, "We figured it out. That's all I can say right now."

Silence. "Is Susan with you?"

Eddie hesitated. "No. I'm trying to protect her. There are a lot of people who want to hurt her."

Loren held her breath. Please don't hang up.

Silence. "Who?"

Eddie looked over at Loren, eyebrows raised.

What to do? Would the man on the phone even know who Treleous was? She shrugged and mouthed, "Tell them, I guess."

Eddie said, "Treleous."

Silence.

Loren held her breath, and glanced over at Emily, who stared at the phone, eyes wide.

The voice came over the line again. "Melrose Park. The first picnic table beyond the Rittenhouse Monument. Three PM tomorrow." Then the line went dead.

Emily grabbed a napkin and hastily scribbled down the information.

Eddie shook his head. "Don't bother. There's no way I'm going there."

Loren nodded. "It's definitely a sticker burr."

Emily stopped writing and looked back and forth between them. "What's that?"

Loren turned to her. "It's a kind of trap. By setting up a time and very specific place—"

Eddie said, "Usually a place they can see from a long way off."

Loren continued. "Right. They get to sit there, wait, and then when you show up, they can observe you from afar. See how you arrive, your vehicle, get some pictures of what you look like."

Eddie added, "And then attach themselves to you."

Loren smiled ruefully. "Like a sticker burr. They set up surveillance and follow you home. It's almost impossible to see and shake a tail in that scenario."

Eddie sighed and sat back down. "So they would know everything about us, and we would have a real hard time not leading them back here. They give up nothing and learn who we are and where we're staying, and we get nothing. It's a common trap to use when the people you're meeting know that you need them more than they need you."

Emily stared at the ground and nodded. "I see. Amazing. What are you going to do, then?"

Eddie frowned. "Two can play at this game. Mind if I invite someone over for dessert?"

She shook her head. "On one condition. I get to keep listening."

Chapter 55

Frank leaned against the hanger wall and watched the jet taxi over lights blinking. Something was going on here, and he suspected that whatever it was that everyone had been looking for was also here, not on that dammed island.

That's why the bastards from Miami showed up. They were still searching as well. Was the senator working with them now, or was this group still freelancing?

The jet stopped, and the engines whined down.

Frank pushed off the wall and ambled over.

Mack was first out the door, and he bounded down the stairs.

Frank shook his head. The kid was happy that it was finally time for some action. He loved to fight.

Mack shivered. "Definitely not Miami. It's chilly."

Behind him, men carried boxes down the stairs.

Frank nodded in greeting. "What you got?"

"Four Falcon drones, weapons, ammo, Chip, and six men. What about you?"

He turned and led him over to his truck. "I've got hotel rooms, ATVs, trucks, and some hiking equipment for you."

Mack jogged a few steps to catch up. "Where am I going?"

"You remember that talented son-of-a-bitch that keeps showing up?"

"Mr. Seaplane? The Hispanic looking one? Mr. Talented?"

"Yep. He drove off into the woods with the girl."

Mack scowled. "Heading where?"

"That's the question."

Marco stood guard in front of two SUVs.

Frank jerked his thumb over his shoulder. "Get the men back to the hotel and feed them. I'm going to take Mack for a ride."

Marco nodded. "Roger."

They slid into the truck, and Frank drove them out of the lot. "Anyway, this guy and Susan went off-road in a Jeep heading east. We've done some research, and they won't be able to go more than about five miles before he has to turn back or head off on foot."

The highway was pitch black and deserted.

Mack said, "With the girl, he won't be able to make very good time." He rubbed his hands together. "It'd be miserable in this cold without equipment. Do they have any?"

Frank shot a look over. "With our experience with them, I'd say yes."

"Going where, and why on foot?"

"I told you about the reception they received. They don't seem deterred, however. We've monitored the woods, and they haven't come back out. Not with that Jeep, at least. So, in the morning, I want you to go after them."

Mack nodded. "To what end?"

Frank continued to stare straight ahead. "Find out where they're going if you can, but either way, I don't want them to come back out of the woods. Ever."

Mack grinned and pulled a pack of gum from his pocket. He angled it over to Frank, who shook his head. He put a stick in his mouth and then his smile faded. "What about Tom?"

Frank puffed out his cheeks as he blew out a breath. "I don't know. Someone took him but left his radio."

Mack frowned. "That's weird. You'd think they'd take it and try to listen in on our communications. Why leave it?"

Frank shrugged one massive shoulder. "I think it was some kind of message, but I'll be damned if I get it."

"So, what are you going to be doing while I track these two down?"

"Well, the people in this town are protecting something. We'll use the drones and see if anything looks out of the ordinary. Do some nosing around."

Mack pushed the gum against his front teeth. "You'd better be careful."

"Yeah, I know. I'll make everyone work in pairs from now on." Frank's phone chirped. He glanced down and grinned.

Mack raised his eyebrows. "What?"

"The pieces are falling into place, my friend. Gemini reached out to his contacts. The guy you chased out of the pipe shop is named Eddie Mason—ex-Ranger and spook. His dossier is on the way."

Chapter 56

As Eddie led Craig out of the elevator and into the main room, his old boss eyed the book cover posters. "Tell me again, how does Jeff know Emily Bryant?"

Eddie looked over his shoulder. "A better question is, how do you know who she is?"

He scowled. "I don't live under a rock. I've even read a few of her books. I like her main character. Again, I ask, how does Jeff know her?"

Eddie shrugged and led him upstairs to the roof. "Jeff knows everybody."

The two women stood when they arrived, and Loren hugged her former boss. "Craig Black, this is Emily Bryant."

He shook her hand. "I've read some of your stuff. You're very talented."

She ducked her head. "That's very kind, and what do you do?"

Craig hesitated for a fraction of a second and then said confidently. "I work for the State Department."

Emily raised her eyebrows. "Uh-huh. Would you like some coffee?"

Craig said. "Please. Black."

They all sat.

Eddie said. "Emily here figured out the pipe shop puzzle."

Craig paused in the act of sipping his coffee. "Really."

Loren nodded. "She realized Leonette didn't go to the pipe shop. He called it."

Craig set down his cup, glancing at Emily. "So, someone has a scrape on the line?"

Loren nodded. "Listening for the word Lanceolate, we think."

Craig scratched the stubble on his chin. "Did they contact you?"

Eddie said, "They want to me to sit at a picnic table in Melrose Park tomorrow at three."

Craig shook his head. "Sticker burr."

Loren leaned back in her chair and crossed her arms. "That's what we thought."

Eddie asked, "Is there a way to find the scrape and trace it, or the number they called us from?"

"Probably not, but we can try," Craig pulled out his phone and then, glancing again over at Emily, paused.

She held up one small hand. "I know you're Bureau, or more likely, Agency. I can keep my mouth shut."

Craig's eyebrows shot up, and he opened his mouth.

Emily looked down her nose at him. "No offense, Mr. Black, but no one from the State Department would wear that blazer. I'm already involved in this. Just keep going."

Loren fought back a smile. "She has been a big help."

Craig furrowed his brow and looked down at himself. "What's wrong with this blazer?"

Emily patted his arm. "Nothing, dear, it's just not State Department."

Craig held her gaze, frowned, and dialed. After a moment, he said into the phone. "Ned, Craig, I need you to look for a scrape on," he raised his eyebrows at them, and Loren handed him a paper he read the number from. "Thanks." He hung up and sipped his coffee. "How did the person on the phone sound? Step me through the call."

They recounted the conversation.

Again, Craig glanced over at Emily before answering. "You asked them about Treleous?"

Emily held up both hands this time. "I knew not even to ask."

Craig held her gaze and then looked over at Eddie. "So, they sounded defensive?"

Loren added, "And guarded."

Craig's phone rang. "Yeah." He listened. "Thanks, Ned. No, leave the scrape alone, don't mess with it. Let me know where the trail leads." He hung up. "There is a scrape on the line that records each inbound call that meets the criteria and sends it to an I.P. address that sends it to another, and so on. It will take a while to find the end, if we can at all."

Eddie sat back heavily. "What now?"

They sat in silence for several seconds.

Craig said to Emily. "This is a perfectly good blazer. This blazer would go fine at the State Department."

Emily smirked. "You know that's bull. When you bought it, you purposely set a price limit that was just below what even the most junior peacock in this town would consider too blue collar for their starched monogrammed shirts. You're making a point, and you know it."

Craig stared at her hard and then grinned. "You want a job?"

She rolled her eyes and looked away. "You couldn't afford me."

Eddie shook his head, fighting back a smile. Was Craig flirting? "You mind if we get back to the problem at hand? Do you think you could put together a team? A set up big enough net to catch them if I go to this meet?"

Craig shook his head. "No. We know nothing about them. Everyone would look suspicious. We'd be chasing geese all over the city. It's the whole point of a sticker burr. No, we have to use the scrape."

Loren leaned forward on her elbows. "We probably can't find where it's going, but can we use it?"

"What do you mean, use it?" asked Eddie.

Craig nodded slowly. "We could send a message. The question is, what should the message say?"

"It has to be good," began Loren. "We might only get once chance before they close the channel down."

Emily stood. "This sounds like it's going to take some time." She turned to Craig. "I have extra bedrooms if you'd like to stay the night."

Craig let out a slow breath and checked his watch. "I might do that. I have a meeting at ten tomorrow morning, so I'd have to leave here by about nine."

Eddie said, "I appreciate it, Craig, because I've no idea what to say to these people."

Chapter 57

It was cold but clear, so Luis rolled out his bag in front of the tent to lie down. Better to have nothing blocking his line of hearing or sight.

Susan began the night in the tent, but after a few minutes moved outside and lay next to him. She whispered, "How do you know trouble is coming?"

Luis shrugged. "Sometimes I can just sense it. It's hard to explain."

The bright half-moon lit up the surrounding ground in a soft glow.

"Is it always right?" Susan asked.

"Do you mean when I feel it, does something always happen? No. At least not to me, but I'm convinced something happened somewhere that I was tuned into." Why did he answer her so honestly? It wasn't like him to share like that. Especially about personal stuff. Why was this girl getting him off his game like this?

"Do you always get a warning before danger?"

Luis sucked his teeth. "No."

Susan turned her head toward him. "Why do you think that is?"

"I don't know. I've learned not to ignore it, but to never depend on it."

Luis could feel Susan hesitate before she asked, "Did you feel it when you got hurt?"

"Yes."

Susan nodded. "I'm sorry to ask about that. I just needed to know if it just warned us or protected us."

Odd how she'd accepted Caveman without a pause, and now she took his strange instinct in stride. He'd never met anyone quite like her. "It's just a vibration. Like the same way you can feel a train coming. If you don't move, it'll still run you over."

He could sense that she was smiling as she curled up tighter in her sleeping bag.

It was getting cold, but not the coldest he'd ever been by a long shot. The night wore on and now and then Susan faded off and snored softly before snapping back awake.

Luis grinned. He liked this girl. He glanced at his watch. Just after midnight. He was just about to pull each knee to his chest to stay limber when he froze. His fingertips vibrated, and he cocked his head, listening.

The wind hissed in the trees overhead, masking much of the night's sound. He slowly slid out of the sleeping bag.

Susan reached over and grabbed his hand.

She was smart. Silent and calm.

With an exaggerated slow movement, he held his finger up to his lips.

Susan nodded, slithered out of her bag, quickly rolled it up, and tucked it under one arm.

Luis handed her his bag and, holding his rifle in both hands, led her away from the camp. He moved slowly, stepping carefully, pleased with how Susan mimicked him. They slid behind the fallen tree and Luis rose and put the thermal scope to his eye. He moved slowly in a circle until he spotted them.

Four men coming from the east, rifles high, moving in a tight-knit group, the last man watching their six. Trained ex-military by their posture and movement. He noted goggles in their silhouettes. If they wore night vision, they'd be okay, but if they were using thermal—well, then Luis and Susan were in trouble.

About fifty yards from the clearing, the men split up without a word.

Luis leaned back and held his finger up to his lips again.

She nodded.

He looked back through the scope. The men arranged themselves around the camp, preparing to enter from each side. Luis focused on the one circling around, coming in their direction.

The soldier turned just before their hiding place and headed toward the clearing. They silently entered camp and checked the tent.

Luis calmed his breathing and moved his finger up on the trigger.

Once the men realized the camp was empty, they quickly moved back-to-back, facing out and sweeping their surroundings.

The one facing Luis swept by them without pausing. Must just be just night vision—thank God.

The men had a quick, low conversation before they formed up again and moved quickly back the way they'd come.

Luis did a quick three-sixty before watching them leave. They didn't pause or stop, just kept moving east at a good clip. He gritted his teeth. For the second time, the enemy knew exactly where they were.

Luis tracked them until they were out of sight, then turned in a slow circle once again, the thermal scope to his eye. Something flared white off to his right. What was it? That was the problem with thermal. Nothing could hide from you, but it showed little detail. You couldn't always tell what it was. He slid his finger back down to the trigger and centered on the object.

Susan whispered, "What?"

Luis held up a finger. The target turned, and Luis relaxed. Side on, he could tell it was small—smaller than a man. It ducked and moved. Luis dialed the focus. Under his breath, he said, "I think it's a fox." He continued scanning, then relaxed and lowered the weapon.

He could just make out Susan's wide eyes in the moonlight.

A surge of anger sprouted in his mind, and Luis quelled it. Through gritted teeth, he said, "That's the second time they knew exactly where we were."

Susan nodded, her attention never leaving his face.

Luis asked under his breath. "How did they know how to find us again?"

"I don't know." She reached out to grab his arm, but stopped short. "I swear, Luis, it's not me."

Was she the problem? Again, even if she was bad, how could she have contacted someone? And, even if she could have, how then could she have directed them right to them? Did she have some sort of tracker on her? If so, it had to be something she'd brought. No one had been close enough to plant something on her.

If Treleous had, then they would have acted in Miami. Used it to find the house in Coral Gables. Since then, she had all new clothes. She never met with anyone outside the group. Did someone pass something to her in the restaurant when they arrived?

Susan broke his train of thought. "Luis, please. I'm telling you the truth."

He frowned. That didn't make sense. If they'd had someone at the restaurant to pass something to her again, they'd have acted then. He put a hand on the top of the pistol at this hip. "Put yourself in my place, Susan. What would you think?"

Susan took a step back. "I don't know." She blew out a breath. "If it was me. I could have just yelled. There were four of them, right? I could have just run over screaming. If I wanted them to get you, why would I stay quiet?"

That was logical. He didn't have an answer for that. And again, he had no idea how Susan could have contacted anyone, even if she wanted to.

"If they're tracking me, then I don't know about it. You want me to take all my clothes off?"

Luis did, but not for the reason she was asking. That surprised him a little. Stay focused. "No. If they were tracking us, they'd have followed the signal here to us behind the tree."

Susan rubbed her face. "Could they be tracking something at the camp?"

Interesting question. "What, though? We took everything but the tent. When could someone have put a tracker on that?"

Susan shrugged. "In the parking lot while we ate breakfast?"

Luis shook his head. "I don't think so. I asked the waitress to put us at a table where I could see everything—the front door, the back, and the Jeep in the parking lot." He looked around. Something wasn't right.

"How come you could see those men, but they couldn't see us?"

"Probably they only had night vision. That just makes it look like dusk, or just shades of gray. It can't see through things or behind a screen, just like your eyes normally." He gestured to his scope. "This is thermal. It sees heat, even if it's behind something."

"Thank God for that."

Luis said, "Agreed. But thermal isn't good for details. That's why it took me a moment to decide that was a fox before. I like knowing something's near us, even if I don't know exactly what it is." He flinched. "How do they keep finding us? We have to solve that soon, or we're in trouble."

She stepped forward, her voice pleaded. "It's not me, Luis. I swear."

He nodded and lifted the scope back to his eye and slowly turned again. Nothing. On a whim, he raised the rifle and focused on the canopy above. Just to the left of the camp, he stopped. About a hundred yards beyond the clearing, something bloomed with a white heat signature about fifty feet above the ground.

Chapter 58

Eddie stood and stretched. For over an hour, they'd batted around ideas and still didn't have a plan. "It's after midnight. I think we're at a dead end. I say we sleep on it and reconvene early tomorrow." He turned to Emily. "Is that okay with you?"

She shrugged. "I'm usually up and eating breakfast by six."

As they moved downstairs, Emily asked Craig, "Do you need anything?"

Craig shook his head. "No, thank you. I always have an overnight bag with me in the car. In my line of work, I never know what might happen."

Emily chuckled. "Yeah, the State Department can be like that."

He grinned. "Yes, it can."

Inside their room, Loren asked Eddie, "Are Emily and Craig flirting?"

Eddie snorted. "I don't know what's going on there and I'm not sure I want to."

They brushed their teeth and settled into bed.

Eddie didn't know what to say to whoever was listening in on the pipe shop. "It's a weird way to communicate, listening for a word on what appears to be a randomly selected phone line."

Loren snuggled up next to him. "I don't think it's random. I'll bet you they lived near here and it was a landmark they all knew. It's paranoid, is what it is. Think about it, it's the ultimate cut out. These people are afraid of something. Probably Treleous. I can't say I really blame them."

"I agree. Then how are we ever going to get them to trust us? This might be our only path to who Caveman is."

"Or who Treleous really is."

He sighed. "I can't shake the feeling that we have just one shot before they disappear. If we lose them, what's our next step?"

Loren adjusted her head on his shoulder. "Don't forget, Luis has uncovered something in Montana."

"That's true. At least we know Caveman wasn't crazy. Both locations led to something just like he said they would."

She lifted her head and looked at him. "Did you doubt him?"

Eddie shrugged. "Not really, but it's good to know both of them panned out. You know?"

She put her head back on his shoulder. "That's true."

"But it begs the question: why was this in his head? I mean, I get them pushing in skills and even knowledge about CIA missions. But the scrape here and the ranch in Montana aren't official or connected to Mendelson. So why does he even know about them?"

"I don't know."

Loren stretched out her legs. "You know what I keep thinking about? The man who gave this information to Sam in the first place."

Eddie frowned. Long before he and his crew were pulled into this Mendelson and Treleous mystery, Sam was the first to get involved. A man named Heinrich Stein approached the senator on the street one day with a packet of papers and vague details about a conspiracy involving all of this. Before Sam could ask a question or tell the man to get out of his face, Heinrich saw something frightening, and he ran. Only to be murdered later.

He looked down at her. "You mean Heinrich?"

She nodded. "What did he think he would accomplish? I've never understood his plan. What did he expect Sam to do? And if he hadn't convinced Sam, who would even know about this? I mean, Treleous would be operating with impunity. Unopposed. It's scary."

Eddie sighed. "Would be? There are. How does all of this fit together—Mendelson, Treleous, Caveman, the pipe shop, the ranch in Montana, and Heinrich Stein? One minute it's getting clearer, and I think we're making progress, and the next we're grasping at straws and getting nowhere."

"I know what you mean."

Eddie stared at the ceiling, trying to get the damn pieces to fit together.

After a few minutes, Loren's breathing evened out as she fell asleep.

Eddie tried to organize everything he knew and find some logical thread. Why did Caveman even know who Susan was? It made sense for him to know her father, but Susan wasn't connected to anything. So why would she be on the green list? Unless it linked her in a way they didn't understand. It was like they were missing some key puzzle piece. Something that would tie everything together.

Eventually, Eddie faded off to sleep, only to be shaken awake by Loren. He bolted up. "What's wrong?"

Loren put a hand on his chest. "Nothing. We're fine. Lie back down. Something occurred to me."

He rubbed the sleep from his eyes. "What's that?

"Well, it seems like some of the scientists had their own little resistance against Mendelson. I mean, someone hid Caveman away, and maybe helped Susan's dad to disappear. Some of the other scientists as well."

"I buy it. What does that get us?"

Loren sat up. "So, if there is this group, was Heinrich Stein one of them?"

Eddie shrugged. "It would make sense that he was."

"If he was with them, then they intended to reach out to Sam. They trusted him."

Eddie nodded.

Loren continued. "So maybe our message should tell them we're connected to Sam. He could be our bridge. The one person both of us trust."

Eddie nodded. That made total sense. He reached up and kissed her. "You're a genius."

Loren grinned. "I have my moments."

Chapter 59

Mack laid out everything for his backpack on the hotel room bed. Never leave a paved road without three days' rations and water—one of the many lessons he learned from the Corps. As a Recon Marine, a lot of two-hour missions ended up being two days long. That only happened to you once before you made sure you always had water and granola bars with you.

Surveying the items, he ticked off his mental list. Ammo was the tricky one. You never wanted to run out, but it was heavy. His quarry included a civilian woman, so he should be able to catch up with them. No problem. He tossed another box of 5.56 on the pile. Then, almost as an afterthought, he put a flashbang in an outside pocket.

Mack glanced over at a tablet on the bed. He'd spent the last hour going over Eddie Mason's life. A spook and at one time an Army Ranger, not too shabby.

He doubted the Hispanic guy was a Ranger, though. He seemed more like Delta, or a Seal. Mack didn't think he was Recon. That was a pretty small community, and Mack believed he would have heard of him, at least by reputation. Maybe not.

He loaded his pack, carefully placing each item in the way he liked it. He couldn't remember a time in his life when he wasn't hiking somewhere to shoot something—whether a deer or a Republican Guard.

This dude Eddie was also at one time on the most wanted list. That was interesting. They needed to know more about that. Was this guy a mercenary now? Could he be bought?

Frank knocked once and entered. "You'd better get some sleep."

Mack glanced at his watch. "I know. What time are we leaving, five? I can still get four hours. I'll be fine." He nodded down at the tablet. "Did you read about this Eddie character?"

Frank eased down into a chair. "Yeah, I already asked Gemini to get us more information about him being a wanted man. I thought I recognized his name, so I looked back through Loren's file. When she was in the Agency, one time she had to run, and guess who was sent out to bring her in safely?"

Mack looked up, eyebrows raised. "You're kidding."

"Nope, our boy Eddie himself."

"You were right. You said if we kept picking, the pieces would come together. Does Eddie have a place in Miami?"

"Gemini is checking on that as well." He frowned. "Be careful out there, Mack. We don't need either of them alive. If you can see where they're going, that would be useful, but just take them out. Don't play around with this guy."

Mack nodded and zipped up his pack.

"I'm serious, Mack."

He looked over.

The older man's eyes narrowed.

"I got it."

Frank looked down his nose at him. "No, you don't. This guy has pissed you off and you want to prove you're better than him."

True. Mack wanted that in the worst way. "I can take him."

Frank snorted. "I know you can. But you know how combat is, Mack. Anything can happen and the best man doesn't always win. Just kill them. Don't play with your food, and I want you to check in without fail."

"Yes, Dad."

Frank said sharply. "Mack."

The younger man looked up. Frank didn't talk to him like that very often.

"There's something going on here, separate from these two. Kill them and come back." He grinned. "I have a feeling this might be more fun, anyway."

Mack knew Frank was manipulating him, but he really didn't want to miss the fun. "I got it. Kill them and come back."

Chapter 60

Luis studied the object in the tree. The thermal image showed little detail, only that it was small and emitting heat. He focused on it for a long time, but it didn't move. A sleeping bird?

He felt Susan move closer to him, sensing he could see something. He leaned down and whispered in her ear. "Look through the scope," he pointed, "At that tree top and tell me what you think that is."

She guided it to her eye like a pro.

Luis suppressed a smile and showed her how to focus.

She studied it for a moment and then said, "I think it's square, or a rectangle."

Luis took the rifle back and looked again. Possibly. He made a motion for her to wait, checked their surroundings with the scope, and then crept closer to the object.

He checked periodically, but it didn't move as he approached. Finally, near the base of the tree, he focused on it. She was right. It was square.

He turned and focused off back to the east, scanning the tops of the tree and discovered another spot. It had to be at least a hundred yards away. He panned through the canopies and then spotted another small heat bloom to the south. Checking his surroundings once more, he moved quickly but quietly to the east, until he neared the second object. Now he could see another a hundred yards beyond that.

Ducking, he weaved his way back to the tree where he'd first spotted the object in the treetop. He pulled a penlight from a leg pocket and then, covering it with his hands, he studied the trunks.

Small, deep gashes dotted the wood at intervals before moving up. Climbing spikes—it had to be. He looked up. Cameras were the only reasonable explanation.

Why would they be here? Luis believed they were still in the national park. Were these used by the park service? You couldn't really see the game from that high up. To keep people out? Then why didn't someone official intercept them during the day? No park rangers during the day but trained soldiers at night? He crouched and made his way back to Susan. "I think it's a camera. There are more stretching off to the south and east."

"But none to the west?"

Luis shrugged. "Only a couple, it looks like."

Susan said, "Then it has to be from the ranch. I mean, the townsfolk were prepared to deal with people asking about it. It seems reasonable that they would have protections on their back door as well."

"It would also explain how they knew exactly where we were."

Susan punched him in the arm. "Told you it wasn't me."

Luis grinned. "I'll let you off on this one." His smile faded. "The question now is, how are we going to get to the ranch?"

They sat back against the fallen tree.

She nestled her head into his shoulder. It felt right there, which surprised him.

His fingers buzzed faintly. Cleary, this was another kind of trap. Again, with the déjà vu feeling. The parallel between the whole Ellen situation and this one continued to nag at Luis. He'd led her into a trap then as well. He still remembered everything like it was yesterday.

It was cool behind the gas station mid-way to Verdun when he parked at the edge of the lot. The temperature had dropped considerably as soon as the sun went down, and Luis rubbed his hands while Ellen turned on her cell phone and checked her messages.

Luis glanced over. "Anything?"

Ellen pursed her lips and brushed her dark hair out of her eyes. "There's a message from Craig, my boss at the Agency."

"That's good, right?"

She shrugged. "At least it's someone I know. But..." She hesitated, "I'm not sure who I trust right now."

Luis shrugged. "Well, we have to start somewhere. Call him and we'll be really careful about the meet."

She looked at him, her eyes wide. Reaching over, she squeezed his forearm. "I can't thank you enough. I don't know what I'd have done if you hadn't been there."

Luis put his hand over hers. Damn, she was a good-looking woman. Was that really why he was doing this? He didn't think so. Something about her called on his sense of duty and pulled at his Latin upbringing about protecting women in distress. He was sure nowadays it would be seen as old-fashioned and maybe a little chauvinist, but Luis didn't think it was that simple.

Ellen dialed and put the phone on speaker.

After two rings, Craig answered. "Hello."

"It's Ellen."

Craig's voice was calm. "Are you all right?"

"I am." Her eyes misted up. "I'm sorry, Craig. I don't know what I did wrong. Something changed today. I could tell they were on to me."

This surprised Luis, and he was unsure how to comfort her.

Craig continued in a calm and measured voice. "It's okay. You did nothing wrong. I'll tell you all about it when you come in. Is someone helping you?"

She glanced over at Luis. "Yes."

Some instinct prompted Luis to shake his head.

Craig asked, "Who?"

Ellen studied Luis' face. "I'd rather not say. Not yet."

Craig hesitated. "Okay. I know a man who owns a wine shop in the town of Verdun. It's called Rouge and Blanche. It's just off the center of town. Can you get there?"

She looked over at Luis again, eyebrows raised.

He nodded.

"Yes. We can get there. When?"

"Tomorrow morning, first thing. As soon as it opens. Is that okay? Will you be okay until then?"

"Yes. Yes, we'll be fine. Thanks, Craig." She hung up and looked over at Luis.

He glanced at his watch: eight o'clock. He figured they were about an hour from Verdun, and Ellen looked exhausted. "We aren't far from Metz. Let's get a hotel and get some rest. We've got hours to kill."

Her eyes widened. "They'll look for my name at hotels."

Luis shrugged. "They don't know mine. I'll check in. Don't worry, we'll be fine."

She sat back with a sigh. "Okay. I can't thank you enough. You didn't have to do this."

He started the Mercedes. "Don't worry, I won't let anything happen to you."

• • •

Susan stirred and looked at him, bringing Luis back to the present.

She seemed to have sensed something in his posture. "You okay?"

Luis said, "Fine, just thinking about stuff. You?"

She nodded, her attention lingering on his face.

"Try to get some sleep and we'll see how things look in the morning."

She nestled back in beside him and yawned. "Okay, but I don't see how it's going to be any more promising tomorrow."

Luis nodded. He didn't, either—he just desperately hoped he wasn't leading Susan into another trap like he had that night with Ellen.

Chapter 61

The sun was just beginning to peek over the horizon as Mack studied the crashed pickup and then looked sidelong at Frank.

He narrowed his eyes. "Don't say it."

"Do you think he knew this drop-off was here?"

Frank smiled. "I don't think so. He seemed scared shitless when he suddenly sailed out into space."

Mack pulled out his rifle and gear. "An orange Jeep?"

Frank slapped him on the back. "Yep. Be careful and keep in touch."

Mack slid down the incline before putting on his pack. Holding his AR in both hands, he waded slowly across the creek and entered the woods.

Ever since he was a boy in West Virginia, he loved the hunt, tracking red stag, turkey, and sometimes a squirrel if the family really needed to eat. He scanned the mountains glowing in the sunrise. Bigger and prettier than back home. Hell, out in the world, everything was bigger and better than home. Not much to do where he grew up, but dig coal and be poor.

He knelt down and studied the Jeep tracks. The mud had crusted over with the overnight freeze. It would melt soon and leave the ground soggy once again. This would be like tracking a herd of elephants through tall grass. Mack cinched up his pack and broke into a trot.

It was unusual for home to come to mind. That rarely happened anymore. He wanted out so badly and he hadn't looked back once. Hell, he was only sixteen when he'd driven all the way down to Princeton to see the military recruiters, where he had one question for them. Which one was the baddest unit, and how could he get into it? Of course, the Army had been coy about Delta and how only a select few men made it in. Same with the Navy and the Seals.

Mack grinned. Not the Marines. They told him that Marine Recon was as tough as it got, and there were fewer of them than either Delta Force or the Seals. That if he wanted to be a Recon Marine, and he was good enough, then he'd be one.

That's all Mack needed to hear. The son-of-a-bitch wasn't lying, either. The Marines saw what he could do and made him one, then sent him off to the fight. He hopped his way down an incline. At the bottom, he crouched and checked his surroundings. Cocking his head, he listened for anything out of the ordinary before continuing to track the Jeep.

War was mostly what he'd hoped it would be—blowing things up and shooting bad guys. What surprised him was after the high of battle, there was always a letdown and a kind of depression.

He'd hunted all his life, but he was still amazed by the amount of blood in a human body. How in battle it splattered everything bright red, and how terrible it was to see your buddies die.

He stopped at a small stream, and out of habit and knelt to examine the bank. A split hoofprint with two dots behind it. Not an elk, must be a moose—and nearby. He looked upstream, following the animal's path.

He'd never hunted a moose before. That would be cool. Forcing his focus back to the tread marks, he decided he'd have to come back after all this was done and bag himself one. He stepped over the water and broke back into a loping jog.

What had driven him out of the Corps were the idiots in charge. Except for Frank. He was the only commander he'd ever had that wasn't full of it. Frank was always straight and cut through the bull. Still, Mack had been hesitant to follow him when his old boss called. As screwed up as the military was, it still lets you blow stuff up and shoot people. Not many jobs let you do that.

Ahead to the left, he glimpsed orange, and hunkered down. Pulling a pair of binoculars from his pack, he focused on the spot. The Jeep. Lots of trees here. He could see why they'd stopped driving. The question was, were they still here?

He slipped along to his left, his rifle up and ready. Stepping carefully, he slowly circled the vehicle, stopping regularly to listen, and then moving a little closer with each pass.

After two full trips, he was convinced that the Jeep was empty and approached it. He checked the door—locked. Shading his eyes, he peered inside. Two duffle bags. He turned, listening again, before squatting.

The Hispanic guy was pretty good at not leaving prints, probably out of habit. The girl, however, was a different story. Small boots, brand new from the looks of the tread. It took only a few steps to recognize how she walked and the signs she left in her wake. Mack grinned. He had them now.

Chapter 62

Loren woke before Eddie, showered, then headed to the kitchen.

Emily was already cooking hash browns in a pair of jeans and a red and white checked shirt.

Loren chuckled. "Do you eat like this every morning?"

"Only when I have guests. I love having people stay over." She pointed with a spatula. "Coffee's there."

Loren poured herself a cup. "Can I help?"

"If you want to scramble some eggs, we can put them on whenever the men decide to grace us with their presence."

Loren grinned and took out the carton.

"So, you and Eddie seem pretty good. How did you two meet?"

"We were both in the Agency. I got in some trouble," she shrugged, "and he saved me."

Emily stopped stirring and looked over her glasses at her. "You have got to be kidding me."

Loren shook her head. "Nope. It's true."

Her eyes widened. "How delicious is that?"

"It was pretty romantic. At least, afterward it was."

Emily tipped her pan, scraping finished potatoes onto a plate. "Is it okay if I ask why you're trying to find this missing person?"

"His daughter asked us to help."

"And did you know this might be more than a simple disappearance?"

"We did."

The older woman held up both hands. "I appreciate your telling me that much. I know when to leave well enough alone. I won't ask anymore."

Craig entered the room. "Good morning, ladies. These smell wonderful."

Loren had the powerful instinct that he'd been standing just outside, listening.

Emily pointed. "Coffee."

Craig rubbed his hands together. "You, ma'am, are a saint and a prophet." He poured himself a cup and inhaled deeply.

Emily drew down her brow. "With bad poetry like that, maybe you do work for the State Department."

Craig waggled his eyebrows.

Loren turned away to hide her incredulous smile.

Eddie entered. "Good morning."

Craig handed him a mug.

"This is too much, Emily," Eddie said. "We thank you so much for your hospitality."

She waved this away but seemed pleased.

They finished cooking and moved the food to the table.

Loren asked. "Are you working on a new novel?"

"Always. Another Blake book—*Cast Off*."

"What does the title mean?" asked Eddie.

Craig frowned at Emily. "It's a spatter type meant to identify blood at a crime scene that was flung from something. Usually the murder weapon."

Her eyes widened. "Very good. I'm impressed. You do a lot of blood splatter analysis at the State Department?"

Straight faced, Craig replied, "It's a very cutthroat business."

Emily fought back a smile and turned to Loren. "I'm almost finished with it. If you have some time later, you can see it if you want."

Loren nodded eagerly. "I'd love to."

Emily pushed back from the table. "Okay. I like to start the day with a little time outside in the fresh air. I'll leave you all to your work." She stood and turned to Craig. "I know you have a meeting this morning, so I probably won't see you. It was nice to meet you, and you're welcome back anytime."

Craig stood. "Thanks again for your hospitality. It was a pleasure."

After she left, Loren looked over at him. "What are you, a teenager?"

Craig scowled. "What do you mean? I was just being polite."

Eddie guffawed. "I didn't know you were even capable of such flirty banter."

"I'm capable of a lot of things you don't know about."

Eddie rolled his eyes. "Loren came up with a good idea last night."

"Let's hear it," said Craig.

She leaned back in her chair. "If we put together all the pieces, I get the sense that at least some of Mendelson's scientists were resisting him and got organized about it."

Craig nodded speculatively. "Organized and sophisticated enough to put on a scrape program."

"Right. So, if there is such a group, is it safe to assume Heinrich Stein was part of it? That they sent him to contact Sam?"

"I see where you're going. So Sam might be someone you both trust. A bridge of sorts. That's a good idea."

Eddie said, "I thought so, too. Let's send a message that says something like, 'I'm sure you understand, but we can't make the meeting today.'"

Loren added, "After all, we know what happened when Heinrich met our friend Sam."

"I like that," said Eddie. "*Our* friend. Then say, we wouldn't want the same thing to happen to Susan."

Craig said, "That's good, but we have to end with what we want them to do. Which is what?"

That stared at each other across the table.

Loren said, "Give them our email address. Ask them to start slower. We want to get to know each other first before any of us take a risk."

Craig frowned. "I think you need to personalize this a little more. Make it a conversation between two people."

Loren said, "Makes sense. How do you suggest we do that?"

Craig looked each of them in the eye before saying. "You need to sign it. Give them a name, a first name at least."

Loren looked over at Eddie, who sighed. "Okay. I'm the one who talked to them, so I guess sign it, Eddie."

Loren turned to Craig. "Can your people feed that message into the scrape?"

He stood. "I'll have them get on that right away and see if they take the bait."

Part 3

Chapter 63

Frank collected his men in a field south of Beaver Ruin, where they unpacked the drones and set up a command center in a cargo van.

Chip adjusted his belly as he sat in front of the two screens and tested the connectivity with each camera.

Frank grinned at the black eye from the run-in with the man at the pipe shop. It was good for Chip to get a little dirty now and then. Make him a better support person sitting behind his monitors.

Chip gave a thumbs up, his eyes never leaving the images. "We're online."

He nodded. "Good. Come on, let's assemble the troops." Outside, he spread a map out on the hood of a pickup and gathered the men around. He pointed to the little town. "Let's start here and break the surrounding area into quadrants. Chip, how much battery can we get out of these birds?"

He shrugged. "We've upgraded them a bit, so we should get a solid forty minutes."

Frank nodded. "Okay. We don't want to lose one of these things, so we fly them out for nineteen minutes and then bring them back here for more juice." He pointed to each pilot as he gave orders. "From downtown you go to the northeast, northwest, southeast, southwest. Be organized and thorough. Look for anything out of the ordinary. Power lines, large structures, cave mouths. I don't know what else. These people are guarding something, so find it." He stopped and looked up, making sure everyone was following him. Satisfied, Frank continued, "Keep the drones high and stagger your take offs so they don't attract attention." He glanced up at Chip. "If anyone asks, do we have an excuse paper ready?"

The tech man patted his shirt pocket. "We have an official-looking work order to check power lines and possible pipeline paths."

Frank folded up the map. "Then let's get going."

One by one, the black and yellow insectoid machines lifted gracefully into the sky and soared off to the north.

Frank followed Chip back into the van and eased his bulk down next to him. Each screen showed an image of the ground streaking by far below. He pulled out a cigar and put it unlit into his mouth. "Are we recording?"

Chip pointed to four red LEDs on a box to his right. "We're rolling. If there's something, it should be easy to find. There's not much out here."

"Lot of country, though."

Chip sighed. "True. Hopefully, whatever they're protecting is near the town."

"It makes sense that it should be." He thought about the call Ben made hitting a tower here in Beaver Ruin. The one data point that led Frank to this town in the first place. It had to be near here. They just had to recognize it.

Chapter 64

Eddie kissed Loren on the top of her head and began to clear the table. "We still haven't heard from Luis?"

She wiped her mouth and stood to help. "Not since yesterday morning." She glanced at her watch. "It's still pretty early in mountain time."

Eddie scraped off a plate. "Are you worried about him?"

She shrugged. "A little. Are you?"

Was he? "Maybe a little, as well." That was unusual—Luis had always been able to take care of himself.

Loren stacked the dirty plates next to the sink.

He studied her. He hadn't really ever been worried about Luis since the first time he'd met him. As he washed the dishes, his mind kept returning to that time like buzzards returning to roadkill. To the morning long ago in Verdun.

Even that early, traffic already clogged the A4 as he and Jeff approached the town. Eddie had slept through most of the five-hour trip from Honfleur, and he sat up and rubbed his eyes.

Jeff glanced over. "I thought you weren't in the CIA anymore."

Eddie yawned, "I'm not."

"So why did we drive across France to save another agent on the run?"

Once again, he marveled at Jeff. This strange little man had become very important to Eddie. He was always up for whatever. Case in point, driving across half of France at the drop of a hat. "That's a good question." He sighed. "I'm not sure."

Jeff chuckled. "Translation, Loren asked you to."

Eddie raised his eyebrows and shrugged. "Yeah, that about covers it." His phone rang, and he examined the number. "Speak of the devil." He answered. "Good morning, Loren."

"We've got a problem." She sounded breathless and panicky.

Eddie sat up. "What's up?"

"You're supposed to meet Ellen at a liquor store in Verdun owned by someone Craig has worked with before," she continued in a rush. "But the meet is compromised. I'll tell you how later. But Ellen must have turned off her phone, and she's not returning my calls."

Eddie glanced at his watch, a little after eight. "What time's the meet?"

"At ten. As soon as the place is supposed to open."

He rubbed his chin. "How is she supposed to know me?"

Loren hesitated, and he could hear her suppress the smile in her voice. "You're supposed to have a red bandana."

Eddie rolled his eyes. "What am I, a cowboy?"

Her smile was evident in her voice. "Ellen has a wonderful sense of style, Eddie." She suddenly turned serious. "I'm worried about her, and you. Be careful."

Eddie hung up and glanced over at Jeff. "Our meet has been compromised. No one is supposed to be involved in this meet but us, Ellen, and Craig, so how is the hell did it get burned?"

"What do you want to do?"

"I don't know. But for starters, I need a bandana."

Jeff looked over at him, eyebrows raised.

Eddie shook his head. "Don't ask."

• • •

The street running in front of the wine store was typical for a French town like this. Shop keepers hosed down the sidewalks while vendors set up stalls with postcards and trinkets for tourists. Eddie's attention was everywhere as he strolled down the road. He glanced at the proposed meeting place as he passed. Closed, but a light was visible in the back room. He glanced at his watch, still fifteen minutes until the meeting time.

He did a wide circuit and then approached again from the rear. No one seemed to be out of place or following him. Stopping at the back door, he cocked his head. Quiet. Eddie picked the lock and eased into the shop. He stood in the doorway, pistol held out and ready, before taking two cautious steps and closing the door behind him.

He stepped behind a rack and stopped to listen. The only sound was the hum from the refrigerators to his right. Then the faintest scuff. He tiptoed back a few steps and circled around the shelves. Holding his pistol low in both hands, he inched toward the door and swung around the find a big man in a black suit standing in the front room holding a gun.

Eddie pulled back just as the man fired. The bullet punched through the wall just above his head.

With a bang, the rear door of the shop flew open, forcing Eddie to scramble to his right, trying to avoid being trapped. He heard the man in front grunt, and then the bottles crashed as they toppled from the shelves. He flopped to the ground, followed by a rain of glass.

The man at the back door stopped, distracted by the sounds in the front.

Eddie stepped out and shot him twice. He quickly crouched down to make sure the man was dead, and then, keeping low, moved forward into the shop.

The large man lay spread eagle on his back. A pool of blood and wine blooming around him.

Eddie inched closer and examined the bullet hole right above the man's dress shirt pocket. The street out front was empty. He leaned down and craned his head upward, noting where the bullet had entered high up on the front window. Someone was helping Ellen. Someone very talented. That was a hell of a shot.

He heard a thump outside. He needed to get out of here. Out the front? No, there were two bodies here. He couldn't be seen here. Running back through the shop, he kicked the back door open and ducked into a roll. He came up face to face with two startled men, guns drawn, about to enter the shop.

They narrowed their eyes at Eddie and swung in his direction.

Eddie put a bullet in one man's chest, causing him to tumble into the second. He dove, rolled again, and fired again as he came to his feet, the bullet striking the wall just above the men, and ran.

He ducked down an alley, holstered his gun, and pulled out his cell phone.

Whoever was helping Ellen was talented. He just hoped he could keep them both alive until Eddie could get to them.

· · ·

Loren set some more plates next to him, bringing him back to the present.

That had been his first exposure to Luis. It really was a hell of a shot.

She put her arms around him. "Thinking about Luis?"

He nodded. "I hope he's okay."

Chapter 65

Luis sat behind the fallen tree eating a granola bar breakfast and watching the sun crest the mountains. He turned to see Susan run her short fingers through her hair and gather it up into a ponytail.

He'd learned a long time ago that on a mission, you had to be a man of two minds. One part focused on the objective, keeping a lookout for danger and always ready to spring into action. You'd go nuts if you functioned like that for days on end, however. You had to find some normalcy and levity in the downtime to maintain your sanity. Hence the second mind, for moments like this.

The men in his unit usually blew off steam with raunchy and sick jokes about the death and carnage around them. It was a way to keep the horror at a distance and find some levity wherever you could. He glanced over at Susan. It didn't seem like that would work with her.

Professionals learn how to move back and forth between these minds as necessary. Would an amateur understand this? Did he need to stay serious and focused all the time for her to understand they were in a tough spot? Or would she react poorly to the constant stress? He didn't know how to find this balance with this strange yet amazing girl.

He rubbed his eyes. "Whenever I'm on a mission, I don't miss my bed, hot food, not even a toilet, but not having a hot coffee to start my day is torture. I'm jonesing for a cup-a-joe."

Susan grinned. "I could use a mug with cream and sugar."

Luis liked her smile, but scowled. "The only way to drink it is black. You should try Cuban coffee. If you need to sweeten up café Americano, then that stuff will definitely curl your toes." He pulled the normal scope from his pack and changed out the thermal one.

Susan shivered and rubbed her hands together. "Were you born here? In the states, I mean."

Luis nodded. "I was. My parents came over before they were married. Both my brother and I were born here."

She crumpled up her wrapper and put it in her pack. "I always wanted a brother or sister. Are y'all close?"

Luis shrugged. "He's my older brother, so I always looked up to him, but we're very different. We don't see each other very much anymore."

Susan frowned and looked like she wasn't sure what to say about that. A shadow crossed her face. Like she was once again questioning what she was doing here.

Luis was wondering the same thing. He rose until he could just barely see over the log. What was the plan now? He'd gone into town asking about the ranch, and the locals responded by shooting at him. Plus, Treleous was already there waiting for him. He believed those were two discrete events. Treleous was using Susan to trap the team. That was a fact. The reaction of the townsfolk was harder to understand. What did that mean?

So, after escaping all that nonsense, they ended up here in these woods. Approaching the ranch from the rear had seemed like a good plan at the time. Was it still? Armed men showed up at their camp last night. He had to assume they were from Arrowhead. Where else would they have come from? Luis sighed. That meant they knew that he and Susan were coming, and they didn't seem thrilled about it.

So what now? If they returned to the Jeep, then what? They couldn't really go back to town, where Treleous would probably be lying in wait for them. Caveman said there were answers at Arrowhead Ranch. Answers they needed. Now Luis wished he hadn't brought Susan along. In this situation, she reduced his options considerably.

He rubbed his face. There was no good choice. They had to go forward, at least a bit, and see what happened. He looked over at her. "As soon as we step out from behind cover, we'll be visible to the cameras again."

Susan sidled up next to him. "You think they'll come out and intercept us in the daylight?"

"I don't know. I need you to be alert and do exactly what I tell you to do. Got it?"

She held his gaze and nodded. "We didn't harm those men last night. That should tell them something, right? That we're not a threat?"

Luis blew a breath out through his nose. "Let's hope so." He turned back to her. "So you agree we still should keep going forward?"

She shrugged and nodded. "If we go back, then what's our next move?"

He didn't really have any other ideas, either. "True, but it's risky."

Susan shrugged. "I know. But this may be as close to some kind of answer as I've ever had. I have to see." She pursed her lips. "I think if we walk normal, and don't look like we're sneaking around, maybe they'll just come out and talk to us."

Luis snorted. "Or just shoot at us."

She punched his arm. "Don't be so negative."

He was getting the feeling that this was her ham-handed way of flirting. "I'm practical. Not negative."

They stood, walked back to the clearing, and packed up the tent.

Susan smiled and waved at the camera.

Luis narrowed his eyes at her. "What are you doing?"

She shrugged. "Sending a message that we aren't threatening."

He frowned up at it. "Or they could see it as us taunting them."

Smile fading, she dropped her hand. "You really think so?"

"I don't know. They don't want visitors. They've made that very clear. Just keep your wits about you and if I tell you to, run north. Got it?"

She nodded and pointed in the correct direction.

Luis gave her a thumbs-up, led her out of the clearing, and they started working their way to the east. "The good news is, we won't get lost."

Susan said, "That's true, we just follow the cameras."

The question was, follow them where? And towards what?

Susan asked, "How far away do you think it is?"

Luis shrugged and gestured at the canopy above. "I figure these can't go on too far. Hopefully less than a mile more."

He snaked their way through the trees—zig zagging so that he passed near bushes and low-growing plants. Always keeping close to something that could act as cover. Glancing over his shoulder, he shook his head at her.

Susan scowled. "What."

"I think you can see that jacket from the airport."

Susan looked down at herself and the powder blue covering. "What's wrong with it?"

"I didn't say it wasn't nice. It just doesn't really," he hesitated, "blend."

She shrugged, feeling the material on one sleeve. "I like it."

Shaking his head again, he continued meandering back and forth as they trudged along—always changing his line-of-sight while constantly checking ahead and behind them. His anxiety slowly rose as they moved forward. They had very little visibility. The enemy knew exactly where they were, and that they were alone. He tightened his grip on his rifle and narrowed his eyes as he studied their surroundings. This was really a crappy spot. If someone lay in waiting ahead, he would have trouble seeing them. Of course, someone could have circled around behind them or be tracking them as well, and they would also be very hard to detect until they were very close.

He glanced over his shoulder and froze.

Susan stilled and looked up at him, eyes wide, but not saying a word.

Good girl. Luis moved his focus over the landscape behind them. Something had alerted his brain—a sudden change in movement. Something had either stilled or moved. A subtle action that his brain was hard wired to notice.

Out of the corner of his mouth he said, "Slowly take off your pack, ease down with me and lie on your stomach.

Susan nodded.

Just before Luis' eyes dropped below the bushes, they caught the unmistakable glint of sunlight on metal.

Chapter 66

Eddie fidgeted nervously as he nursed his second cup of coffee. They seemed to have a decent hypothesis, but it was all conjecture. Every piece was logical, but entirely based on circumstantial evidence. They could conceivably also support a completely different conclusion.

What had led them to this point was Susan's father. He was the one who'd called the shop to activate the scrape. Maybe this wasn't connected to Mendelson at all. Hell, they could just have stumbled across some secret group that helped people disappear for a price. Call the pipe shop and vanish for two hundred grand.

At least they were making progress. This replenished in Eddie that sense of purpose that he'd discovered he really needed. His team was back on track, with a direction. Hopefully, the right one. He hated his current lack of activity, though. If the scrape didn't produce some return communication soon, then what was next?

Should he go help Luis? He glanced at his watch. They hadn't heard from him in a while, but Eddie wasn't sure where he would even go to help him. He sighed. Another problem on his list that he couldn't do anything about at the moment.

Loren sat across from him, engrossed in the loose pages of Emily's latest novel.

She was also on his to-do list. She was "the one", and he couldn't imagine being with anyone else. Some part of him, however, felt a little guilty about the current arrangement. He was from a traditional small-town background, and this just living in sin, so to speak, was nagging at some part of him. He felt a need to legitimize this.

Loren's background was anything but traditional, and she often struggled with the regular progression of a normal relationship. She's told him once that she'd always dreaded the moment when some man would say he loved her, but when it finally came, it was from Eddie, so it had been okay. She said it back, but that it had been "okay" was less than encouraging. Especially with the thought of progressing their relationship further.

He ran a hand over his chin. How would she respond to the thought of marriage? Would that be also be *okay* if it was with him, as well? Or would that be the final thing that pushed her away? She was sometimes hard to predict. Eddie had to risk it, however. He wanted this and felt it was right. It was a bridge they were going to have to eventually cross, but as with everything, timing was critical.

She sensed his attention and looked up from the book.

Eddie raised his eyebrows. "Is it good?"

She nodded. "Very. I'm always surprised by her—"

Eddie's cell phone rang.

He glanced down and furrowed his brow. "It's Sam." He answered the phone on speaker. "You're on with me and Loren. What's up?"

Sam's voice came over the line, "I take it you attempted to contact someone?"

Eddie exchanged a look with Loren. "Yes, why?"

"They called on my private line and asked if I knew and trusted you. Eddie, I mean."

Loren asked, "What did you tell them?"

"That I knew you and trusted you implicitly. He asked your full name, but I refused to give it, and when I asked what this was about, he hung up." A beat passed. "What is this about?"

Eddie pursed his lips and leaned back. "You remember Heinrich Stein?"

Sam hesitated a moment. "The man who told me about Treleous?"

"Yes. We believe he was possibly part of a group of scientists who worked for Mendelson and, I don't know, organized, for lack of a better word. That maybe Leonette disappeared to join them."

"I see. Well, this is good, then. We might be making progress."

Loren said, "Maybe, but we're trying to get them to trust us. Hence why we dropped your name."

Eddie added, "Sorry, we would have told you, but we didn't expect them to reach out to you directly, at least not this fast."

"Not a problem. Well, at least I did what you wanted me to. What now?"

Eddie sighed. "I don't know. We're just dangling some bait in the water. Calling you was them taking a nibble, but we need them to take a bite."

"That would be amazing. All this time, I just assumed Heinrich was acting alone, which was why no one else contacted me."

Eddie glanced over at Loren. "Let's hope."

Sam said, "I have to go into a meeting. Please keep me in the loop."

Eddie assured him they would, then hung up.

Loren glanced up at Eddie. "If we're dealing with a group, it begs the question why hadn't anyone else followed up after Heinrich?" She sat back and sighed. "Maybe we have this all wrong."

Eddie adjusted the phone on the table. "I was having similar doubts. But now that they called Sam, at least we got some kind of response."

They considered this a moment, then Eddie's cell phone rang again.

Chapter 67

Mack grinned. Through his scope, he had just glimpsed Mr. Talented and the girl as they dropped below the bushes. This guy was good. They'd noticed each other at almost the same time. They knew he was here, so now it really was a hunt. He slid behind a tree and closed his eyes, relishing the almost sexual thrill he got from the chase.

Reaching up, he tweaked his scope's focus and frowned. His quarry was about 150 meters away. Easy shooting range with the Ruger AR he carried. Mack hunkered down and eased around the tree. He had the advantage. There were two of them. She was a civilian—he grinned—and that jacket. Adjusting the scope again, he caught just the smallest flash of movement and squeezed off a round.

A rush of excitement filled him as he ducked and rolled to his right, scrambling away from the shot point before Mr. Talented could return fire. Which way would they try to escape? North was uphill, and Mack doubted they would come toward him. That only left forward and downhill to the south. What was their destination, and how close was it? Would they be able to get help from there? Some instinct told him they wouldn't push forward. So that meant they would move to his right.

He rose just above the line of foliage and scanned the horizon beyond his targets. Nothing. No cover at all in that direction. Grinning, he dropped back down and crab-walked behind a massive ponderosa pine. Peering around the edge, he held still and waited. A gentle breeze rustled the leaves overhead. Mack looked past all of that background movement. Beyond the natural motions around him, to the unnatural ones. The hesitant stop and start movements that prey makes. The telltale signs of fear.

Just to his right, he caught a flash. A powder blue streak. He smiled as he lifted the rifle and rotated his eye to the scope. He panned the direction she was moving and then squeezed the trigger.

Chapter 68

Frank paced outside the command trailer, twirling a lit cigar between his thick fingers. The air was cool and dry—much better than the humidity they'd had to deal with in Miami.

Chip called out from inside. "Hey, Frank, we've got something."

He hustled up the stairs and dropped into the empty chair next to his technical wizard. Two large screens sat on the desk, the left one split into quadrants, each displaying the camera feed from one drone. Frank frowned at the images of endless forest and farmlands.

Chip pointed to the top right. "Look at this."

A large barn came into view from a very high altitude.

Frank frowned. "What am I looking at?"

"This is a cow ranch northeast of town. But check out this structure. It's huge, and the cows don't seem to go here." He moved his finger. "And look at these lines going in the side here. That's some serious power." Chip squinted at the screen. "Looks like some big ass telecom going in there too, but that's not what caught our eye."

Frank glanced over.

Chip typed in a command and all the images on the right-hand monitor minimized. He pulled up a grainy still image of a man standing on a balcony holding an assault rifle. He clicked his mouse, and it switched to another picture of an armed man outside the side door.

Frank took a puff on his cigar. "Well, I'll be damned."

Chip clicked through three more photographs of armed men. "Somebody really wants to protect something in that barn."

"They sure do."

Chip clicked back to the view from the drone as it continued to circle the structure.

Frank tapped an ash into a cup. "Where exactly is this?"

Chip pulled out a map and spread it out on the desk. "I drew a red box around it."

Frank studied the mark and its proximity to the town of Beaver Ruin. "Bring everyone home. I don't want anyone at this ranch to know we're onto them yet."

Chip clicked a button and talked into his headset. "This is Tiger Tech. All birds back to the nest. I repeat, everyone come back home. Over."

They had something. Now he just needed Mack to get back. Where the hell was he? "Good work." He clapped Chip on the shoulder, stepped back outside, and called his boss.

Gemini answered on the second ring and listened as Frank filled him in on the discovery. "Holy crap."

Frank chuckled. "Agreed. The question is, now what? Do you want us to just reconnoiter and gather intel, or do you want to take it?"

Gemini was silent for a moment. "I *want* whatever is in that building, Frank."

"Are you sure? That's going to attract some attention."

"I know. Be smart about it, but I want whatever's there."

Frank blew out a breath. "We'll need more men."

"You'll have them. I'll get the rest of the team and we'll be in the air in under an hour. I'm on my way."

Frank hung up and walked back inside the trailer. We'll be? Gemini was coming with them. That was unusual. He studied the ranch's location on the map again and frowned. This was it. He could feel it in his bones.

The question was, what was it? His first mission for Treleous has been to find and kill Heinrich Stein. Was this the culmination of all the missions he'd run for them?

He'd had Chip mark each cell tower, and only one was close enough to cover the ranch. The same tower Leonette hit when he made a call just before his disappearance. The one that led Frank here.

How to take a target like this? First, you'd have to cut it off from the world. Isolate it and then surround it. He looked over at Chip, still seated in front of his computer. "Is it possible to jam up a cell tower?"

The large man looked up, adjusted his glasses, and shrugged. "Just one tower? The one near town?"

Frank nodded.

"Yeah, that one's just an old 3G tower. We've got a device that can connect to a port on it and hold that line. Then it can grab another and another. An old tower like that can only support thirty, maybe forty at a time. It'll take a few minutes for others to drop off, but before long, we should have all the connections. That way, we can essentially jam up the whole tower."

Frank scratched at the puckered scar on his neck. "Would it look weird? I mean, would it attract anyone's attention?"

Chip shook his head. "I don't think so. It'll just be like when a cell tower near a stadium gets overloaded during a football game. How long do you want to hold it like that?"

Frank folded up the map. "A while. How long can we maintain it? A day or two?"

"Maybe, but eventually someone's going to come and investigate."

"We'll deal with that, then. How long will it take to get ready?"

Chip bobbed his head from side to side as he considered the question. "Maybe half an hour."

Frank said, "Come on, let's put together a plan." They walked over to the team standing nearby in a tight circle.

Not counting Mack, who wasn't back yet, and Chip, who didn't count as a field man, they didn't have enough people to even surround the place.

They'd seen pictures of at least three different armed men at the ranch. Assuming that they were guarding it round the clock, that had to be at least nine men, probably double that. On their home turf, in a compound.

These are the bastards that had Tom. Frank had to assume that he was alive, otherwise they'd have left his body. So he had to take that into account when storming this place as well. If Tom was alive, then they needed to keep him that way.

Damn. He really wished he knew more about what was inside that building.

Frank sighed, wondering if the team Gemini was bringing was enough. With the element of surprise—probably. Of course, Tom was a wild card. Would they use him as a bargaining chip? Only if they had the time. He had to cut these people off, then hit them hard and fast.

He evaluated the little group in front of him. There was Marco. He was a good, steady man but lacked imagination. The only other notable resource was Ricky. A tall, lanky, bald man, who could think on his feet and ask the right questions. The rest were just good solid soldiers, which was both good and bad. He needed more intel. "All right, I want to take this ranch building we discovered. We're pretty sure they're holding one of our men, and we want whatever is inside."

Everyone stopped fidgeting and looked up at Frank. Play time was over.

Ricky said, "Just so you know, there are probably at least ten armed men at the house and around the barn. Most likely more."

Frank said, "I know, that's why I want a plan. I'll get us some more men, but we need to have a full plan of assault by the time they get here." He pointed to each man as he gave commands. "Send one drone at a time to reconnoiter the ranch. Carefully and cautiously, don't be seen. I want to know about possible sniper spots, egress points, including footpaths in and out, anything else that might be useful. A plan for attacking the place and holding it." He pointed at Marco. "I want you to find the telephone trunk that serves the ranch. Make sure there aren't any landline telephones connected to the place and if there are, what it will take to sever them? When we're ready, I want them completely cut off from the world."

Marco nodded. "No problem."

Frank frowned. "What about power? I want that cut, too."

Ricky said, "The building has two large commercial generators, and there's another by the house."

Frank scratched his scar. "These are out in the open, though, right?"

Ricky nodded.

"Then pay attention to them on the drone runs and come up with a plan to knock them out, too." Frank pointed to the next man. "The nearest real police station is in Harlow. Manny, I want you to go down there and get the lay of the land. Put together a plan to cut communications and sabotage all the police vehicles there." He had turned to leave when Frank grabbed his arm and said, "Just put together a plan and don't get caught. The rest of you, grab some rest. It's going to be a long night."

Chapter 69

Eddie stared at the ringing phone in surprise. He didn't recognize the D.C. area number on the screen. He leaned forward and put it on speaker. "Hello."

The voice that came across the line was deep and guarded. "Is this Eddie?"

"It is. Who's this?"

"You can call me Burk. You want us to trust you, but then you ignore our invitation to meet."

Eddie said, "I have to protect myself as well. It's not a reasonable request that I show all of my cards, and you don't have to show any."

The line was silent for a moment. "I'm not the one who wants to meet. You're the one who seems to want something from us."

Eddie exchanged a look with Loren. "That's true, but that doesn't mean I have to give you all the advantage. I'm looking for a compromise."

Burk snorted. "That's why you sent us a barely veiled threat."

Eddie frowned. "What threat? That was not my intention."

"What I am supposed to think when you remind me what happened to Heinrich and what could happen to Susan?"

Loren's eyes widened.

Eddie leaned forward. "Again, that was not my intention. I was merely pointing out that you and I are up against a ruthless and powerful enemy. I only meant I didn't want Susan or myself to end up like that."

"Susan is fine, and I suggest you stay away from her."

Eddie rubbed his forehead. "Susan is not fine, and wherever you think she is, you need to check. I'm trying to help her."

The line was silent for a beat before Burk's deep voice returned. "Why?"

Eddie sighed. "She came to me, asking for help. Help to find her father. Searching for him is how we found the scrape on the line for the pipe shop."

Burk asked, "Why would she come to you? How does she know you?"

Eddie frowned at Loren. That was a good question. How was he supposed to answer it? He couldn't very well tell them that Treleous used her as bait in a trap. What could he say then? How *would* she know them? "We help people. Help them when no one else can."

Burk asked, "Who's we?"

Eddie sat back and rubbed his face. "This is too one sided, my friend. I think I'm showing good faith, but you won't give me anything in return."

"Can I talk to Susan?"

Another reasonable question that Eddie couldn't comply with. "Not at the moment, but soon."

Burk's response had an air of finality about it, like he was about to hang up. "Then I guess we have nothing to discuss—"

Eddie shouted. "Wait!" His mind raced, searching for something to say. Anything to keep him on the line. "Listen, we know about Arrowhead."

The line went dead.

Chapter 70

Luis lay prone on the forest floor, his head cocked to one side. Looking over at Susan, he put a finger to his lips.

The wind rustled in the leaves overhead, masking all other sounds. He mimed to her they should crawl on their hands and knees, keeping low.

She nodded.

He crept downhill a bit, Susan right behind him. Suddenly, a shot rang out and splintered a trunk just above them.

Both Susan and Luis dropped to their bellies.

So, someone *was* after them. He'd known it in his bones, but it was good to have confirmation. Unfortunately, he also now knew, without a doubt, that their intentions were hostile. Who was it, and how had they found them? Couldn't be a park ranger. Shooting without warning wasn't really a park ranger approach. What about the men last night, the ones presumably from Arrowhead? They came in force last night, but this seemed somehow odd compared to last night. Remembering their posture, Luis didn't have the impression that they came to inflict violence. It struck him as more of a mission of discovery. Besides, this person came from behind, not the direction of Arrowhead.

That left Treleous. If so, then why did they wait so long to pursue? They saw where he and Susan entered the woods, and tracking them wouldn't have been a difficult task.

Luis shook his head. His instinct had been to worry about them coming, but it had taken so long, he'd assumed that they lay in wait ahead instead.

That was a mistake, obviously. He twisted around until his mouth was near Susan's ear and whispered, "Are you cold?"

She shrugged and whispered back. "I'm all right. Why?"

"This jacket is like a marker for whoever that is. Will you be okay without it for now?"

She nodded and slowly pulled the zipper down, wincing at the soft rumble it made. "Who do you think it is?"

He shrugged. "I'm guessing the people who used you to get to us."

She nodded, and keeping low, shrugged out of her jacket.

Underneath, she wore a dark blue sweatshirt that would be much harder to see.

Luis pointed to a large pine about ten yards further on.

She nodded, and they commando-crawled in that direction.

Every few strides, he would stop and listen, his rifle cradled in his right arm with the trigger down, where he could roll and fire quickly.

They were in an imaginary canyon. He couldn't push on towards the ranch and who knows what kind of reception. He couldn't really go uphill, as it would give his adversary too good of a sight line to them. That only left downhill, but surely, whoever was out there knew that as well. He really was in a crappy position.

They inched around behind the tree and sat side-by-side, backs against the massive trunk. He asked sotto voce, "Take out the pistol I gave you."

She nodded and pulled it from her pack.

Luis checked his rifle and then leaned slowly out and looked behind him. He caught the quickest flash of a blond mohawk, before yanking his head back.

The forest rang with sound as three shots embedded themselves in the wood behind him.

Chapter 71

Eddie looked over at Loren as he hung up the phone.

She said, "They called on your personal cell."

"Yep. Not a good sign. They must be spying on Sam somehow."

Loren took his phone and wrote the number of the incoming call on one of the loose novel pages, then pushed in her chair and started for their room. "So it's a good bet that they're tracking the phone. You wanna go ditch it?"

Eddie nodded. "Yes, I think Emily would be more comfortable with you."

Loren nodded and took in his dark polo. "I'll get our gear and you something lighter to wear."

Eddie walked down the opposite hall. "Emily!"

The author appeared, brow furrowed as she pulled reading glasses from her face. "What is it?"

Eddie said, "I'm sorry, but we might have led the," he hesitated, "the bad guys to your house. Do you have a car I can borrow? I want to lead them away from here if I can."

She nodded. "Of course. I have a little Isuzu pickup for transporting plants and such."

Loren returned and gave Eddie one of the two pistols she held, a burner phone, and a light-colored jacket. "I'll call Craig and get us some help."

Eddie nodded and turned to Emily. "The keys, please?"

She led Eddie into the mud room outside the elevator and retrieved them for him.

Eddie said, "Thank you. I'm so sorry about this."

Emily waved this away. "Don't worry about it. Let's just deal with the problem. We can worry about that later."

Eddie kissed Loren. "I'll call when I know something."

She nodded. "Be careful."

"You, too." Eddie stepped into the elevator. As the doors closed, he could hear Loren ask Emily, "Do you have an alarm system or a panic room of some sort?"

At the ground floor, Eddie stepped out into the long, narrow area that led outside. He opened the door to his right, exposing an empty one-car garage with bags of potting soil stacked on a pallet. He turned and raced over to the other side, where he found a small red pickup truck. Not the world's best getaway car. He pushed the button to raise the garage door and backed the Isuzu out.

A dark Suburban came to a stop at the end of the alley. The driver, a large man in sunglasses, made eye contact with Eddie.

Damn it. Eddie swung the nose around and raced away from him. He careened onto the main road, causing the driver of a blue Volvo to slam on their brakes and yell at him. Eddie rubbed his face. They had a bigger, more powerful vehicle, probably knew the city better than he did, and more than likely had help. He dialed Loren's burner from his.

She answered right away.

"They already know where the house is, but they saw me and are giving chase. Be careful."

"Let me know how I can help."

"Will do." He hung up the phone.

At the last minute, he turned down a side street, causing the Suburban to skid to a stop and back up before continuing after him.

Eddie turned again and noticed a garbage truck working its way down the block. As he whizzed by it, he lobbed his cell phone into the back of it.

What now? They already knew where Emily's house was, so he needed to escape and then find a place where he could meet up with Loren and Emily after.

How were the women going to slip away unnoticed? Eddie shoved this thought away. Loren was very capable, and she'd have Craig's help. He needed to stay focused on his own problems. He glanced up in his rear-view mirror and gauged the distance to the rapidly closing vehicle, and tried to bring up a mental map of the area. Where was the best place for him to shake these guys?

A second large, dark Suburban pulled into the street ahead and raced toward him.

Chapter 72

Mack grinned, moving parallel to his prey, until he found a suitable spot and placed his rifle on a small rise. He'd been right. Mr. Talented and the girl in the stupid coat had moved south downhill, using the vegetation and shrubs as cover while moving from tree to tree.

He put his eye to the scope and studied the enormous trunk they were using as a shield. Once sure they weren't moving, he strained his neck up and glanced to his right. About another hundred yards further on, the ground leveled out and the low plant life all but disappeared and the pines were spaced further apart. His quarry moved toward open ground, where there would be nowhere to hide.

He had to give this guy credit. He was careful, smart, and skilled, only moving when he had to. Mack would have killed anyone else already. He took a deep breath and forced his mind to still. The advantage was his, if he could just remain patient and wait for Mr. Talented to make the first move.

He glanced to his right again. His target had to realize he was running out of room as well. Soon, his only option was going to be to fight back. Mack grinned. Then the real fun would begin.

He wondered if he should try to capture this guy. He was trying to escape and keep the girl alive, putting him at a disadvantage. Why didn't Frank ask him to capture him if he could?

They'd spent the last year trying to get their hands on anyone connected with the island. Hell, they'd used this damn girl for just this purpose. Now Mack had one here in his sights. Why just kill him?

Mack's smile faded. Because this bastard was just too capable, and too much trouble. Now, with the trap at the pipe shop, they had the name of this dude's partner, Eddie. So they'd gotten what they needed, and Mack didn't have to risk trying to bring this guy in anymore.

His smile returned. That was fine with him. He'd wanted to kill this guy for a while. Besides, whatever Frank had stumbled onto in this little town was more important.

As Mack suspected he would, Mr. Talented suddenly swung around the tree, fired twice, and tried to move back uphill. Mack pivoted and squeezed off two more rounds, forcing his quarry back.

He shook his head. Damn, this guy was good. That girl was going to end up being his undoing. Alone, this would be one hell of a contest, but trying to move, stay out of sight, and keep her alive would be too much for anyone in this position. No matter how good.

Mack craned up and studied the ground between him and the tree Mr. Talented was hiding behind. It was about forty yards slanting down and to the right.

Twenty yards in his direction was the rotting trunk of a medium-sized pine that had fallen years ago. It was a good spot to squeeze his targets and make it harder for them to escape.

He put his eye back to the scope and studied the tree, calming his breath and lowering his heart rate. Come on, look out again. Check to see if I've moved.

A head snapped around and back five or six feet off the ground, much higher than Mack had expected. He rocked the stock up and fired, driving Mr. Talented back.

In the same motion, Mack was on his feet, the rifle still tight to his shoulder as he ran forward, hunched over. Weaving a bit, he covered the ground and then dove in feet first, right behind the fallen tree.

His grin returned. He had them now. There was no escape. The only move was for Mr. Talented to sacrifice himself to help the girl escape.

He leaned up and put his eye back to the scope. Not today, amigo.

Chapter 73

Eddie darted his attention between the SUV behind and the one ahead that was barreling down on him. He was about ten seconds from being trapped. What resources or advantages did he have? He had to be a foot narrower than the two pursuers. Maybe he could use that.

He slammed on his brakes and turned into a narrow alley to his right. The bigger vehicles could probably pass as well, but it would be a tight fit and should slow them down. The pickup's little engine rattled as Eddie raced down the passage. His right mirror clipped a garbage can, causing it to spin and fall in his wake. He burst out onto a larger road. As another driver laid on their horn as he passed, he glanced in his rearview mirror. Nothing. Eddie swallowed. Had he lost them? Looking up again, his heart sank. One of the dark SUVs rushed onto the road, spitting the can from underneath as he swerved to follow.

Eddie turned again and noticed a patrolman two cars ahead. That was good. He doubted that whoever this was would do something overt with a cop around.

The first dark SUV slid in behind Eddie and kept pace. Where was the other one?

Following this cop was good, but he couldn't stay with it too long. He didn't want them to get bored and turn their focus back on Loren and Emily. He had to keep their attention for as long as possible.

Was he in real danger? What did they want? He went back over the conversation. Clearly, Eddie had mishandled things, and these people felt threatened. This didn't strike Eddie as a defensive move, however.

The cop turned at the next light and Eddie followed him, thinking he would stay close to him a little longer.

Showing up at Emily's house was an aggressive, offensive response. Why? What was their endgame? Scaring him and Loren away? Eliminating them? It was hard to predict his adversary's strategy when he didn't know them or their motivation.

He followed the police car another block, evaluating his options. Would he be in better shape on foot? Eddie considered that. Would they try to grab him in public? How sophisticated were they? Sophisticated enough to put a scrape on a public line and bug a U.S. senator. So they could be capable of anything. No, he needed to stay with the car a little longer. He glanced at the gas gauge and smiled to himself. Of course, Emily's car was full. At the next light, he left the patrolman and turned onto a highway.

Out of the corner of his eye, he detected the second SUV turning onto the road ahead of him. Trying to box him in again. To what purpose? Maybe the plan was to kidnap him. To learn who he was and why he was after Susan's dad?

Eddie's mouth tightened. That wasn't going to happen. He slammed on his brakes, making the little pickup shudder, and spun the wheel. He completed a clumsy U-turn and shot back the other way.

This caught the trailing SUV by surprise, and they hesitated before responding. He heard more horns blaring from angry drivers behind him.

As he passed over Rock Creek, he noticed the park on his right. It dredged up memories of the area as snippets from his training came to mind. When your enemy has a resource advantage, you need to change the situation, and keep changing it until you've taken away that advantage.

He wouldn't be able to get away from the two of them in this pickup. He had to get the enemy out of their cars. Once on foot, he would be outnumbered, but he would have more options at his disposal. Then maybe he could get some other wheels.

He glanced over at the park again. Running along the other side were several hotels. One of them would be a good place to ditch the vehicle, and the activity and confusion would make it easy for him to blend into the crowd. He slogged through a roundabout; the SUVs falling behind in the merging traffic. He pulled on the light jacket Loren had given him and zipped it up.

Then, turning south, he accelerated, paralleling the creek and zigzagging through traffic until he noticed the Fairmont. She'd do.

Rocking his body to one side, he pulled out his wallet before swerving into the hotel's short little driveway and slamming on the brakes. Pulling out a fifty-dollar bill, he handed it and the keys to the valet. "Remember me." Then he raced past the wide-eyed young man into the lobby.

Chapter 74

Luis pulled the magazine from his rifle and scowled. Thirteen rounds. He was in a crappy spot. The boxes of ammo he'd left in the Jeep weren't helping him, but there was nothing he could do about that now. After more than a day, he was again surprised that Treleous had suddenly shown up tracking him like this.

Especially since the only person he saw was the big man, which is partially why he assumed they weren't coming. Luis hadn't seen Mohawk back then, or he might have acted differently. He still couldn't explain the delay, however. He closed his eyes. No sense second guessing now. It was what it was.

Susan looked at him wide-eyed and whispered, "We're in trouble, aren't we?"

Luis shrugged. "A little bit. Listen, when I tell you, I want you to run toward the ranch. Follow the cameras."

Her eyes narrowed. "What are you going to do?"

"Cover you. Each time I rise up and fire a shot, you sprint east toward the next tree. Got it?"

She shook her head. "I don't want to leave you." She glanced down at his weapon. "How many bullets do you have left?"

Luis suppressed a sigh. Why wouldn't this girl just listen? She was going to get them both killed. "It doesn't matter. You—"

Susan leaned in closer and whispered fiercely. "It does matter. I'm not leaving you."

Luis stared into her wide hazel eyes. She was a fighter. He really did like this little white girl. Taking her chin between his thumb and forefinger, he said, "Listen, don't worry about me. I can't protect you and fight this guy at the same time. Once you're safe, don't worry. I'm going to kick his ass."

Her brows drew down. "I don't like it."

Luis pushed the magazine back into the rifle. "Your complaint is noted." He mentally shook his head. When did he start sounding like Eddie? Hunching down close to the ground, he leaned out.

Instantly, a shot rang out.

Luis yanked his head back in the nick of time. Damn, he was close. The son-of-a-bitch had moved. Smart. He rubbed his chin. This changed things. They were now in a much worse situation. He looked to his right. The ground gave way to a plain with no coverage. He couldn't really move back uphill the way they'd come. He sighed and looked back toward the ranch. It was too far, and the trees were too far apart. Just too little cover. Not to mention he didn't know the reception he'd receive if they got there.

Susan's eyes darted around on his face.

He was going to have to make his last stand here. It was a crappy place to do it, but he seemed to be running out of options. He turned to tell Susan his new plan when he heard movement from Mohawk.

Chapter 75

Loren perched on the edge of the tub in the master bath, her pistol held loosely at her side.

Emily sat on the closed toilet, her eyes wide and focused on her. "Sorry, this is the most secure room I have."

Loren glanced around and forced a smile. "We're the ones who are sorry. This will do. It really is a beautiful room."

Emily nodded. "Thanks. It took me a couple of tries to get it right. But I do like how it turned out." She frowned. "If someone gets in, can you kick their ass?"

Loren snorted. "Probably not." She smiled and lifted her pistol. "But I can put a nice grouping of holes in them. The pistol is the greatest female empowerment tool ever invented."

Emily grinned. "I like that. Do you mind if I use it?"

"Not at all." Loren studied her. Emily was a tough bird. She'd give her that.

A clock chimed in another room.

Emily said, "So, who are these guys? Can you tell me?"

Loren shrugged. "We don't really know. That's kind of the problem. If they're connected to the men waiting at the pipe shop, then the only thing we really know about them is that they're up to no good. Maybe on a grand scale." She sighed. "If it's not them, then we don't know who we're dealing with."

Emily nodded. "I see."

"I'm really sorry we brought this to you."

Emily crossed her feet at the ankles and studied her tennis shoes. "Actually, it seems like it was Sam who led them to me." She looked up and smiled faintly. "You and Eddie are a pretty impressive team. Smooth and coordinated under fire."

Loren nodded. "We are."

"So, you gonna marry him or what?"

Her eyebrows flew up. That was unexpected. It was the question, though, wasn't it? Sadly, Loren wasn't really sure how to answer it.

Emily held up her hands. "Sorry, that was an indelicate question. I'm a nervous talker, I'm afraid."

Loren shook her head. "No, it's okay." She frowned. "I'd like to. It's just..."

"He doesn't want to?"

Loren chuckled. "No, he's a pretty traditional guy. I bet he'd love to marry me."

"So it's you who has doubts?"

"That's not it. I have no doubts about Eddie or how I feel about him. It's, well." She shrugged. "He may never ask me." She leaned back and looked down the hall, listening for a beat before continuing, "I've had a bit of a strange life and, well, I sort of give off the impression that I'm gun shy about all this relationship stuff."

Emily titled her head to one side. "Are you?"

Loren shrugged. "Yes. Well, I was. Before Eddie."

Emily grinned. "Then that's the only thing you need to know, dear." She opened her mouth to continue when the phone rang.

Loren dug it from her pocket and glanced at the screen. "Hello."

Sam's voice came over the line. "I just got out of committee. What's going on?"

Loren sighed. "I think they were watching you or spying on you, and it led them to us."

"My God, are you okay?"

Loren shrugged at Emily. "We're okay. Eddie led them away and Craig is sending over some help."

"I am so sorry. Is there anything I can do?"

"Not yet. Give me a bit to get things settled and I'll call you. Be careful, though." Her phone beeped, and she glanced at the screen. "Listen, Sam, that's Craig. I'll call you back." She switched to the other call.

Craig's voice came over the speaker. "Hey. One of my men is coming up to your door. Don't shoot him. His name is Moe. He's tall with a ponytail."

The doorbell sounded.

Loren replied, "He might be here. Hold on." She led Emily back down the hall. In the mudroom outside the elevator, they studied the exterior camera monitor. A tall, muscular man in a green tank top stood at the door, holding a pistol to the head of a shorter man in black tactical gear.

Loren said into the phone, "He's here and he has a prisoner."

Craig replied, "I told him to check your perimeter. Let him in before he attracts the cop's attention."

Loren pushed the intercom. "What's your name?"

"Moe. Craig sent me. Now open up before someone sees me."

Emily pushed the button and the outside door opened. She exchanged a look with Loren as the elevator whined and the car rose.

The doors opened.

Moe looked to be in his fifties but was fit and muscular. He reminded Loren of an older Luis, only taller, with a longer ponytail.

Loren pointed her pistol at the prisoner's chest.

Moe nodded, shoved the man inside, and slid his own gun into his waistband. "I'm Moe. Moe Seaver." He pulled zip-ties from his pocket and was about to secure the man's wrists when she forestalled him. "I'm Loren. Thanks for the help." She turned to Emily. "You have any handcuffs?"

Emily scowled. "Of course."

Loren fought back a smile. "Get them, please."

Emily hustled out.

Moe frowned. "You don't want to just zip him?"

Loren shook her head. "I'm not sure who he is yet, and I don't want to just treat him like an enemy."

Moe tilted his head to one side as if he didn't understand what she meant.

Loren led them into the living room. Next to the couch was an old radiator caked with years of paint. She pushed the couch a little closer to it. Then turned to the prisoner. "Sit."

The man hesitated a moment and Moe pushed him down.

Emily returned and handed Loren the cuffs.

She closed one cuff around his right wrist and locked the other side to the radiator. She tugged on it and, when satisfied it was secure, stepped back.

Moe jerked his head over at the prisoner. "Alex here was watching your place." He handed her his wallet.

She opened it, took out the license, and read aloud. "Alexander Marks. Why are you here, Alex?"

The man stared straight ahead, remaining silent.

Moe asked conversationally, "Want me to break a bone?"

Alex's eyes darted to the side for a fraction of a second.

Loren shook her head and walked back to the table, lifting the page where she'd written the phone number from earlier. "No. I'm hoping to avoid making an enemy of these people if I can."

Moe looked from the posters on the wall back to the older woman a few times. Then he motioned with his head for the two women to follow him to the kitchen. In a low voice, he asked. "Are you Emily Bryant?"

Her eyes flew open wide, and she nodded.

He fist-bumped her. "Far out. *Powder Burns* is my jam." He pursed his lips and nodded. "That's exactly how it is when someone gets shot. It's like you'd really done it before." He thumped his chest twice with his fist. "Respect."

Emily looked startled and proud. "R-really? Thank you, you don't know what that means to—"

Loren cut them off with a look.

Emily pulled her head down into her shoulders and mouthed, "Sorry."

Loren squeezed her arm and glanced over at Moe. Where the hell did Craig come up with this guy? She frowned back at the wall posters. She appreciated that he'd brought them here to the kitchen. He was trying to keep Emily's identity a secret, but that cat was out of the bag now. What a mess.

Chapter 76

As Mack studied the ground between him and his targets, a warning scratched at his mind. The skin on the back of his neck tightened, as it sometimes did. He turned and surveyed the trees behind him, and then slowly scanned in a circle. Something was wrong.

He pulled his legs up under him. Was this a trap? Had Mr. Talented been leading him on until reinforcements arrived? Where would that help come from, though? Something was definitely off. He could feel it.

He put the scope up to his eye and slowly worked uphill to his right. Then he spotted him. A little over a hundred yards away, a man holding a rifle to his shoulder moved along at a steady pace parallel to Mack.

The man's posture and gait were familiar. He moved the way the U.S. military taught soldiers to move—quickly but carefully into hostile territory. Whoever it was, he was no amateur.

Mack pulled his head back from the scope and studied the woods behind him again. The question now was, how many were out here?

Frank wouldn't have sent someone else after him, Mack was sure. Besides, the man was coming from the opposite direction. From the direction Mr. Talented and the girl were headed.

He put his eye back to the scope and pivoted in the downhill direction. After a minute, he spotted a second tango, further away and moving parallel to the first.

Did they just miss him, or were they moving to flank him?

He looked back through the scope at the first man he spotted. This time, the target was looking in this direction. Mack sank down a bit. He was low and well camouflaged, and he felt confident that the man couldn't see him, but the hostile had stopped and looked directly at this spot. How did they know where he was? Was it the shots? Had the sound attracted their attention?

Mack spun and looked back at the tree Mr. Talented was hiding behind. Damn it. It was time to get out of Dodge. He grimaced. He was so close to killing that bastard. It would just have to wait for another day and time. Mack needed to go now. Staying low and casting one last quick look over his shoulder at his quarry, he moved a few steps and stopped. He scanned back the direction he'd come from and froze. A third and then fourth man were coming toward him. So they *were* trying to trap him.

His only real recourse was to strike before they could converge on him. The closest target was the first one he'd identified uphill. He stepped out, lifted the rifle to his shoulder and centered the crosshairs on the man's head.

Chapter 77

Putting his pistol in the back of his waistband under his jacket, Eddie crossed the wide marble lobby and walked out the back door to the courtyard. The small restaurant was just finishing up breakfast, and he stood near a group that was gathering their stuff to leave as if he was part of their party.

Eddie felt completely unprepared to fight this unknown enemy. As far as he knew, they weren't anything official, and he didn't believe they were with a government agency. Were they some kind of organization like Treleous? Possibly, but to what end or goal? Without this kind of information, it was hard to predict how far these men would go. How desperate or ruthless they were.

A large black man in a blazer strode in the middle of the foyer, talking into his sleeve, while his attention darted around the lobby.

Eddie recognized him as the man from the first SUV. He forced himself to remain in profile to his pursuer, appearing natural and uninterested. Not looking at him or away from him. Careful to avoid all the visual cues that a professional would zero in on.

A middle-aged woman in the group noticed Eddie and furrowed her brow.

He leaned in. "I'm sorry. I was sitting at this table earlier and I was wondering if I left my cell phone."

Her suspicious expression cleared, and she glanced back. "I don't think so."

Eddie shrugged. "Thanks anyway."

He casually meandered over to the pool at the rear of the courtyard. He stopped at a closed outside bar and acted as if he was reading the menu and looked back to the lobby out of the corner of his eye.

Three other men dressed in dark, more tactical looking jackets were talking to the man in the blazer. He pointed in both directions, and the men dispersed and started the search.

Whoever these people were, they were secretive, paranoid, and easily upset. At every step, they took offense to almost everything. Why was that?

Eddie moved carefully to the edge of the courtyard. About a block down the road, he could see an entrance to Rock Creek Park through the windows. Lots of trees and green, possibly a good place to lose these guys and regroup. He'd gotten them out of their car, neutralizing their primary advantage. But they still outnumbered him. Now he needed to change the game again. Hail a cab, or somehow grab a vehicle, and catch his pursuers flat footed.

Checking behind himself once more, he slipped outside and turned right down an alley between this arm of the hotel and the building behind it. He pulled out his burner phone and pretended to talk as he strolled to the corner and peaked around. All clear. He stepped out and headed toward the park.

Two people ahead of him stopped to talk. An elegant older woman with a very tall and thin dog like some kind of Russian wolf hound. A younger man laughed at the woman while he stooped to scratch the dog's ears.

Eddie smiled and nodded as stepped around them and then continued using them as cover back to the hotel.

He stopped at the edge of the main road next to the park, waited for a break in the traffic, and then jogged across. His heart sank.

Beyond a screen of bushes was some kind of dog area, wide open with very few people. It was maybe a hundred yards across, offering no cover, and nearly empty in the early morning.

Eddie looked back over his shoulder.

Two men spilled out of the hotel onto the street behind him, looking back and forth, then one pointed in his direction.

Chapter 78

Frank gathered the team around the map spread out on the hood of one of the pickup trucks. Glancing at his watch, he said, "I want a fully blown out plan before the rest of the team gets here. How are we looking?"

Marco answered, "We're ready to jam the cell tower, and cut land lines and connectivity to the building whenever you give the word. I noticed on the drone footage that they have a short-range two-way radio tower attached to the building, though."

Frank frowned. "What's the plan for that?"

Marco shrugged. "We could shut out the power, or have a shooter take out the tower itself, once we make our move."

Frank turned to Chip. "What's the range of those things?"

Chip blew out a breath through his nose. "With the tower on top of the building like that?" He shrugged. "Maybe five miles line of sight. The mountains would wreak some havoc with it, though."

Frank scratched at his scar. "Could they contact the police station with one of those radios?"

Chip furrowed his brow. "In Harlow?" he shook his head. "I don't think so."

Frank said, "That's not good enough. We'll have to kill the power and take out the generators, maybe the radio tower itself." He turned to Ricky. "Can you do that?"

He nodded and pointed to the map. "The building sits down in a low area, which helps us. There are good sniper spots here and here. Paul and I can be in place at these spots inside a half an hour." He slid his finger across the map. "There are only two ways to get vehicle traffic in and out of the ranch. This main road here and an old dirt road leading out of the back."

Frank frowned. "Where does that go?"

Ricky shrugged. "It's not much more than a dirt road —"

"Where does it go?" Frank asked again, narrowing his eyes.

"It meanders on a long way, like seventy miles or more. I don't know what condition it's in, but it appears to run all the way to east to Highway 87."

In a speculative tone, Frank asked, "Could they escape that way, or could reinforcements come in?"

Rich grinned. "They could, but it's easy to watch. If we're ready, we could deal with them if they did."

Frank nodded. "Then be ready." He turned to Marco. "What about Manny? Is he ready to handle the police in Harlow?"

He gave him a thumbs up. "He's in place with a plan, just waiting for the word."

Frank went over every question in his mind again, checking for any hole, concern, or unknown. He had the element of surprise, and by the time they moved, he'd have superior firepower. Everything was in place.

Chapter 79

Loren filled a glass with water and set it on the ground next to Alex's foot.

Her prisoner glanced down at it and then back at her.

Moe crossed his arms and leaned against the wall, his brow furrowed.

Emily kept stealing glances over at Craig's mysterious man from a seat at the kitchen table.

Loren turned and frowned at Moe. She was glad he was here, but right now, he was doing more harm than good. They were trapped in a trust paradox, and she needed to get them out of it.

This was the toughest part of the whole spy game for her. How did you establish trust? It almost always required one party making a leap of faith. Making themselves vulnerable to prime the pump, if you will. This was risky in a game as dangerous as this one. But if someone didn't break the ice soon, then they would all freeze to death.

She turned to Moe. "Why don't you go check the perimeter again? Make sure we're clear."

He nodded, but the look in his eyes told her he knew she was just getting him out of the way.

She forced a smile. "Be careful."

Moe nodded again, then shot a quick look at the prisoner. "You, too," he answered as he turned his attention back to her.

When he was gone, Loren looked over at Emily. "Why don't you go write for a while?"

Emily started. "Oh, right. I'm sorry, my dear." Nodding rapidly, she stood and walked down the hall.

Loren suspected the author was eavesdropping, which was fine. She'd sent her away mainly to establish to their captive that the author wasn't involved in all of this. She pulled a seat over in front of Alex. "Let's see if we can start over."

His eyes narrowed. "That's quite a goon you've got there."

Loren pursed her lips. She understood that most people had predicable hot buttons. It was one thing her con-man father had drilled into her. With women, it was usually flattery, and a deep-seated need for protection. With men, it was primarily ego, and a similar fear of getting old and weak. Loren had learned to use these, sometimes lightly brushing them with a mark, but sometimes you just had to poke the sensitive area.

She looked down her nose at Alex. "You're just mad that he got the best of you."

He narrowed his eyes and then shrugged one shoulder. "So, I'm supposed to like that?"

This was a very good response. The answer of a person Loren could work with. She leaned back. "As you can probably tell from our conversations, he's not part of our team. Your aggression surprised us, so I had to outsource some protection."

Alex shot a glance over at the elevators. "From where?"

Loren smiled. "That's my business." She held his gaze. Intelligent eyes full of defiance. She had to get through to him somehow. "So again, let's see if you and I can start over."

Alex pulled his arm, pulling the handcuff chain tight. "Then take me out of this."

She sighed. "When I'm convinced that you aren't a threat to me, I'll undo it. You have my word."

He tilted his head to one side. "And just how would I prove that to you?"

"I'm not sure yet. Let's begin by just having a conversation. Someone has to make the first move, so I'll start. The group I work with is friends with Senator Sam Hawthorne. We're working against a group called Treleous."

Alex showed no recognition.

Why didn't he know that name? Who were they worried about, if not them? "We're working against some bad men, who we're afraid of. That's why we're acting this way."

Alex quickly mastered his face and looked back at her, expressionless and maybe trying to seem uninterested.

Loren bit her lip. This was the moment of truth. She had to take a risk here. A risk that would either plant a seed of trust or put the entire team in danger. But this was the only way forward that she could see. If someone didn't make the first move, they would be in a standoff forever. She sighed. "Susan didn't find us. Treleous tried to use her as bait to get to us."

Alex's attention shot back to her.

She continued, "We were able to get her away from them, and we," she shrugged, "well, we believed her and decided to help. She really is looking for her father. Through one of our sources, we found out about the pipe shop and Arrowhead."

Alex blurted out, "From who? No one knows that information," then seemed to catch himself and set his mouth back into a hard line.

Loren raised his eyebrows. "Then how are we here? How do we know this?"

He looked down, but he seemed troubled.

Loren hid a smile. She'd just formed her first little crack in the ice.

Chapter 80

Luis's sixth sense suddenly flared to life. His fingertips vibrated, and a sense of danger suddenly flooded over him. He found this both odd and ironic. It was a little late for this kind of warning—wasn't it? Unless something had changed. Had the situation suddenly become more dangerous?

He darted his head out from behind the tree to check on Mohawk. From behind his adversary's cover, Luis was just able to detect the barrel of a rifle poking out, but not pointed at them. He snapped his head to the right and noticed a black clad soldier about fifty yards away, hunched over, stepping carefully in Mohawk's direction.

That's who Mohawk was aiming at.

Without really thinking about it, Luis stepped out, bringing the rifle to his shoulder. Then, rolling his eye to the scope, he fired into the fallen tree Mohawk hid behind. Twelve rounds left.

Jerking back, Mohawk fired, and the black clad man fell.

Luis stage-whispered over his shoulder to Susan. "Run! To the ranch!" He then continued to his right and yelled out to Mohawk, "Hey!"

Mohawk fired blindly at where Luis had been standing.

He heard sounds as his adversary rolled away and reset his potion. Luis continued moving toward the fallen man, rifle ready to fire.

The blond head popped up again.

Luis ducked, and the two fired past one another. Eleven bullets left. Staying low, he looked out of the corner of his eye at the prone man on the ground.

Mohawk fired twice more, but Luis could tell by the sound that they were in a different direction. He was firing at someone else. Must be more of this fallen man's friends out there. They had to be the guys from last night. The ones he assumed were from Arrowhead.

The man on the ground moved slightly.

Luis snapped his head and rifle around to face him.

The man lifted both of his hands off the ground in surrender.

"Are you hurt?"

The man shook his head. "I'm wearing a vest. It just hurts."

Luis nodded. "I think I saved your life."

The man shrugged and nodded. "We saw him tracking you on the cameras, and we came to help. So I think we're even."

Luis pursed his lips. "Fair enough." He was out from cover, on hostile ground, outnumbered, and with limited ammunition. He was definitely committed now. Damn this whole situation.

Several shots rang out further away, and Luis glanced in that direction before returning his attention to the man. "Can I let you get up without you trying to shoot me?"

The man nodded. "It seems like the least I can do." He rolled to his knees and stood.

Luis took a step back, his gun pointed at the ground between them.

The man gestured to his radio mic on the upper left part of his vest. "Can I check in with my team?"

Luis nodded.

The man clicked his radio. "This is Fire One to Fire Team. Report in. Over."

A man's voice came over the radio. "This is Fire Two. Fire One, are you okay? Over."

He clicked his mic again. "10-4 whole and not leaking. You? Over."

"This is Fire Three. This blond bastard is tricky. We're going to lose him, copy? Over."

The man glanced over at Luis and said into his radio, "Let him go, team. Repeat, let him go. Report to me, I am talking to last night's tango. Over."

The man held out his hand to shake. "I'm Rob."

Luis glanced down at it. He was in a weird situation. He'd set out to find this ranch. Presumably to find the very people he now stood in front of. But Luis wasn't quite ready to get within reaching distance of this man. Not yet. "I'm Luis. If you don't mind, I don't think we know each other well enough to shake."

Rob dropped his hand. "Understood."

Luis sensed someone walking behind him to his right, not trying to be quiet. He shot a quick look over his shoulder.

Susan picked her way toward them.

Luis said, "I thought I told you to run for the ranch."

She stood next to him. "I did, but then I came here."

Luis shook his head. Sensing others approaching, he tensed and brought the rifle back to his shoulder. "Your men are getting close. Want to tell them not to shoot me?"

Rob clicked the mic. "Fire Team, stand down. Report to me, but stand down. Over." He looked over at Susan, but asked Luis, "Who's this?"

Luis kept his eyes on the tree line as he answered, "This is Susan. Susan, this is Rob."

They nodded at one another.

Three soldiers emerged out of the woods and assembled behind their boss.

Rob said, "This is Luis and Susan."

She asked, "Are you the ones who visited our campsite last night?"

Luis looked sidelong at her.

Rob nodded. "Pretty slick job of slipping past us. So, what do you want?"

Luis asked, "Are you from Arrowhead?"

Rob studied him for a long time before he answered. "Why?"

Luis took that as a yes. He tilted his head toward Susan. "We're looking for her dad."

Rob furrowed his brow. "Who's her dad?"

Susan said, "Benjamin Leonette."

Rob shrugged and furrowed his brow. "I've never heard of him."

Chapter 81

Eddie turned and strolled south, studying the two buildings ahead on either side of the street. They looked like condos. Such places probably had security of some sort. Could he use that to his advantage?

Eddie gauged their distance and glanced casually over his shoulder. The men pursuing him had not made it to the corner yet.

The central question now was, how well did these men know what he looked like? There probably hadn't been time for them to research him before they arrived at Emily's apartment, even if they knew his name. Probably not enough time to even see his driver's license photo. In all probability, they only got a brief glance at him during the car chase, especially the men in the second vehicle. They'd only have a vague idea of what he looked like—a white man with dark hair. They wouldn't know his height or his build.

He had the light-colored jacket on before he left the car in front of the hotel. So he could shed it and go back to the dark shirt, changing his profile. His burner phone rang, and he answered.

Loren's voice came over the speaker. "Craig sent over some help, some guy named Moe, and we got one of them."

Eddie could hear the smile in her voice, and his brow furrowed. "One of who?"

"One of Burk's men. He and I are having an interesting conversation. I called Burk, but he didn't answer. I think he's still hoping to catch you and nullify our advantage before he answers. So don't get caught."

Eddie snorted. "I'm doing my best. Do you trust this guy Craig sent?"

"I think so. He caught one of them for us. Why?"

"Then send him to the Rock Creek Park near M Street. I'm going to need a ride."

"I'll have him leave now. Be careful." She hung up.

Eddie reached the building and once again shot a look back as he reached the corner. The men were at the street, looking back and forth.

He turned, and as soon as the building blocked their view of him, Eddie shed the light-colored jacket, dropping it into a garbage can as he passed. Then he sprinted to the end of the block, across the street on the other side of the condo and into the woods surrounding Rock Creek.

He'd changed his profile, but if they saw him here, it would immediately attract attention and make him look suspicious, squandering that advantage. He forced his way deeper into the foliage. There were maybe twenty feet of trees and the bank down to the creek was steep. No easy way to cross here. He returned north, parallel to the creek, and back toward the Fairmont.

How was he going to hook back up with this guy from Craig? And who the hell was he, anyway? Moe? Eddie shook his head. What a mess. He looked over his shoulder. He didn't see anyone pursuing him through the trees.

What would he do if he were the hunter? He'd run along the edge of the tree line, knowing that Eddie couldn't cross the river yet. So he'd search for them along the street through any break in the foliage.

His burner phone rang again, and Eddie answered.

"This is Moe. Where you at?"

Eddie stopped to catch his breath. "I'm running along the tree line next to Rock Creek, away from M Street. Where are you?"

"I'm on M crossing Wisconsin, so like six blocks from the river. Which side of the creek?"

"On the far side, you have to cross it to get to me."

Moe asked, "How hot are you?"

"I've got several following me, at least two on my tail. I lost them coming into the woods, but I'm not clear."

"Got it."

"Turn left on 25th Street when you get there. Keep an eye out for two guys in black."

Moe chuckled. "Just like their buddy, huh? 10-4, I'll call back when I'm there."

Eddie hung up and kept moving until he was opposite the empty dog park again. He stopped behind a large tree and leaned out cautiously, searching for signs of his pursuers. He spotted one of them walking along on the opposite side, clearly searching for him among the trees.

Eddie looked back at the creek. It was still a steep drop, but he could cross if he had to. But that would put distance between him and Moe. What was further down? He could just see some kind of building on his side of the street, just beyond the dark park. Keep moving in that direction?

He heard a racing engine and turned toward it. A late 60s Chevy Impala roared down the street in Eddie's direction. Just before he reached the man searching for Eddie, it swerved over, and the driver's door opened. It smashed into the man with a sickening bang. He crumpled to the ground, and the Impala kept driving.

Eddie's phone rang, and he answered. "Was that you?"

"Totally. Where are you?"

"In the woods across from you."

The Impala slammed on its brakes.

Eddie looked both ways and then ran to the car. He shot a quick glance at the man on the ground, rocking back and forth—in pain, but alive.

As Eddie neared the car, he called out, "Moe?"

He nodded. "The one and only."

Eddie jumped into the passenger's seat.

The Impala shot forward.

Looking over his shoulder, Eddie said, "Thanks. How did you know that was him?"

Moe shrugged. "He looks just like the one I nabbed this morning."

Eddie snorted. That wasn't a lot of information to justify such an act. "Thanks." He held out his hand. "I'm Eddie."

He shook it. "Moe. Glad to help. Can I ask who those guys are?"

"We don't know."

Moe furrowed his brow. "They're kind of weird."

"What do you mean?"

"They're obviously ex-military, but they aren't very good at this spook stuff. I caught the one outside Emily's house in about two seconds."

Emily's house? Did this guy know her already, too?

Motioning over his shoulder with this chin, Moe said, "And this guy. I roared down the street and the dude didn't even look over." He looked sidelong at Eddie. "Amateur hour, you know what I mean?"

Eddie nodded.

Moe glanced at his watch. "I've still got to make it to North Carolina today. So if you all don't need me anymore, I'm going to drop you back at Emily's and then blow. Cool?"

Eddie suppressed a smile. Who the hell was this guy? "Cool. I really appreciate the help."

Moe waved a hand. "I'm always down to help someone in Craig's crew."

Eddie looked out the window. Was he part of Craig's crew? Uh, definitely not.

Chapter 82

Luis and the small group of soldiers all took a step back as Susan lost it.

She threw her hands in the air and stomped around in a circle, shouting. "What do you mean you don't know my father? I don't understand!" She bore into Luis with wide eyes. "Then why are we even here? Why am *I* even here? What's going on? How did I even get into this?"

Rob, the lead soldier, looked over at Luis with a worried expression. "Why did you think he'd be here?"

Luis shrugged. How the hell was he going to answer that? "We had a source that told us about Arrowhead, and that her father was somehow connected to it."

Rob opened his mouth to respond and then put his fingers to his earpiece. His eyes narrowed and the rifles of the men behind him lifted a fraction.

Luis took a step back, lifting his left hand, hand palm out, while keeping his right finger on the trigger. "What just happened?"

Rob said, "One of my men noticed a drone casing the ranch."

Luis compressed his lips. That was a very bad sign. He'd assumed that Treleous had come here to catch whoever Susan brought here. Of course, he still didn't know how they knew about this place. They didn't need a drone to find them, so they were looking for something else. "It's the people with the mohawk dude."

Rob narrowed his eyes. "How do I know they're not with you?"

Luis rolled his eyes. "They chased us out of town here." He quickly added, "And then tracked us through the woods. You saw him. You know we're not with him."

Susan had stopped ranting, suddenly remembering the trouble they were in. She added, "Ask the guy in the bar, the mule bar, whatever it's called. He was there and saw them chase us."

A flicker of recognition flashed across Rob's eyes. He knew that. Once again, he titled his head, listening to his earpiece.

Luis said, "I can help. These are bad guys, and they're well trained and well financed. You're going to need my help."

Rob rubbed his mouth. "What do they want?"

Luis shrugged. "I'm not sure. We know about them, and have tangled with them in the past, but I have no idea how they know about this place."

One of the soldiers stepped forward. "Sir, we should get back to the ranch."

Rob looked at Susan. "I'm sorry, someone misinformed you. We don't know anything about your father." Turning back to Luis, "Please stay away from the ranch. You have no business there and we would like for you to go back the way you came." With that, he turned on his heel and led his men away.

Susan watched them go, her face falling. "What now?"

Luis sat down on a log and frowned toward the ranch. "I don't think it's safe to go back the way we came." He sighed, "Also, I don't believe that the ranch isn't connected to your dad." He held her gaze. "And I think those guys are about to be in a world of hurt."

She sat down next to him. "So we wait?"

He pulled out a granola bar and handed it to her, then dug out his satellite phone. "I think it's time we had a chat with Eddie."

Chapter 83

Eddie stepped out of Moe's car and exchanged a fist bump with him before pressing the intercom button. As soon as the door opened, Craig's strange friend drove away. Eddie stepped inside, holding his pistol loosely at his side. The ante room was quiet and still, and he listened intently for a moment before striding forward and calling the elevator.

None of this had gone as planned, and Eddie was unsure what to do next. The people who'd responded to the message on the scrape, whoever they were, were his only path to Susan's dad. He sighed. Somehow, they kept ending up in some sort of conflict. He needed to deescalate the situation and get them to just talk to him.

To Eddie's surprise, Emily gave him a big hug as soon as the doors opened. She led him into the living room, where Loren sat having a conversation with a man in black tactical gear handcuffed to the radiator. He suppressed a smile. When Loren decided to work her charms on someone, especially a man, she was something else.

She stood, and, taking his face in her hands, kissed him. "You okay?"

Eddie nodded. "Thanks to Moe." He shook his head. "Were did Craig dig him up?"

Loren grinned. "No idea, but he's an Emily Bryant fan."

Eddie looked at Emily and chuckled. "Who isn't? Evidently, I'm the only loser in the game."

Emily blushed and waved his comment away. "There's still time."

He turned back to Loren. "Have you gotten in touch with Burk?"

Loren shook her head. "I left him a message, but he hasn't called me back."

Eddie sighed. "Who's our guest?"

Loren led him over. "Eddie, this is Alex."

The prisoner held his gaze with an expression that appeared more curious than hostile.

Eddie nodded. "Pleased to meet you, Alex. We've all gotten off on the wrong foot, and I'm hoping to get this all straightened out."

Alex replied, "I'm listening."

"I'm serious. I want to start over. What's the best way to get in contact with Burk and work this out?"

A moment passed before he replied. "The number he called you on, the one she called, is the right one." He shrugged. "If he hasn't called back, it's because he doesn't want to talk to you."

Loren pulled out her burner phone. "A lot's happened since then. Let's try again." She dialed, put it on speaker, and handed Eddie the phone.

It rang four times before Burk answered it in a low voice that sounded menacing and a little resigned. "What do you want?"

Eddie replied. "Just to talk. I have your man Alex here, and we need to get him back to you."

Burk snorted. "Well, I have your man, too. The one you sent to Montana."

Eddie's eyebrows flew up. He very seriously doubted that these amateurs had captured Luis. "If that's true, then you have Susan as well, and she can vouch for us."

"I told you I know where Susan is, and she's safe."

Eddie blew out a breath. "That's not true. She's with my man in Montana, so if you have him, then you have her. I'll happily trade Alex here for him. Come back to the house and let's talk."

"Look, you threatened us, kidnapped one of my men, and put another in the hospital, but you just want to talk?"

Eddie grimaced. "Is the guy by the road okay? I'm sorry about that. That wasn't my intention. That wasn't done by one of my team. You surprised us by coming to the house, and I had to ask for help."

The line was silent.

"Seriously, let's try to make peace. Your man Alex can hear you." He looked over at the prisoner. "Tell him you're okay."

Alex's shoulder sagged. "Sorry, boss."

Burk replied, "That's okay. You all right?"

He looked from Eddie to Loren and back. "Yes, and I think they're telling the truth. I think they really do just want to talk to you."

Eddie looked at Loren, eyebrows raised.

She shrugged and flashed him a self-satisfied smile.

Burk sighed. "Okay, I'll be there in ten minutes. And my boy better be fine."

Eddie's shoulders relaxed. "He will be. Thanks."

Part 4

Chapter 84

Luis dialed the chunky satellite phone and waited for the connection to go through.

Eddie answered, sounding a little breathless. "Luis? Are you okay?"

"We're okay. Why do you ask?"

Eddie said, "Someone just told me they had you in custody."

Luis scowled. "Uh, no. Who said that?"

"Some people we think are connected to Susan's dad and the ranch. We contacted them through the shop."

Luis said, "If you know someone connected to Arrowhead, you need to tell them that Treleous is here, and I think the ranch is in danger."

There was a brief pause before Eddie asked, "Do you think they're after whatever's there?"

Luis said, "I do. We ran into someone from the ranch," he glanced over at Susan, "and they say they never heard of her dad, but I'm not sure I believe them. They also won't accept my help, and they're not up for what is about to happen to them."

"Trained, but not really experienced?"

Luis frowned. How the hell did Eddie know that? "Yeah."

"Same thing on our end."

Luis nodded. "I think you need to get here pretty quick. I mean, it's going to go down soon."

"And there're going to help?"

Luis sighed. "They don't want it, but I think I have to try to help them. It's our only connection to Susan's father, and whatever's there, Treleous wants it pretty badly. Agreed?"

"Yeah, I hear you. Okay, stay safe and we'll be there as fast as we can."

Luis glanced at his watch. "I'll call you in a bit. I have no way to charge this thing, so I'm going to turn it off."

Eddie replied, "10-4," and hung up.

Luis looked over at Susan, who stared back defiantly, eyes narrowed.

He raised his eyebrows. "What?"

She folded her arms over her chest. "Go ahead. Say what you're going to say. That you need to get me someplace safe while you handle this."

Luis froze. That was exactly what he was going to say. The problem was, he didn't know Mohawk's location. Treleous was almost certainly waiting in town, and probably at the airport as well. He was a multi-hour walk back to the jeep, in the middle of a forest he didn't know, with little civilization to speak of for miles in any other direction. Not to mention the hostility she was showing right now. He didn't understand her. "What do you want me to do?"

Susan's eyes widened. She threw her hands up in the air and started pacing. "I don't know. I'm stuck here now. You people are like a whirlwind. I come to get y'all to help me find my father." She spun back, pointing her finger at him. "Do you know how that usually works?"

Luis took a step back and shook his head.

"I give a man a check," she wiggled her fingers, "And he goes off and looks for a while, and then gives me a report. They don't whisk me away, dismantle my only car, fly me to Montana of all places and," she held up her forefinger, "And not once did anyone shoot at me or chase me," she finished breathlessly.

Luis fought back a smile. "And how many of those men made any progress in finding your father?"

Her eyes blazed, and he immediately regretted the comment.

She snapped her arm and pointed back toward the ranch. "They didn't even know who my dad was. So you haven't made any progress, either."

Chapter 85

It surprised Eddie when, ten minutes after their call, Burk stood alone at Emily's back door. On the screen, he recognized the large, square jawed man in a blazer as the one coordinating the search for him in the hotel lobby a short time ago. Not obviously armed, but he had some sort of weapon, Eddie was sure of it. He didn't blame him. He and Loren held their pistols loosely at their side as she pushed the button to open the door.

As the big man crossed to the elevator, Eddie studied his carriage and stride on the screen. He was mad. Angrier than when they talked on the phone a short time ago.

Eddie furrowed his brow and grabbed Loren gently by the arm, pulling her back a step.

She looked over, her eyebrows raised.

Out of the corner of his mouth, he muttered, "Something's changed."

The elevator doors opened and Burk stepped out. His jaw rigid, he immediately fixed his attention on Eddie and growled, "Where is she?"

Eddie resisted the urge to step back and asked calmly, "Who?"

Burk narrowed his eyes. "Susan. There is some evidence that she isn't where we thought she was." A muscle flexed in his jaw.

Eddie rolled his eyes. "With my man in Montana. I told you that, and I told you she wasn't where you thought she was."

This seemed to take a fraction of the wind out of Burk's sails and he moved from foot to foot as if he was trying to find some way to vent his anger and frustration. "Is she safe?"

Eddie sighed. "Yes. She's in a weird situation out there, but she's with the most dangerous man I've ever met."

Loren motioned with her head toward the next room. "Come on. Let's go in here and talk. See if we can figure all this out."

After a brief hesitation, Burk reluctantly followed, with Eddie bringing up the rear.

He shot a look over his shoulder at Eddie, and once comfortable that it wasn't a trap, continued on into the living room. He took in Alex as he entered the open space. "You okay?"

His man sighed. "Just embarrassed, Cap."

Burk once again scowled at Eddie. "Who's the strong arm that keeps getting the best of my men?"

Eddie said, "Sorry about the man back at the Fairmont. We didn't expect you all to respond like this." He shrugged, "So, we had to ask for help."

Burk pursed his lips. "From whom?"

Loren answered, "The CIA."

His shoulders slumped, and he said under his breath. "Damn it." He looked up at Eddie and Loren. "Who are you guys?"

She placed a hand on his forearm, "Why don't you have a seat, and we'll tell you."

Eddie sat at the breakfast table and motioned for Burk to join him. They needed to find some common ground. Something to work back from. "Did you serve?"

Burk ducked his chin and looked down his nose at Eddie for a beat. "I was in the Army, then the Secret Service for a while."

Eddie nodded. "What unit?"

"Rangers."

Eddie's eyebrows flew up. "Me, too. What battalion?"

He blew out a slow breath through his nose. "The 75th Regiment."

A smile crept across Eddie's face. Burk was a badass. "Benning?"

Burk's eyes narrowed. "No, McChord. You with the Regiment?"

Eddie nodded. "Before I got pulled into the Agency."

They studied each other with different expressions now.

Loren rolled her eyes. "You boys can compare tattoos later." She looked over at Eddie. "I told Alex over there the story about how we got involved in the whole Treleous thing."

Eddie held her gaze for a moment. His team was not a dictatorship. He trusted and depended on each member and their instincts. He knew that at some point they were going to have to take a risk, to make an overture. If Loren believed that this was the moment, he would follow her lead.

After a beat, Burk, back to being wary, took a seat across from him and Loren sat down at the end.

Eddie considered the man. Could this still be just an outfit that helped people vanish? Completely unconnected to the Mendelson and Treleous affair? No. Not once had Burk asked about Susan. Now he was certain this was all connected. They had finally found a thread to unravel, and Eddie needed to pull it carefully. "How well do you know your bosses?"

Burk held his gaze, his mouth compressed to a thin line. "I'm not sure what you mean."

Eddie shrugged. "I'm going to tell you our story. What I want to know is, do you know enough to connect some dots yourself, or are you just a man whose only job is to protect someone?"

"What does it matter?"

Eddie kept his attention steady on Burk but did not respond.

Burk finally blew out a slow, deep breath. "I know enough."

"Do you know who Heinrich Stein was?"

A flicker of recognition flashed across Burk's eyes, and he nodded.

Eddie continued. "A few years ago, he reached out to Senator Sam Hawthorne to get help. Help fighting a group called Treleous."

Burk shifted in his seat, his attention riveted to Eddie now, but he remained silent. Eddie thought he detected just the smallest flash of recognition.

"Sam reached out," Eddie gestured at Loren, "to us to help him in this cause. So for a while now we've been working with Sam behind the scenes," he shrugged. "To resist them, I guess you'd say."

Burk stayed focused on Eddie. "Who's us?"

Eddie shrugged. "Just a team of ex-government types who sometimes help people." He shot a glance over at Loren. "Treleous knows about us, and they've been trying to find out who we are and stop us." He shrugged again. "Trying to find out what we know."

He remained focused on Eddie, eyes narrowed, still not saying a word.

Eddie scratched the table. "Another thing I don't think you know is that Susan Leonette has been looking for her father for some time."

Burk shook his head. "That can't be." He frowned at the two of them before continuing. "She was told where he went and was provided for."

Eddie and Loren exchanged a look.

She said, "I don't know what broke down where, but something did. She's been using every resource she has, and I'm guessing a few she doesn't, to find him. For a long time."

Burk frowned.

Eddie continued, "Treleous found her and tried to use her as bait in a trap to catch us."

A crease lined Burk's forehead, his shoulders tensed, and he looked like he was preparing to stand.

Loren held a hand out to him. "We were able to get her away from them."

Eddie said, "And we've been trying to help her. That's why we came to the pipe shop and why I sent Susan with one of our team to Montana."

Burk's brow furrowed. "How could you know about those things?" He shook his head. "How could you know about the ranch?"

Alex sat hunched forward on the couch, his wide eyes never leaving the conversation at the table.

Eddie hesitated. "We've developed some sources as we've worked on this problem."

Burk's mouth thinned. "What sources? No one knows about the ranch."

Eddie tilted his head to one side with a look that said, "You know I can't tell you that." He sighed. "Why don't you reach out to your bosses? Tell them the story I just told you, and let's see what they say. Maybe we can help one another."

Burk pursed his lips and stared at the table between them. "Okay." He looked up. "Give me a second." He stood and glanced around.

Eddie gestured toward the mudroom.

Burk nodded and walked back there and closed the door.

Loren came up from behind Eddie and rubbed his shoulder.

Burk's low rumbling voice floated from the other room, but Eddie was unable to make out his words.

After a few moments, the big man returned, looking perplexed. "My bosses say that if everything you say is true, then you should," he hesitated, glancing at the floor before continuing, "then you should know the password."

Chapter 86

Luis was unsure how to calm this suddenly angry and assertive Susan. She was right, and he supposed that she'd gone along in the beginning because she'd do anything to find her father. But now things had changed, at least from her point of view. He could understand that.

He liked this new side of her. She'd always been tough, but—he let this train of thought fade. He had bigger problems. The first of which was, what to do with her? Mohawk was somewhere back the way they had come. Treleous was almost certainly still watching the town and probably the airport. Luis had no safe place to hide her for now.

Treleous was going to raid the ranch, take whatever was there, and most likely kill everyone. He couldn't just stand on the sidelines and let that happen. He had to help these people, even if they didn't want him to. And secondarily, they were their only connection to Susan's father.

Rob had told them he didn't know who her father was, and Luis believed him. That didn't mean that the ranch didn't somehow lead to him, possibly in a way he didn't know or understand.

A drone whizzed by far to the west, and Luis followed it as it passed.

Susan's scowl faded a bit as she tracked the craft as well. "You think that's those guys who are after us? What did you call them—Treleous?"

He turned back to her. "Yes."

She took a deep, cleansing breath. "I know you're trying to help me, but this is out of control, and I deserve some answers."

Luis frowned. She did. He had to admit that. Standing, he said, "Okay, have a seat, and I'll tell you what I can."

She narrowed her eyes, but complied.

"There was a scientist named Mendelson, who worked for the government. He was a dangerous man, and he worked on some projects that people thought were," he shrugged, "evil."

A crease formed at the top of Susan's nose. "And my father worked for him?"

Luis nodded. "Yes, but I don't think he knew what Mendelson was doing, or if he did, then shortly afterwards, decided he wouldn't be part of it. I think that's why he disappeared."

She nodded slowly. "So he wouldn't have to do that work anymore?"

"I think so. Any man who raised you—well, that's why I believe he did what he did."

A small smile brushed her lips.

"Anyway, the government shut Mendelson down, and eventually, he committed suicide." He rubbed his face. "But some people wanted these projects to go on."

Susan's eyes widened. "Treleous."

"Treleous. They started working in the shadows, trying to keep his work going."

"Why are they called Treleous?"

Luis shrugged. "No idea. We really know nothing about them." He paused and slowly took in their surroundings, moving in a complete circle before turning his attention back to her. "A man named Heinrich Stein was another of the scientists that worked for Mendelson. He wanted to stop them, so, he—uh, told a friend of ours about them."

"The friend with the plane?"

Luis nodded. "Yeah. And we've been working against them ever since." He sighed. "Anyway, there's supposed to be a secret cache somewhere with all of Mendelson's work. All the experiments, designs, data, and stuff like that. That's what Treleous is looking for."

She looked over toward the ranch, shading her eyes against the sun. "And you think that's what's there?"

Luis shrugged again. "It seems like a safe bet. What else would be there? What else would require guards?"

Susan turned back to him. "And why do they want y'all?"

"To find out who we are. What we know. They think we may know where Mendelson's work is. To make sure we can't be a threat to them."

The crease returned to her forehead. "And we led them right to it?"

Luis shook his head. "I don't think so. They were already here when we got to town."

She frowned. "That's true. That really is strange. How did they find this place?" She picked up a pinecone and threw it. "So, where is this Stein guy?"

Luis snorted. "Someone killed him, right after he told our friend."

She threw her hands up in the air. "Of course they did. Okay. At least I have a sense of what's going on. I appreciate you confiding in me." She studied her hiking boot and then looked up at him. "What about the guy at your house? Cayman?"

Luis closed down all expression. He trusted this girl, but that was a line he wouldn't cross. Not yet at least, and not without the rest of the team's blessing. "Just a member of the team." He could see she didn't believe him, but let it go.

Susan said, "This all just doesn't seem like my father. He's very smart, and well, he's a bit like an absent-minded professor. I don't see him planning his own disappearance, or even knowing people who know how to do that kind of thing." Her eyes misted up. "I just can't see him doing any of these things." And then almost to herself said, "Not without at least telling me."

Once again, Luis wasn't certain how to comfort her, and resisted the urge to hug her, not sure if that was the right thing to do. "I don't know. But nothing has changed. We will help you find out."

She wiped her eyes. "Okay. I know you want to protect me, but I don't know of any place I could go." She pointed off to the mountain side of the ranch in the distance. "What do you say we go up there, find a good vantage point and check out Arrowhead? It would keep me out of the way and safe, keep you near in case they needed you. In the meantime, you could check the place out, get the lay of the land or whatever."

"You mean reconnoiter?"

She nodded quickly. "Oh yes, that sounds much better."

Luis sighed and shook his head at her. She was trouble, no doubt about it. But he didn't have a better idea. He reached into his pack and took out a granola bar. "Okay, let's eat and then we'll go see what this place looks like."

Chapter 87

Eddie looked over at Loren, dumbfounded. What password? What were they talking about? It was so sophomoric and once again spoke to this group's amateurish tilt.

She shrugged and mouthed, "Ask our friend."

Eddie nodded and turned to Burk. "Give me a second."

He walked into the bedroom. Obviously, Loren was right. The next logical step was to call Caveman, but that worried Eddie. Asking about Leonette had knocked him out for a whole day. They were nearing some answers now. He could feel it. But he was also apprehensive that the wrong question could hurt Caveman. What if it even knocked him out permanently?

He rubbed his face. Eventually, they had to cross this bridge. He knew that, so he pulled out his burner phone and dialed.

Caveman answered immediately. "How's it going?"

"We're fine, but this keeps getting stranger."

The smile in Caveman's voice was audible as he said, "Well, did you really expect all of this to suddenly become normal?"

Eddie grinned. "Not really. Is Jeff there with you?"

"Yeah, you're on speaker."

Jeff's voice came over the line. "I'm here. What's up?"

Eddie said, "I just want you there in case what I'm about to ask Caveman makes him pass out or something."

The amusement evaporated from both their voices as they agreed.

Eddie hesitated. "We've come across some people who we presume are connected to Susan's dad, and they're asking for a password."

Caveman snorted. "A password?"

Jeff added, "That's a weird thing to ask for."

Eddie's heart sank. Caveman knowing the password was their only way forward. If he didn't know it, then he didn't know what his next step was.

A moment passed, then Cavemen chuckled. "Wait a minute." He barked out a laugh. "I think, I think that might mean something to me."

Eddie's heartbeat quickened. "What?"

Caveman continued, still on the edge of laughing, "I think the password is Bressler's." He chuckled. "Yeah, I think it's Bressler's. Like the ice cream place in Daytona. I used to go there as a kid all the time." He immediately stopped laughing.

Holy crap! Caveman remembered something from his past! Something personal. From a childhood.

A silent moment stretched between them.

Caveman sniffed and said in a hoarse voice, "I'm from Daytona. I grew up in a little house west of the beach." His voice caught in his throat and then he choked out, "Eddie, I finally remember something useful. Something about me."

Eddie's eyes misted up as well. "That's great, man. It's amazing." It really was amazing, and Eddie wanted to unpack this completely with his friend. Unfortunately, he had to get past his current obstacle first. "Is that all you remember?"

"Yeah. It's sort of fuzzy."

Jeff's voice sounded over the phone, talking to Caveman in the background. "Do you remember your name?"

"No. Not my name, or my parents, or anything like that. I just have vague memories of going there and of Mr. Bressler's funny mustache and amazing ice cream."

Eddie broke out into a grin. They were getting somewhere, but as always, it was terrible timing. "Okay, we'll talk about this more later. Do you really think that's the password?"

Caveman chuckled again. "I know, it's weird, but, yeah, it should work. I don't know why, but it should."

Eddie said, "Okay, I have to go. I'm sorry."

Caveman said, "No, it's fine. Go. Keep us in the loop." He hung up.

Eddie stared at the phone. Could this really be the password? And if so, it brought up many questions. This was a place, supposedly from Caveman's past, so why would it be the password for this whole weird group? Was everyone in the organization from Daytona? If not, then how else would they all know about the place?

Or was it just a password for Cavemen? Something he wouldn't forget. This led to another problem. If it was Caveman's password, and his alone, what would happen when Eddie used it? He obviously wasn't Caveman. Would it immediately expose the team, or worse, Caveman, or at least their knowledge of him?

Once again, Eddie found himself suddenly at a threshold he wasn't prepared to cross yet. He reluctantly walked into the other room.

Loren, Burk, and Alex looked up expectantly.

Eddie hesitated. "The password is Bressler's."

Chapter 88

After lunch, Luis led Susan around the northeast side of the ranch. The steeper, more rugged terrain slowed their progress, but Luis figured they were really only killing time until Eddie could get here or Treleous attacked, anyway. Moreover, this was the best way to keep Susan safe and distracted.

He knew they were going to show up on the ranch cameras, but he hoped that by not heading directly toward them, it would keep the soldiers there from reacting. Besides, those guys had other problems to deal with.

As they picked their way around trees and large rocks, his mind once again turned back to the other time he'd waited for Eddie to come save him.

He'd come through then as well, and, like now, it was in less-than-ideal circumstances. Susan differed from Ellen, however. She was more down to earth.

He remembered it like it was yesterday.

Ellen checked her reflection in the window behind the check-in desk at the hotel in Metz. She was a beautiful woman, but acutely aware of it and always primping and adjusting her hair and clothes. If Luis was honest, it was a bit off-putting. She wasn't like anyone he'd ever met. She was more like a fancy doll who sat on a shelf.

She also wasn't shy and innocent like Susan, either. As soon as they were in the room, Ellen was kissing him—hard. After a moment, he held her at an arm's length, trying to get a read on this woman.

She held his gaze. "I just need this right now."

Luis believed her and understood that there was nothing more to it than that. She wasn't really interested in him, just in some kind of release. He checked the door, peeked out the blinds, and then returned to her as she unbuttoned her blouse.

Afterward he sat on the edge of the bed thinking, while Ellen lay on her stomach breathing quietly.

Luis didn't like going to this meeting with just the pistol and the few rounds he had left, but he couldn't think of any way to get any more firepower. He was in a foreign land, way out of his element, and with no support. He was a soldier, not a spy.

Just before five the next morning, while it was still dark, he gently woke her, and they collected their stuff.

Ellen was still paranoid that her phone was being tracked, so she kept it off as they climbed into the Mercedes and drove into Verdun.

Parking near the meeting place, Luis noticed a man in a black suit. He was big, with more fat than muscle, and had a suspicious look about him. Luis marked him and then put him out of his mind until he saw him again seated at a table in front of a closed restaurant about a block down from the liquor store.

He carefully checked the front and rear of the wine store as best he could, with Ellen in tow. Needing a better view, he studied the three-story building across the street.

There was still very little activity in the early morning, and Luis found a third-floor apartment for sale across the way and down from the shop meeting place. Not quite sunrise yet, the place was still and quiet. He carefully broke the door with a swift, quiet kick. Empty. The small rooms were even devoid of furniture. He gently pushed Ellen inside and closed the door behind them.

Moving to the window, Luis looked around the curtain without touching it. He could see through the big front window into the still dark liquor store. He had good visibility to his left, but only about a block to his right.

A cigarette glowed and then faded at a table in front of a closed restaurant beyond the liquor store. Luis' fingertips tingled. The smoker had a good vantage point to watch the store that was their intended meeting place.

As the sunlight slowly filled the alley, Luis realized it was the same guy in the black suit. This meeting Ellen had set up was definitely a trap.

Chapter 89

Loren's eyebrows shot up, and she suppressed a smile.

Burk frowned. "The password is," he paused, "Bressler's?"

Eddie nodded.

"All right. Let me see what they say."

He stepped into the other room and Loren glanced over at Alex before leaning into Eddie. "Bressler's?"

He shrugged and whispered back to her. "That's what he says." Grabbing her elbow, he pulled her over into a corner. "It's an ice cream place in Daytona. He remembers going there as a kid."

Her eyes opened wide. "Really?"

He nodded.

Loren suppressed a smile. Caveman had remembered something. Something real. A lump formed in her throat. After all this time, they were finally making some progress. She just hoped it didn't come to a screeching halt if Burk returned and Bressler's wasn't right. Which was possible because it was the dumbest password ever.

If it was wrong, then she didn't know what their next move was. They would have even less credibility with these people than they did now.

Her thoughts returned to Cavemen and her eyes misted up. He remembered something real. She couldn't believe it. She hastily wiped a tear away with a finger.

Eddie noticed and took her in his arms for a quick hug. It was reassuring to be in his muscular arms and surrounded by his familiar smell. They separated and stepped apart when Burk walked back into the room.

He snorted and shook his head. "Okay. Bressler's was right. I'm supposed to help you in any way I can. So what the hell is going on?"

Thank God. Eddie's shoulders sagged in relief. "First, I'm sorry we hurt your man back there at the Fairmont."

Burk shrugged. "It's all right. It's just a sprained knee. He should have been watching his six."

An awkward silence stretched between them.

Alex sat forward and asked, "Can I get unlocked, then?"

Loren compressed her lips. They only had Burk's word that they were friends now. The big man was clearly armed, but at the moment, she and Eddie had him outnumbered. The instant Eddie uncuffed him, that situation changed, even with Alex unarmed. She exchanged a look with Eddie. If this new peace was real, she didn't want to mess it up by refusing, but it was an awful risk.

Burk sensed their hesitation. "Not yet, Alex. I think if I were them, I'd want a little more than this before I did that."

Alex sighed and slumped back against the couch.

Loren nodded. "Thanks."

Eddie gestured to the table. "Let's have a seat again. My man thinks there's trouble brewing in Montana."

Chapter 90

Frank glanced at his watch. It was a little after two, and Gemini wouldn't be on the ground for hours. He didn't have enough men to start without them, so he had no choice but to wait.

His men were getting antsy. He could feel it. Hard to blame them, but they were all used to the hurry up and wait of military life and had settled into rotation of work and rest with little direction.

He wanted Mack before all this got off the ground, anyway. Where was that boy? As usual, he hadn't followed directions, and they hadn't heard hide nor hair from him since he'd trotted off into the words. Frank shook his head. It was always this way with him. He should be back already.

His radio squawked. "Five to Actual. Come in, Actual. Over."

"This is Actual. Go ahead, Five. Over."

"Actual. The tangos from the ranch are on the move. I think they're looking for us. Repeat, tangos are moving in small groups and appear to be searching. Over."

Frank gritted his teeth. "Damn it." Someone had gotten sloppy. It was bound to happen, with so much time to kill. He clicked the mic. "Solid copy Five. Good work. All units, we have to wait for the rest of our team. Pull back gently. Repeat. All teams, pull back gently, and don't be seen. We still want the element of surprise as much as possible. Over and out." He sighed. The longer you waited at the target zone without acting, the worse it got, every time. Frank spat. Where the hell was Mack? He climbed back into the truck and retrieved his handheld radio. He held the button and said into it, "Actual to One. Come in, One." Silence. His chest muscles tightened with worry. He couldn't wait for him any longer. Four reserve men stood nearby, awaiting orders. Frank pointed at one of them. "Go to the spot where we sent Mack into the woods. You know where that is?"

The man nodded.

"Go there and make sure he doesn't need help." He frowned. "Don't go into the woods. He's liable to shoot you. Just go check it out and report back."

The man gave a perfunctory salute, but stopped as Frank's cell phone rang.

He glanced at the phone with a scowl. "Mack, where the hell are you?"

"Pulling up now."

He hung up and shaded his eyes as he looked down the road. A truck pulled up and Mack stepped out.

Frank's shoulders slumped. "About damned time. What happened?"

Mack flinched and held his hands up, miming holding his rifle. "I had him dead to rights, Frank. Both of them. And then these damn soldiers showed up, and I had to bug out. I'm guessing they're from this ranch you've discovered?"

Frank frowned at him. Was that the complete story? Probably not. It was always a mixed bag with this kid. Maybe that's why the people at the ranch were getting antsy. They'd seen Mack. He frowned. "They seem like they were with Mr. Talented?"

Mack shook his head. "Not really."

"How did they know you were there?"

Mack shrugged. "No idea, Frank. I dropped one, but Mr. Talented engaged me, so I don't think I killed him."

Frank pursed his lips. "But you don't think they were together?"

"No. I don't think so."

So could Mr. Talented and the girl be their prisoners, too? Could they have taken them, like they took Tom?

There was too much he didn't know, and Frank hated unknowns on a mission. Nothing he could do about it now. He gestured at the map on the hood. "I think this is it, kid. Gemini is on his way. I think this is what we've been looking for."

Chapter 91

Eddie held his gaze as Burk digested his warnings about trouble in Montana.

"I talked to my man in Montana on the way over. He seems worried as well, but he didn't really give me any specifics. He said they'd taken custody of someone yesterday who was causing trouble in town, but he won't talk. You're sure he's not your man."

Eddie nodded. "I just talked to him. Your men do not have him."

"Well, who the hell do they have? What kind of trouble?"

Eddie pulled out his phone. "Let me try him again." It rang until it went to voice mail.

Loren said, "He was in the woods, where he didn't have much signal, and he's trying to save battery on the satellite phone."

Eddie pursed his lips. He knew they needed to go, and soon. He looked over at Loren. "You said Treleous was there waiting for Luis when he arrived in Beaver Ruin, right?"

Burk half stood, his eyes wide. "What! You led them there?"

Eddie scowled. "I just said they were *waiting* for us."

He slowly sank back into his seat. "How? How do they know about the ranch?"

Loren shrugged. "We don't know that, either."

Burk narrowed his eyes. "Do you have a mole?"

Eddie shook his head. "There are only three of us and we've been together for a long time. The only outsider who knows about all of this is Susan, and she seems like an unlikely spy."

Burk's eyes widened. "Are you sure it's her?"

Loren said, "We are. We checked that out as well."

Burk rubbed his face with both hands. "There are only three of you. If this Treleous is at the ranch, then we are well and truly screwed." He glanced over at Loren. "Sorry, Ma'am."

Loren shrugged and said with the hint of a smile, "It isn't crude if it accurately describes the situation."

Eddie said, "We have access to more resources than that, but it seems like we need to get to Montana as soon as possible." He turned to Loren. "You want to call Craig, see if he can help?" He grimaced. "I'd even take Moe's help again."

Loren nodded and took a few steps away, putting the phone to her ear.

Eddie looked up at Burk. "How many men do you have?"

"I've got two down the street," He tilted his head over to Alex, "Him and me. Maybe a dozen at the ranch. How many do you think they'll have?"

Eddie thought back to the island and the resources Treleous brought to bear. "More than that."

Loren walked back. "Craig is sending Moe back. He'll be here in ten."

Burk narrowed his eyes. "Who's Craig?"

Eddie answered, "Our friend at the Agency."

Burk's eyes widened. "You don't mean Craig Black? You sure you trust him?"

Eddie shrugged. "I'm sure he's not with Treleous, if that's what you mean? But beyond that..." He grimaced.

Burk threw his hands in the air.

Eddie shrugged and tilted his head toward Alex. "Well, we might as well let him out and get your team over here."

Loren nodded and dug the key out of her jeans pocket and handed it to Burk.

Eddie said to her, "I'm going to call Jeff. Can you reach out to Sam and get his jet?"

She nodded.

He dialed, and Jeff answered.

Eddie said, "Hey, man, Luis is in trouble in Beaver Ruin. We're headed in that direction, but we need transport, guns, help—whatever you can get there in the next six hours before we land."

"I figured you might ask me that, so I've already been working on it. It's the middle of nowhere, but I know an extreme organic rancher in northern Wyoming who owes me a favor."

Eddie pinched the bridge of his nose. What did that even mean? "Whatever you can get. I think Treleous is there, and I think we might have to rescue a group. So, we'll need a big vehicle and anyone that can fight. Guns, anything that would help."

"I'm on it. You getting in the air?"

Eddie shrugged. "As soon as we can." He hung up.

Loren said, "Jet is ready and waiting. All you and I have are the two pistols."

Eddie frowned. "That's true."

Burk said, "When they get here, my team has extra equipment."

Eddie scowled. "You have any plans or pictures of the ranch?"

Burk nodded. "I can get them."

Eddie said, "Good, get them. I want to be in the air in thirty minutes."

The back door buzzed, and Emily stuck her head into the hallway.

Eddie looked over at Loren.

She nodded and headed in her direction. "I'll talk to her."

Alex asked, "Is there a bathroom?"

Eddie pointed as he led Burk back into the mudroom. They needed to get moving now.

Two soldiers stood at the back door.

Eddie jabbed the button, letting them in. "How good are these men?"

Burk shrugged. "They're trained, but none of them have any actual combat experience."

Eddie raised his eyebrows.

Burk shrugged. "I didn't think I needed those skills. We mostly do security work."

The elevator doors opened. The first man held up two black duffle bags and said with a grin, "I brought toys."

Burk made a quick introduction. As Eddie was ushering the group into the living room, the buzzer rang again. Seeing Moe standing at the back door, he let him in.

When the elevator doors opened, Eddie said, "I thought you had to go to South Carolina."

Moe said, "It was North Carolina." He shrugged. "Plans change."

Eddie looked past him. "No Craig or anyone else?"

Moe shook his head. "He says that the Agency can't get involved in domestic stuff."

"You're not CIA?"

Moe took a step back. "No way, man, I'm strictly freelance."

Eddie rubbed his eyes. Why was he even surprised? "We have some friends in trouble in Montana, so we're going to fly down there and try to help them. We're up against trained mercs, and we'll be outnumbered."

Moe's craggy face slowly split into a smile. "Sounds like my kind of game." He held up a fist.

Eddie bumped it and raised his eyebrows. "You sure?"

"Craig says help, I'm in. Oh, and he says he'll have more help waiting for us when we get to Montana. Better help than he gave last time, whatever that means."

Better than last time? That was a low bar. Last time, he didn't really help at all.

Eddie waved into the living room. Where did Craig find these people? He'd better come through this time, or they were heading into a world of hurt.

As Moe walked into the other room and saw the group of soldiers, he leaned into Eddie and said under his breath, "You know, these guys are lightweights."

Eddie sighed. "I know."

Loren, Burk, and the soldiers looked back expectantly.

The men eyed Moe warily as he walked in and took Loren's hand and kissed it.

Loren looked down her nose at him. "Cool your jets, Romeo."

Eddie narrowed his eyes. "Seriously?"

Moe looked over at Eddie and held both hands up. "Just being polite, amigo."

Eddie rolled his eyes. Where did Craig find these guys? He said to the room, "Everyone ready?"

They all nodded.

He turned to Burk. "You can get these plans pretty quickly?"

"Yes, I'll pick them up on the way. Loren told us where, so we'll meet you at the airport."

Eddie said, "Make it quick."

He nodded and led his team out of the room.

Eddie asked Moe, "You have your car?"

"Yeah, want me to get it?"

Emily ventured hesitantly into the kitchen and nodded at Moe.

Moe grinned at her. "I have a message from Craig."

Emily's eyebrows flew up. "Oh, really?"

Moe nodded. "He told me to tell you not to worry, you're perfectly safe here. He'll make sure you don't get any trouble from being dragged into the middle of this mess. Personally."

Emily placed a hand on her chest. "Well, thank him for me and tell him that really isn't necessary."

Moe gave her a two-fingered salute and walked out.

Eddie and Loren exchanged an amused look, and she turned and gave Emily a hug. "Thank you so much. We can never thank you enough, and we are so sorry if we brought you any trouble."

Emily grinned. "Don't be silly. It was so exciting." She hugged Eddie. "All I ask is, when it's all over, you'll have to come for dinner and tell me the story. Now go help your friend."

Loren smiled in return. "It's a deal."

They gathered their bags and rushed out the door.

Chapter 92

Luis stopped at the top of a rise and waited for Susan to catch up. She was in good shape, but her legs were shorter, and she had to work to match his pace. He suppressed a smile and turned to apologize and poke fun at her when he stopped dead.

Tears streamed down her face. Not the fight back the sorrow, misty eyed, melancholy he'd seen from her before. This was something different, and she looked haunted and full of despair.

Luis rushed over to her.

Susan turned away, wiping both cheeks with her palms.

"What is it?"

She squeezed her eyes shut and shook her head.

Luis vacillated for a second and then took her into his arms.

She fell into him, holding on tight, as she sobbed into him with deep, wracking convulsions.

He held her, unsure where this rush of emotions had come from. He glanced around, worried that this moment was making them vulnerable, but it was open and rocky here and it would be hard for someone to sneak up on them.

She gradually calmed down and eventually pushed away from him, wiping her face. "I'm sorry."

"It's okay. What brought this on?"

She bit her lip. "For the first time, it hit me. I think my dad might actually be dead." Another tear snaked down her cheek.

Luis wiped it away with his thumb. "Why?"

She shrugged. "I've just been thinking about the whole situation now that I know more. Now that we know that bad men really were after my dad." She shrugged. "They must be after all of Mendelson's old scientists, right?"

Luis couldn't lie to her, and he knew she'd know if he even tried. "Probably."

"There's no way he could escape people like that. He just wasn't that kind of man. And even if he did, there's no way he wouldn't reach out to me for five years."

He furrowed his brow. "First, you don't know that. Your dad disappeared. If they had him, then they wouldn't need us, right?" This sounded good, but it wasn't the entire story. "Second, you yourself just realized how dangerous Treleous is. It would be deadly for you and him if he tried to contact you."

She wiped her eyes again and nodded. "But he would have left a note some kind of message. He would have left me money, or someone I could turn to. He wouldn't have left me like this. With no word, help, nothing. Not if he was still alive."

Luis had no answer for that. What she said made sense, but he still hoped the man was okay. He studied her face and then, without even thinking, took her into his arms again. He could feel her small breasts crush against him as she clung to him. Why did this woman affect him so? "This is what I learned in war. Never give up hope until you have to. Always believe until you see it with your own eyes. God can surprise you sometimes, and hope doesn't cost you anything."

She kept her head pressed against his chest as she nodded.

Luis stroked her hair. "And I'll do everything in my power to take you to the truth."

Chapter 93

Eddie shook his head as Burk's men loaded all their equipment underneath Sam's jet and then clambered aboard. He, Loren, and Moe made the group larger, but he was still afraid they wouldn't be enough. But this was all they had at the moment, and they had to get going.

Once inside, he collected everyone around a coffee table in the front of the cabin.

Burk raised his eyebrows at his surroundings as he spread out a map of Wheatland County. "Just how rich is your friend?"

Loren answered, "Rich enough."

Moe stretched out his legs in front of him. "I like it. I was born to travel this way."

Burk pointed at the map. "We're landing here. Our friends are on a ranch here."

Moe sat up and frowned at the map. "That's kind of in the middle of nowhere."

"It is. The closest police station is Harlowton, but it's a very small force."

Eddie met Burk's gaze. "They want whatever's in the warehouse."

Moe tilted his head. "What's in it?"

Burk's lips compressed.

Eddie continued to Burk, "Look, I don't care what's in there. I just want us to be on the same page." He looked around the plane. "We don't have enough people to drive these guys off. We're going to save as many of our people as we can and then bug the hell out. We can't save whatever's there. Got it?"

Moe shot a glance at Eddie before looking back at Burk.

Loren asked. "What about the Bureau? Can we say this is some sort of domestic terrorism?"

Eddie shook his head at her. "The nearest field office is in Salt Lake, and even if we could convince them to come, by the time they arrived, it would be all over. Even if Craig was willing to call." He looked back at Burk. "And then *they* would know whatever was there as well."

Loren scowled and asked Moe. "Speaking of Craig, he didn't offer any help aside from you. No offense."

Moe shrugged one shoulder. "None taken. He said he can't be seen doing anything on American soil, but he'd make sure there'd be some help there when we land."

Loren rolled her eyes. "He's such an asshole."

Eddie looked at Burk. "Are we on the same page?"

Burk nodded. "Yes. Not that it matters. We couldn't do anything else, even I wanted to."

Moe asked, "No one's going to tell me what's in the warehouse?"

Eddie glanced at Burk and then said to Moe, "A bunch of paper. Files that are important to a small group of people. They're too heavy to carry, and too few people want them, for them to have any street value."

Burk's eyes widened. Eddie must have hit the nail pretty close to the head.

Moe grinned. "Now see, that's all you had to say."

Eddie shook his head, and continued to Burk, "Do you have a layout of the compound?"

Burk rolled a set of blueprints out on the table. The area was a long rectangle with a triangle at the end. He gestured across it. "It sits in the middle of a large ranch, but here in the middle is a twenty-acre compound. The main road runs from the town of Beaver Ruin into the camp about a mile away."

Eddie didn't like the look of this at all. Who picked this location to hide something? It was terrible. Very difficult to defend.

Burk continued, "There's a dirt road coming out of the back."

Loren frowned. "Going where?"

Burk shrugged. "I don't know. It just goes on and on to the east. It's in awful shape. This area up here in the triangle is trees, like a forest. Chain link surrounds the entire place."

Eddie frowned at the two shaded areas on either side of the road leading out the back of the ranch. "What are they?"

Burk shrugged. "They're rises."

Moe's brow furrowed. "Like a hill?"

Burk nodded.

Moe tossed his hands in the air.

Loren snorted. "So we can assume there's a sniper on each of those. Who picked this place?"

Burk scowled. "Not me."

Loren said, "How many people are there?"

"Fourteen guards. Plus a cook, a computer guy, a maid, and the handyman."

Eddie furrowed his brow. "Who's the man your team nabbed? The guy you thought was with me?"

Burk shrugged. "I don't know, but they took some prisoner. Rob, my head guy, has been away from the compound, so I really haven't had time to talk to him."

Loren said, "Maybe they got one of Treleous' men?"

Eddie sighed. "Maybe. I wondered why they hadn't moved on the ranch yet. That might explain it."

She continued, "Luis said it was only a small group. Maybe they're waiting for reinforcements, too?"

Eddie rubbed his face. "We have to assume they'll get there before we do. The question is, how long before?"

They all frowned at the blueprints.

Eddie shrugged. "Anyway, from what we know about them, they'll have at least twenty men arranged around the compound. And Loren's right, more than likely a sniper on each rise."

Moe said, "There's forest here, and outbuildings all along here. If their men are already in place, it's going to be very hard to approach without being seen, even if they don't have drones, which they probably do."

Eddie nodded. "So we have three problems. Getting in, gathering as many people as we can, and then getting back out. And I don't see how we do any of them at the moment."

Chapter 94

Luis led Susan higher up the slope and to the east until they came to a clearing that afforded a good view of the ranch below.

Surprised, she commented, "It's bigger than I expected."

Luis nodded in agreement.

From this vantage point, they could see a large two-story house, a massive barn, and seven outbuildings in the middle of at least twenty acres. A tall razor topped fence encircled the entire place.

Someone was protecting something here. The question was, what? It was the middle of nowhere. Could it be the Mendelson depository?

They stopped and sat on a large flat rock, sipped from a canteen, and stared at the compound below. There was nothing to do now but wait. Luis asked Susan about her life and answered her questions about his. It was a good way to keep her mind off the things she couldn't answer, and problems she couldn't solve as the sun moved across the sky.

After a while, Susan stood and stretched. "Before long, we're going to have to think about dinner and where we're going to sleep tonight."

Luis narrowed his eyes at the ranch. Why hadn't Treleous attacked the place yet? He studied the long shadows stretching out in the valley below. Were they waiting for nightfall? For reinforcements? He didn't think they'd brought very many men with them in the first place, so they must be waiting for more. Where would they come from?

Eddie and Loren had better get here soon.

A screech from up the mountain behind them made Luis whirl and grab his rifle. "Did you hear that?"

Susan nodded, eyes wide.

The slope uphill was rocky and steep. He stood still, slowly moving his attention from one side to the other. Treleous was here, but he was also acutely aware that this was the wilderness. A wood full of large, extremely dangerous, and aggressive animals.

Suddenly, his fingertips vibrated, and a powerful instinct flared. He needed to get to the compound. Now. What could he do with Susan, though? It would be dark before long, and neither of them knew this area. He couldn't just leave her here alone. He looked over his shoulder. Of course, down there was Treleous and more danger.

Susan read his face. "If your instinct says go, take me." She glanced warily back up the hill. "What other choice do you have?" He opened his mouth, but she pressed on. "You have no choice. I'm probably safer with you, anyway. So, let's go."

Luis ground his teeth, but she was right. He turned and started downhill, heading directly towards the compound. All was still quiet, but he could feel it. Something was about to happen.

Chapter 95

Frank's phone rang. "Hello."

"It's Gemini. We're on the ground and already moving in your direction."

A smile touched Frank's lips. "We're ready to go."

"Great. We'll be there shortly."

He hung up and glanced at his watch. Earlier, he'd moved the command trailer to a small depression nestled in a cluster of foothills near the ranch. He took a moment to pace back and forth in front of it. He twirled an unlit cigar between his thumb and forefinger as he collected his thoughts. "Chip!"

The heavyset man stuck his head out of the trailer. Frank pointed at him. "Take down the cell tower."

Mack rolled out of a pickup's bed, rubbing the sleep from his face. "Ready?"

Frank nodded and glanced at this watch again before turning to Mack. "Reinforcements are here. We need the element of surprise, so we're not ready to move yet, but I want the two snipers in place before we cut them off. Get them in unseen and then come back to me." He looked down his nose at his second in command. "Unseen and unheard."

He rolled his eyes. "I got it. Stealthy and quiet." Motioning to the two snipers nearby, the three of them trotted up the path.

Chip stuck his head out again. "The cell tower will be jammed in the next twenty minutes."

Frank nodded. "Good." He turned to the other men. "Gear up and do a comms check. It's almost game time." He searched the crowd for Marco.

"Call Manny and tell him to cut off the police station in Harlow." He opened his mouth to continue, but Marco replied, "And don't get caught. I'm on it."

• • •

Later, Gemini and the extra men rolled in and piled out of their trucks. Frank began to execute his plan. After briefing the new soldiers on their roles and sending them to their position, he glanced over at Gemini, whose gray eyes were wide and looking inward. "Last chance."

"Do it. I want whatever is in that warehouse." He turned, focusing on Frank. "You've got a job to do, and you don't need me looking over your shoulder." He nodded to his personal bodyguard, and the compactly built bald man stepped in behind him. "I'm going to find some coffee. Get me that building, Frank." He started to walk away before turning back. "In one piece. Make sure Mack understands that."

Frank nodded and leaned into the command trailer.

Chip sat inside, directing the troops with information he was receiving from overhead drones.

Frank's earpiece crackled.

"Twelve to Actual. I am in sniper position One. Over."

He glanced at his watch. "Solid copy, Twelve." That was the farthest vantage point. His other sniper should have already reached his nest. What was the problem? He touched his throat mic. "Actual to Eight. What's your status? Over."

The response was immediate. "This is Eight. I'm in position, Boss, just waiting for two tangos taking a smoke break to clear out before settling in. All good. Over."

Mack's voice sounded next. "Actual, this is One. I'm covering him. All good. Over."

Then after a minute, "This is Eight. I'm in place. Over and out."

Frank stepped into the trailer and sat next to Chip. He slid his cigar into his shirt pocket and studied the feed coming in from the two drones circling overhead.

This was his last chance to adjust things before the ball got rolling. From long experience, he understood that once the action started, you couldn't control it anymore. The method Frank had developed over the years to counteract that was to control everything he could until the last possible second. Without taking his eyes off the screen, he said into this throat mic, "This is Actual. Monitor the perimeter. Make sure no one slips away on foot. Over."

Chip frowned and pointed at the screen. "Anyone leaving the two structures would have to egress through here, here, and here." He pointed to the west, south, and east fence lines. "We have men watching each point. And they should be easy to pick out with the drones, regardless."

Frank frowned and pointed to the northern boundary. "What about here?"

He shrugged. "It's a lot of area to cover and there's nothing that way but the mountain, so we're thin there. Do you want to move someone up there?"

Frank ground his teeth and glanced at this watch again. "No time. It'll be dark soon." He touched his throat mic. "This is Actual. Kill the power and cut communications. Seal the perimeter. No one gets out of that place, starting now. Over."

Chip adjusted his glasses. "Power is out." He glanced over at Frank. "Want the snipers to take out the two generators?"

He nodded and lifted his radio. "This is Actual. Take out the generators and the radio antennae. Over."

A shot immediately rang out, echoing in the canyon. It was immediately followed by a second and then a third.

Chapter 96

Luis and Susan were more than a mile from the ranch, and it took them a while to wind their way down to flatter ground. About halfway there, he saw the small group of men leave the compound below and head in their direction. He said over his shoulder, "Here they come."

The two groups stopped about thirty feet apart.

Once again, Rob led the contingent. He frowned at Luis. "Done sightseeing?"

Luis shrugged. "Just staying out of your way, but nearby, in case you need me."

Rob sighed. "Need you for what?"

Luis nodded at the ranch beyond them. "Treleous is coming. I promise you."

Rob hesitated. "We have seen some odd activity, but how do I know you're not with them?"

Luis and Susan both rolled their eyes.

She said, "Didn't we already cover that this morning?"

Rob began to reply, but then suddenly held his fist up. He touched his throat mic and said, "This is Fire One. Go ahead." He tilted his head and listened to his earpiece for a moment, then his eyes narrowed. Several shots rang out and echoed off the mountains. "Fire Base, come in. Fire Base, do you copy?" He looked up at Luis. "Someone took out the generators and." He glanced around at the other men. "And now I've lost radio contact. Can anyone else reach home base?"

The other soldiers tried their mics and then shook their heads.

Luis frowned. "I'd say you were under attack."

Rob's eyes flashed. "No kidding."

Luis continued, "The question is, what's at the ranch? Are they after whatever's there," he gestured at Susan, "or are they after us?"

Rob took a half pace back and moved his weapon a fraction in Luis' direction.

Luis stepped in front of Susan and quickly darted his attention over the group, measuring each man's posture and expression. "Whoa, whoa."

Rob asked, "What did you mean by that?"

Luis darted a look toward the ranch. "Don't you think we need to deal with whatever's going on there first?"

Rob ground his teeth so hard Luis could hear it. "Team, go to the ranch. Keep me in the loop. I'll be along shortly."

They hesitated.

"Go."

With one last look at Luis, the men turned and moved away.

Rob asked again, "What did you mean?"

Luis shrugged and answered in a calm, even tone. "Look, I don't care about whatever secret you've got here." He tilted his head toward Susan. "I'm only interested in finding her father. But after the reception we got in town from your little band of brothers, it doesn't take a calculus teacher to realize you're protecting something." Luis paused, but Rob remained silent. "When Susan and I arrived, apart from the reception we received from the townsfolk, the men with Mohawk back there were waiting for us."

Rob's eyes narrowed. "Then I think it's safe to say that they're after you."

Luis leaned in and said in a low, menacing voice, "Then why did they send only one man after me and take the rest to attack your ranch?"

Rob's eyes widened.

A shot ran out, echoing off the mountains. Then a second and a third, all coming from that direction.

They all turned toward the sound.

Through gritted teeth, Luis said, "Come on, man. We need to help your guys. Let me help."

Rob looked back at Luis for a beat and then shook his head. "Come on." He turned and took off in a run toward the ranch, Luis hot on his heels.

He called over his shoulder to Susan, "Drop your pack. Follow us, but at a distance."

"Got it."

Soon, Luis could just make out the outline of the two larger structures through the trees. A moment later, a high chain-link fence topped with razor wire came into view.

Rob veered to his right and Luis followed.

Ahead, the four soldiers from earlier stood clustered around a door-shaped gate in the fence. One kneeled in front of the keypad, a second man leaned over his shoulder, and the other two stood guard.

The one facing their way noticed Rob approaching and called out softly.

He asked, "What's the problem?"

The man working on the keypad responded. "The system goes into a dead man mode when the ranch's power is out."

Rob narrowed his eyes. "Why? Doesn't it have a battery backup or something?"

The man working on the pad said without looking up, "Because it assumes that in the event of a power outage, we'll be on the inside."

A muscle bulged in Rob's cheek. "So, how do we get through it?"

The man glanced up. "We can put it in override mode. The problem is, to do that, it sends a text verification code to one of our cell phones."

A second soldier said, "And the cell tower is down or offline or something."

Rob rubbed his eyes. "What kind of dumbass..." He trailed off.

Luis rolled his eyes, grunted, and shrugged off his pack. This was going nowhere, and time was of the essence. These amateurs would be here all day.

He unzipped it and pulled out his bolt cutters.

All five soldiers looked up at him, and Susan turned to hide her smile. The man working on the keypad asked, "What are you doing?"

Luis put the cutters up to the fence.

A second man grabbed his arm. "You can't just cut it!"

Luis scowled. "Why the hell not? Your friends are under attack," he shook his head, "what's it going to do, set off an alarm? Let's cut the dammed fence."

Rob nodded. "Let him go."

Luis began methodically cutting strands until there was a hole big enough for a man. He kicked the section out and stepped through, the other soldiers close on his heels. Over his shoulder, he told Susan to wait out of sight.

Chapter 97

Frank paced back and forth in front of the command center, chomping on an unlit cigar and holding the radio close to his ear.

The door to the trailer banged open and Chip leaned out. "I got something on the drone feed. There's a group of soldiers at the ranch's northern gate—not ours. They're trying to get through it now."

Frank clamped down on his cigar so hard that the muscles in his cheek bulged. He tossed the shredded tobacco onto the ground. This was the worst possible time. They'd already committed themselves, and he could not let his team get surrounded. Into the radio he barked, "This is Actual. All teams hold Position Two. Repeat. Hold at Position Two. We have a group of tangos approaching the northern gate. Repeat. Tangos at the northern gate. Over." Frank's forehead creased. Hostiles outside the ranch, trying to get back in? Where had they come from? Was it Mr. Talented? Or his friends? Had reinforcements arrived?

Over the radio came Mack's voice, his tone laced with frustration. "This is One. We've split the forces inside the perimeter, one tango down, and I've forced three into the house. Repeat. Three in the house and we've driven the rest into the barn. We can take them. Are you sure you want us to hold? Over."

Frank strode over to a stack of aerial photographs of the ranch stacked on the truck's hood. "Affirmative, One. Stay covering the snipers. Repeat. Hold position. Over."

Mack sounded petulant. "Solid copy, Actual. Over."

Frank studied the map until he located the gate Chip had indicated. He traced with a finger from there to the interior of the compound. The house was too far, so Frank assumed they would make for the barn. He clicked the mic. "Actual to Ten. Come in, Ten. Over."

"This is Ten. Go ahead, Actual. Over."

"The tangos coming in the western gate will most likely move to the barn. Repeat. Tangos, probably moving to the barn. Over."

"Solid copy, Actual. Understood. Over."

"Move to the outbuildings just to the north. You should have a direct shot at them. Get as many as you can. Over."

"Solid copy, Actual. I'm Oscar Mike. Ten, over and out."

Frank pulled another cigar from his pocket and clamped it between his molars. Hopefully, it was a small force, and he could trap them, but one against four was too much. He lifted the radio again. "Actual to Ten, over."

"This is Ten. Go ahead, Actual. Over."

"I don't want these guys moving around, harassing us, and fighting with guerilla tactics. Take out the furthest tango and force them into the barn. Repeat. Into the barn. Copy? Over."

The radio crackled and then Ten replied, "Solid copy, over."

Frank frowned. He opened the door to the command trailer and said to Chip, "You said soldiers. Is the girl with them?"

Chip furrowed his brow. "What girl?"

Frank gnashed his teeth and quelled a wave of anger. "When Mr. Talented got here, he had a girl with him. Is there a girl with the group at the western gate?"

Chip looked back at the screen. Leaning in close, he frowned at the image. "I don't think so."

Frank turned and pointed to three of his reserves standing nearby. "You boys are Oscar Mike."

All eyes swiveled to him.

"Go skirt around the ranch on the west side and come up to the north. Make sure no one is waiting outside the fence. Specifically, there was a girl with them earlier and I don't see her now. Stay frosty. She might be guarded. Kill anyone you see and force the rest inside the compound. Got it?"

All three nodded.

Frank continued, "Also, make sure this new group doesn't run back the way they came. Squeeze them between you and the other men like a vise. Got it?"

The men nodded again.

"Get moving."

They turned and jogged into the woods.

Chapter 98

Luis and the other soldiers fanned out and crept toward the structures another fifty yards ahead. Their movements were more deliberate now, each man holding his rifle ready. The forest continued a short distance into the compound's interior before giving way to a wide, grassy area surrounding the inner buildings.

The trees made Luis nervous. There were a hundred good places for an ambush. Poor lines of sight, especially at dusk, and no sense of where the enemy was. Luis rubbed his fingertips against his thumb, feeling the slight vibration. His whole body knew that this was a dangerous situation. He could now make out the two-story house off to his right, the large, tall barn straight ahead, and several small outbuildings to his left.

The open area appeared deserted and there was no movement on the house's balconies, either. How many men were here, and where were they? None of them on guard?

The soldiers began to close ranks behind the man on the right, who was focusing on a door in the barn.

Luis followed suit, bringing up the rear. He didn't like everyone clumped all together, so he slowed, allowing some space to grow between him and the group. It was too quiet and too still.

A shot rang out and the last man of the group grunted and fell. Then a second doubled over and crumpled.

Luis dropped, rolled to his left, and came up, rifle to his shoulder. A tall, slim figure in fatigues took another shot in their direction from a spot near one outbuilding. Luis tilted his head, sighed, and put a bullet in the man's forehead. Ten bullets left.

The other soldiers shot quick glances at Luis as they ducked and took cover. Luis had been through this before when soldiers unfamiliar with him suddenly realized his skills. He didn't like the attention, but at least now they might listen to him. It also didn't hurt that they now knew he was on their side. He sidled up to Rob. "What now?"

The barn was about thirty yards away across open ground, with the house another thirty beyond it.

Rob pursed his lips and moved his attention around the area. "I don't know where my men are."

A shot rang out, followed by two more.

Luis said, "They're still fighting somewhere."

Rob nodded. "The barn is the closest."

Luis studied the roof and the hills beyond it and pointed. "There's a good sniper position there, and probably over there. We have to assume we'll be sitting ducks crossing that yard."

Rob blew out a breath. "Probably."

Luis looked over at the house again. What was his end goal here? They could certainly fade back into the woods, ease out the gate, and go for help. They wouldn't be back for hours, and Luis knew that by then it would all be over. He couldn't just let these men die like this. But how could he best help them? Not by barricading himself in the barn with the rest of them, that's for sure. He should stay outside and wreak havoc from the shadows. What about Susan, though? He looked back over his shoulder, searching for her. After a moment, he detected movement.

He put his hand on Rob's arm and nodded his head in that direction. He put his rifle to his shoulder and stepped to the side, scanning the area behind them.

Susan stuck her head around a tree and then darted behind another one.

Luis furrowed his brow. He'd told her to stay outside. "I'll be right back." He jogged to her and said under his breath. "I told you to stay back."

Susan nodded and jerked her head in the direction she'd come. "I know, but there are men back there. Coming this way."

Luis looked over her shoulder and frowned. Damn it, he should really take her and run. In about two minutes, they'd be trapped with everyone else in that building, which he did not think was going to be a good thing at all. He frowned back toward the west and then detected another movement. Then another to his right. It was already too late. "Okay, come on and keep your head down."

She nodded, and they returned to the men.

Rob looked at Susan.

She said, "Sorry, but more men are coming from that direction."

He grunted in frustration.

Luis nodded. "It's time to move." He once again studied the area and pointed to a side door on the barn facing them. "Let's make for there. I'll put suppressing fire on that sniper's nest, and you have one of your men do the same on that one. Make sense?"

Rob nodded and motioned his men into a tighter group. "All right, we're making for the barn door. Stay in a tight group," he gestured toward Susan, "keeping the girl in the middle. Al, you concentrate fire there. We're worried there could be a sniper. Luis here will do the same there. Stay sharp and keep your head on a swivel."

The group formed up around Susan. Luis looked down at her and she gave him a weak smile. She really was beautiful. He leaned in closer to her, the ghost of a smile on his lips. "You'll be fine." Then, turning serious, he said, "But keep your head down, and no matter what happens, keep moving forward. No matter what. Got it?"

She swallowed and nodded.

Luis looked up and met eyes with Rob. "Any time."

Rob surveyed his men. "Let's move."

Chapter 99

Frank stared at the ground, his meaty hand gripping his radio as he listened to the action unfold.

"Actual, this is Ten. Five tangos coming through the woods. Repeat, five tangos. They're armed and appear to have at least some military training. No woman visible. They're approaching the tree line opposite the barn. Engaging. Over."

A shot rang out. Then two more. Then another that echoed off the mountains in the distance.

Frank pulled the radio closer to his ear. Silence. "Ten?" Nothing. "Ten, do you copy?" He gritted his teeth and shook his head. It was Mr. Talented. It had to be. He clicked the mic again. "This is Actual. Does anyone have eyes on Ten, and does anyone have eyes on the tangos coming from the west? Over."

"Roger, Actual, this is Fourteen. I'm close to Ten's position. I can check on him."

Frank said, "Solid Copy. Carefully, Fourteen, carefully. Over."

"Copy that, over."

"Actual, this is Eighteen. I can just see the barn door where you think the tangos are heading. Want me to engage? Repeat. Engage tangos at the door? Over."

Frank clicked the mic. "Roger, Eighteen. Engage, over." He continued pacing.

A volley of gunfire echoed through the air.

"Actual, this is Fourteen. Ten is gone. Repeat. Ten is KIA. Over."

Frank closed his eyes. "Solid copy, Fourteen." Frank pulled out his cigar and ran a hand over his mouth. "Fourteen, are any tangos still visible? Over."

"This is Fourteen, no one else visible. I cannot get any better look without being exposed. Repeat. No clear line of sight. Over."

"Solid copy. Fourteen, stay put and look for targets of opportunity. Over." If they could just get them into the barn. Better to have his enemy all in one place rather than moving around causing havoc, which he was sure Mr. Talented could do.

"Actual, this is Eighteen. I'm moving in their direction, behind good cover. Over."

Damn it, they'd been two minutes away from taking the damn place clean. Now the enemy was barricaded, and this just got way more complicated. Frank lifted his radio. "Roger, Eighteen. All units, this is Actual. Make sure that all hostiles are in a building. Ensure no one is outside. Repeat. Corral all tangos into the barn or house. Over." He scratched at the scar on his neck and clicked the mic again. "Actual to Seven, what's the sitrep in the woods?"

"Actual, this is Seven. No sign of a woman or any other tangos in the woods. Repeat, no tangos in the woods. We went through a hole they cut in the fence and are now about halfway to the barn. Do you want us to keep going? Over."

Frank frowned. He always preferred to keep a few men in reserve. "Seven, two of you hold tight and make sure no one escapes that way. And Two, flush all tangos to the barn. Repeat. Two, flush tangos inside. Over."

"Solid copy, Actual. Seven out."

"This is Eleven. I see movement at the tree line. Over."

"This is Twelve. I see them from up here on the rise. Over."

Frank narrowed his eyes. This was the chance he'd been waiting for. It was time to kill one of these bastards.

Chapter 100

Eddie looked down his nose at Burk, who sat slumped in his seat. "Still nothing from the ranch?"

Burk shook his head. "Not by cell, text, or email." He looked up at Eddie. "I even called the police station in Hawley, but I couldn't get in touch with them, either."

Eddie grabbed his shoulder. "We'll just have to wait and see. My man is with them, and he'll be a big help. They just need to make it until we get there. Let's just make sure we're ready when we do."

Burk nodded.

Eddie turned back and frowned down at the blueprint where they'd marked all the likely placements of Treleous' men. "Assuming we have a reasonable sense of the force that they have, that's how I'd have them laid out if it was me."

Moe furrowed his brow and nodded.

Eddie glanced over at Loren. This was not good. It was a large area, and the enemy's troops were certainly more skilled than Burk's soldiers. They were outnumbered, out skilled, had no good communications with people inside, and the bad guys had to at least suspect that they were coming.

Moe said, "The one cool thing is that we should have people on both the inside and the outside, forcing them to fight on two fronts."

Loren shrugged. "True, but we have no way to coordinate with anyone on the inside and no sense of where they are in the building. Hopefully, we can call Luis on the satellite phone, but he can't give us continuous intel during the fight. We're liable to shoot each other like this."

Eddie added, "And we have no way to approach in stealth. They'll see us coming."

Moe sat back. "Okay, you're right. It really is a crap taco, isn't it?"

Eddie glanced up at Burk. "Will the people in the town help?"

He nodded. "I think so, but they're untrained and undisciplined and would probably do more harm than good."

Eddie rubbed his chin. "You're probably right, but maybe we don't need them to do that much. They could just keep their eyes open, help," he shrugged. "Maybe create some sort of distraction?"

Burk nodded slowly. "Yeah, I see where you're going. We're going to need all the help we can get. I'll call the bartender in town when we get closer. He's kind of like their unofficial leader."

Eddie pointed at the dirt road leading out of the rear of the compound. "This is still our best bet. Somehow, we create a diversion, maybe with the help of the people in town, coming in here from the west with one team, while a second gets the people and gets them out of Dodge along that dirt road to the east."

Burk asked, "In what vehicle?"

"That's just one of many problems we don't have an answer for yet."

Moe said, "Even if you're able to do that in whatever vehicle you dream up—that's a long assed road with no way to get off it for a while. They can mosquito you the whole way." He shrugged. "Maybe even race down the highway ahead of you and lay a trap."

Loren leaned back. "And all of this will be in the dark, in territory that we've never seen in the daylight, much less scouted."

Moe scowled. "This is bumming me out. I need a positive point to balance my brain, man. I mean, like now."

Eddie stared at the plans. "We might have one ace in our hand."

They all looked up at him.

Loren asked, "Luis?"

Eddie grinned. "No, Luis is the wild card. We just have to hope that they want what's in the warehouse more than they want us." He glanced over at Burk. "Sorry about that."

He shrugged. "The only real protection it had was secrecy, and that's already blown."

Loren sighed. "Then let's all hope that they want what's in there pretty bad."

More furrowed his brow. "What's the ace, then?"

Eddie grinned. "Jeff."

Chapter 101

Luis put a round into the possible sniper's nest as the group broke the tree line and made for the barn. Then, after a beat, another, and yet another, as they crossed the area. Ten, nine, eight. He noticed movement by an outbuilding and shot a round there for good measure. Seven.

They made it to the door, and Luis and two of the other men turned and faced out.

Rob banged on the door twice. "It's Rob, don't shoot me!" As soon as it opened, he ushered Susan inside.

Luis followed them through the opening and came to a stop. The massive open-air building was cool—almost cold. Skylights dotted the ceiling, and emergency lights spaced along the inside were the only illumination.

The dim interior was open, with three rows running the length of the building. The one closest to Luis was a line of hundreds of beige file cabinets sitting next to one another, stretching off into the distance. There had to be two hundred of them in that row alone. The next was the same. What the hell? This had to be the cache of Mendelson's work that everyone was after. What else could it be?

The third row was a long rack with computers, side by side, green and red lights shining and blinking. How did this still have power?

Luis looked from the file cabinets and computer servers to Susan.

Her eyes were wide, but she just shrugged. "I don't know what I expected, but wow."

"I know."

A red-haired man in fatigues jogged over, with two soldiers behind him. He shook Rob's hand vigorously. "Sarge. It's good to see you."

Rob grabbed his shoulder affectionally. "You, too. Mike, meet Luis and Susan. They're here to help."

He raised an eyebrow at Rob but shook their hands as well. "Good, we're going to need it."

Luis looked over the cabinets and computers as they crossed the barn to a pair of glass walled offices. He leaned down to Rob, glanced once around himself and then said, "I need some ammo."

Rob's eyes darted to the objects, but he didn't comment on the barn's contents. He said to of the men, "Go get this man some ammo."

The man nodded and jogged away.

Rob turned back to Mike. "What's the sitrep?"

Mike's smile faded. He darted a glance at Luis. "Ed's dead and Freddie took a slug to the thigh, he's in pretty bad shape. Big and Little Tony and Adam are all stuck in the house. We can talk to them on the handhelds. I've got a man at every entrance and," he pointed up at the corners, "one at each roof vent. We're in a bad way, Sarge. We're trapped, or effectively surrounded. Every time we try a door or a window, someone shoots us back inside."

Rob gestured to the remaining men he brought with him. "Send them wherever you need reinforcements."

Mike stepped over and directed the men to their posts.

Luis craned his head around, noticing a catwalk near the ceiling going the length of the building along the ridgeline. If he was assaulting this place, now would be a good time to attack, when lookouts would turn to greet the new arrivals. Luis turned to Susan. "You still have the pistol I gave you?"

She nodded, pulling it from her waistband.

He pointed. "Go stay by those offices, with your pistol out and ready."

She nodded and jogged over. He turned to Mike and Rob. "Get on that radio and tell everyone to stay sharp. We're vulnerable right now."

Rob nodded and took the handset.

Luis turned to Mike. "Let's look at your setup."

He nodded and led them across the barn and down the long aisle of servers and computer equipment.

Luis's attention took in everything as they walked, categorizing both assets and liabilities.

Rob spoke into the radio as he followed, telling them that Luis was here to help and for everyone to stay sharp.

Luis pulled his satellite phone from his pack. "Let me check in and see how far away our help is."

Chapter 102

Frank paced back and forth outside the command trailer. He missed being in the action, but liked the control that came with this role. Moving the pieces around the chessboard, adjusting to the action.

"This is Eight—"

The sound of gunfire cut him off. Steady continuous fire.

Frank squeezed the radio and waited. He wanted desperately to ask what was going on, but his men needed to stay focused on the fight.

"Actual, this is Thirteen. Over."

"Go ahead, Thirteen. Over."

"Tangos firing on Eight and Twelve as cover. Repeat, chasing snipers down while they move. Over."

Frank resisted a surging impulse to throw the radio against the trailer. "Solid copy, Thirteen. Over." It was Mr. Talented. It had to be.

"This is Eight. I'm good, but tangos made it to the building. Repeat. Tangos in building, over."

Frank clicked the mic. "Roger, Eight, solid copy. Twelve, what's your sitrep. Over."

"This is Twelve, I'm good. That son of a bitch is a meat eater, for sure. Over."

Frank nodded. No shit, a snake eater would be his guess.

He flinched as another surge of anger bubbled up inside him. He could not believe that his smash and grab plans had gone to hell. Now he had a damned siege situation, which always sucked. He scratched the puckered scar on his neck. At least he had them in one place, where he could control them. He could dictate the action, which Frank always preferred.

He strode over to the map spread out on the hood of a truck and studied it. Now he could tighten the circle by moving to secure locations closer in. He traced these with his finger. Yeah, that was good. With them all inside, he had options.

He only had two worries still snagging on his thoughts. One was Tom, the man they'd nabbed. Presumably, he was still alive and being held somewhere inside. Frank was convinced that if they were going to kill him, they'd have left the body as a message. So where was he? How would they rescue him? If this all went to hell, he could just set these buildings on fire and force everyone out into the open. Mow them down like rats. But that would mean sacrificing Tom, so he would leave that to the last possible moment. Also, Gemini would not like that. He really wanted whatever was in that building. Frank spat. He hated limitations and rules of engagement.

The third thing worrying him was Mr. Talented's friends. Where were they? Gemini told him that the FBI had arrested one of them. What was his name—Eddie, that was it. Was that slowing them down? If so, it wouldn't last forever.

He lifted his radio. "This is Actual. Reinforcements could come to help the hostiles at any time now." He hesitated. No, he had to keep moving forward. "All teams, prepare to move to your second position closer in. Repeat, Position Two. It's time to tighten the net. Over."

The sun was just disappearing behind the mountains as Frank frowned at the map. The whole situation was a mess. Which was costing him time, and this all needed to be over by morning. Ultimately, people were going to ask questions. And their reinforcements would be here, eventually. He knew that much about these bastards, at least. They would come. The only question was, how would they get here?

He'd recalled the three reserve soldiers from the back gate once all the tangos were in the building. He turned to them. "Listen up. Pogue, you go into town and keep an eye. I want to make sure the villagers aren't getting restless. Make sure no one's thinking of investigating the gunfire."

He nodded and trotted off.

"Trammel, go back to the airport. That's probably where the help will come from. Keep your eyes peeled and let me know as soon as they arrive."

He also nodded and left.

Frank nodded. That made the situation a little better now. He would not get caught flatfooted again.

Chapter 103

Luis frowned at the satellite phone. No answer from Eddie or Loren. He hoped that meant they were in the air and on their way.

He studied the barn's outside walls. Normal studs and drywall on the inside with one-by slats on the outside. None of that would even stop a pistol bullet, much less a sniper rifle. Suddenly, he stopped and grabbed Mike's arm. "Hey, is it always cold like this in here, or are the heaters just off with the power?"

Rob shook his head. "No, actually, it's kind of warm right now. We keep it really cold," he gestured to the rack, "because of the computers and stuff."

"So then these walls are insulated?"

Rob nodded and gave him a quizzical look.

Luis returned to walking. "If the walls are thin like maybe normal with this kind of building, you can sometimes see the studs and internal structure on a thermal scope. I've seen the hot-water pipes in an apartment wall like that before. These insulated walls should help." He gave him a rueful smile. "I'm looking for any advantage I can get."

Rob nodded. "Okay, Mike, tell us what we got going on here."

Mike pointed and spoke mostly to Luis. "There's a door at each corner, and one in the middle of this side wall facing the house. I've got a man at each one with the door cracked, so they can see anyone coming." He gestured to a catwalk overhead. "There's an opening to the roof at either end, and I have a man with a rifle in each."

Not bad. It was a crappy situation. The number of egress points spread the team too thin. He didn't really see any better choices than the current layout, though.

Luis studied the surrounding area as best he could through the door cracks. He didn't detect any movement, so at least for the moment, the enemies' plan wasn't immediately breaching the barn. Probably because they had no intel on the interior. No point rushing in blind when you held all the situational advantages.

At each stop, he studied the men. They were in a decent position, and looked calm and focused, which was good, but they clearly weren't used to combat, and he could see the fatigue in their eyes.

The three men walked back to the office. Susan stood up and joined them.

A tall, willowy man in a flannel shirt and wire-rimmed glasses sat at a terminal typing. He was pale and sweating, and appeared like he could come apart at any minute.

Rob put a calming hand on his shoulder. "What's the story, Randy?"

The man swallowed. "We've got no power, both external generators are down, no connectivity, no phone lines, no nothing."

Luis asked, "Then how are the servers still running?"

Randy glanced up at him. "Because we have the baddest UPS in the world." He noted Luis' confused expression and added, "Uninterrupted power source." He pointed off to his right. "That's what's in those racks at the end. Lots of batteries." He glanced at his watch. "We've got maybe twenty-seven more minutes before they're dry."

A soldier ran up and handed Luis ammo.

He nodded his thanks.

Susan took one of the boxes, opened it, and extended her other hand out towards Luis.

He studied her for a second and then popped out the magazine and handed it to her, the ghost of a smile on his lips.

She began to thumb in rounds.

Luis turned back to Randy. "But you can't communicate using the backup power?"

Randy shook his head. "I mean, we could, but we're not connected to anything. The outage is outside the ranch. Probably at the trunk in town."

Susan pointed. "Who's that?"

They all followed her finger to a man seated in a chair, hands and feet bound.

Rob sighed. "That was one of the men who chased you out of town."

Luis frowned at him. So this was one of Treleous' goons. He was short and broad, with thick arms and legs, and only a patch of short black hair over each ear.

The man said in a low, confident tone, "That's right. My people are going to kill every last one of you if you don't let me go right now."

Luis raised an eyebrow, turned his back on the man and said into Rob's ear. "You grabbed him?"

Rob shrugged. "We didn't know what else to do. We chased him out of town with the others, and I guess his truck broke." He sighed. "So we cuffed him but left his radio in the truck."

A creased formed in Luis' forehead. "Why?"

"Because we don't really know how to handle a situation like this."

Luis nodded, squeezed his shoulder, and turned to Randy. "So we have no way to communicate with the outside world, not even through the cloud or something?"

Randy gave him a withering look. "Sure, but how do I talk through the cloud without connecting to it?"

Luis smiled. It was a fair point. He unbuckled his pack. "Let me try my friends again." Down the way, he noticed a man in jeans and a flannel shirt sitting on the floor beside a woman in an old-fashioned light blue dress. She had her head in her hands and was quietly sobbing.

He shrugged off his pack, and glanced over at the prisoner, then jerked his head for Rob to follow him. They walked a few steps away, and he asked, "How many men do you have?"

Rob said, "You mean soldiers?"

Luis rolled his eyes. "Yes. I'm not counting Randy or the couple down there."

"Still able to fight? I don't know. I think ten now, including the men in the house."

Luis guessed Treleous had at least twice that, all hardened soldiers. Plus, they had Mohawk. This was not good. "How experienced?"

Rob shrugged. "They're all ex-military, but they have little combat experience. Those guys end up at Blackwater, places like that, not on guard duty in Montana."

Luis nodded and pulled out the satellite phone. "Trained but not tested."

Rob nodded.

Luis glanced around the room. He believed Treleous wanted something that was in this warehouse. Why else would they have put more resources into capturing it than him and Susan? That was good. It meant that they wouldn't just burn the place to the ground, which bought him some time, but not much.

Rob glanced at the phone. "Who do you keep calling?"

"Some friends of mine. Why, do you have someone you could call?"

Rob shrugged. "Yes, but they're a long way away."

Luis frowned. "Let's hope mine are getting close."

Part 5

Chapter 104

The pilot had just announced they were on final approach when Eddie's phone rang. He glanced down at the screen. It was Luis. Thank God.

Burk looked over, eyebrows raised.

Eddie said, "It's our man in Montana, on his satellite phone." He answered on speaker. "Luis, how are you and Susan?"

Luis snorted. "Not so good. We're at the ranch and the place is under siege. Treleous has us surrounded and has cut our power and comms. We need help soon."

Eddie looked up. "We're on final, but we still need to get to you."

Burk leaned forward, eyebrows raised, and Eddie gave him a go-ahead gesture.

"This is Burk. I work with the people at the ranch. Who are you there with?"

Loren leaned in, her brow furrowed.

They heard sounds of Luis fumbling with the phone, and then Luis said, "I have it on speaker. I'm here with Rob."

Rob's voice came over the line. "What's up, boss? Glad you're in the loop."

"I am. Hang tight, Rob, we're coming." Burk looked over at Eddie, his brow furrowed.

Eddie glanced at his watch. "How long can you last?"

Luis sighed. "As long as we have to, I guess. But hurry. I think we're on borrowed time. Let me go, I've got to save juice on the phone, I've got no way to charge it. I'll call you in thirty and see where you're at."

Eddie replied, "10-4. Hang in there."

"We will." Luis hung up.

Burk furrowed his brow, and a sadness crept into his eyes. "I haven't told you everything. I'm sorry, I didn't know if I could trust you, and now—well, things are looking a little grim. I feel like I owe you this, at least."

Eddie's attention was riveted to him, and Loren and Moe leaned in.

"Part of the purpose of the ranch, or I guess I should say part of the original intent, was to be a mechanism for getting people out secretly and into hiding." He held up his hand. "I don't know who, so don't bother asking me." He shrugged. "We named it the Arrowhead Protocol for whatever reason, I never knew why. The contact would call the pipe shop just like you figured out, and we would set up a meeting in Beaver Ruin and make them disappear. We only used it once." He looked down. "It was Susan's father." He met Eddie's eyes. "Actually, from what I understand, he helped set it up, did a dry run, things like that. When he used it himself, I wasn't involved after the meet. I don't know what happened to him after that. Or even if he made it or is still even alive." He looked over at Loren and Moe. "I'm sorry. That's all I can tell you."

Chapter 105

Luis hung up and turned to Rob. "Okay, we've got to make it for a couple of hours. What are our resources?"

"For starters, thank goodness we're in here. All the guns and ammo are stored back there." He pointed toward a closet in the rear.

Luis nodded. "What about the three men at the house? Can we get them over here? We're going to need all the help we can get."

Rob turned to Mike. "You said we can talk to them?"

Mike nodded and handed over a handheld radio. "Rob to Team Fire. Come in, Team. Over."

Luis frowned. "Team Fire?"

Rob shook his head. "You don't know the half of it. The man who hired us wanted us to be Team Pfeilspitze."

Luis' eyebrows shot up. "What the hell is that?"

Susan said almost to herself, "It's German for arrowhead."

Rob and Luis turned to look at her.

She shrugged and looked away. "What? I know stuff."

Rob turned back to Luis. "So, I shortened it to Fire."

"Fair enough."

The radio crackled. "This is Big Tony. Glad you're okay, Sarge. Over."

Rob looked over at Mike. "These are encrypted, right?"

Mike nodded.

Rob continued, "10-4, Tony. What's your sitrep? Over."

"Pinned down, but okay. You in the barn? Over."

"10-4. Maybe you should join us. Over."

"I'm game, Rob, but we're hemmed in by three shooters. Repeat, three shooters. The worst is up where we saw that coyote, over."

Luis raised his eyebrows.

Rob said into the radio, "Solid copy. Hold on, over." To Luis he said, "There's a rise on the east side of the camp. Where you were worried about snipers when we ran over here."

"There's a lot of ground between us and them. Okay, tell them to hold tight."

Rob clicked the mic. "Hang tight, we're working on a plan. Over."

"Solid copy. Over and out."

Luis said. "That sounds like someone who's used a radio in a combat zone."

Rob nodded. "Big Tony is my best soldier."

"Another reason we need to get him over here." He glanced up at the ceiling. "Can you see this rise from up there?"

Rob nodded. "I think so."

"I want to see. How do I get up there?"

Mike said, "I'll show him."

Luis held up a finger. He had just squatted down in front of Susan to tell her he'd be right back when he froze.

Susan sat looking at the floor. A tear brimmed at the edge of her eye, threatening to spill down her cheek. He kneeled in front of her. "What?"

She shook her head quickly and wiped her eyes. "I'm fine." She looked up at him and then shrugged. "I just thought that something inside would be connected to my dad." She shook her head slowly. "This is all just a lot."

Luis hesitated, unsure what to do, and then took her into his arms again.

She fell into them, holding on tight and sobbing into his shoulder a few times, before pushing back. She took a deep breath and nodded. "I'm okay now, thanks. I just needed a moment."

Luis' attention lingered on her face.

She leaned forward and kissed him clumsily, then looked away. "For luck or whatever." Her eyes darted back to him.

Luis grinned. "Thanks, I'll take all the luck I can get." He winked at her. He really did like this girl. "I'll be back in a moment." Standing, he said, "Let's go."

Mike led him to the back of the barn.

Once again, he couldn't help but compare Susan to Ellen back when he first met Eddie. That was the first time he'd laid eyes on Eddie Mason. From the window of the empty apartment, Luis saw him ease into the wine store. It was as clear now as if it was yesterday.

Looking across the street at the liquor store, he whispered over his shoulder, "Ellen, how are you supposed to know your contact again?"

She leaned over his shoulder and looked out the window. "He's supposed to have a red bandana." He could see the shadows of someone inside the shop already. The big man from earlier waiting in the front. Then he spotted another figure in the rear slowing working their way forward. If this was their contact, then he was their only way home, and he was now walking into a trap. Luis had to protect him, but he was a long way from the target on a downward angle. With a pistol. And limited ammo. Luis snorted. "I still can't believe you chose that as your identifier."

She scowled at him. "It's perfect. How likely is it that someone else is going to be wearing one?" She squinted down at the figure in the shop's rear. "He doesn't have it."

Luis chuckled and pointed. "Yes, he does. He's got it wrapped around his right fist."

She leaned forward and nodded. "Oh, yeah. Why isn't he wearing it? You sure it's him?"

Luis nodded. "He's being very sly about it, but he's checking out the meeting place. He's one cool customer."

Ellen covered her mouth with one perfectly manicured hand and said under her breath, "He's walking into our trap. That big man is going to kill him."

Suddenly, the flabby man in the black suit walked across the front window of the wine store. Heading for the contact. In one fluid motion, Luis leaned out the window, lifted his pistol, and fired two shots. The big man spun and full backwards into a rack of wine bottles.

The reports echoed in the quiet early morning street.

Ellen grabbed his arm, her brown eyes wide, but she was a trained professional and there was no panic in her.

From this hidden position, no one could have seen him take the shot, and it would take a long time for the police to arrive and then turn their attention to the rooms across from the crime scene. They had time.

"Do you trust this Eddie character?"

"Loren does, and I trust her."

Two men ran up to the store and peered in through the broken window. One walked out into the street and looked down the opposite way from which they'd come.

The second man, however, turned and looked up at the apartment building across the street. He slowly scanned each window.

Luis pulled slowly back, putting a hand on Ellen's arm as he did. "Time to go."

She nodded.

They burst out the back door and ran for the Mercedes. He only had four rounds left. They had to get away, or they were in a world of hurt.

Two men appeared to his right around the far corner of the building.

Luis slid to a stop in front of Ellen's Mercedes.

Another darker car he couldn't see very well picked up more men off to his left. Damn it.

He started the car and screeched out into the open street, the dark vehicle hot on his heels. "Turn on your phone and check for messages. It doesn't matter if they're tracking it now."

She did and then looked up, eyes wide. "I have seventeen messages."

Luis sighed. "Well, we might as well listen."

The first message came over the speaker. "Ellen, this is Loren. The meeting has been compromised. I'll explain later, but be careful. I can't get in touch with Eddie, the man who's supposed to meet you, either. Please call me and tell me you got this."

Each successive message was nearly the same, except Loren's urgency and worry rose with each one.

Luis frowned. "At least it seems we can still trust them." He shrugged. "He obviously wasn't working for them."

Ellen nodded and ran her hands through her thick sable hair and closed her eyes.

Her phone rang.

"This is Eddie. Are you all right?"

Ellen said, "Yes. Are you?"

"I'm fine. Thanks to you, I think. Are they on your tail?"

Luis motioned for her to hand the phone over. "Yeah, we've got one car on our tail and probably another trying to catch up."

"Damn. Which way are you heading?"

Luis ducked and glanced out the windshield. "Northwest. I'm almost to the D603."

Eddie's response was immediate. "No. Stay on the surface streets, but keep going that direction. I'll meet you up where the river turns. I know a place. Keep going if you can."

Luis cut between two cars, grabbed the parking brake, and slid around a corner, gaining some distance on his pursuers. "How far?"

"A few miles. I'll be there. I promise."

Chapter 106

Mack stood up from lacing his boots back up after changing his socks. Number three on his list of things he'd learned in the military. Change your socks and underwear whenever you can. Lessons learned the hard way, and this damn situation looked like it was going to go on for a while.

The sun was just below the horizon and already the air was turning chilly, the stars sprinkled across the sky like sugar.

He walked over to the command trailer.

Frank stood staring down at the map spread out on the truck's hood. "We've got everyone surrounded in the two main buildings." He looked up. "It's time to make our move. Eventually, people will start asking questions. We ready?"

Mack shrugged. "We're in position. The longer we wait, the less focused we'll be. You know how it is."

Frank folded his arms. "Yeah, and their friends are going to show up, eventually."

Mack ground his teeth. That was true. These bastards always seemed to come to each other's rescue. "How would they get here? If they're still in D.C. or Miami, they'd have to come by plane, right?"

"You'd think so. I have Trammel watching it."

Mack frowned at the map. "How many do we think there are again?"

"Most everyone is in this barn. I'm guessing fifteen to twenty with some civilians, and three in the house."

Mack frowned. "The ones in the house, they're all soldiers. The ones in the woods were also trained, but not very experienced or skilled."

Frank nodded. "We've observed the same thing."

Mack shrugged. "So, burn them out."

Frank ducked his head and looked around. "We can't"

Mack spat and shook his head. "Because of Gemini."

Frank said, "He wants whatever's in the building—and bad."

"I know." He hated limitations. "Then let's whittle them down. Why don't we get the three in the house? We've got numbers and then we'd have everyone else in one structure before dark." He shrugged. "Baby steps."

Frank tucked his cigar in the corner of his mouth and spoke around it. "That's not a bad idea."

A prickling sensation raced across Mack's neck. Something was wrong. He could feel it. Like a tug to action pulling on his whole body, it was time to move.

Frank looked up at him and narrowed his eyes. "What is it?"

Mack rubbed his chin. "We've got to strike the house now."

He pulled the cigar out of his mouth and frowned at him. "Why?"

Mack shifted his weight from foot to foot. He knew Frank trusted his instincts. They'd been right in the past. "I got a feeling."

Frank nodded slowly and lifted his radio. "This is Actual. Heads up, boys. It's go-time. Check your areas and let me know if anything seems off. Over." One by one in numerical order, the men checked in all clear.

His two remaining reserves wandered over.

Mack put in his earpiece, grabbed his rifle, and said to them, "We're going to head down this path to the edge of the house, then split." He looked over at Frank. "Who's watching the house?"

Frank glanced at his map and read. "Eleven on the south, Three on the east, and Twelve up high."

Mack turned back and pointed at the first man. "You hook up with Three, help cover us. Dave and I will breach from the front. You mow down any rats we drive outside. Got it?"

The man nodded.

Mack exchanged a nod with Frank, then led the men down the darkening path at a trot. Frank's voice came through his earpiece, "This is Actual. All right, we are Oscar Mike. Repeat. We are Oscar Mike.

Reinforcements are coming your way, so don't shoot them. Twelve, you're our eye in the sky. We are hitting the house. Repeat, we are about to hit the house. Over and out."

Mack held up a fist and stopped the group at the fence line. The only movement was the gentle swaying of the pine trees off to his left. With two fingers, he pointed twice, and one man moved slowly in that direction.

He led the other soldier forward, crouched low, rifle ready until he was twenty-five feet from the house, and stopped. His whole body was thrumming now. His skin was on fire, his very nature driving him to action.

Mack put his finger back on the trigger. Go-time.

Chapter 107

Luis climbed the ladder and stepped out onto the catwalk. There was a dormer and a small window built into the gable at either end. The roof design was for Montana winters, with a very high peak and a steep slope on either side.

A lone soldier stood leaning against the wall, his head tilted so he could see out the window.

He straightened at Luis' arrival.

Luis asked, "Anything?"

The man shook his head.

Luis leaned down and looked out. "Can you see the spot where the coyote was?"

The man smirked. "Barely." He pointed. "It's right there."

Luis lifted his binoculars and studied the spot. He waited and then noticed just a slight movement. The barrel of a rifle, he bet. He glanced down at the man's Remington 30.06. "Are all the rifles here like that?"

He nodded. "Yeah. We mostly use them for hunting."

Luis patted it. "It'll do just fine." He leaned down and looked again. They needed to do this before it was too dark. "Stay alert. We're going to make a move here soon. When we do, I need you to shoot there, keeping that sniper down. You need to cover the men coming over from the house. Got it?"

The man nodded.

Luis thanked him and climbed back down, then returned to Rob, who stood with Susan and Mike. "I think we can drive the sniper up on the rise back long enough for them to get across, but he said there are three shooters."

Rob lifted the radio. "Rob to Big Tony, come in. Over."

"This is Tony, go ahead, Rob."

"I'm going to put a friend on the line." He handed over the radio.

Luis clicked the mic. "Hey, Tony, I think we can distract the sniper. What else do you need to make it over here? Over."

"There's at least one other at ground level on that side. Maybe someone at the barn door can help keep them down. Over."

Luis replied, "Solid copy. I don't like us being split up, and I'd like to bring you over here before full dark. What do you think? Over."

"Agreed. It's either we try to get out, or they try to get in. Over."

Luis looked over at Rob and Mike, who both nodded.

"Okay, Tony, are you ready? Repeat, can you go in a minute or so? Over."

"10-4. How do you want to coordinate? Over."

Luis turned to Rob. "Tell the man up top, when he's ready, start shooting into that rise there. In a steady rhythm like boom, boom. Just to keep the sniper down. Got it?"

Rob nodded.

"That'll be our signal." Luis lifted the radio. "Tony, this is Luis. Stand by. When we put some fire on the rise, that's your signal to move. Copy? Over."

"Solid copy, Luis. We're ready. Over and out."

Chapter 108

Loren leaned back and examined their list of issues. She shook her head. They were short on options, resources, time, and hope at the moment. Reading aloud, she said, "Okay, so we've agreed that the pilot will drop us off, then immediately take off for Billings and wait there until we tell him where to pick us up."

Eddie nodded. "If we make it out on that dirt road as far as 191, there's no place else for him to go, really. If we get out, we'll have to meet him at Billings."

Burk sighed. "It's at least two hours to get there on a road like that."

Eddie said, "Yeah, but if we make it that far, hopefully they won't be hot on our heels."

Moe said, "It all goes back to Eddie's comment earlier. If they really want what's in that barn, then they won't want a bunch of resources further and further away from it. It really is the only ace we have."

Loren returned to her list. "We need a vehicle that can make it over tough terrain and hopefully carry close to twenty people. In reality, that's got to be at least two vehicles that can cover rough ground."

Moe sat forward. "Maybe tweak the plan a bit. If they really are that interested in the barn, then we should split everyone up. Get the principals and less capable people out in whatever vehicle we can get, and then the rest of us scatter." He folded his arms. "If they won't like chasing a truck a long way from the barn, they won't like chasing after rats scattering out into the night."

Loren looked at Eddie. Rats? It was a good idea, though.

Burk frowned at him. "You willing to be one of those people?"

Moe leered at him. "Of course. They don't want to come after me in the dark, I promise you that. Your men from the ranch should run, too. They know the area, probably better than these jokers waiting for us." He counted on his fingers, "That leaves you, Eddie, Loren, Luis, Susan, the maid, the maintenance man, and the computer dude. So that's only nine?"

Burk asked, "So why don't we all just scatter, then?"

Eddie was starting at the blueprints as he spoke. "Because the civilians will never make it."

Moe nodded. "A lion will leave his lunch if a rat scampers too close by."

Rats again? What the hell did that mean? They all stared at him a moment before Eddie turned to Burk's men. "Can you all find a way to safety?"

After a moment, they nodded.

Burk said, "The easiest landmark will be the Martinez farm. They have a big red barn up on the hill. You can't miss it."

Eddie said, "The big red barn it is, then."

Loren rolled her eyes. "So that means we only need to find a ten-passenger vehicle that can go over rough ground as soon as we land, and we still don't have an idea for a good distraction."

The group was silent for a moment, digesting the enormity of their situation.

Loren felt the plane begin to descend. As everyone started collecting their gear, Eddie turned to Moe. "So. What's your story, and why are you helping us?"

The Agency man shrugged. "It's my job. I do freelance stuff, mostly for Craig."

Eddie asked, "So, what's your background?"

"This and that."

Loren narrowed her eyes. "And Craig has enough work like that to keep you busy?"

Moe pursed his lips and nodded. "The CIA can't do any official work domestically and," he hesitated. "You know how it is. Presidents come and go, political tides change, it can create a lot of chaos. So parts of the

Company live outside the books, know what I mean? That's where I come in."

Loren frowned. Outside the books? Did he mean off budget? Some sort of independently funded black ops? She looked over at Eddie. How much could they trust this guy? Once again, it was clear that Craig was playing his own game.

Chapter 109

Luis eased the door open a crack, hoping the slow movement was not obvious to the men watching in the near darkness. He'd once again fitted his AR with his thermal scope and panned around as much as the space would allow.

He could see a brief flash of white now and then on the rise. At the far corner of the house, he could glimpse the heat halo of someone just out of sight.

His fingertips vibrated. It was time. Come on, get going. The feeling intensified. They had to act now. He couldn't wait any longer and he was just about to move on his own when a shot sounded above him, followed by another.

Luis pushed the door open and stepped outside. Rolling his eye to the scope, he put two rounds in the corner with the haloed figure behind it.

The side door to the house banged open. Luis could see the brightly silhouetted figures of three men hunched down and running in his direction.

Then, just beyond them in the house, he saw two figures behind them moving fast. Luis yelled, "Run!" as he fired one shot. He could make out the shape of the ridge along with one of their heads. Mohawk! Stepping further away from the building, he fired. Another movement caught his attention, and he ducked. Pivoting right, he fired twice at that corner of the house again. To keep the other men flanking him, he dropped and rolled, coming up rifle ready and chased them back behind that corner with another round.

The first of Rob's men made it to the barn and dove inside.

Luis swiveled back to the house, backpedaling but keeping his attention on the door. A figure darted its head out and Luis fired again, driving it back.

The second man made it to the barn.

Luis slid in that direction, looking to follow the last man in, his rifle trained on the house.

Mohawk popped up in a different window to the far left.

Luis crouched and whirled in that direction.

Mohawk fired, and the last man's head snapped back as he crumpled to the ground.

Chapter 110

Mack sidestepped out of the room, still looking down his sight at the barn beyond the window. He estimated the enemy had eighteen soldiers. Make that seventeen now.

He should have gotten two of them, but Mr. Talented was a worthy opponent. If Mack hadn't thrown himself to the side after the kill, Mr. Talented's return fire would have hit him. He grinned. Now was the fun part. He touched his throat mic. "This is One to Actual. One tango is down, the rest are all in the barn now. Repeat. All tangos now in the barn. Over."

"Solid copy One. All first units should be in the second position. Tighten the noose around the barn. Actual over and out."

Mack continued into the dark kitchen, looking through his thermal scope at the other structure. The power was off, but he could see fuzzy blobs of heat through the walls. Too hot to be people. Electronics next to the wall, maybe. Did they have another power source?

His earpiece cracked. "Actual, this is Twelve, over."

"Go ahead, Twelve."

Mack stopped, putting his hand to the ear.

"When the tangos ran for barn, I could not engage because I was taking fire from the ridgeline of the barn. Repeat, my position is compromised. Do you want to relocate? Over."

Mack leaned down to look out the window at the barn's roofline. They may have chased twelve down so the people could cross, but in doing so, they gave away their position.

Frank's voice came over the radio. "Negative, Twelve. Stay put, but keep your head down. Actual to One, come in. Over."

"This is One. Go ahead."

"What's your twenty? Over."

Mack stepped closer to the window, studying the top of the barn. "I'm in the house. Over."

"Are you in a position to engage their sniper position? Repeat, can you engage in enemy position? Over."

Mack leaned down. He put his thermal scope up to his eye and he could just make out the halo of a heat source just inside an opening there. Maybe a window. "10-4 Actual. If Twelve and I hit it at the same time, we have a good chance. Repeat. High confidence if we both engage. Over."

Mack settled the stock tighter against his shoulder and adjusted his neck.

"This is Actual, engage when ready. Repeat, engage when ready. Over and out."

Chapter 111

Luis stood next to Rob, staring at the still form lying on the ground not fifteen feet from the door.

Big Tony, one of the two men to make it across safely, looked over his shoulder. "You sure he's gone?"

Luis sighed and nodded. "He hit him in the head. That Mohawk bastard doesn't miss. Who was it?"

Tony turned away. "Adam."

He really was big, with broad shoulders, a thick neck, and a black buzz cut. The other man, Luis deduced, was Little Tony. He was a good-sized man as well and would only be called little when compared to his friend. He shook his head. "Sorry about that."

Big Tony gripped his shoulder in a massive fist. "Don't be. They were obviously coming for us. Without your help, we'd all be done."

Rob added, "At least we're all together."

Luis sighed. "And surrounded. They'll tighten the noose on us now for sure."

Little Tony asked, "Is any help coming?"

Luis nodded and glanced at his watch. "Yes, but we're not sure when it'll get here. Probably at least another hour."

Big Tony sighed. "Well, that sucks." He waved a hand at the computers and file cabinets. "I figure the guys out there are here for this." He focused on Luis and Susan. "What brings you here?"

Luis jerked a thumb at Susan. "We came here looking for her father."

Big Tony frowned at her. "Who's your father?"

A crease formed at the top of her nose. "Benjamin Leonette."

No flicker of recognition crossed his face. "Never heard of him. Why you'd think he'd be here?"

Luis shrugged. "We had some intel—maybe bad intel—that he was here. Or that you'd at least know where he was."

Little Tony said to Rob, "I'd be really concerned that his source knew about this place, but I guess the party outside makes all that moot." He glanced back at Luis. "Did they follow you here?"

Rob shook his head. "No, the people outside were here first. They want this stuff," he pointed at Luis and Susan, "and them, too. We can figure all that out later. You two come with me and let's get you plugged into our defenses."

The group walked off.

Luis leaned against the wall and then slowly slid down it until he was sitting on the ground beside Susan.

She took his hand and leaned her head on his shoulder. "We're pretty well screwed, aren't we?"

He put an arm around her. "We just need to hold on until help arrives."

Gunfire erupted again.

Luis leapt to his feet, rifle ready, tracking the sound. It came from overhead on the catwalk. He started running in that direction.

Big Tony and Rob appeared from the opposite end.

Luis called out as he ran by, "Pay attention to the egress points. This could be a distraction."

Big Tony nodded and headed in the other direction. "Roger."

Luis checked each door at the end before hustling up the ladder and jumping onto the grating.

The soldier stationed here lay motionless on the ground, his blood-stained body in a crumpled heap.

Luis turned and ran down the catwalk toward the other end, screaming, "Down, get down! You're next!"

The man dropped just as bullets tore through the wood frame of the window. He then commando-crawled to him.

Luis studied the roof line for windows, openings, or any other way for a shooter to see them. Nothing seemed obvious, so he stood and motioned the other man down the ladder.

This group were damned amateurs. Everyone was already exhausted, and they were all going to get killed. He wondered how he could play for more time and plan. This kind of attack inside the United States would not go unnoticed for very long. Treleous needed to end this tonight.

Rob was waiting for him when he reached the bottom of the ladder.

Luis just shook his head.

Rob flinched and closed his eyes for a beat.

"I'm sorry."

Rob looked up, his face drawn. "I can't believe this is happening."

Luis put a little steel in his voice. "Well, it is, so let's get through it."

Rob nodded and then straightened his spine. "They're taking positions closer in. We can see movement, but not enough to take a shot."

Luis's mouth twisted. "Tell them to shoot at movement, anyway. Don't waste ammo, but let's stress *them* out a little for a change."

Rob nodded. "I'll pass the word at the far end. Can you tell the men here?" He handed him a handheld radio. "That the only way we have to communicate is with these. They're point to point, so they still work."

Luis nodded. This sucked. The building was long and wide, which made it hard to defend. He went to the closest corner door. In the pale light, he could see the faces of the two sentries. They looked tense and worried. "What are your names?"

"I'm Bart. He's Dub."

"You boys okay?"

Dub looked over from the door. "I don't see how we get out of this, sir."

Luis grinned. "I work for a living soldier, and it ain't over until it's over."

They nodded and smiled weakly.

He handed them a radio. "If you see movement, take a shot. Even if you aren't confident of hitting anything."

Dub looked sidelong at him. "Like now?"

Luis nodded. "If you see something."

The rifle bucked in the young man's hands.

Their unseen opponent returned two shots, causing the three of them to duck, and immediately the night filled with gunfire.

Chapter 112

Frank sat down and frowned at the black monitors.

Chip looked sidelong at him. "I'm bringing the last drone in. We can't see anything with them anymore, anyway."

"We need to get some drones with night vision or thermal cameras."

"I'll add it to the list."

Mack was convinced that the attack at the ridge window at the barn had taken out a man. In addition, he didn't detect any thermal haze at the window at the other end. They'd probably chased the one at the other end down, as well. So. They'd hurt the enemy and reduced their visibility. Things were moving along nicely.

His radio crackled. "Actual, this is Nine. Come in. Over." Frank didn't like how that voice sounded, and he kicked the trailer door open and bounded down the stairs. He looked at his chart for the man's location—watching the town. He clicked the mic. "Go ahead, Nine."

"Actual, there is a convoy of semis rolling through town in your direction. At least five of them repeat semis inbound to you, over."

Frank narrowed his eyes. Five trucks? From where? He lifted his radio. "Actual to One. Mack, get your ass back to base. Repeat One to base. Over."

Mack sounded petulant, leaving the fun. "Solid copy, Actual. On my way. Over."

Frank could hear them now, rumbling down the road in his direction. He waved to his reserve soldiers to follow and spread out. What was in them? If they were full of troops coming to help, they would have stopped outside of town and distributed the men where they were not so obvious.

Sustained gunfire suddenly rang out from the barn, and Frank ducked and looked back over his shoulder. He clicked the mic. "This is Actual, what's the sitrep?"

"This is Thirteen. Just giving it back to them in kind. Over."

Frank saw the headlights and started walking toward them, pulling his Glock from its holster.

The gunfire came to a stop, and the night was quiet again.

Mack trotted out of the woods and fell into step with him. "What the hell is this?"

"I don't know, but we're about to find out." He said over his shoulder, "Eyes open, boys."

The first truck came to a stop on the main road at the turnoff.

The passenger door opened, and Gemini stepped down.

Mack dropped his head.

Frank let the tension go out of his shoulders. "Pardon me for saying so, sir, but that's a good way to get shot."

Gemini dusted off his hands. "I knew I could depend on your restraint."

Frank scratched at his scar. "This for whatever's in the barn?"

Gemini nodded. "As soon as we're in, we'll start to load out."

He looked down the line of trucks. "This is attracting a lot of attention in the middle of the night."

Gemini nodded. "I agree. So, you had better take this place soon. I want whatever's in that warehouse."

Chapter 113

The plane landed and as it taxied over, Eddie still didn't know what he was going to use as a distraction. Glancing back at the men, he asked Burk, "They going to be okay?"

The big man shrugged. "Most of them don't know the area at all, but they've all had training. Hopefully, they just have to make it until morning, and this will all be over."

Moe snorted. "One way or another."

This was a disaster. They had no chance to reconnoiter the area; it was dark; he had men with little to no combat experience, and they were running out of time.

He exchanged a worried look with Loren, who pursed her lips and asked, "What's the temperature on the ground?"

"A balmy thirty-seven degrees." Eddie raised his voice and addressed the entire plane. "Okay, listen up. You've all been briefed. We just need to cause enough of a distraction until we can get to the people inside. We'll send some kind of signal, I haven't worked out what yet, and then everyone attack them at once. Just to keep their attention while we get the people out and to safety. I know it's late, and this is a crappy situation, but if you push through for a few more hours, it will all be over. Copy that?"

The men nodded.

Eddie continued. "Okay, we'll figure out how to get you to the locations, but once again, Team One, you attack from the south, two from the north, three from the west, and Team Four is our getaway team to the east.

Remember, the plan is to harass them and attract as much attention as possible. Any questions?"

One man in the rear, with hair a little longer than a military cut, raised his hands.

Eddie nodded at him.

He asked with a grin, "We're getting hazard pay for this, right?"

The room filled with a nervous chuckle.

"Count on it."

The aircraft came to a stop and Eddie released the handle, and the stairs folded down to the ground. As he stepped out, he noticed two pairs of people standing twenty feet apart, arms folded, glaring at each other. The two on the right were solidly built men, armed and dressed like soldiers. The two across from them were mammoth men dressed like bikers, also armed, and looked like they knew how to use the weapons.

One of the military men looked over. "You Eddie?"

He continued down the stairs. "I am."

"I'm Hawkins, this is Grant. We owe Craig a favor, so we're here to help."

One biker looked over. "My name's Big Dog, and this is Trent. We owe Jeff a favor, and so we're here to help, too."

Hawkins snorted at the man's name.

The biker looked over. "You got a problem? You want to see why they call me that?"

Eddie reached the bottom. "Cool it. If you're really here to help, then we have a real situation, and not much time to solve it." The rest of Eddie's group assembled behind him.

Moe narrowed his eyes at the second soldier. "Hawkins?"

"Moe? This has to be a low rent operation if you're here."

Moe grinned. "You know it, brother." To Eddie, he said, "These guys know what they're doing. They'll be a big help."

Eddie nodded and turned back to Big Dog. "What's your story?"

He frowned and shifted his weight from foot to foot. "We're in organic farming."

Hawkins rolled his eyes.

Big Dog narrowed his eyes. "It's a cutthroat business."

Eddie held up his hand again. "I've got friends in trouble if you're really here to help. We need it, but we got to get going."

The two sets of men still glared at one another, but nodded.

These were obviously capable men, and they needed all the help they could get, but this was not starting out well at all.

Eddie continued. "All right, listen up. We're in a crappy spot, so pay attention, I'm going to go over our sad little plan as fast as I can, and then we got to get moving."

Chapter 114

Staying low, Luis corralled all the civilians, including Susan, between the two rows of file cabinets to get them some cover. After a brief respite, the men outside began to harass them again as the attackers pressed their advantage and the men at each door pushed back.

Luis said, "Stay low and stay put. Susan, keep your pistol ready." She nodded and met his eyes, so earnest and determined. He leaned in and gave her a quick kiss.

Her eyes flew open wide, and she grinned. Then she gave him a shove. "Go on."

He turned and moved back to the office.

Bullets tore through the walls and whizzed by with a high-pitched whine. Shards of wood and fragments filled the air, and something grazed his cheek, sending a line of pain behind it.

He slid in next to Big Tony at the office window. The house was the closest structure to the barn, and Luis was convinced this was where the vanguard would be. It was close and would provide cover until the moment of attack. Translation—this is where Mohawk would be.

Big Tony rose, panned, and fired twice in quick succession. He growled out the side of his mouth. "We're in the soup here, man. This ain't good."

Luis put his eye to the thermal scope and slowly moved from left to right. He stopped at the far corner of the house. He could just see the halo of a heat signature hiding behind the corner. From the size of the haze, he guessed it was more than one.

He pointed.

The large man swung his rifle around.

The attackers stuck their heads out and Tony and Luis quickly fired, driving them back.

Big Tony gritted his teeth. "They're just toying with us."

Shouting broke out in the far corner. "Attackers! We need help!"

Luis sprinted the length of the building. This was what he'd feared. They were testing the defense, feigning at one spot, and then attacking in numbers somewhere else. He slid to a stop and stuck his rifle through the door with the two sentries here.

The targets were close and trying to get a little closer.

Luis aimed and squeezed the trigger, driving one and then another back behind cover. They were holding their own but not injuring any of the enemy. He aimed and shot again before shouting started at the far corner of the barn.

Chapter 115

The two soldiers and the two bikers frowned at the blueprints when Eddie finished laying out the strategy.

Big Dog arched an eyebrow. "That's not much of a plan."

Eddie nodded. "No, it's not."

He grinned. "I like it. What are we going to do for a diversion?"

Hawkins crossed his arms and flashed a self-satisfied smile. "We've got a little C4 in the truck. If we blow something up, someone's going to notice."

That was a good idea, and certainly better than any idea they'd had before that suggestion.

Hawkins looked over at Big Dog with a "what've you got" expression.

The big biker motioned to his buddy, who jogged around the corner. With a roar, a motor started, and a big World War II 6x6 Army truck drove in and came to a stop.

Big Dog grinned. "We'll handle the escape plan out the back of the compound." He opened the passenger door, then hauled out a broad man in a denim shirt who was hog-tied with thick rope. The captive struggled as Big Dog dumped him unceremoniously onto the tarmac, his protests muffled by the duct tape that covered his mouth.

"I'm pretty sure they know we're coming. This is the spy they sent to warn them of our arrival." He grinned broadly. "He did not complete his mission."

Hawkins resisted a smile for a moment and then broke into a grin. "All right. I can work with you crazy bastards." He gave the biker a fist bump.

Eddie said, "I'm glad we achieved world peace. Let's get moving and kick some ass."

Chapter 116

Luis reconvened with Rob and Big Tony by the offices.

The big man said, "This is not working."

It was true. If they stayed here like this, they were dead. They had no situational advantages. He rubbed his forehead. "We're spread too thin, and we'll never make it until help arrives. We have to change the game."

Rob said, "I'm all ears."

Another volley of gunfire shattered the night.

To encircle the entire barn, Treleous had to be spread pretty thin as well. Could there be a weak spot? Luis asked, "The buildings that surround us, are they evenly distributed?"

Rob frowned. "What do you mean?"

Big Tony shook his head. "No. Most of the buildings are on either side," he pointed east, "but there is only one that way. A shed with a few motorcycles and a snowmobile."

That was something. "What's beyond the building?"

Rob said, "About thirty yards of open ground and then the fence."

Big Tony added, "Beyond that is just a dirt road."

Luis nodded. "Not great, but I'd rather be out there than just waiting in here for them to come get us."

Rob scowled. "It's our job to guard," he hesitated, "what's in here."

Big Tony shot him a look. "This place is burned, Rob." He turned back to Luis. "The real problem is, that side is under the rises with the two snipers."

Luis sighed. That was a problem. If those guys had thermal scopes, they could just pick them off one at a time. Hell, in the time it took them to cut through the gate, they could drop at least a third of the group. He rubbed his forehead. He had to find a way to get outside, where he could fight.

Luis studied the group of civilians huddled between the filing cabinets. There were just too many of them. How was he going to get out of here dragging them all along the way? He turned to Rob. "I think we should move everyone there against the back wall. We're too spread out and the dirt road behind us here is the only way we can escape."

Rob frowned at the rows of cabinets for which he was responsible.

"Look, I know your job is to protect whatever this is, but it's over. We've got to get as many people as possible out of here alive. If we're all together, at least we have numbers."

Rob hesitated before nodding reluctantly. "Okay, you want to bring them back now?"

Luis rubbed his face. "Yeah, let's see if we can build a barricade." He wondered if the enemy would use a grenade, but he didn't think so. Even with a flash, he had to believe they'd be worried about damaging the stuff in here. After all, the contents had to be their goal.

He looked down and met eyes with Susan. A fresh wave of anger surged through him. He would not let them hurt her. Turning back to Rob, he said, "Yeah, let's pull back now."

Would a bullet go through a filing cabinet full of paper? From the front probably not, but from the side, maybe. He glanced at his watch, then pulled out his satellite phone and dialed Eddie.

After three rings, he answered. "How are you doing?"

"Not good. You close?"

"We're probably thirty minutes out still. Sorry. We're getting there as fast as we can."

Luis scowled. That was too long. "It is what it is, man. Just get here as fast as you can."

From behind him, more gunfire erupted, and Luis turned off the phone and brought his rifle up.

Chapter 117

Loren rode with the organic warriors in the big truck, searching for the dirt road at the rear of the compound, while Eddie was off with Moe and the other soldiers to create the diversion.

Big Dog said, "I love this no plan stuff, it's totally my style."

She chuckled and shook her head. "Can this thing get down the dirt road even if it's in awful shape?"

He nodded. "Oh, she'll make it. The question is, how fast? She isn't built for speed, if you know what I mean."

Loren nodded. This plan sucked. They didn't really have a way to coordinate with Luis. It involved too many civilians, and the unknowns were beyond counting. She closed her eyes and prayed that everyone was still alive by the time this ridiculous operation even got going.

Darkness settled over the land as the massive vehicle rumbled along.

She leaned over and looked at the speedometer. Sixty-two miles an hour. She glanced up at Big Dog.

He shrugged. "Slow and steady wins the race."

She raised her eyebrows. "Does it, now?"

His face suddenly turned serious. "We have to believe that's true and hope we get a little help from the man upstairs."

Loren's eyebrows raised. She hadn't expected that from this strange man. He was right, though. She said a little prayer and tried to keep her worries at bay. "How do you know Jeff?"

He glanced over and shrugged. "He knew our lawyer when we were," he hesitated, "doing a different kind of farming. I met him at some lawyer's party, and you know how Jeff is. In like two minutes, he knew my entire life story."

Loren snorted and nodded.

"Anyway, he told us how much money we could make in organic farming. That he knew some people that could set us up."

"Of course he did."

Big Dog grinned. "He was right, too. Especially if you take into account—uh, how much we reduced our overhead. Legal costs and the like. We're in a much better place."

Loren shook her head. "That's Jeff." She glanced at her watch and grimaced. Looking out across the empty dark landscape, she willed the truck to go faster.

Chapter 118

Eddie, Moe, and Burk rode with Hawkins in one of the two black Ford Explorers they'd arrived in. The rest of Burk's team and Hawkins' partner went to its twin. They raced out of the parking lot and headed towards Beaver Ruin.

Hawkins looked sidelong at Eddie. "This plan sucks."

Eddie nodded. "It does. If you've got a better idea, I'm all ears."

Hawkins shook his head. "I'm not saying I have a better one. I just don't like not having a plan, you know? I'm better with a plan."

Eddie shrugged. He needed to alter the way the man was thinking about the mission. To keep him from getting caught up in the process and to stay focused on the objective. "Look at it this way. We have a plan. Blow as much stuff up as you can, shoot everyone who's not a friendly, and draw the enemy off into the night."

Hawkins's mouth slowly broke into a grin.

Moe chimed in from the back seat. "That is a much better sounding plan. I like that version."

Hawkins glanced up at the rear-view mirror. "Me too, Moe. It reminds me of Bogotá."

Moe nodded. "Fun times."

Burk exchanged a look with Eddie, but still had to repress a smile.

Hawkins said to Eddie, "You want to try your man inside again?"

Eddie nodded and dialed the satellite phone. It rang and rang with no answer.

Chapter 119

Frank finished penciling in each team member's new location on his map. Their circle around the barn was nice and tight, and it was time to end this. People were going to notice and eventually come and investigate the gunfire, and they still had to load up whatever was in there and get it out of here.

How long would that take? What if someone showed up before it was done? They would have to at least hide the bodies. He shook his head. No, he had to believe that no one would come until morning, so their only shot was to be out of here by then, and the only way to make that happen was to move now.

He lifted his radio. "This is Actual to Team. Get ready. We are about to pop this pimple. If anyone is black on ammo, get some now. Repeat, we move soon. One, report to base. Over."

A few minutes later, Mack jogged up, a grin on his face. "We ready to rock and roll?"

Frank nodded. "We are, indeed." He turned and gestured to the map. "How do you want to proceed?"

Mack narrowed his eyes. "We've got more resources than they do, so let's use that."

Frank looked over. "Hit them from all sides?"

Mack nodded. "Fast and hard from all sides. Force them back from their positions and get inside."

Frank held his gaze. "Without—"

"I know. Without messing up what's in there. I'm cool."

Frank said, "All right. Let's go kick their ass, then."

Chapter 120

Luis supervised as soldiers used hand trucks to hustle metal cabinets into a rough semicircle two rows deep at the eastern end. They repeated the process against the back wall, creating a semicircular area of protection with a space at each end to enter and exit.

As Luis examined it with a critical eye, his brain kept bringing up comparisons to the Alamo. The last stand at Fort Filing Cabinet. Not an encouraging thought.

Rob and most of the soldiers assembled around him. "Where do you want to put the men?"

Luis frowned and looked over the group. Tired but resolute. That was as good as he could hope for in this situation. "Four at the doors down at this end, and the rest filling the gaps we left here facing the far wall. Hold them at the outside as long as you can, and then give way back to our structure here."

He looked from face to face, ending on Susan and the group of civilians already inside the protective arc. "Our only hope is to escape as soon as they get hold of what's in here. Force them to defend it and retreat outside. But our timing has to be perfect."

One man asked, "What happens once we get outside?"

Luis shrugged. "One problem at a time. We just need to get there," he turned back to the civilians and pointed toward the rear of the property. "And no matter what, once you get outside, keep moving east along the dirt road. Got it?"

Everyone nodded.

Luis clapped his hands. "Then let's get in position."

Rob leaned in and said under his breath, "What do we do if they want us more than what's in here?"

Luis looked sidelong at him, shrugged, and grinned. "Kill as many of them as possible."

Someone yelled, "Here they come!"

Chapter 121

Mack moved down the trail to the front of the barn, his thermal scope to his eye as he swept back and forth. "This is One. I'm approaching the target zone from the southwest. Everyone ready? Two minutes to go. Repeat. Two minutes. All area units check in. Over."

One by one, each member of the team checked in over the radio in numerical order.

The process was an old habit, but a good one. There was always the possibility that there was an unknown bogey, or that Mr. Talented's friends had arrived and taken out a member of the team.

Stopping at the edge of the woods that faced the western end of the barn, Mack panned from one door to the other, then frowned. He wasn't getting any type of glow at all. Like there was no one behind either cracked door. With even just one man, he should see a thermal halo. He changed the settings on the scope. Nothing. All black.

He waited, but no one ducked their head out for a peek, or moved anywhere near the space between the door and the frame. He touched his throat mic. "This is One to Four. Any signs of activity at the side door? Over."

"This is Four. Negative, One, all is black. Over."

Mack scowled and spoke into the radio again. "One to Twelve, any activity at the east end? Any signs of life? Over."

A moment passed, and then he answered. "This is Twelve, One. 10-4. We have signs of at least one tango at the door. Over."

Why down there and not here? What would he do if he was in Mr. Talented's position? That was a good question. The man was in a crappy spot. Mack's answer was the same as it always was—attack. But he wouldn't care about the civilians, and he bet Mr. Talented would. So, pull back? Make some sort of barricade at the far end? Why there? Mack's eyes widened, and he chuckled. Because it was near the dirt road? That was a pipe dream. There was no way they'd be able to escape like that. He grinned. It was a bad plan, but he had to admit that he didn't see a better one.

He clicked his mic again, "This is One. All units, when we crash this place, I want everyone to the east to hold position. Repeat. Eastern units, hold your position. We're going to hit the barn from the west and sides. Call in your understanding. Over."

Again, the units answered in order. This was a good crew. No questions, no push back. No one even asked why.

He glanced at his watch. Game time.

Chapter 122

Luis kept a mental track of where each attack was happening. Where the enemy was probing and where he wasn't. He pivoted and ducked as the enemy stuck machine guns through the door cracks at the far end and sprayed bullets, trying to get a man inside. They were only attacking at the west end now. Nothing at this end for a while. Was that a feint?

Two enemy soldiers slipped through and took up positions behind some of the file cabinets at the far end.

Rob yelled out, "They're inside!"

Luis glanced over his shoulder. No one was attacking at either door here at the east end. Why? They must have guessed this was where their last stand would be.

Moving along the line, he kept repeating, "Only fire at a target. Be smart! Hold them back." At a corner door, he leaned out, scope raised. A bullet drove him back, but not before he picked up one enemy behind an outbuilding. Luis leaned over to the guard. "Only one?"

He nodded. "That's all I see."

Luis looked back at the makeshift barricade. It made sense. If he led a line of civilians into dark, unknown terrain, they would be sitting ducks.

He looked back at the western door as two more enemies slipped through and took up positions behind cover. Luis clapped a man on the shoulder and moved back to the others. It was time to turn the tables a bit. To become the aggressor. The enemy had them backed against a wall, literally, but they were also coming at him down a canyon. A funnel, if you will.

He slid in behind the barrier of file cabinets, settled in, and rolled his eye to the scope.

When one enemy soldier stuck his head out, Luis put a bullet in his forehead, then pivoted and hit another in the shoulder. That should slow them down.

Chapter 123

Eddie's heart hammered in his chest as the seconds drained away like blood from a dying body. He had to get to Luis.

Hawkins pointed ahead to the left. A fire flared up, illuminating the great ball of smoke floating up from it.

"It looks like the people in the little town are helping."

Eddie replied, "If it's them."

"Let me call our man here and find out the situation." He dialed. "It's Burk. Good. Good man. We're two minutes out." He hung up. "Apparently, there's a line of semis near town, and our friends set fire to one of them."

Eddie nodded. He hoped that had drawn the enemy back, rather than forcing them forward. "Let's get ready."

Burk lifted his radio. "Okay, boys and girls, we are coming into town. Remember your assignments and your job. These are much more seasoned warriors than most of you. Your job is to distract and fall away—not to engage. Cause as much irritation as you can and give us time to rescue as many people as possible." He released the button, sighed, and then clicked it again. "Also, remember, at daylight, fall back to the Martinez farm. For those of you who've never been here before, you can't miss it. It's due west of the ranch, with a big red barn up on the mountainside. Good luck."

Hawkins roared down the highway, Beaver Ruin appearing around a bend to the right. At the edge of town, he slammed on his brakes and the SUV slid to a stop.

Eddie was out the door before it came to a complete stop and headed toward the ranch, with Burk close on his heels. He glanced over his shoulder and saw the other men spreading out behind him.

Keeping to the side of the road just inside the tree line, they ran past the town.

Chapter 124

Frank's radio crackled.

"Six to Actual. There is a fire at the rear of the convoy. Repeat. Fire in the convoy. Over."

He kicked the trailer door open and bounded down the stairs. Flames licked up from the trailer of the last truck in the line. He hustled over to the map. Five was covering the town. He clicked the Mic. "Actual to Five. Come in, Five. Over." Silence. "Come in five. Over." Nothing. Shit. Did that mean that Mr. Talented's friends had arrived? If so, what happened to his man at the airport? "Actual to Ten. Come in, Ten." Silence.

His radio crackled. "One to Actual. Want me to come back?"

Frank clenched his fist. There was no way he was losing this prize now. He lifted his radio. "Negative, One. Stay put and get me that barn. I don't care about anything else. I want that barn and what's in it. Copy?"

"Solid copy. Over."

He turned and yelled, "You drivers get the other trucks to safety!" He pointed to his two reserve soldiers. "You two cover them. Now!" He looked back at his map. Who should he move to answer this threat? It was clearly intended to attract his attention, possibly to lure him into a trap. He narrowed his eyes. If help had arrived, then they had the element of surprise. Why would they give away that advantage? Did they have fewer numbers? Did they need more time?

Either way, Frank felt like if he responded now, he could neutralize the threat before his team became surrounded. But every move in combat was a tradeoff. He decided the men watching the sides of the barn were the least important. If he kept the teams at each end of the building, Mack's team attacking from the west, and a second team keeping anyone from escaping out the other end, he should be okay.

He clicked his mic again, reading from the map. "This is Actual. Units Three, Four, Six, Fifteen and Seventeen, report back to the trailer double time. Repeat. Those units, pull back to me. Everyone else, hold your ground. Kill those bastards and get me that barn. Over and out."

He picked up an AR, leaning against the truck's fender, and checked the magazine. They wanted some sort of response. Well, that's what they were going to get, and they would not like it.

Chapter 125

Luis' mind fell back into his training. In every situation, you needed an objective, something you were trying to accomplish—otherwise, your actions were random and unproductive. The only aim he could come up with right now was simply to make it out of this alive. Not much of a goal.

Once again, the two groups had settled into a game of cat and mouse. The enemy would shoot covering for each other and try to advance, while Luis' team did its best to push them back.

What was he working toward? Angling for an escape? Buying time until help arrived? He bit his lip. Neither was a good option, but if they just stayed here, they would all die. That was for sure. They had to make a move, but no options presented themselves.

Even if Eddie and Loren arrived soon, they would have to fight their way in here. That would be very difficult. The enemy was settled in and knew the area better. Luis shook his head. His rescuers would be in a dark, unfamiliar area against entrenched and prepared enemies. It would take time to break through that. Time Luis didn't have.

Susan sidled up beside him, holding a full magazine up towards him. He popped the one from his rifle and traded with her.

Glancing down at her, he fought back a smile. Her hair had escaped the ponytail and was framing her face. With her pistol tucked into her waistband and her eyes ablaze with defiance, she was a far cry from the frightened girl he'd met only a few days before.

She stood on her tiptoes and kissed him before pulling back.

Wow. She really was something else. He had to figure out a way to keep her alive. All of them, but especially her. He'd promised to find her father and get her out of this, and that was what he was going to do. Even if he didn't know how.

A flare of vibration shot across his fingertips. He whipped his attention back to the opposite end of the barn.

The enemy let loose with a wave of fire, and then Mohawk slithered through the door and behind the cover.

Chapter 126

Loren braced herself against the door as the big army truck rumbled down the dirt road. If you could even call it that. It was really just two tire ruts snaking on and on through rolling, uneven ground.

The two weak pillars of light from the headlights danced across the darkness as the vehicle bounced its way over every rise and fall.

Big Dog asked, "How much further?"

Loren lifted the GPS and squinted at it. "Still thirteen miles to the back gate of the ranch."

He glanced over at her. "What then? It's not like we're going to sneak up in this thing. We'll be sitting ducks."

She sighed. "I know. We just need to hope and pray that Eddie's team will be enough of a distraction by the time we get there." The truck suddenly fell as the ground abruptly sloped down, and her stomach leapt up into her throat. She pushed herself back into the seat. A distraction wasn't enough. For them to get inside the compound was going to take something bold. Drastic. Unexpected. In her bones, she knew that was true, but she couldn't, for the life of her, come up with an idea to accomplish that. This noisy, lumbering old truck was just too easy a target for anyone with a weapon.

Loren rubbed her forehead. Getting back out was going to be even worse. She pushed that thought aside. One problem at a time. There was no point in wasting thoughts on getting away if they couldn't figure out a way to get into the compound in the first place.

She clenched her teeth. Hang in there, guys, we're coming.

Chapter 127

Keeping low, Eddie led Burk around the town, while the others headed west to create distractions and chaos. He needed to get to the back gate and somehow help Loren and Jeff's bikers to get in. How they were going to get back out again, he didn't know, but he had to focus on this problem first.

He stopped on a rise outside of town and got his first look at the compound, just able to make out the details in the bright halfmoon. He said under his breath, as Burk came up beside him, "It's big."

"Too big. Their people have lots of cover and concealment."

It was true. Going in here would be a maze, and the enemy would have all the advantages. Off to his left, a rattle of gunfire suddenly rang out and muzzle flashes flared in the distance. "Let's hope that works." Eddie pulled down his night vision goggles and scanned the area before nodding to Burk and easing down the slope.

The muffled pop, pop of more gunfire suddenly erupted ahead of them. Inside the barn. Where Luis was.

Eddie scanned the area to his left and right and then broke into a trot. The fence line loomed ahead of them, twelve feet high and topped with razor wire—stretching off in both directions.

Burk tapped him on the shoulder and motioned him to the right.

Keeping low, they jogged along until they came to a door in the fence line. A dark electrical keypad locked it, but there was a large hole cut in the fence next to it. Glancing both ways, they stepped through it.

Chapter 128

Frank left three men to guard the trucks at their new, more secure location. Gunfire sounded from the west side of the compound, and his radio crackled.

"Actual, this is Fifteen. I am taking fire at the southwest fence line. Over."

More shots sounded.

"This is Nine, gunfire at the northwest corner as well. Over."

Frank ground his teeth. He didn't know what size force he was facing. Were they really under attack or was a small group just pestering them? He clicked his mic. "This is Actual. Are they engaging? Over."

"This is Eighteen. Negative, Actual. More like harassing fire moving down the line to the north. Over."

Frank responded, "Any idea on numbers, Eighteen? Over."

Several more shots rang out.

"No idea, Actual. At least five, but numbers unknown. Over."

What was to the north? That's where Mr. Talented broke through the fence. But if the enemy had numbers, why not a frontal assault? Unless it was a diversion. He looked east and tilted his head. Nothing. Not a sound. Then more shots from the west. Frank turned back.

"Actual, this is Eighteen. I'm taking fire again. Over."

"Five, are they trying to breach?"

"Negative, Actual. Not yet. Over."

Frank scowled. Why?

"Actual, this is Thirteen. I have tangos at the north fence gate." Several reports echoed off the mountain. "Repeat. I have tangos at the north gate."

More sounds of combat.

Frank waited a moment, and then said, "What's the sitrep, Thirteen? Over."

"I've forced them back outside, Actual. Do I pursue? Over."

Frank frowned. He forced *them* back out? By himself? "Negative, Thirteen. Hold your position. All perimeter units, hold your position. Repeat. Hold and keep any tangos outside. Over and out." Come on, Mack, get me that barn.

Chapter 129

Now that Luis knew Mohawk was inside, everything had changed, and he needed to keep track of him at all times. He shot a quick glance over at the side doors at this end. It would be a good time to attack from there as well and squeeze Luis's little rag-tag band. All was quiet, however.

Susan handed him another magazine, and he swapped it with the one in his rifle as she thumbed rounds into the empty one. "Is help coming?"

He nodded. "It's on the way." He leaned up, putting his rifle to his shoulder, but a volley of bullets pushed him back down. He ground his teeth and slid his gun into the space between two filing cabinets and squeezed off two rounds. It was too little, too late, and the attackers had moved a little closer once again, advancing and taking cover behind a cabinet again.

Luis glanced over his shoulder. They were losing ground at a steady pace. The enemy had enough soldiers inside now that it was impossible to slow their advance. Moving down by Rob, he said into his ear, "Which door is closer to the dirt road?"

Rob pointed to the southern one.

Luis rubbed his forehead. How to handle this? Send a couple of soldiers out first to clear the way? Then try to cover the civilians as he ushered them out in groups?

Could they keep them safe like that? Should he go first, or protect from the rear?

He blew out a breath through his nose. No. He would have to stay, and hope that the other men could handle whatever was outside.

Big Tony exclaimed, "We've got to get out of here!"

Luis nodded. "I know. I'm going to have to send you and a couple of your guys first, and then I'll bring up the rear. Okay?"

A worried expression passed over Big Tony's face, but he nodded.

Luis clapped him on the shoulder, then leaned up, rifle ready, to recheck the situation.

Four enemy soldiers broke from cover on his right, firing as they advanced. As Luis turned in their direction, a sudden movement caught his eye. Mohawk was sprinting towards him from the left, firing as he ran.

Chapter 130

Eddie held up a hand to stop Burk, who crept along behind him. They had made it to one of the two outbuildings on this side of the house. Leaning around the corner, he could see its dark outline about twenty yards away, and beyond that vague shape of the barn. He didn't like it. Approaching the house from this point would leave them too exposed. He gestured to Burk, indicating that they should move down to the next outbuilding to the east.

The big man nodded and led the way back in that direction. Here at the corner of a small storage building, the house was only about fifteen feet away.

Eddie lifted his rifle and looked through the night vision scope. Nothing. At least nothing he could see.

The two men exchanged a nod and then sprinted across the space.

Just as they reached the opposite corner, shots rang out, and bullets tore into the wood. They dove behind the building, rolled, and came up ready to fire.

Eddie moved to the near corner. As soon as he peeked out, another report sounded, and bullets once again punched into the wood above him.

He yanked his head back and glanced down at Burk, who shook his head.

Damn it. They were pinned down in the dark with no sign of the enemy.

The sound of muffled gunfire continued inside the barn for about thirty seconds before coming to an abrupt halt.

Eddie took a deep breath and held it, trying to calm his heartbeat. He could hear constant irregular fighting off to the west. Hopefully, that helped. He moved down to Burk, leaned into him and said, "We've got to get past these guys."

"I know. But I'm not sure how to do it. Did you get a location on any of them?"

Eddie shook his head. "Negative."

Burk rubbed his face. "I was hoping our other team out there would have dragged more of them away than this."

"Me too." He sighed. They had to get past this. Luis was running out of time. "We're going to have to rush them. Want to try it from this corner or that one?"

Burk stared at him for a long time, his expression hidden in the darkness. He shook his head. "I think this one is better, but it ain't going to be good."

He was right. But it was worse for Luis, and he couldn't leave him there any longer without trying to help. "Let's go."

Chapter 131

Luis yelled over his shoulder, "Watch the north side," as he moved to intercept Mohawk.

All the enemies had them outclassed, but Luis knew he was the only one who could match the stupid blond-haired SOB trying to flank them.

Noticing Luis approaching, Mohawk pivoted and squeezed off two rounds before veering left.

Luis ducked behind the cabinets, rolled, and came up firing. It took him a fraction of a second to locate his target in the dim interior. That was all Mohawk needed to close the gap and dart behind another set of filing cabinets. Luis ground his teeth. It was a good move, and the closer Mohawk got, the worse it was. He wouldn't be able to both fight him and keep his charges behind the barrier alive without some distance to work with.

Mohawk popped up and fired one round before ducking back.

It struck the steel a mere four inches from Luis' head. Damn, this guy was good. What were his options? The enemy was too close now. Getting this large a group safely out the door seemed all but impossible now. Not to mention, they had no clue what type of reception they'd receive outside.

Could he take Susan and get her out? Was that even possible? And if it was, should he? No. He had to stay, but they were out of time.

His only hope was to kill Mohawk, but how? The man would not make a mistake. Luis looked out between the cabinets to confirm that his target was still there, shuffled down a bit, then popped up and fired three shots.

Instead of driving Mohawk back, however, he dove forward and scrambled behind a cabinet closer.

Luis pivoted and fired, just missing the man. Damn it. That was unexpected. This guy was crazy. As if the situation needed any more problems. He rifled through all the options in his mind and came to the only terrible solution. He was going to have to match crazy in kind and rush Mohawk. Pray it was unexpected, and that he really was better than his enemy. He gathered his feet underneath him and was just about to spring forward when the night vibrated with a deep, sustained horn.

Chapter 132

Loren clung to the truck's doorframe handle for dear life as it rocked and bounced down the uneven road. She looked over, amazed that Big Dog could keep control of the steering wheel and his foot on the gas. Of course, he was holding it with both hands, the massive muscles in his arms bulging under the strain.

He leaned forward. "There it is."

Loren snapped her attention back forward. She could just make out a fence and the outline of buildings inside. She pointed. "That big one must be the barn."

Big Dog nodded.

Over the radio she'd learned that the soldiers were distracting the enemy, but unable to draw many of them away, and Eddie and Burk were pinned down just beyond their destination.

Big Dog glanced over. "What's the plan?"

Loren forced down a manic chuckle. "Ram it. Ram through the fence, and then keep going until we crash into the barn."

Big Dog looked over with a grin. "You sure? What about the people inside?"

That was a good question. It would suck to show up as the cavalry and run over the people they were trying to rescue. She didn't really have a lot of options, though. "Lay on the horn the whole time and let's hope they get the message."

"You got it." He pushed his foot down a little further and the massive truck jarred and bounced more, making it almost impossible to control it over the last fifty yards. When they finally reached a bit of flat ground before the fence, Big Dog was able to let go and jam down on the horn. It resonated out into the night, deep and throaty.

They crashed through, pushing the fence forward. It strained against the truck, threatening to stop it. Just when it looked like it would, part of it slipped under the tires and, with an awful screech, it disappeared underneath.

Big Dog pulled himself back straight in his seat with one hand on the steering wheel, the whole time holding his other mashed down on the horn.

He altered course a fraction, aiming for the corner of the barn, and pushed the gas some more. A maniacal grin spread across his face just before they smashed through the wall.

Chapter 133

Eddie grinned as Burk snapped his head back and forth, trying to detect the source of the wail. "What's that?"

"That's Loren. Come on, let's go." Firing as he advanced, he darted around the corner, betting that the sudden unexpected sound would distract the enemy. He was right. They'd covered half the distance before the other men responded, and that was all the time they needed.

Eddie and Burk each took one down and stopped at the corner of the outbuilding closest to the barn. He rolled his eye to the night vision scope and panned back and forth, looking for anyone else.

Burk asked, "You see anything?"

"No. It's clear as far as I can tell."

"Now we just need to let the people inside know that we're friendlies."

Eddie nodded. "It would suck to finally make it there and have them blow our heads off."

Burk barked out a laugh. "That would suck indeed."

The wailing sound was now underpinned with a deep throaty growl, and they turned just in time to see the hulking shape of the army truck crash through the fence with a terrible screeching and crunching sound.

It strained against the wire for a moment and then the fence was sucked underneath.

Eddie and Burk stumbled back as the truck accelerated and turned towards the barn.

Chapter 134

Luis stopped himself just as he was about to leap and dropped back down behind the barrier. What the hell was that sound? Was it the enemy? More reinforcements? Some sort of psychological warfare ploy? Something to distract and discourage his men? Somehow, he doubted that.

He moved down and then stretched up to see over the barrier and locate Mohawk. He'd retreated a step and looked confused and leery of the sound as well. So it wasn't on his side. Then it must be help.

Luis' eyes widened. He leaped up and fired, driving Mohawk back as he yelled over to the corner, "Get away from the walls! Fall back to me! Run!"

Mohawk hunched over and moved behind a cabinet and came up on the other side, rifle ready.

Luis ducked just as Mohawk fired. He slid to a stop and moved back in the other direction before coming up, firing again. Out of the corner of his eye he could see his men running toward him and he slid more to his left before coming up firing at Mohawk, giving them cover.

The back corner exploded and a massive army truck burst through the wall. Shards of wood, metal, and glass sprayed in all directions.

Luis moved toward it, holding an arm protectively over his head.

The passenger door of the 6x6 opened and Loren leaned out. Leveling an assault rifle at the far end of the barn, she began to shoot.

Out of the other side, a massive biker-looking dude stepped out with a pump shotgun. He calmly took aim and fired again and again.

Luis turned back and yelled, "Everybody to the truck!"

Chapter 135

Eddie's face broke into a grin as he watched the truck crash into the barn. He clicked his throat mic. "All units, this is Eddie. Let them have it. Repeat. Go."

Burk shook his head, and the two men sprinted for the barn.

Ten feet from the structure, however, shots rang out from overhead, forcing them back behind cover.

Eddie rolled to the edge of the wall, put his back to it, and searched for the source.

Burk crawled over next to him.

He looked back and forth through the night vision scope. Nothing. Where had the shot come from? Two more reports sounded, and Eddie just barely caught the muzzle flash above him. The rise! They thought there might be a sniper there. In the chaos, he'd forgotten. Damn it! He pointed and Burk nodded.

They stood flat against the wall and, leaning out, tracked up to the rise through their night-vision scopes.

Eddie asked, "Got him?"

"No."

They separated, moving to get a better angle and a shot.

Eddie couldn't see over the lip at this angle.

The sniper fired again, and Eddie could see the flash. They both stepped out and fired.

The sniper slumped over, then lay still.

Eddie lowered his rifle and motioned Burk over. Leaning towards him, he said, "Let's get the one on the other side."

Chapter 136

Luis narrowed his eyes. It was time to deal with that stupid white-haired bastard once and for all. He sidestepped to his right, between Mohawk and the people scurrying to the truck, and moved forward. A flash of movement caught his eye. He fired, ducked, and kept moving behind a row of cabinets and muttered under his breath. "Not so easy now that it's just me, is it?"

Mohawk rose, fired and sprinted to his left, deeper into the barn.

Luis had expected that, so he rolled and put two rounds just a fraction ahead of him, forcing Mohawk to skid to a stop. He scrambled back and sent two shots over Luis' head as he moved around behind a cover.

Luis sprinted forward, kicking over one of the metal cabinets, exposing another soldier. He put a bullet into his forehead before bursting into the alleyway.

Mohawk saw him coming and lowered his shoulder, bowling over the wall, sending file folders sliding across the ground. He shot wildly as he ducked back behind cover.

Damn it. He was moving back toward the civilians loading into the truck. Smart. Luis glanced over his shoulder, and then, staying hunched over, pursued. Suddenly, the west side of the compound erupted in gunfire. Luis slid to a stop. What the hell was going on there? Eddie and Loren's plan, he guessed. Which was good, but bad because it caused him to lose the exact location of Mohawk.

He eased forward and to his right, making sure he could step into the open and cover the civilians if Mohawk attacked. He moved a few more steps and then stopped. Where was that bastard?

Chapter 137

The sounds of battle rang out from the west. Frank needed to make a decision—and now.

Gemini, tall and thin in his hunting jacket, paced back and forth behind him. Abruptly, he halted, his eyes narrowing. "We have to get what's in the barn now. Everything else can be handled later."

Frank clicked his mic. "Actual to One. Come in, One. Over."

The irritation was obvious in his voice. "This is One. Go ahead."

"One, let them go. Top priority is we hold the barn. Repeat, top priority is the barn. Copy? Over."

"But I have him!"

"Mack, do you hear me? Our top priority is the barn. Over."

There was a long pause. "I copy."

"No bullshit, Mack. This time you have to listen."

"Solid copy Actual."

Frank spat the mangled tobacco remains on the ground. "This is Actual. All units fall back into the barn. Repeat, let all tangos retreat, but fall back and secure the barn. Over and out." He tossed the radio up on the hood of the truck.

Gemini walked over and placed a hand on his shoulder. "Don't worry, we'll get these bastards all in good time." His phone rang, and he walked a few steps away, listened for a moment, and then looked back at Frank. "A team will be here to clean the site and load everything up in 30 minutes. This has to be over by then."

Frank glanced at his watch, a muscle in his cheek bulging. What a cluster.

Chapter 138

Eddie led Burk through the jagged hole in the building's corner, guns raised and checking back and forth. They came up behind the army truck. A massive man helping people climb in whipped around.

Eddie lowered his rifle and yelled, "Friendly!"

Burk pushed past him and waved. "Tony. How's it going?"

Big Tony gave him a relieved grin and shrugged. "We ain't dead yet."

Eddie clapped Burk on the shoulder and gestured that he was heading forward. He rounded the truck and found Big Dog and Loren providing cover. "Where's Luis?"

She pointed. "Off hunting."

Eddie looked back over his shoulder at Burk, who gave him a thumbs up. Time to go. Eddie put his middle finger and his thumb in his mouth and released a high, shrill whistle. A second later, he did it again.

Luis appeared out of the darkness, firing over his shoulder. As he came even with them, he said to Eddie through clenched teeth, "I almost had him."

Eddie nodded. "Another time." He turned to Big Dog. "Let's get out of here."

The biker nodded and ran back to the truck.

Eddie pointed to Loren. "You and I can cover from the front." He turned to Luis. "Get in the back. We're going to be exposed as we get out of here."

Loren climbed in first, and Eddie had just made it onto the seat when Big Dog jammed on the accelerator and the truck lurched backwards.

Eddie closed the door while she pushed the windshield down on its hinges and continued to fire her weapon as they roared back into the night.

She asked Eddie without turning, "What about the snipers?"

"Burk and I already took care of them."

Big Dog wrestled the wheel and backed the truck around in an arc, before jamming it into first gear, and they lurched forward. His biceps bulged as he strained hand over hand, turning the truck back toward the hole in the fence. He jammed it into second gear and the truck surged forward into the night. "Here's hoping that they want whatever that was back there more than us."

Chapter 139

Luis crouched behind the tailgate, gun ready as they rumbled and bounced their way out of the compound. He panned the thermal scope back and forth, but it was difficult to keep it steady.

The big black guy who had arrived with Eddie crouched beside him. "Any pursuit?"

"Not that I can see."

"I'm Burk, these are my guys. I wanted to thank you for all the help." He offered his hand.

Luis shook it. "I'm Luis. My pleasure."

Big Tony was standing near the cab. He glanced over the roof at the road ahead of them, looked back, and gave them a thumbs up. All clear.

Luis panned the darkness behind him one more time before allowing himself to relax.

Huddled in the center of the bed were the cook, the maintenance man, and the computer nerd. Rob and the four remaining soldiers sat along the sides, holding their guns ready.

Susan came up behind Luis. Wrapping her arms around him, she kissed his shoulder.

He leaned back. "I'm sorry we didn't find your father."

She laid her head on his shoulder. "It's all right. We found something here. I'm not sure what it is, or how it's connected to my dad, but we found something." She shrugged. "So maybe that's progress."

The truck bounced and pitched back and forth as it roared down the dark dirt road.

Luis continued to pan back and forth with his scope until he finally felt safe enough to sit down.

Burk followed suit with a sigh. He turned to Susan. "I don't want to get your hopes up, but a long time ago, we used that barn back there to smuggle people out to somewhere." He shrugged. "I don't know where to, and I don't know if your father made it to anywhere safe, but he did pass through here a long time ago."

Luis turned to see Susan nod, clearly trying to keep a rein on her emotions. She nodded. "Thank you."

He folded her into his arms.

Big Tony asked, "What's the chance that there's a trap up ahead?"

Burk shrugged. "You got me." He motioned back behind them with his head. "I think what they really wanted is back there, so I'm hoping we're safe for now." He made his way back to Rob, and the two bent their heads toward one another in conversation.

Susan took Luis' face in her hands. "Thank you for saving me."

He shrugged. "Well, I can't help but feel like we were the ones who got you into danger in the first place."

She shrugged again. "You could also say *I* got you into the danger."

He grinned. "That's true."

The truck suddenly dropped as it passed over a dip in the road. It then strained up the other side, and they rumbled on through pitch blackness on all sides.

She leaned in and looked into his eyes.

He could just make out her features in the moonlight.

She said, "I don't know what lies ahead, and I'm not very good at this kind of thing." She shrugged. "I don't have much experience, but is there something kind of happening between us, or is it just the danger and stress? Just tell me straight, please."

Luis took a moment to examine his feelings. There was something about her that just affected him. He smiled and nodded. "I think something might be happening here. I don't know what, but it's something."

She leaned into him and rested her forehead against his shoulder. "What now?"

"I've no idea," replied Luis, as he tilted her chin up with his thumb and pressed his lips against hers in a gentle kiss.

Chapter 140

Loren turned as Big Dog said, "We must have missed the turnoff. It didn't take us this long earlier."

She looked around the darkness and nodded. He was right. This was further than they had come before.

Eddie asked, "Where does this road take us again?"

She rubbed her forehead, bringing the map back to mind. "Eventually, 87, but hopefully we can find a way off and down to Highway 12 sooner."

Eddie nodded and glanced over his shoulder. "Did we get everyone?"

"I think so. Everyone we knew about, at least." She leaned back. "But we didn't find Susan's father."

Eddie sighed. "I know."

She glanced at her watch. It wasn't even midnight yet. It felt like four in the morning.

The truck rocked and swayed its way on into the night until finally Big Dog pointed. "That looks like a road going south right there, doesn't it?"

Loren leaned forward. "It does to me."

Eddie nodded.

Big Dog turned onto the road, which thankfully had a much smoother surface. Before long, they reached Highway 12, where he was finally able to stop. Everyone got out of the truck and stretched their legs.

Burk took the civilians aside and spoke to each of them.

Loren gave Susan a hug. "Glad to see you again."

The younger woman quirked a smile. "And in one piece."

Loren hugged Luis. "Sorry we took so long."

Luis snorted. "Better late than never. Thanks for coming."

Eddie turned to Big Dog. "We couldn't have done it without you."

The big biker waved away the comment. "Anything for Jeff. Besides, it was a rush."

Loren looked around the group. How the hell had they gotten caught up in all of this? And what was their next step? Looking over at Eddie, she asked, "What now?"

He ran a hand through his hair. "I have got no idea."

Burk's phone chimed, and he looked down at it. He said a few more soothing words to the civilians and then walked over to them. "I told my bosses what happened." He rubbed his chin. "They'd like you to come see them." He blew out a breath. "Which is unusual. *I've* never even met them."

Eddie's lips thinned. "When?"

"Tonight."

Eddie held his gaze. "Okay. Where?"

"Maine." He gestured over at Susan. "And they'd like for us to bring the girl."

Loren looked over at her, eyebrows raised.

Susan chuckled. "Oh, I'm following this all the way to the end. I'm in."

Eddie nodded and turned to Big Dog. "Can we get you to drop us off at the airport in Billings?"

The biker twirled a finger in the air. "Let's load her up."

Chapter 141

As the truck pulled back onto the highway, Luis finally allowed himself to truly relax a bit. They were out of that damn barn and away. Eddie had arrived in time, just like before.

Susan sat in front of him, leaning back against his chest, and he wrapped his arms around her.

He placed his forehead against her hair and sighed. He had known that Eddie would come this time. The first time, he hadn't been so sure. He closed his eyes and remembered racing away from the wine shop in Verdun all those years ago.

Luis wasn't sure about Eddie. He just wanted to get on the expressway, let Ellen's Mercedes loose, and run. But Eddie asked them to keep going, to stay on the surface streets and head north towards the Meuse River. Luis didn't want to do that, but on some instinct alone, he complied.

The phone rang again, and Ellen answered. She listened for a second, then looked over at Luis. "He wants us to meet him at a warehouse ahead. He has directions."

Luis nodded. "Okay, just tell me where to go." He glanced up at the rearview mirror. There were two cars on his tail now.

She pointed toward an intersection. "Take that left."

Luis continued as if he was going past the street, then at the last second grabbed the parking brake and slid around into the turn. He glanced at the mirror again. That bought them a few seconds.

Ellen held tight to the armrest, her knuckles white. "Turn right after that Leclerc."

Luis down shifted and cut the corner across the parking lot.

Ellen moved her hand to the handle on the door frame. "Next left. It's number 1742."

Industrial buildings lined the street, and Luis desperately searched for building markers as he raced past.

Ellen pointed and yelled, too late, "There it is!"

Luis slammed on the brakes, jammed the car into reverse, swinging the nose around, then shot forward again.

Ellen was out of the car before it even came to a stop, running for the building's brown wooden door. She yanked the knob, but it wouldn't open.

Luis raced up and, without stopping, leaped, and hit it with both feet. It burst inward.

The two cars slid to a stop outside.

Luis pushed Ellen in. He turned and shot the first pursuer in the chest, and then rushed after her. Three rounds left.

The interior was wide open, with nothing to hide behind.

Ellen turned to him, wide-eyed. "What now?"

He directed her against the wall they had just come through. "Watch my back."

He leaned out. Five men rushed toward the door. Luis shot the first two before pulling back. One round left. Damn it. Reaching around, he pulled Ellen closer. They only had one advantage: their pursuers had to come through the door. He inched closer to the opening.

An arm snaked inside, trying to shoot blindly.

Luis seized the wrist and bent it savagely, but it pulled back before he could grab the gun. Damn it. Now they knew what side of the door he was on. They would rush them. He lifted the pistol.

The three men burst around the corner.

Luis shot the closest, threw his pistol at the face of the second, and turned too late to stop the third one from shooting him.

A crack echoed around the interior.

Luis flinched but felt no impact.

The last man closed one eye and then stumbled to a knee.

Luis glanced over his shoulder at Ellen.

The man fell forward and was still.

A man leaned in, then pulled back. "Friendly. I'm Eddie. Are you okay?"

Luis's shoulders relaxed. "Yes, we're fine."

Eddie leaned in again, his pistol ready, entered, and then lowered his weapon. He gave Luis a once over and spoke to Ellen, "You good?"

She nodded and then rested her head against Luis' back.

Luis remained tense and ready as Eddie checked outside once more before extending his hand. "Nice to meet you."

•   •   •

The truck bounced as it turned into the airport, bringing him back to reality, and he grinned at the memory. Luis had joined up with Eddie and Jeff that afternoon, and they'd been together ever since. He kissed the top of Susan's head and blew out another relieved breath. He'd known Eddie would come—he always did.

Part 6

Chapter 142

Eddie eased back into the seat as Sam's jet leveled out and headed east. They'd left Rob and the other soldiers from Arrowhead to deal with the civilians and then rendezvous with everyone else at the Martinez farm. Eddie didn't know what would happen next for all of them, or how Burk's people were going to handle the civilians, but that was their problem. Eddie had enough to deal with. He glanced over at Susan asleep curled up next to Luis and raised his eyebrows.

Luis shrugged, and the ghost of a smile crossed his lips.

Eddie considered the pair. He definitely thought Luis needed someone; he was just surprised that Susan was the one. Not that he had anything against her, she just wasn't who he would have imagined for Luis. Then again, he really didn't know what type of woman he'd choose for Luis, so there was that.

Burk sat stretched out, fingers laced on his stomach, snoring softly.

Loren came back from the bathroom and sat next to Eddie. "You, okay?"

He shrugged. "Hopefully, we're about to learn something." All the time, effort, and anxiety had led to this. Was this connected to Caveman? Maybe. Connected to Mendelson? Probably.

Were they closer to finding Susan's father? Who knew? What else was ahead? Was anything they'd discovered through all of this helpful? Did they need people connected to the mad scientist? Yes, to help with Caveman. But did that help them fight Treleous? This gave Eddie pause. What was his primary mission? Caveman, of course. When had stopping Treleous become almost as important as that?

The answer was, today. What Treleous had done at the ranch was beyond crazy. The risk, the scale of the attack. The pure audacity of the exposure, murder, and destruction spoke of a sense of impunity. These people thought they could do anything and get away with it. That no one could stop them. Hell, no one but Eddie's little team was even trying.

Loren nodded over at Burk. "You believe that he's never met his employers before?"

He shrugged. "Why would he lie about that? To what end?"

Loren shook her head. "I don't know. This whole situation is so weird."

Eddie rubbed his forehead. It was weird. Was this a trap? If so, it wasn't a very practical one.

• • •

The sun was bright, and the morning crisp and cold when they landed in Maine. As everyone stood and put on their coats, Eddie leaned down to Luis. "Keep your eyes open. All right?"

He nodded and patted the pistol at his hip.

The jet taxied over to the main hangar. As soon as it came to a stop, Eddie opened the door and pushed down the ramp.

The airport was deserted except for an elderly Asian man standing in front of a classic turquoise Chevrolet Suburban.

Eddie looked first one way and then the other before turning his attention back to the lone figure standing in a dark suit. The man had bright silver hair with a matching thin mustache.

Eddie descended the stairs, followed by the others.

The Asian man walked past Eddie. "You are Mr. Burk?"

The big man nodded.

"I am Mr. Ling. They sent me to bring you and your friends to the house. Do you have any luggage?"

He snorted. "No luggage."

Mr. Ling gestured and then led them over to the Suburban.

Burk said, "This is a nice ride. What year?"

Mr. Ling ducked and nodded. "Thank you. Very nice. 1963."

Luis and Susan took the middle row, and Eddie and Loren the back, while Burk sat in the passenger's seat.

Mr. Ling drove them out of the airport and onto a highway heading south.

Burk looked over his shoulder at Eddie, eyebrows raised. He turned back to Mr. Ling. "Where are we going?"

"To the house."

He raised his eyebrows. "And where is that?"

The driver's attention never left the road. "Down this road, about an hour or so."

Eddie took Loren's hand and looked out at the scenery. This man didn't appear to be any kind of threat, and even though they didn't know where they were going, it seemed like an awful lot of trouble for a trap. Who were they going to see, though? A secret club of former Mendelson's scientist? Susan's father? He looked over his shoulder. She was awake and alert as she studied the passing countryside.

Eddie leaned into Loren. "Pretty place."

She nodded. "The question is, what's here?"

Mid-morning clouds had collected on the horizon by the time Mr. Ling finally turned off the highway. He drove through a tall iron gate and down a long driveway to a sprawling white house perched on the waterfront. Two large outbuildings of similar architecture flanked the primary structure.

The front door opened, and a lanky man with unkempt gray hair stepped hesitantly outside, still remaining partially behind the door. "Susan?"

Shocked, Susan yelled, "Daddy!" She flung open the car door and rushed into his arms.

He held on while she sobbed into his chest, her body convulsing. "It's okay, sweetheart. What's wrong? It's okay. I'm fine."

She stepped back, wiping her eyes with the backs of hands. "What do you mean, what's wrong? I've been looking for you for years. I thought you were dead."

Eddie and everyone else climbed out of the car and gathered behind her.

Her father drew his bushy eyebrows together. "No, sweetie. I left you a note, in our code, at your apartment, with access to money."

Her eyes widened. "No, you didn't." She looked through him for a second. "Well, I didn't get it. When I finally made it back to my place, I'd been robbed. I never saw any of that."

A crease formed in his forehead. "No. They couldn't have. I checked every semester, and you're still enrolled at Duke."

Susan shook her head. "No, they kept doing that, so I'd know I could always come back. Your friends in the administration, I mean. I haven't taken a class in years."

A look of horror clouded her father's face. "That's why you never reached out to me. I thought you were mad. That you were ashamed of me."

Susan looked into his eyes. "How could you think that? I've been looking for you all this time." Her eyes filled with tears again, one breaking free and snaking down her cheek. "Why did you leave me?"

He took her back into his arms. "No, sweetie. Sh, sh, sh. I had to protect you. The people after me are…" He faltered. "Well, I guess you know what they're like now. I'm so sorry. I stayed away to protect you."

Luis took a half step forward, his eyes riveted on Susan.

Her father continued, "I'm so sorry, sweetheart. So, so sorry."

A stern voice with a slight accent said from the top of the stairs, "We should continue this indoors. We have much to discuss."

Eddie looked up to a see a severe looking Asian woman standing in the doorway. Her face was just beginning to line, her dark hair pulled back tight with one streak of silver running through it. She nodded at him, turned, and walked back inside the house.

Chapter 143

Susan and her father, still clinging to one another, followed the unknown woman inside, but Eddie hesitated. He looked over at Luis, who shrugged.

Loren put her hand on his arm. "We're here. Might as well see what the story is."

They walked up the stairs, Burk on their heels, and into the massive well-kept house. They passed fine antique furnishings and bookshelves covering every wall, following Ben and Susan into a wide-open glass sunroom at the rear that stretched the entire width of the house.

A dozen high-backed wicker chairs sat spaced around, facing the ocean. The Asian woman came to a stop beside a short man in a white suit with a thick, gray beard, who rose from a chair and stood beside her.

The two groups stared at one another in silence. After a moment, the bearded man said in a gravelly voice, "Sit, please. I know you have lots of questions, as do we. So, with a little effort, I believe we can shed light on some things."

A short elderly man in a denim shirt and jeans entered from a side door.

The man with the beard looked over. "Ah, Freddy. Some lemonade and some kind of simple lunch for," he scanned the room, "for a large contingent, please."

Freddy saluted with two fingers and left the room.

Eddie and the rest of the group sat down, but the bearded man and the Asian lady remained standing, facing them.

Stroking his whiskers he said, "Where to begin? I guess names are as good a beginning as any. My name is Calvin," he gestured to the woman next to him, "and this is Chin."

She gave her head the slightest nod.

"Over there is Benjamin. I must thank you for reuniting him with his daughter." He nodded at Susan.

Chin's forehead creased just a fraction.

Calvin continued, "Ah. Though we've never met, I recognize Burk. We thank you for your years of service to us."

Burk fidgeted and nodded but remained silent, his brow furrowed.

Calvin's dark brown eyes settled on Eddie. "So, if you'd be so kind as to tell me who you are?"

Eddie considered the question. In their war against Treleous, anonymity had been their greatest defense. He didn't know these people, so wasn't sure if he might need this same protection in the future. But it was too late for that. They'd come all this way looking for some answers, and they wouldn't find them without some risk. "I'm Eddie. This is Loren, and Luis."

Calvin bore into him with implacable eyes before nodding. "Pleased to meet you."

After a long minute of awkward silence, Chin asked in a tone just short of an accusation, "How did you find Susan?"

Eddie sighed. "Actually, she found us."

Susan nodded. "It's true."

The conversation faltered again.

This was going nowhere. Eddie recognized the names. These were all Mendelson scientists. Two of whom were supposed to be dead. "Does the name Treleous mean anything to you?"

Calvin shook his head. He raised his eyebrows at Chin and Ben. Both shook their heads as well.

Eddie looked over at Burk. When he'd mentioned the name before, he thought he detected a sense of recognition. Had he misread that?

Calvin asked, "Should it?"

Eddie frowned and turned back. Why didn't they know about Treleous? Or was it just the name they didn't know? "That's what we call the people trying to continue Mendelson's work."

Chin took an involuntary step back, and Calvin's eyes grew round.

Eddie held up a hand. "We're not with them. In fact, we work against them. I suspect you do, too. I think that's why you left Mendelson and went into hiding."

The color drained away from both Chin and Calvin's face, and they stared at him in openmouthed horror.

Eddie stood and stepped forward. "It's okay. We're working against them too. We work with Senator Sam Hawthorne."

At the name, Calvin's shoulders sagged a bit. "Why do you call them Treleous?"

Eddie shrugged. "I don't know. That's what Sam called them." He gestured over at Susan. "Whatever they're called, they used her to find us."

Ben's eyes widened, and he turned to her. "I'm so sorry, sweetie." He took her in his arms again.

Calvin asked, "Why did they want to find you?"

Eddie hesitated, unsure how to answer. Loren stepped forward. "I think they were looking for whatever was at Arrowhead. They thought we knew where Mendelson's work was."

Chin narrowed her eyes and tightened her lips before snapping accusingly, "So you led them there?"

Loren shook her head.

Susan said, "They were there before us. We just went there looking for Dad."

Calvin frowned. "I don't see how they could have found it." His thick brows furrowed. "And how did you know to look for Ben there? How did you know about..." he trailed off, exchanged a look with Chin, and then studied the floor. "You knew the password. I'd forgotten that in all of this." He looked up. "You have Jason, don't you?" The faintest smile touched his lips. "You found Jason, didn't you?"

Chapter 144

Loren looked from Luis to Eddie. Jason? Did they mean Caveman? It had to be. Was that a secret they were willing to reveal now? She raised her eyebrows.

Chin studied this exchange and said briskly, "They don't know his name." She looked over at Calvin. "He doesn't remember his name, so how could they know it?" She stepped forward and said to Loren, "You have him, though, don't you?"

Eddie gave her a barely perceptible nod and then Loren said, "We call him Caveman."

Calvin crumpled into a chair.

Ben barked out a laugh.

Chin closed her eyes. "How did you find him?"

Eddie asked, "How did you lose him?"

Calvin took in a huge breath and stood. "Good. You should be reticent to share too much, too quickly." He exchanged another look with Ben and Chin. "Since you already seem to know. Yes, we are scientists who escaped from Mendelson and have been hiding for years from the people you call Treleous." He hesitated. "But we're not of a clandestine persuasion. All of this cloak and dagger stuff is beyond us. We would never have been able to…"

Chin picked up the thread. "Only one amongst us could really think like that."

Loren slowly nodded. "Heinrich."

Chin's eyes widened, and she nodded. "You seem to know an awful lot."

Eddie said, "There's a reason Sam came to us for help."

Calvin said, "Then you probably know it wasn't really Heinrich. It was his brother Kurt, who was with the GRU or something like that, and then the CIA, I think. He's the one who got his whole family out of east Germany. Kurt and Heinrich planned all of this, set up this place for us, hid Jason away in a spot none of us knew about, and reached out to Sam."

Chin shrugged. "When Heinrich died, we were at a loss. We've never heard from Kurt again, either."

Ben nodded. "We didn't know what to do. But we knew we were in danger, so we stuck with the plan and stayed here."

Chin looked over at Susan. "After they got to Heinrich, we were terrified. I'm the one who told Ben he couldn't have any contact with you. I thought it was for the best. They seemed to be everywhere. If you have anger, direct it at me. I'm to blame."

Susan looked from Chin to her dad.

Ben shrugged. "I wanted to keep you safe, too, but when I weakened, Chin helped me to stay strong."

Calvin frowned. "So how did you find Jason, and where is he?"

Eddie ran a hand through his unkempt hair and looked over at Loren.

She said, "That's a long story. But rest assured, he's safe."

Eddie's eyes suddenly widened. "You're Calvin Arturo."

The bearded man raised his unruly eyebrows and nodded. "Yes."

"You're number one on the green list."

Calvin grinned, looked over at Chin, and said, "They do have Jason."

Chapter 145

Eddie studied Calvin as the elderly man shook his head and said, "Jason was part of Heinrich's experiment. That's why he's the one who hid him." He snorted. "His foolish green list contained all of us," he gestured over at Susan, "Even her and other members of our families. Me being at the top was meant as a joke, I assure you."

Chin frowned. "He never could be serious."

So, Caveman's name was Jason. That was actually a bit disappointing. Somehow, it didn't quite seem to fit him the way Caveman did.

Calvin's smile faded. "But Jason knew nothing about Arrowhead. You couldn't have found it even with his help."

Luis said, "Actually, Jason is exactly how we found it."

Loren nodded. "As soon as we told him the name Benjamin Leonette, he—well, he remembered a bunch of stuff. And one of them was that there was a path. Like a railroad called Ling Track." She looked over at Eddie for confirmation.

He nodded. "From the Paleo Pipe Shop in Georgetown."

Luis said, "To the Arrowhead ranch in Montana."

Chin exchanged another look with Calvin. "Ling is my last name. Lingtrack100 is an email address I once had. There was an email I sent to everyone on the team using that address when Kurt finished setting up the escape route. I don't know how that could have ended up in Jason's brain. It wasn't part of any load we tested."

Calvin frowned. "That we know about. It seems that Heinrich put a few extra factoids in on his own."

Chin nodded. "So it appears. The ranch was supposed to be a secret we told no one about."

Calvin nodded, and the conversation stalled.

Luis asked, "All that stuff in Arrowhead. It's backed up somewhere, right?"

Chin scowled. "Of course."

Loren's brows drew together. "Then why keep all that paper? All those filing cabinets? Why go through all the trouble?"

Chin shrugged. "Heinrich was adamant that we needed to keep them. When we saw where Mendelson was headed, we were horrified. We wanted to stop him." She sighed. "And when we realized he was working with some outside people..."

Ben picked up when she trailed off. "We all started collecting information, eavesdropping on conversations, things like that."

Chin continued, "We used codes to communicate with one another. Pass on what we found or overheard."

Calvin nodded. "We would scribble coded messages in the margins of papers, hiding them as innocuous doodles. All of us were worried about two things. Getting killed and someone trying to continue this work."

Ben nodded. "That's when they started knocking us off."

Chin said, "Heinrich was convinced that if we collected all the paperwork, and combined it," she shrugged, "it would contain the secret to stopping—what did you call them, Treleous? If we pored over each of our codes, we could piece it together. So, we kept the originals, even after everything was scanned in."

Ben shook his head. "He could never figure it out before he died. It's all just been sitting there since then. We never found this key he was looking for."

Eddie asked, "So, what have you been doing all this time?"

Calvin shrugged. "We have several laboratories set up here. We do our work, collect patents, so that we can pay for Burk and all of his men, and..." He looked over at Chin with a helpless gesture.

She finished for him, "We've tried to find some answers to everything at Arrowhead, but we found nothing. We can't go back into the world or these Treleous people would kill us, so we've just been waiting."

Loren asked, "For what?"

Calvin raised his eyebrows. "For someone to come."

Luis said, "To come and do what?"

Chin hesitated, exchanged a look with Calvin, and shrugged. "We don't know."

Eddie glanced at Loren. She saw it too. That was a lie. He didn't detect any malice or danger in her statement. It just wasn't, at the very least, the whole truth. What were these people hiding?

Silence again stretched between the two groups.

Loren said, "Well, we found Susan's father. That's what we set out to do."

Susan wiped away a tear with one finger. "I can never thank you enough." She rushed over and hugged Eddie and Loren fiercely. Then walked over and took Luis' hand and pulled him over to Ben. "Daddy, I'd like you to meet my boyfriend."

Eddie's eyebrows shot up, and he looked over at Loren, who was trying unsuccessfully to hide her surprised smile.

Chapter 146

Luis didn't believe he'd ever met a girl's dad before.

Ben's eyes were wide with surprise as he shook his hand, but Luis didn't detect any anger or judgement. He looked bewildered more than anything else.

Luis glanced over at Eddie. He could tell his friend didn't believe these scientists were telling them everything, either. Something was wrong.

Susan hugged Ben again. "I've missed you so much."

It still surprised Luis that they'd found him. When no one at the ranch knew who her father even was, Luis had feared the worst. He was really glad to be wrong.

Susan turned back, sliding an arm around him, and rested her forehead on his chest. "I can't ever thank you enough." She looked up into his face and frowned. "What's wrong?"

This gave Luis pause. He didn't like how she was able to read him so easily, so soon. He leaned in and said under his breath, "They aren't telling us everything."

She shot a look over at her father. He had wandered over to Calvin and Chin and the three of them were talking to each other quietly. She frowned at them and then patted Luis' chest. "Give me a moment." She returned to her dad.

Eddie met eyes with Luis and gave him a "what the hell" expression.

Luis shrugged. A noise drew his attention. He turned to see the older Asian gentleman who'd driven them here enter, then disappear through a door on the far wall. A kitchen?

When Luis turned back to Susan, she and the three scientists were quietly disagreeing about something. Eddie and Loren came over to him.

The scientists kept glancing up to see if they were being overheard.

Susan said something urgently to the group, then they fell silent. She turned to Luis, Eddie, and Loren. "I think you guys should hear this." She glanced over her shoulder. "They haven't told you everything. Well, they told you what they thought applied to you, but…" she trailed off.

Calvin cleared his throat. "Heinrich knew he was in danger," He exchanged a look with Chin, "and he left us instructions." He hesitated. "We—well, he didn't expect you to be the ones to come."

Susan walked over and took Luis' hand, getting out of the middle of the conversation.

Eddie furrowed his brow. "Who did he expect?"

The group of scientists stared at the floor.

Susan said, "Heinrich left a letter for the FBI."

Chin frowned at Susan and then nodded.

Eddie raised his eyebrows. "He expected the Bureau to come here? Why? What did it say?"

Calvin said, "We don't know. We didn't open it."

Chin interjected, "And we're not sure you should, either. He told us only to give it to them."

Again, silence stretched between the groups.

Loren said, "We know people in the FBI and the CIA. We can help. Besides, it's been a long time. If they haven't come by now, they may not be coming. We probably need to help Heinrich's plan along a little."

The scientists huddled again before Calvin nodded.

Chin walked over to a drawer and retrieved a large manila envelope. She handed it to Eddie.

"FBI," was written on the front in blocky, masculine script. The envelope was heavy.

With a final nod from Calvin, Eddie tore it open and pulled out a single letter and a paper-clipped bundle of pages.

Eddie read it aloud. "To Whom It May Concern, the included document contains everything you need to know about the Kamata Case. We're sorry, we truly meant no harm."

Eddie looked up at the scientists. "What's the Kamata Case?"

They looked genuinely befuddled by the letter's contents.

Chin answered, "It is a city in Japan." She shook her head and glanced at the others. "But other than that, it means nothing to me."

Eddie turned to the clipped papers, which were just pages of code.

He handed it to Calvin, who showed it to Ben and Chin.

Ben said, "We're not really computer people. That was Koji's role for the group."

Chin spoke without looking up from the pages. "This is some sort of hack. It's how someone defeated a very tough firewall." She met Eddie's eyes. "I've no idea what this is about."

Loren ran a hand over her mouth. "So, if we bring in the FBI, this isn't anything that's going to get the three of you in trouble?"

Calvin's eyes widened, and he shook his head. "It's not anything we did, but if we're discovered..."

Chin handed the papers back to Eddie. "If those Treleous people find out about us, we're as good as dead."

Eddie passed them to Loren.

Luis looked over her shoulder at the document. What the hell did this mean? Every time they got an answer, it created two more questions. "So you've just been waiting here for the FBI to come? All this time?"

Calvin nodded and looked at the floor. "It's what he told us to do. I thought it would be something about these Treleous people. Something the FBI could use to help us."

Chin scowled. "Instead, it was admitting to some other crime Heinrich and his brother committed." She shook her head. "We've been waiting all this time for nothing." She suddenly snapped her head around and pointed at Eddie. "You have doomed us!"

In a flash, Luis put a hand on his pistol and took a step toward Eddie.

Calvin and Ben retreated a step.

The skin around Chin's neck flushed red. "You brought those people to Arrowhead."

Eddie said to Loren out of the corner of his mouth. "You wanna watch behind us?"

Loren nodded and turned.

Eddie held Chin's gaze. "We did *not* lead them there. Why would Susan lie to you?"

Calvin stepped forward. "Chin."

Chin worked her mouth and lowered her finger to point at the letter in his hand. "That has nothing to do with Treleous or whatever you call them. Heinrich and his brother broke lots of laws. They were decent enough to not leave us holding the bag, but we will *not* be discovered." She trembled a bit and her eyes brimmed with tears. "As soon as you let anyone know we are here, we're dead."

Susan took a step closer to Luis, who shot a glance at her before returning his attention to Chin.

Eddie said, "Ms. Ling. We told Susan we'd find her father, and we did." He lifted the pages. "I'll find out what these mean, and I won't expose you. You have my word."

Chin lowered her hand. "And how will you do that?"

Eddie looked over at Luis and shrugged. "I don't know yet."

Chapter 147

The next morning, Eddie adjusted his mug on the cracked linoleum tabletop at a coffeeshop just down the street from the Bangor International Airport. He looked around the interior one more time, pulled out his cell phone, and dialed.

Craig answered on the second ring. "I'm guessing you're all right. Moe said things got a little hairy up there in Montana."

"Yeah, we're fine. Thanks for the help. I'm assuming he's okay?"

"No problem. He's fine, he's a lot like Luis, hard to kill. Did you learn anything useful?"

Eddie stared out the window at the deserted street. "A little. But Treleous got what they were after."

Craig said. "I see. I still don't understand why they would want it. But that sucks, regardless. I'll put out some feelers to see if we can learn something from all of this. Anything else?"

How much should he trust Craig? That was always the question. "Have you ever heard of the Kamata case?"

Craig was silent for so long, Eddie wondered if he'd lost him.

When he finally answered, his voice was low and almost menacing. "Why are you asking about that? Is this connected to Montana?"

"This has nothing to do with the ranch. Do you know the case?"

"Of course, I know about the case! What do you know about the case is the question and, more importantly, why are you asking me about it?"

"I gather it's important."

Craig sighed. "You might say that." Another long pause. "We need to talk about this face to face. Where are you?"

Eddie drummed his fingers on the table. Craig could easily track the phone. That's why he left the house. "Bangor."

"Maine?"

"Yes."

Craig was silent again. "What the hell are you doing there?"

"That's where the trail led us."

"What trail? Never mind, don't tell me yet. Can you get back to me? Here in D.C.?"

Eddie sighed. "Not for a while. Do we really need to talk in person?"

"Crap. Yes. I'm on my way. Can you meet me near the airport there?"

Eddie was surprised. What was Kamata? And why was it so important that Craig felt the need to talk face to face? And right now? "Yes."

"I'll be there in under three hours. I'll call you when I'm close." He hung up.

Chapter 148

Eddie called Loren and filled her in on the situation, then paid the bill and walked outside. The classic, turquoise Suburban sat parked out front, the driver asleep, his hat covering his face.

Eddie knocked gently on the fender and the elderly Asian gentleman who'd collected them up at the airport sat up. Chin had told him in Chinese to take Eddie to the airport, and the man had spoken very little since then.

Eddie and the driver studied one another. "You speak English, yes?"

The man nodded.

Eddie offered his hand. "I'm Eddie."

The driver hesitated, then shook it. "I am Jianguo."

"Pleased to meet you." Eddie glanced at his watch. "We've got some time to kill, several hours. Do you know some place we can get ammo, and a good place to eat?"

The man frowned and then nodded. "Come on, I know a place."

Eddie got in and they pulled away. "I'm assuming that Chin Ling is your daughter."

He nodded. "Yes." He looked back. "Very much trouble."

Eddie grinned.

After an excellent authentic Chinese lunch and a stop off to restore the team's ammo reserves, Jianguo drove them back to the airport. The entire time, he said less than ten words, and Eddie was growing tired of the man's stoicism.

They parked and settled in to wait.

Eddie said, "When we pick this person up, I need someplace that he and I can go to have a private conversation. Do you know of such a place?"

Jianguo nodded. "Good place, not far."

•   •   •

When Craig finally arrived, he took in the old vehicle and the Asian driver with a "what the hell" look as he climbed into the back seat.

They rode in silence for a short way before pulling into the parking lot for the Ecotat Gardens and Arboretum.

Jianguo eased the seat back and placed his hat over his face again.

As Eddie led Craig into the park, the CIA man glanced over his shoulder toward the Suburban. "What's going on?"

Once again, Eddie was at a bridge he wasn't yet ready to cross. He didn't like deciding things because he had no choice. Of course, that's how it always was with his old boss. Over his shoulder, he asked, "What about Montana?"

Craig glanced around before answering. "I sent Moe back there to check it out. It was totally clean."

Eddie furrowed his brow. "What do you mean, clean?"

"Nothing was there. Nothing inside the barn, no bodies, no people, just a bunch of bullet holes and nothing else."

Eddie blew out a breath.

Craig nodded. "They do have resources, don't they?"

"How do you even fight that?"

"We have resources too, you know. We just need to discover where we need to direct them."

Eddie looked out over the landscaping. That was the question, wasn't it? Where to go next? He didn't know. Deep within the park's interior, they stopped at a pair of rustic benches facing one another deep in the interior and sat. They seemed to be the only people in the expansive park.

Eddie sighed. "Okay, I'm a little nervous about letting you in on all of this. I need your word that you won't act on anything I'm about to tell you without my agreement."

Craig dropped his chin and looked down his nose at Eddie. "You know I can't do that."

Eddie shook his head. "Okay, let's just say if it doesn't affect national security, something like that. I need you to give me some assurances before I continue."

His old boss frowned. "Okay. I won't do anything with the information you're about to give me without discussing it with you first." He held up a finger. "But I have to tell you, Eddie, Kamata is serious. The kind of thing I can't just ignore."

He nodded. "Okay, I don't even know how that fits in yet. So I'm more worried about some of the other things I know." A gust of wind rustled the trees all around them. Eddie gathered his thoughts. Kamata was something serious. That was unwelcome, but not unexpected news. Craig had come here to talk face to face after all. How would he tell him all this? He handed over the letter. The Agency man glanced at the handwritten "FBI" on the front and raised his eyebrows. He pulled out the paper, read it, and looked up.

Eddie leaned forward. "What the hell is Kamata?"

Craig brandished the letter at him. "Where did you get this? Who wrote it?"

"I'll get to that. First, tell me what it is."

Craig sat back heavily. "In about 1999 or 2000, someone hacked the police department in Kamata, Japan. Not unheard of, but it was well done, professional work. The American powers-that-be took notice and put this type of hack on a watch list."

Eddie tilted his head to one side. "What's in Kamata?"

"Nothing. It was just a brag, some kid showing how good he was." Craig looked around again and lowered his voice. "The only reason anyone really cares about it is, in 2014, someone hacked the CIA."

Eddie's eyes widened.

"Exactly, and they used a similar process, code, tool—I don't know what—that was used in Kamata. It had the same fingerprint."

Eddie rubbed his forehead. What was Heinrich into? Why would he hack the Agency? For what? No wonder he thought the FBI would come knocking one day. "What did they get?"

Craig scratched at his stubble. "That's just it. Nothing really. They stole a placeholder for some Agency projects. Just a list of project names for budgetary purposes. It didn't have any agent names, assets, or sensitive information. We didn't really lose anything."

"But it scared the hell out of everybody."

Craig pointed at him. "Exactly. So what do you know about it?"

"Okay, let me try to tell you all of this linearly."

"This sounds like a long story."

Eddie rocked his hand back and forth. "I hope not. So, the D.O.D. installs Mendelson over a bunch of black projects sometime around 2010."

Craig nodded. "Close enough."

"This dude is a sicko, and even the scientists begin to distance themselves from him, believing this is all going to get shut down. At some point, they realize that someone else is working in the background, trying to keep this work going in secret."

Craig asked, "Treleous?"

"That would be my guess. Some of the scientists sort of organize. Collect information—leaving notes to one another in doodles with codes in them in the paperwork. Something—or someone—gets on to them or realizes that the plug is about to be pulled. Then, as you've already told me, at some point the scientists began to disappear."

Craig's attention was now riveted on Eddie.

"Heinrich Stein, you remember the scientist we talked about?"

Craig nodded. "He's the one they found murdered in D.C."

"Yeah. He becomes like the ringleader of the resistance. He seems to have a head for it, and he has a brother in the CIA."

"Kurt. I put that together since the last time we talked. The two of them and some of their family members escaped being held by Putin's people. Kurt went to work for the Agency and Heinrich caught on with the D.O.D. science division."

A couple walked past in the distance, laughing.

Eddie continued, "Well, at least you've validated some of this. Anyway, Heinrich organizes a resistance, and with Kurt's help, smuggles three scientists out, and sets up a safe-house for them."

Craig pursed his lips. "Here in Maine. That explains why you're here. Which three?"

"Calvin Arturo, Chin Ling, and Benjamin Leonette."

Craig's dark eyebrows flew up. "Really?" He chuckled, "So he is alive, and you found him. Impressive. What was in Montana?"

Eddie waved away the question. "That's too far down the path. I'll get back to that in a minute. So he sneaks these people out, installs them here, and goes to enlist help from Sam Hawthorne."

"Why Sam?"

"I don't know. As we've already established, we're assuming Treleous catches up to Heinrich in D.C. and kills him. The scientists here don't know what to do next, and they're understandably terrified of Treleous."

Craig scowled. "He didn't leave them anything? No back-up plan, or anything like that?"

"Nothing. He just left them that." Eddie pointed at the letter in Craig's hand.

Craig studied the envelope. "Heinrich wasn't a computer nerd." He shook the pages. "This work is beyond him. Meaning, he had to recruit someone to help. What I really don't understand is, the list they got was worthless, certainly not worth the risk. And it's not like the hacker, whoever he was, grabbed the first thing he came across." He lifted the pages again. "They went after this specifically." He shrugged. "What would he do with it?"

Eddie wiped his mouth. Now was the time he'd been dreading, but he didn't see a way forward with any of this unless he let Craig in on Caveman. The Treleous problem was too big. Eddie didn't believe that Heinrich had had anything else going on. So that meant that Kamata had to be connected to all of this—though Eddie couldn't imagine how.

This also meant that maybe the information in Caveman's head, at least the CIA information, wasn't nearly as valuable or dangerous as they were afraid it was. Just a list of project names. So maybe he could convince Craig to forget about Caveman, or at least let him stay with Eddie's team. "That's the other thing I need to tell you, and where I don't want us to get crosswise. Was my project, Project Lighthouse, on the list the hacker stole?"

Craig narrowed his eyes. "Yes."

That was good. It validated assumptions Eddie was basing this decision on. "Do you know what Heinrich's specialty was?"

"No, not really."

"He ran a project called Afterimage that tried to push data directly into someone's brain. Not successfully, but that was the goal."

"Okay."

Eddie said, "When Sam and I went to that island in the Caribbean looking for the Mendelson repository, obviously we didn't find it, but we did find a man living there. A man who couldn't remember his own name. But he knew what Lighthouse was."

Craig furrowed his brow. "So you think he was, what, a failed After Image subject?"

Eddie shrugged. "It seems so, yes."

"But that makes even less sense. What purpose would that serve?"

"I agree. I've no idea."

Silence stretched between them, and then Craig asked, "That's what you're afraid of? That I'll take this amnesiac person from you?"

Eddie nodded.

Craig sighed. "I don't love that he knows the names of some of our projects, but," He shrugged. "The Mendelson scientists didn't really know anything else critical." He raised his eyebrows. "Does he know about the Mendelson projects?"

Eddie shook his head. "No, nothing about himself, or what happened to him, or the experiments themselves."

"Okay, so far, I've heard nothing to make me feel like I have to take action. What else is in his head?"

Eddie snorted. "Skills in construction, stuff like that. Nothing else national security, I don't think." Eddie lifted one shoulder. "But he had information that led us to the ranch in Montana."

Craig's eyebrows shot up again. "Really? What's this guy like?"

Eddie said, "Odd. So we're on the same page. I said I would protect Caveman and I will."

Craig chuckled. "Caveman?"

Eddie shrugged. "I found him in a cave. I had to call him something." He tilted his head to one side. "Of course, now we've learned his name in Jason, so I'm going to have to get used to that. We good?"

Craig nodded. "Yeah. For now."

"And the scientists?"

"If I believe they really don't know about Kamata, I'll leave them alone too."

Eddie stood. "Thank you. Let's go meet them."

Craig followed suit. "What's with your driver?"

"He's Chin Ling's dad. He doesn't talk much."

Craig brushed off his pants. "Good."

Chapter 149

Loren stared at the ocean from the backyard of the safe-house in Maine. Worried about Eddie's meeting with Craig, she'd walked out here to get some fresh air and clear her mind.

This new relationship they had with her old Agency boss was still fragile, mostly because Craig was always playing multiple games at once. That's why Eddie was the one who had to go—the two of them had to work out their differences for this to work.

The central question of all of this wasn't Kamata. She wasn't worried about that for some reason. It was Caveman—or Jason—now. She didn't see a way around telling Craig about him, and once the genie was let out of the bottle, there would be no putting him back in. Out of the corner of her eye, she saw Luis scouting the property, a pistol held low at his side.

With a sigh, she turned and walked back into the house. Susan and her father sat in one corner, heads close, talking. Loren smiled to herself. They'd found him—that was at least something.

She walked into the kitchen where Calvin and Chin were making a pot of tea.

He looked up, raising his eyebrows. "Would you like a cup?"

Loren said, "Please."

Chin stared at her with narrowed eyes. "I don't like this."

"I know. But this will help us figure out what Kamata is, and it will get us closer to stopping Treleous."

Chin sniffed. "You will never stop them. They are too big. Too powerful."

Loren accepted a mug from Calvin and spooned some sugar into it. "Maybe. But you might be surprised."

Chin's expression tightened into a glare and her voice rose a bit. "Might be is not good enough. All you will do is make us end up like them."

Loren stopped stirring. "Like who?"

"Like the other people working on Mendelson's dammed projects."

A shiver ran up Loren's arms. "What do you mean?"

Chin turned her back on Loren.

Calvin said in a softer tone. "Lots of scientists worked on the Mendelson projects. As far as we know, aside from the three of us, all are dead or missing."

Loren's brow furrowed. "What do you mean, missing? All of them?"

"All of them."

"So, what, you think they killed them all?"

Chin's eyes widened. "Worse. They have them somewhere."

Calvin stared into his mug and nodded.

Loren frowned. "You mean locked up somewhere? In a prison?"

Chin shrugged one small shoulder. "Locked up, but not just being held." She shivered.

Calvin said, "Continuing his work. Continuing all that evil."

Chin said through gritted teeth. "I will not be part of that. I will die first."

Loren put her hand over her mouth, horrified. "We will never let that happen,"

Chin snorted. "Will you be able to stop it? The three of you? If they discover us, you cannot stop them."

Loren set down her cup. "Like I said. You might be surprised."

Chin shook her head. "You haven't made a dent in them yet. Not that I've heard about. Such talk, but nothing to show for it." She turned and walked from the room.

Chapter 150

When Eddie finally led Craig up the stairs and into the safe-house on the coast, everyone was in the sunroom waiting. He studied their expectant and worried faces. "This is Craig Black. He's with the CIA and has been helping us work against Treleous."

Loren and Luis looked over the group, but none of the scientists displayed any kind of reaction at all.

After an awkward moment, Eddie was about to speak again when Craig said, "I know you're scared, I understand. Most of the Mendelson scientists are dead or missing—"

Chin stepped forward. "Who is dead?"

Craig pursed his lips. "Matheson, Elliot, Gordon, Karlsson, Koji, and Stein."

Calvin and Ben exchanged a look and Chin stared through him as she slowly crossed herself. "We knew about Heinrich. The rest, we feared the worst." She looked up sharply at Craig. "What about the others?"

He spread his arms. "I'm sorry. I've searched, but I cannot find any of them."

Calvin raised his eyebrows. "You've searched?"

"I have. I really am working against Treleous, and I won't let anything happen to you."

Chin sighed. "They must have the others someplace. Continuing the work."

Craig nodded. "That's my belief as well."

Color crept up Calvin's neck. "We must find them."

Chin asked, "What about Kamata? Did that help?"

Craig studied her for a moment and then shook his head. "I don't think so. It was a hack of the CIA, but all they took was a list of CIA projects. No details, just names. Do you know why he would do this?"

She exchanged a look with Ben and Calvin before shaking her head. Her mouth twisted in anger. "Perhaps. First, it wasn't Heinrich. This would have been beyond his skills. He must have convinced Koji to do it." She sighed. "Before his death, Heinrich and Kurt became obsessed with some CIA project called Madera." She threw up her hands. "They became convinced that it was the key to figuring all this out." She focused on Craig. "Of course he already had the name, so what he planned to do with a list with no details is anyone's guess."

Luis scowled. "Wood? It's Spanish for wood, or timber."

Eddie asked Craig, "What is Madera?"

He shook his head. "I don't know. Give me a second." He took a few steps away and spoke quietly into his phone, before he returned frowning. "It was some unimportant project in Cuba that went bad. It was closed before this breach."

Loren said, "So it wouldn't have been on the list that Koji stole?"

Craig nodded. "Those were the only active projects."

Eddie turned to Craig. "Do you have any idea how it could be connected to all of this?"

"None. I don't see a connection at all."

Calvin said, "Heinrich could be rash and impulsive, but he was not stupid. If he was convinced there was a connection, then there has to be. We just have to figure it out."

The back door opened. Burk and one of his men entered and walked over to the kitchen.

Craig stared after them with a crease in his forehead.

Eddie was intrigued to notice that his former boss seemed concerned by Burk's presence. He turned to Loren, then noticed her worried expression. "What's wrong?"

She asked Craig. "You're sure that they didn't get any details about any of the CIA missions? Just active project names?"

Craig turned his attention back to her. "Yes. Why?"

"Then how is my name in Caveman's head? How does he know me?"

Her former boss frowned. "I don't know."

Chapter 151

Loren smiled, remembering Luis' hesitation when Craig and Burk secured the safe-house, and it was time to go. Susan really had an effect on him. He was clearly relieved when they decided he would stay behind and help Burk's men protect the scientists. They were a cute couple, and Loren thought she was good for him.

Someone had to go watch Jeff and Caveman, so she and Eddie were on their way. She turned her attention back to Eddie, who stared out the window, brooding. "What's wrong with you?"

He turned back, shrugging. "We didn't accomplish anything. No, actually we went backwards. Treleous now has the repository."

She took his hand. "That's not true. We found Susan's dad, which is what we set out to do. We found the missing scientists and have them under Craig's protection now, and hopefully, they can help with Caveman. I mean, Jason. That's going to be hard to get used to."

"I know and all that is good, but none of that gets us any closer to stopping Treleous." He sighed. "Somehow, along the way, that's become almost as important to me as helping Caveman." He smiled ruefully. "I'm not ready to call him Jason yet."

"Me, either. But we have the name Madera. That and Heinreich's brother's connection to Cuba is a start."

"I'm not sure what we can do with that. Craig said he'll see what he can dig up, but he's not hopeful." His eyebrows went up. "And did you see Craig's reaction to Burk?"

Loren nodded. "Yeah, he was definitely not telling us everything there."

Eddie shook his head. "What else is new?" He looked out the window a moment and then turned back, his eyes haunted. "And now they know my name."

She nodded as a shiver of worry passed through her. That was not good, and even though they appeared stuck, it didn't diminish her dread that a storm was coming.

Epilogue

Frank stared out the truck window as Mack pulled into the parking garage across from the building here in Richmond. This was the first time Gemini had summoned both of them. It had always been just Frank in the past. What did that mean?

The way it all went down in Montana was still like swallowing bile for Frank, but Gemini had ruled the entire operation a success. So why the summons so soon? Now that they'd found Mendelson's stash, was the job over? Did Treleous no longer need Frank and Mack's services? Were they expendable?

He scratched the puckered scar on his neck. This would be a dumb place to try to kill them. Would they pay them off and send them on their way? Doubtful with all that they now knew.

Mack parked and looked over at Frank. "Why are we here?"

He shrugged. "I don't know, but keep your eyes peeled."

Mack had been sulking since he'd called him off from killing Mr. Talented. Frank understood, but it was growing old. He needed to get this kid some action soon.

They descended the stairs and crossed the street to the building. Both men searched the rooflines and alleys, looking for any kind of threat. As they approached the door, Frank said, "We have to give up our guns when we get inside."

Mack shied away from him. "Like hell I will."

Frank narrowed his eyes. "You will. We're going to give them our guns and go see what Gemini wants."

Mack's eyes darted around the area. "Why me? Why bring me this time? I don't like this, Frank."

The big man stopped and looked at him. "You got a feeling?"

Mack shook his head.

"Then quit your bellyaching and keep your eyes peeled." Inside, the same man in a blazer gestured to a gray plastic tub. Frank placed his Glock in the bin, and after giving Mack a hard look, the younger man placed his inside as well.

They walked down the boring, brown rubberized stairs, their footfalls echoing in the space until they reached the bottom. Frank exchanged one last look with Mack and then stepped inside. The room was the same. Animal heads on the wall, a big wooden desk on one side, and a long marble bar on the other. Gemini was the same as well, in khaki hunting gear as always.

He looked up from his computer and smiled. "Have a seat, both of you."

They sat.

Gemini leaned back and steepled his fingers, studying the two men for a beat. "We've been looking for that repository for a long time, as you know. What you don't know is why." He pursed his lips and looked at Frank. "Do you remember when you first came to work for us? Your first assignment? I wanted you to find a scientist named Heinrich Stein. You remember?"

Frank nodded.

"Heinrich had a brother named Kurt who worked in the CIA. Someone, we're still not sure who, tipped him off about some of our operations. Kurt sent an email about this to Heinrich that we intercepted. It was in a kind of code that we believe contained many of our secrets. About parts of our organization that neither of you even know about yet. It was a danger to us. Possibly even including the locations of our secret operations. Shortly after you dispatched Heinrich, I had another team deal with Kurt." He frowned. "At sea not too far from that damned island."

Frank exchanged a look with Mack.

Gemini stared off into space for a beat. "Heinrich loved to leave little puzzles and hints in his work. All of those damned scientists did. Shortly after we eliminated the brothers, we discovered the existence of this repository. We were worried that persons unknown were working on discovering what the email meant. Trying to decipher the code."

Gemini stood, and nodding for them to follow, walked over to the bar. He poured scotch into three cut crystal tumblers. "We were worried that someone could figure it out and be a danger to us." He handed each of them a glass and raised his own in toast. "My people have gone through all the information in that repository you found using the latest technology. We even breached their cloud backup, where they had every page digitized. We looked at it all."

He clinked glasses with each of them and swallowed down the burning liquid.

Frank and Mack followed suit.

Gemini grinned. "I'm happy to report that it wasn't there. Not the email, not the code, none of it. There is no evidence they are working on any of it, or even knew about it."

He gestured to Frank with his glass. "After Heinrich's death and your recovery of his laptop, it seems that the email stopped there. If anyone else happened across it, they don't seem to know what they were looking at, without the proper context." He took another sip. "My friends, that threat to us is over. We won."

Frank nodded. So far, so good.

Gemini set down his glass. "Now, for your fine work on all of this, we're going to bring you in on the other side of the business. Where the real work is being done." He grinned. "Where the real money is made." He looked over at Mack. "But first, another reward for a job well done. You deserve a little bit of fun before the next phase." Gemini handed him a piece of paper.

Mack looked down at it. "What's this?"

Gemini smiled. "It's Eddie's Mason's address in Coral Gables, Florida. It's their hiding place." He grinned. "Now you can go kill Mr. Talented and all his friends. Think of it as another bonus, before your work on phase two." Mack looked up, eyes wide, and a smile slowly crossed his face.

About the Author

Bret Hurst loves stories of all kinds and reads everything he can get his hands on, regardless of genre. He has always dreamed of being a writer and has been working on novels and screenplays for as long as he can remember. He grew up in Miami and worked a variety of places—from construction, nuclear power plant, ice cream parlor to Walt Disney World. Bret has degrees from Auburn University and Florida International University and is the CIO of a healthcare company. He loves to travel all over the world and resides outside Atlanta with his wife and three children.

ARROWHEAD | BOOK ONE
THE
CAVEMAN
CONSPIRACY
BRET
HURST

Note from Bret Hurst

Word-of-mouth is crucial for any author to succeed. If you enjoyed *The Arrowhead Protocol*, please leave a review online—anywhere you are able. Even if it's just a sentence or two. It would make all the difference and would be very much appreciated.

Thanks!
Bret Hurst

We hope you enjoyed reading this title from:

www.blackrosewriting.com

Subscribe to our mailing list – *The Rosevine* – and receive **FREE** books, daily deals, and stay current with news about upcoming
releases and our hottest authors.
Scan the QR code below to sign up.

Already a subscriber? Please accept a sincere thank you for being a fan of
Black Rose Writing authors.

View other Black Rose Writing titles at
www.blackrosewriting.com/books and use promo code
PRINT to receive a **20% discount** when purchasing.